Demon

Julia Guroff

JHG Books

Contents

Chapter 1

Zombie

December 2001

Jonathan's

I am...

Gabe

When we get back from Jonathan's house, my sister asks me if I want to come upstairs to her room. "Yeah, sure," I say, trying to sound casual. Mom and Dad don't pay much attention to us, and just head into the kitchen together. I'm already starting to get used to the idea that we have secrets to keep from our parents. It's crazy to think that Natalie's been doing this her whole life.

She waits for me to go first, and follows as I use both of my crutches with one hand, and hold the banister with the other. I've gotten really good with my crutches in the last few days, but stairs are still a bit challenging.

I sit on the side of her bed when we get in, while Natalie closes the door behind us. "Why don't you lie down," she suggests. "Angel says your ankle is starting to hurt again."

Woah. Will I ever get used to that? Maybe not. I stare at her, and she rolls her eyes, then comes over and gently pushes me back against one of her pillows. She lifts up my foot with the cast on it, and tucks her other pillow underneath. Huh. Maybe I can get used to this.

"Better?" she asks, sitting down on the chair in front of her desk.

"Um, yeah, thanks."

She looks to the side and smiles. Angel must be there.

"Angel wants you to know that he only tells me what you are thinking or feeling if he thinks I should know. Only if it will help."

Oh. Well that's good to know, I guess. Since Natalie told me last week about being able to talk to her guardian angel, I've started wondering if I would ever have any privacy again. It hasn't exactly been bothering me, but it does feel weird to realize that Natalie can always know whatever I'm thinking.

"Only when it will help," she repeats, obviously knowing exactly what I was just thinking. "Angel says that he will always respect your privacy, and only tell me things if he needs to." She waits for me to nod, then adds, "That's how it works with Timothy. Although I guess with Jonathan, Angel has been trying to tell me everything for a while. Since I started the Jonathan Project."

I still haven't been able to really wrap my head around all that. Natalie decided to start hanging around with Jonathan to try to get him to stop being mean to her. To stop being mean in general. I always knew my best friend had a nasty streak, but he never used to do anything bad to me, so I tried to ignore it. But it started bothering Natalie and she tried to do something to change things. She called it the Jonathan Project.

But then apparently Jonathan's guardian angel got mad at her for it, because he didn't want her to change Jonathan. He liked it when Jonathan was being mean. So he controlled Jonathan into trying to hurt her a couple of times, especially when she wanted to explain to him about guardian angels. I couldn't even protect her when he went nuts and tried to push her off the jungle gym. He and I both ended up falling off. That's how I broke my ankle, and how Jonathan ended up in the hospital.

And how his guardian angel disappeared. Demon, Natalie says she calls him. I thought getting rid of him was a good thing, but she told me that Angel says it is a problem. After seeing Jonathan tonight, I have to agree.

I know Jonathan didn't hit his head when he fell, since I caught him before he could. They took him to the hospital because he was unconscious and nobody had any idea why. But Angel told Natalie it must be because his guardian angel had gone missing, after all the other guardians yelled at him to make him stop controlling Jonathan.

Now Jonathan doesn't even seem like himself at all. I hadn't seen him since he woke up in the hospital, so I was excited to go over to his house finally tonight and visit him, hopefully get the chance to play. But he didn't seem like he wanted to play. Or to do anything at all. He was just strangely quiet. He answered any questions I asked him, but he didn't start anything. He didn't try to do anything. He was like a weird zombie.

I don't know why his parents don't seem more worried about it. I guess they just figure he's being quiet, and that's fine with them. But I can tell there is something missing.

It's Demon. That's what's missing. Jonathan isn't himself without his guardian angel.

Natalie watches me quietly while all of this runs through my head. I realize it and ask her, "Did you hear all that?"

"No, I told you Angel won't tell me what you're thinking unless he thinks I need to know. But I don't need him to tell me now anyway. I know you're worried about Jonathan. So am I. So is Angel."

"I wish I could understand why he's being so weird. It's really because his guardian angel is missing?"

She bites her lip and shrugs. "That's got to be it. There isn't anything else to explain it. Like when he wouldn't wake up in the hospital. You were there, you know there wasn't anything the doctors could find wrong with him."

"And he woke up because our guardian angels talked to him?"

"Yeah, like I told you. Your guardian and Mom's guardian used energy to talk to him. Timothy asked Angel to tell them to try it, and it worked. He woke up, but he still doesn't have his own guardian. They don't know where he is."

I shake my head. This is all so strange. Maybe I won't be able to ever get used to it after all.

Stefanie

"Good night, sweetie." I kiss Jonathan's forehead and make sure his blankets are tucked up over him. He gazes at me while I smooth his hair, then closes his eyes. So I turn out the light and quietly close his door behind me.

He's been so still since he was released from the hospital. We had a follow-up appointment with his pediatrician today, to see if anything is actually wrong, but there isn't. He's eating and sleeping, talking and playing with his dog. But so much more quietly than usual. I'm worried about it, but the doctor assures me there isn't anything to fret over.

Brad thinks it's because Jonathan is spending time thinking about the fight he had with his friend last weekend, and trying to act better. That was actually the whole point of grounding him from watching t.v. for a week, after he fought with Natalie and Gabe at the library last weekend. Although we had forgotten all about it after the whole playground accident and Jonathan spending Monday in the hospital. He hasn't even asked about t.v. since he got back though, so I suppose maybe he remembered he was grounded? I don't know, and I didn't want to mention it to him for fear of setting him off. Normally he can be a bit challenging, and lately he's gotten to be a real handful. So this new milder Jonathan is something of a relief.

But it's still strange. I can't help having a little prickle of worry, my mommy instincts tingling. I guess I'm glad Christmas break has started, and he has a couple more weeks to rest before returning to school for the remainder of third grade. Hopefully he'll be back to normal by then. Well, maybe not all the way back. I'd like him to maintain some of this compliant behavior. But I miss his little spark.

Stefanie's

My beloved is more right than she knows. Her instinctual sense that something is wrong with her son is accurate, but it isn't anything human doctors will ever detect.

The astonishing truth is that Jonathan's Guardian has somehow vanished. It is utterly baffling. Neither I nor any Guardian nearby has ever heard of such a thing. The Guardian of a human is tied to the human's soul. There is no severing such a bond. Or at least there never has been before.

Without Jonathan's Guardian, the child seems like a shadow of himself. His soul, which had blazed more vibrantly than almost any other, has dimmed to the point of invisibility. It lingers feebly, barely glowing. Jonathan does nothing to feed the flame, having no Guardian to encourage him, no motivation to take any action at all. He survives, but does not thrive. He lives, but without animation.

It is impossible to know how long such an existence can be sustained. As it is impossible to understand where his Guardian could have gone, how the soul could have been left behind with the sad shell of a human which Jonathan has become.

I have never beheld anything more tragic.

Yet, I cannot lose hope. I must believe, for the sake of my dearest one, that her child's Guardian will return. *"My darling, take comfort in the knowledge that your beloved child survives, and he is safe here with you. If only his Guardian returns, Jonathan will return as well. We must all cling to this hope."*

Chapter 2

It's My Fault

Natalie

Poor Gabe. This has been a hard week for him. First Jonathan went all crazy and bad and they got into a fight last weekend. Then I had to tell him about guardians, which was a super strange thing for him to accept. Then the whole fight happened with Jonathan on the jungle gym, and they both fell off. Gabe's ankle is broken, so he's wearing a cast and using crutches. But he isn't worried about that at all. He's only worried about Jonathan.

I want to try to make him feel better, and I think distracting him from thinking about Jonathan for a while might help.

"How's your ankle feeling?" I ask him. I think that having him lay down must be helping.

"It's all right," he says. "It doesn't hurt as much as it did at first."

"You know," I tell him, "Angel can see how it's doing. Want him to check it out for you?"

His eyes get big. Poor thing, I just can't stop surprising him.

Gabe

What? "Seriously? Yeah, sure."

She waits for a minute, then tells me, "Angel says the bone is already starting to mend. He says everything is in the right spot, and the cast is making sure nothing can move while it is healing. He thinks you'll actually be all better before your six weeks in the cast are over."

"Oh. Well, cool. Thanks." I guess that's good to know.

She goes over to her closet for some reason, and gets out a metal hanger. I watch, befuddled, while she struggles to unbend it. "What are you doing?" I ask her.

"Just a minute," she says, concentrating on her task, her little tongue poking out of her mouth. Once she gets it more or less straight, she wraps a bunch of masking tape over one end. "Here," she says, once she's done. She hands it to me. "Angel knows your foot is starting to feel itchy inside the cast. He said you can stick this down inside to scratch it. Not too hard, though, you don't want to scrape your skin."

Ooh! Well, that's useful. I guess being able to talk to her guardian angel can be pretty handy.

While I'm gently stuffing the hanger down in there, and getting all the right spots, she is looking to the side and listening to Angel. She nods, then looks back over at me.

"Gabe, Mom and Dad are trying to decide whether to keep going back and forth to their houses over Christmas break. Now that school's out it doesn't make much sense to have the week at Mom's and the weekend at Dad's."

Oh, okay. Again, I guess her guardian is useful.

"I think we should stay here," she says.

"You don't want to hang around with Timothy?"

"I know that we can get our Moms to drive us to visit each other. And Angel talks to Guardian all the time, so I'll always know what's going on with Timothy. I think we should stay closer to Jonathan. I'm trying to figure out what to do to help him."

Her little face crumples, like she has gotten sad all of the sudden. "It's my fault," she says, staring down at her hands. "Everything that happened to him is because of stuff I decided to do. I have to try to fix it."

I yank the hanger back out of my cast and put it down, then reach over and grab her hand. "Don't blame yourself, Nat. He was being really rotten to you."

"Yeah, but even that was kind of my fault. If I hadn't started the whole thing about trying to get guardians to talk to each other, they wouldn't have found out how to use energy, and Demon wouldn't have learned how to control Jonathan. It all comes back to me." Her lip quivers, poor thing. My little sister is so sensitive. She always wants to make everyone else happy, and I can tell this is really eating at her.

"Not all of it, Nat. Jonathan started it, a super long time ago. He's the one who was always teasing you and Timothy. I think that was way before your guardians learned about energy. It was already happening before you did that."

She nods and looks up at me. "Yeah, I know. But I still have to help him. I just don't understand how yet. I know if we go over to Mom's again I won't be able to see him much until school starts again. And Angel won't be able to hear him from over there. I need to be close by."

"All right, sure," I say.

"Good," she says, and jumps to her feet like she's on a mission. "I think we should go tell Mom and Dad we want to stay here over Christmas, before they finish talking about it." She takes my crutches which were leaning against the bed and hands them to me. "Come on."

Oh, okay. Boy, when she makes up her mind she really springs into action, doesn't she?

Brenda

I'm about to go call up the stairs for the kids to come down for dinner, when I hear them coming down anyway. Gabe's crutches thunk on the stairs as he uses them and the banister to navigate the stairway. He hasn't complained at all about any of it, not the pain or the crutches or anything. I think he was so relieved when his friend woke up that he is completely disregarding his own injury.

Ron is setting plates around the table, and I bring over the casserole dish and put it on the trivet. "Good timing," he tells the kids, "have a seat."

Before we get the chance to introduce the topic which we were discussing, Natalie pipes up with, "Can we stay here for Christmas break?" Gabe snorts a little laugh and looks down at his plate.

I start ladling tuna casserole onto everybody's plates. "Well, actually, we were just talking about that." Natalie and Gabe meet each other's eyes in a strangely meaningful way. Oy, those kids. What are they up to now?

Ron takes his full plate back from me and says, "We weren't sure how you guys would feel about it. You want to stay here, Natalie?"

"Yes, please," she says primly, pushing her food around on her plate with her fork.

"Why?" he asks, somewhat baffled. We were assuming Natalie would prefer being at my place, so she could play with Timothy all the time over Christmas break. We were worried that she and Gabe would be in conflict over where to stay.

"I think it would be nice to set up all the Christmas decorations here," she says, "since the living room is bigger. Maybe we could bring over the stuff from Mom's house so everything can be together."

Really? That's what she's thinking about? I catch Gabe giving her a glance and a slight roll of his eyes. Okay, what is going on here? The kids are clearly in league together here. But why? Doesn't she want to play with Timothy?

Natalie looks to the side, then back over to me, and quickly adds, "I'm not worried about seeing Timothy. You'll bring me over there sometimes to play, right? Maybe when we go to get your decorations? And he's already coming here tomorrow."

Why do I get the sense that she's trying to talk us into something?

Ron asks Gabe, "What do you think?"

"Yeah, I'd like to stay here," Gabe says, stuffing a bread roll into his mouth.

Ron looks over at me and chuckles. "Well, okay then. I guess that settles it, right?"

"Sure," I say. "This house it is."

Chapter 3
Let's All Go

Timothy

Dad's driving me over to Natalie's, since Mom is already working at the salon. We're not talking in the car. That's fine with me. I think it's fine with him too. We don't really usually have much to talk about, especially since he got home from deployment a week or two ago. It has been okay to have him back. I was worried that it would be hard, and he'd try to get me to do stuff I don't care about, like playing ball or something. But he hasn't. He's been pretty mellow, and hasn't bothered me at all.

He pulls the car up to the curb in front of Natalie's Dad's house. "Do you need me to come in with you?" he asks.

"No, they know I'm coming."

"Okay, your Mom will pick you up later. I'm going to work."

I guess I knew that, since he's wearing his uniform again, for the first time since he got back. "Thank you for the ride," I tell him. Natalie has reminded me that I should always be as polite as possible with my Dad, since Angel told her it is important to him.

He nods, and I'm not sure he really heard me. "Bye," I tell him, and get out of the car and close the car door behind me. He pulls away before I even walk up to the house.

Before I get to the front door Natalie opens it and pokes her head out. "Your Dad dropped you off?" she said.

"Yes. He's going to work."

"Oh, okay." She waits for me to come in the door, then closes it behind me.

Her Mom is in the living room, and she looks up and says, "Hi Timothy. Is your Dad coming in?"

"No, he's going to work."

"All right, then. Welcome."

Natalie's

Timothy does not seem to have noticed, but his father has been exhibiting signs of significant mental stress ever since he returned from deployment. Guardian and I have both witnessed his sleep disturbances, triggered by nightmares. His Guardian constantly tries to bring him comfort and peace, but Michael's mind appears wounded by his recent participation in the country's current war effort. His subconscious mind seems to be trapped in a repeating cycle of memory and imagination. He does not perceive any of the reassurances being transmitted by his Guardian.

As it is apparently not impacting Timothy, and I can think of no constructive action the Seer could take to alleviate Michael's distress, I refrain from mentioning it to her. However, Guardian and I will continue to monitor the situation, and I will alert her if necessary.

In the meantime, the children have more pressing concerns. Gabe again joins Natalie in her room once she and Timothy enter. "Hey, Timothy," he says, swinging over on his crutches to sit on her bed.

"Hello," Timothy responds, sitting on the floor. Natalie takes a seat at her desk.

Timothy immediately proceeds with the topic on all of their minds. "Did you see Jonathan last night?"

"We did," Natalie says, "and he definitely is missing Demon. When we went over there we thought we'd be able to play with him, but he didn't want to do anything. He was sitting there barely moving, being really quiet. All he was doing was petting his dog."

Gabe affirms this with a nod, his brow wrinkled with distress.

"Did Angel say whether he could see Demon anywhere?"

"No, he's still missing. They can't find him at all."

Timothy takes his notebook out of his bag and starts writing.

"What're you doing?" Gabe asks.

Natalie responds. "He's taking notes. He always takes notes on all our experiments."

Gabe is taken somewhat aback. He asks, "What? This is just an experiment to you?"

Timothy pauses in his writing and looks up. "Yes, of course. This is all part of the same ongoing experiment."

Natalie is concerned that her brother is offended. "Gabe, this is the best way to learn. If we are going to find a way to help Jonathan, we should approach it scientifically. Don't you think?" She looks at him earnestly.

"Um, yeah, I suppose." In his mind, Gabe thinks Natalie and her friend truly are very strange little kids, but of course there is no benefit in repeating this to my beloved.

Timothy completes his notations and lays his pencil down. "Well," he asks Natalie, "what should we do next?"

She wrinkles her nose. "I hoped you would have an idea."

Timothy nods. "I do, but I wanted to ask you first. Since the Jonathan Project is your experiment."

"Oh, okay," she says.

Gabe looks back and forth between them as they speak, laughing softly. "Is this always how it is with you two?" They both stare at him, and Natalie shrugs.

"Well, Timothy, what's your idea?" she asks.

"Obviously we need to monitor Jonathan today. Angel, what is he doing now?"

"Jonathan has eaten breakfast and is inside his home watching a cartoon on television. This is the first time he has been allowed to watch television since the incident at the library last weekend. The privilege had been revoked by his father for a period of one week as a consequence for his actions in fighting."

Natalie repeats this information to the boys, and the children regard each other in some surprise.

"Huh," Gabe says, "I didn't know he had gotten in trouble." It bothers Gabe that he has been so distant from Jonathan since the previous weekend. Normally a detail such as this would have been known to him.

Natalie understands Gabe's concern. "It's all right, Gabe, you haven't had any chance at all to talk to him. You both stayed home from school all week and we've been over at Mom's. There's no way you could have known about it. I think maybe you should go over there and play with him again today?"

Gabe sighs. "I'd like to, but I don't know what we'd end up doing. I couldn't really ride bikes or the stuff we usually do with the crutches. And anyway, after seeing how limp and lifeless he was last night, I doubt he's really going to want to do anything. Maybe only watch t.v."

Natalie says, "I don't know if you could get a good sense of how he is doing if you are only watching t.v. together." She considers a reasonable alternative. "All he wanted to do last night was pet his dog. So probably going over there and playing with him and the dog would be best, right? Then you can come back and tell us how it went." She sighs softly, wishing she was able to go as well, but feeling that she should not while Timothy is here as her guest.

However, Timothy states, "I think we should all go."

Natalie is startled. He has never before expressed a desire to go to Jonathan's house.

Timothy explains, "As long as Jonathan doesn't have his guardian, I think we're all perfectly safe. If he doesn't want to do anything but pet his dog, he won't be able to do anything mean to anyone, right? I'd like to see for myself what is going on."

Natalie's face lights up. "Oh yeah! You should be fine with things this way." Then she laughs, remembering. "I was right after all. You thought I was crazy when I told you that if the Jonathan Project worked you could hang out with us too."

Timothy snorts. "This isn't exactly what you meant."

She giggles. "Doesn't mean I was wrong."

Gabe looks at the two of them and shakes his head. Weirdest second-graders I have ever known, he thinks, feeling a mix of humor and affection. Rising from the bed, he takes his crutches and says, "Well, let's all go, I guess."

Chapter 4

Glimmer

Jonathan

Dad left to go to work this morning after breakfast. Mom told me it's been a week since I was grounded from t.v., so I could watch it again if I want. I hadn't thought about it at all. I told her okay, I guess I'll watch t.v.

So that's what I'm doing. I'm staring at the t.v. but I have no idea what show is even on. Socks jumped up on the couch with me and I'm petting him. He is the only thing which has seemed interesting to me since I got home from the hospital. I don't really care about anything else.

I hear somebody knocking on the door. I don't care. I don't move. Mom glances over at me, then goes to open the door.

Gabe comes in. Natalie comes too. Timothy is behind her.

"Hi Jon," Gabe says to me.

"Hi," I say. I keep petting Socks and looking at the t.v.

But then Socks jumps down off of me and runs over to Natalie, and jumps up on her. I look away from the t.v. to watch. She kneels down and gives him a hug. "Hello Socks! You're getting bigger, aren't you! Yes you are!"

She looks over at me, while she is holding him. He is wagging his tail and squirming all over her. She says, "Hi Jonathan. How are you?"

"Fine."

"Do you think we could all go outside and play with Socks? Maybe throw the ball for him?" I see Gabe and Timothy looking at each other.

"Okay." I get up from the couch. If she's taking Socks outside I guess I'll go too.

Timothy

Last time I saw Jonathan he was unconscious. He is awake now, technically, but I'm not sure I would really call this "conscious". It's like he's barely functioning. Every time I ever saw him before, he was full of energy, constantly in motion. He always had something that he wanted to do. He would seem excited about every single activity, especially when he was teasing me.

Now it seems like Jonathan doesn't care about anything at all. "Guardian," I think to him, "please monitor everything he is feeling, so that you and Angel can describe it to us later." I open up my mind so I can feel Guardian's agreement.

Natalie puts the dog back on the floor and starts to walk towards the patio door, saying, "Come on Socks! Come on! Let's go outside!" The dog follows after her, wagging its tail. She looks up to make sure Jonathan is coming too.

I wasn't sure he would, since he seems so listless, but he gets up off the couch and follows after her. Gabe and I follow him out. I see his Mom watching us, then going over and turning off the t.v.

Gabe finds a tennis ball on the ground outside, manages to lean down on one of his crutches to grab it, and says, "Hey Jon, want to throw the ball for Socks?"

Jonathan doesn't take the ball. He just stands there and stares at Natalie, who is sitting on the ground and petting the dog again.

Gabe watches this, and I think he's trying to get Jonathan to start acting normal again. He says, "Here, Jon, catch!"

He tosses the ball over to him. But Jonathan doesn't react at all. He keeps staring at Natalie, and the ball hits him on the arm and bounces off. He reaches over to rub his arm, but otherwise doesn't move.

I have this bizarre sense of deja vu, and a flashback to when the same thing happened to me a couple of months ago. We were in Natalie's yard, and Jonathan and Gabe were playing ball. Jonathan threw the ball at me and said, "Catch," but of course I couldn't catch it so it hit me in the arm and rolled away.

I can see that Natalie remembers too. She sucks in her breath and looks over at me with wide eyes. I start feeling sorry for Jonathan for the first time ever. Seeing this happen to him makes me realize more than anything else how broken he is because Demon is missing. Natalie isn't the only one who wants to fix Jonathan now. I actually want to as well. I guess I am all in on the Jonathan Project.

Even if he goes back to being mean, it's better than seeing him like this, basically an empty person. Like he doesn't even have a soul any more. I wonder about that. I know the guardians are here because of the souls. "Guardian," I think to him, "can you tell us later about how his soul is doing? Did Demon take it with him?"

Natalie puts the dog down and stands up. She goes over to where the ball had rolled and picks it up. She walks over to Jonathan. He watches her the whole time. She lifts the ball up for him to take, and says, "Here, Jonathan, you can throw the ball for Socks, all right?" But he still doesn't take it. So she reaches out to grab his hand, lifts it up and puts the ball right into it. Then she holds the ball and his hand in both of her hands, and stares right into his eyes. "Jonathan, here's the ball. I think Socks would like for you to throw it for him, don't you?"

And Jonathan seems to come to life, at least a little. He looks down at the way his hand is inside both of her hands, and he gets a tiny little smile on his face. Not the kind of smile I've seen on him before, not bright and huge and excited like usual. It's a gentle little smile. It's almost sad to see. "Thank you," he says. Then he actually tosses the ball over to the dog, who frantically rushes over to pick it up. It's the most action I've seen from Jonathan yet today.

That was all very interesting. I take mental notes, so I'll remember later to write everything down.

Natalie's

Guardian and I regard each other, startled. We have both been scrutinizing Jonathan throughout this interaction, observing both his actions and his mind. And of course his soul, the sad remnant which Demon left behind. From the moment on the playground nearly a week ago when we realized Demon had vanished, we saw that Jonathan's soul was almost quenched. It was diminished from the blazing, towering aura it had become, shrinking into a barely perceptible flicker. Its continued presence alone is astonishing considering the absence of the Guardian who had carried it to Jonathan at the time of his birth. But in its reduced state it is pitiable. Jonathan's lethargic actions and sluggish mind are nothing compared to the catastrophic waning of his soul.

But the moment Natalie touched him, his soul flared. Like a dying ember trying to reignite as a breeze blows across it. His soul began to glow, feebly still, but with a dim glimmer which had not been present since the playground incident. For the time that Natalie held his hand in hers, his soul emitted the tiny gleam.

The moment their physical contact ended, so did the soul's glow.

This is not something that we have seen before. Of course, this entire situation is utterly unprecedented. But we are both deeply perplexed by this new event. Physical contact does not, in itself, impact the strength of the soul. It is the psychic byproduct of actions which can change the soul. The soul cannot respond to physical stimuli any more than Guardians can. Only emotions, thoughts, desires, are effective tools in forging the soul. As we are intangible, so the soul is intangible, and so must be the mechanisms used to craft it into something fine and strong.

But, somehow, Natalie's touch reinvigorated it, although only for the duration of the physical contact.

How is this possible? I consider other times I have seen Natalie touch others, and know that I have not seen it have a noticeable effect on their souls. However, her touch has often had a soothing or comforting impact on the emotions of the person she has contacted.

Also, Guardian notes, following along with my thoughts, every other person she has touched has a present Guardian and an intact soul. Perhaps the effect of touch can only be seen on a damaged soul.

However, I add, it is not any touch. We have witnessed both of Jonathan's parents touch him over the last few days, and their contact had no impact.

It must be both. The Seer's touch, and the damaged soul. Together, their contact is meaningful.

But to what extent? What does this signify? Why did it happen?

I observe the children, who are playing together, not as boisterously as usual, but still seeming to enjoy themselves. Jonathan and Gabe alternate throwing the ball to the dog, while Natalie applauds their efforts and Timothy carefully observes. Jonathan is more animated now, although he is still very quiet and has not laughed or resumed other such normal mannerisms. But he is participating in an activity, whereas before Natalie touched him it seemed unlikely to occur.

Guardian and I realize, together, that we are eager to discuss this later with the children, and particularly with Timothy, who has so many times been able to develop lines of questioning which lead to important answers.

Answers which we must have.

Chapter 5

New Tradition

Stefanie

I'm so relieved to see Jonathan playing with his friends. This last week has been so strange, starting with the trip to the hospital and then the last several days of his unusually lethargic behavior. But now he's in the yard, throwing the ball to his dog, and apparently having a good time. It still seems a lot quieter than usual, but maybe that's because Natalie and Timothy came along. They're younger, and generally less boisterous, so it might be influencing the way they are all playing.

I feel a weight lifted from me. Phew. I think I can start believing that Jonathan is going to be okay. Good thing, because I have so many other things to think about. I managed to get through finals week, but I still have to prepare for Christmas. We haven't even put up the tree yet, we've been so rattled with everything going on. So I have to do that, wrap presents, generally prepare for the holiday.

I'm also anticipating my final semester starting next month, along with my internship. I feel a little burp rising in my throat, and cover my mouth even though nobody is in the house with me. And that, of course. The baby that's on its way. I feel gassier than last time. A lot of this pregnancy is different, possibly because I was a teenager then and I'm a lot older now. Well, I'm only 25, but that still is a big difference from being in high school.

Lots of things are changing. For the better, it seems. I feel more hopeful now that Jonathan is definitely improving. I pull out a piece of paper and start making a list of stuff I need to get done.

Ron

Brenda and I have hauled the boxes of Christmas decorations out of the attic to go through them. We figure we'll go get the tree tomorrow, but she wanted to check out what I have here before she decides what to bring over from her house. It seems like while the kids are all over at Jonathan's house is a good time for us to do it.

I was a little worried about them going over there, after all the drama that happened last week. But Gabe and Natalie assured me with total sincerity that it will be fine, everybody will be able to get along perfectly well. And last night they seemed to be okay together when we visited. I've decided to trust them, and hope for the best. After all, the fight at the library was a complete aberration. Although I've seen Jonathan tease the kids a few times, it had never escalated into a fight before. I'm crossing my fingers it doesn't happen again. After the accident at the school playground Monday where Gabe and Jonathan both got hurt, I'm pretty sure that whatever set them off last weekend has been long forgotten.

I'm watching Brenda go through the boxes of decorations. It doesn't take her very long, since I don't really have a lot. She looks up at me with a crooked smile on her face. "I'm thinking I'll want to pretty much bring everything over. These are fine, but mine are the ones with all the memories."

I chuckle. "Are you dissing my divorced dad decorations?"

"Well, maybe," she laughs.

"Good. This stuff is all generic and boring." I peek into the box in front of her, and see the one unique ornament. I pull it out and hold it up. "Except this one, of course."

She smiles and takes the little luminaria. "Ah, yes."

"That's the ornament which started it all. When Natalie saw it last year, she asked me about it, and then she hatched her scheme to have you come over to set up luminarias with us."

Remembering that night, I am flooded again with love for Brenda, and I lean across the box to give her a kiss. She reciprocates tenderly.

We are in such a good place right now.

"Let's do it again this year," she suggests, after several minutes of smooching. "The luminarias. We'll all be here again. Really here. I'm sure the kids would love it."

"Yes," I agree, reaching up to tuck a stray lock of her dark hair behind her ear. "Let's do it. A new tradition."

Gabe

We've been playing and throwing the ball to the dog for an hour or so, I guess. I'm taking turns with Jonathan. He's doing it, but not goofing around like usual. He seems happy enough. But still very different.

Natalie is watching and helping get the ball from Socks, especially when it's my turn to throw it. It's hard for me to bend down to get the ball with the crutches. My ankle is starting to hurt, but I don't want to say anything about it.

Natalie, though, apparently gets the heads up from Angel. "Jonathan," she tells him, after Socks drops the ball in her hand, "I think it's time for us to go home now. Thank you for playing with us." She hands the ball to him, and touches his shoulder as he takes it. "Bye, Jonathan. We'll see you again soon. Probably tomorrow, okay?"

"Okay," he says.

"Bye, Jon," I tell him. "I'm glad you're feeling better."

"Bye."

As we're heading home, Timothy says, "That was very interesting. We'll have a lot to talk about. I asked Guardian to monitor his feelings."

"Angel was watching everything too," Natalie says, walking next to me as I swing along on my crutches. "I got the sense that he wasn't expecting everything that happened, but he hasn't told me what yet. We'll talk about it when we get home."

Sometimes I can't believe how much is going on that I never knew about before. Here my sister and her friend have this whole other life of guardian angels going on, which nobody else knows about. It's so strange. I'm glad I'm part of it now, though.

Chapter 6

New Mystery

Natalie's

As we arrive home I know Natalie's parents are waiting in the living room with boxes of decorations, and I anticipate that the children will be distracted by the prospect of decorating for the upcoming Christmas holiday. Our discussion, therefore, will be delayed.

Natalie, in entering the front door, immediately goes to where her parents have the open boxes of decorations on the floor. "Oooh! Is it time to decorate?"

Gabe, although not as excited about Christmas decorations as his sister, enters the living room as well. He drops onto an armchair and lifts his injured ankle to lie on the footrest.

Her mother responds to Natalie, "Not quite. We'll go and pick out a tree tomorrow. I need to get the decorations from my house, too."

"When?" Natalie asks. Timothy remains standing in the entryway, waiting for this conversation to end, wishing to proceed with the discussion regarding Jonathan. He is focused on the fact that they are mid-experiment and the data needs to be analyzed.

"Well," Brenda responds, "I'm thinking we can take Timothy home later, and then go to my house to get out the Christmas stuff."

"Okay," Natalie says brightly. Then her eyes fall on the luminaria ornament, and she seizes it with a sharp intake of breath. "Ooooh!" she begins.

But her father, realizing where she is going with this, preempts her with a grin. "How would you guys like to set up luminarias again this year on Christmas Eve?"

"Yes!" she enthuses, a brilliant smile lighting her face. She looks eagerly to her brother and friend for their agreement.

"Sure," Gabe says.

"Okay," adds Timothy.

Her expression of joy dims slightly. They are clearly not as thrilled as she is.

"My dearest, do not be disappointed that they do not seem as enthusiastic as you. This is an activity which will be enjoyed by all, once again this year. I believe your ability to find exceptional delight in all things is one of the many very special things about you." I smile fondly at her.

She sighs, shrugs, and sets the luminaria ornament back in the box. Looking at the boys, she suggests, "Want to go upstairs?"

"Yes," Timothy replies. This is what he was waiting for.

Gabe gets his crutches and hauls himself to his feet. His ankle is experiencing some discomfort after spending the morning standing and throwing balls.

When the children arrive in Natalie's room, I tell her, *"Your brother's ankle is painful. Perhaps he would be more comfortable lying down again."*

She immediately sets about ensuring his comfort. She invites him to lie on the bed, elevates his foot with a pillow, and asks if she can get him anything.

He grins. "Nope, I'm all good now. Thanks, sis. So, what did you all learn about Jonathan?" He is eager to discuss our findings as well.

Timothy retrieves his notebook and waits with a pencil at the ready. Natalie looks to me, and says, "Angel, what was going on that you were confused about?"

Yes, of course she noticed my perplexity. More and more, the sharing of feelings between us is becoming mutual. It is not only I who knows her emotions, but she seems to be growing in the ability to sense mine. She still needs me to speak directly to her, though, in order to know my thoughts. I wonder, briefly, if this might ever evolve as well.

"It has to do with the state of Jonathan's soul."

"I was actually wondering about that," Timothy interjects. "I asked Guardian to check out how his soul was doing without Demon, or whether Demon had even taken it with him when he left."

"A very astute inquiry, Timothy."

Gabe observes from the bed, his head and foot both resting on pillows. He asks, "What?" He is not as familiar with this topic as are Natalie and Timothy, who after all have been avidly pursuing the topic of Guardians for months. Therefore, I begin with a summary of what the children know so far.

"When a human is born, a Guardian brings to them a soul to share. The human's actions in life develop the soul, and the Guardian whispers encouragement throughout the lifetime of the human. Once the human lifetime is complete, the soul returns to the Guardian, to be held forevermore."

Gabe listens to Natalie repeat my words, trying to comprehend. This all still seems very new and strange to him.

"The Guardian is tied to the soul. Never before have I, nor any of the other Guardians who have witnessed Jonathan's current circumstances, beheld a human whose Guardian has apparently vanished, leaving the soul behind."

Natalie continues to relay my words, primarily to Gabe, to help him understand as well as she and Timothy do.

"In answer to your question, Timothy, no, Demon did not take the soul with him. Jonathan retains his soul."

Timothy nods and writes in his notebook.

"However," I continue, *"his soul is greatly diminished. As a human's life unfolds, their soul increases, glowing with power as the human's actions nourish the growing soul. To a Guardian, the soul is visible as a sort of glowing light within and surrounding the human."*

Natalie's brow creases with concentration, as she imagines the sight. "Do you mean, like, an aura? I read about those somewhere. That some people can see other people's auras?"

"Yes, exactly, an aura is an apt way to describe the appearance of the soul to a Guardian. It is quite unlikely that many humans have really been able to perceive this, however. It would certainly be very unusual. The soul is also comprised of matter which cannot interact with the physical world, and therefore is not visible to humans."

The children all glance at each other, wondering if they might be able to detect the souls' auras. *"No, my children, you cannot see each other's souls. I do, however, as do all Guardians."*

Timothy returns the conversation to his line of questioning. "So, you said something about Jonathan's soul is confusing?"

The child's intelligence continues to impress. He does not forget any detail, even without taking notes. *"Yes, something unusual has occurred. More unusual than the mere fact of Demon's absence. From the moment Demon vanished, Jonathan's soul has been extremely small, very dim, barely visible."*

Gabe is following along, and asks, "Is that why he's been acting so weird? Because his soul shrank?"

"It is unclear whether his decreased level of activity is due to the absence of his Guardian, or the reduction of his soul, or both. Likely it is both."

"The whole reason his soul shrank is because Demon is gone, though, right?" Gabe inquires. "So it really isn't two different things, is it? It's just one thing."

His observation is quite accurate. Although I have grown accustomed to both Natalie and Timothy making statements which display a deep understanding of the world, to see Gabe do so is both a pleasure and a surprise. I must give him more credit in future.

Gabe's Guardian, who has been named Aaron by the Seer, regards me wryly, of course already being familiar with Gabe's high level of intelligence. I shrug and smile to indicate my concurrence.

"Yes, Gabe, you are correct. Jonathan's soul is only smaller because of the absence of his Guardian. It can be described as aspects of a single event."

"You already knew his soul was smaller, though, right?" Timothy asks. "Was there something else confusing that happened today?"

The young scientist pulls the discussion back to the specifics of the experiment. *"Yes, Timothy, something new happened, something very surprising."* The children stare at each other, waiting breathlessly to hear what new development I have to report. *"We do not know why, but when Natalie touched him, his soul briefly brightened again."*

The children seem interested in this information, but clearly do not grasp the import. Timothy writes in his notebook. "So," Natalie muses, "touching Jonathan can help him?"

"Perhaps, my dear. However, when others have touched him, including his parents, there was no improvement in his soul. It was only your touch, Natalie, which made any difference."

Gabe looks over at his sister, thinking that the more he learns about her, the stranger it gets. *"Ah, my darling,"* Aaron whispers to him. Gabe, like always, will not sense the message, but as with all Guardians, this does not dissuade the effort. *"Your sister is unique, and marvelous, and it is wonderful that she has chosen to include you in the group of people who know about Guardians. I am so pleased you have learned of our existence, and that your knowledge continues to expand."*

"Why only her?" Timothy asks, wanting more specific information.

"I do not know, Timothy, but your Guardian and I have speculated about this. We assume it is because, as a Seer, her ability to perceive her own Guardian must extend to a further ability to interact with the matter which comprises a soul. But we do not understand how, or why."

"Huh," Timothy says, his mind racing. He has been presented with a new mystery, which is as equally puzzling to Guardians as to humans. Timothy does not view this as a satisfactory answer. He will not allow a mystery to remain unexplored. To Timothy, this is simply an invitation to devise an experiment to uncover the secrets. His mind begins crafting a series of questions, and he speedily writes in his notebook.

Natalie watches him eagerly, anticipating the process which she knows is about to unfold. Gabe looks quizzically at his sister, and she smiles and puts her finger to her lips. He shrugs and lays back against the pillow, figuring he'll just have to wait to see what is happening.

Chapter 7

Souls

Timothy's

My beloved is doing exactly what he loves, exactly what he excels at. He is planning the next step in the experiment. The endeavor which began months ago with the discovery of the use of energy to allow Guardians to speak to each other at a distance, has metamorphosed into Natalie's Jonathan Project. It is one ongoing discovery of all things relating to Guardians.

I send him my feelings of approval and admiration, but I do not whisper to him. Even I wish to be still, to support his concentration.

The room is silent but for the scratch of Timothy's pencil against the paper. After several minutes, he finishes writing and reads back over the last few pages in his notebook. He nods, satisfied with the plan.

Looking up, he says, "Okay, I have some questions." Natalie grins.

"First," he says, "I would like a more precise description of souls in general. Then I want to move on to what is going on with Jonathan's soul. Angel, what else can you tell us about how souls work?"

Natalie's Guardian smiles, pleased that my dearest has taken control of the questioning. It is this process which has, many times, led us to a deeper understanding of important topics.

This will be very difficult to explain, though. The nature of Guardians and the nature of human souls have been so entangled, for so long, that Angel must pause for a moment to consider how to begin.

"I believe, my children, that to answer this question, I must provide some background information about Guardians."

Timothy nods, expecting this. This is not the first time Angel's explanations must start with a deeper history, before Timothy's questions can be answered.

"A long time ago, very very long, many thousands of years before the bible was written, even long before humans began building cities, is when this story must begin."

Natalie perks up at the mention of the bible. This has been a subject of her intense interest and study recently, ever since Angel imparted to her and Timothy the shocking news that humans invented the concepts of God and religion. She has wished to understand how religions develop, and then to find a way to bring other humans to a place of understanding and peace in which there is no longer any reason or desire to battle each other over their religious beliefs. Part of her process has been to learn about the historical truth of the biblical stories. She has been somewhat stymied in this effort by the events involving Jonathan, and has not yet been able to obtain books about biblical archeology as she has wished. Therefore, she hopes that this discussion will provide additional insight. However, the events Angel is referring to occurred long before humans ever imagined the concept of religion.

Angel considers how to proceed, then adds, *"I must take you still further back into the past, before we can even begin the account of souls. Are you all familiar with the concept of evolution, my children?"*

Timothy raises his eyebrows, not expecting this to enter into the discussion. He has read of evolution, in the upper level science books which his teacher makes available to him when he has finished his second grade assignments. Natalie and Gabe look at each other, each having heard the word but not fully understanding the concept.

Timothy sees the perplexed expressions on their faces, and attempts to enlighten them. "Evolution is the idea that creatures change over time. They grow stronger legs or faster wings or something else useful. When a creature develops a new feature that helps them survive better, they are more likely to live long enough to have babies, then their babies can have the new feature too. Eventually when enough of these little changes happen, they end up being a different species. Like the way you've heard humans evolved from apes." He wishes to have this description confirmed. "Is that right, Angel?"

"Yes, Timothy, your definition is accurate. With evolution, a species will continue to grow and develop, generation by generation, gaining advantages over time. This is how humans came into being. Millions of years ago, apelike creatures adapted to their changing environment by developing new abilities, such as how to walk upright. Their bodies changed over many generations, eventually creating legs more suited to walking, hands more suited to grasping, and so on." Angel pauses to allow Natalie to finish repeating the words, and to ensure that each of the children is following along with the information.

"As the human body slowly came closer to the way it is shaped today, so did the human mind adapt to the changing conditions. The brain grew, and achieved new skills and understanding. The new abilities were passed down through the generations, each new individual acquiring the adaptations of their ancestors."

Timothy is rapt with attention. He wonders how it is that Angel is able to teach this lesson, when he has previously told the children they must be the ones to achieve their own learning, because Guardians can only help them understand what they have studied. Angel wishes to clarify this.

"There is no human course of education which could enlighten you regarding matters involving Guardians. As a Guardian I would not be familiar with many of the topics you might study, and it would be best to allow you to learn academic subjects on your own, then discuss them with me later. However, I am able to provide this particular instruction, because this knowledge is deeply ingrained in the identity of all Guardians. This is a fundamental part of who we are, and why we are here."

Timothy and Natalie begin feeling a sense of wonder, realizing they have touched here upon one of the deep mysteries of reality, and that they will be learning information unavailable to other humans. Gabe listens, accepting the lesson without considering the deeper ramifications.

Angel waits a moment to ensure that the children have understood him so far, then continues. *"As early humans adapted to changes in their environment and gained new skills, the glimmers of their first societies began to emerge. They had long known how to use tools, for instance, but began making more advanced versions. They began building more intricate shelters. They began creating other objects to assist them in their lives, such as containers and clothing. Many of their skills grew, as their brains developed and changed over the generations."*

The children follow along with the recitation of their early history, Timothy nodding as each new piece of information is absorbed.

"The evolution of humans continued, assisting them in their development, until one day a new adaptation arose, the most significant evolutionary change yet. A human was born whose brain had an innate ability to attract the matter of which Guardians are made."

"Dark matter," interjects Timothy.

"Yes, my child, your scientists refer to it as dark matter." Timothy and Natalie look at each other, having been told before of dark matter and its relation to Guardians. *"This new human adaptation drew a bit of dark matter to it. There was something about the human's mind which attracted this matter, gathered a tiny bit, and held it within. This was the beginning of the human soul. It was rudimentary compared to how it has evolved today, but it made all the difference to the human who possessed it."*

The children listen with wide eyes, enraptured by this description. It had not occurred to them previously to speculate about how souls came into being. This is wondrous news to them. As always, Angel pauses after every sentence or two, in order to allow Natalie to repeat the information to the other children.

"The first human soul added to the abilities of the human who bore it. This human had enhanced creativity, and was therefore able to conceive of new ways to do things. This assisted the human's community, and improved their mutual chances for survival. This individual was admired by the other humans, due to their innovations which added to the comfort and success of the community. When this human reproduced, the adaptation allowing for a tiny bit of dark matter to be incorporated into the mind was passed down to their children."

I lovingly observe as Timothy's mind processes these facts, busily categorizing each facet of the new information, considering further avenues of questioning to expand his understanding of the subject.

Angel continues. *"The descendants of the first human who had the rudimentary soul were equally as creative and useful to their communities. The other humans began to revere them, and attempt to imitate their designs. Within a few generations, many humans possessed the dark matter characteristic, and human society had begun to blossom with creativity, and with new innovations. Humans began to conceive of using art to enhance their products, and there was a veritable explosion of inventions and changes to the products which they used in their daily lives. This occurred some fifty or sixty thousand years ago, and modern archeologists have noticed that at this time human society underwent a significant transformation. Thus began the earliest hints of human civilization."*

Natalie and Timothy are fascinated, while Gabe is becoming somewhat overwhelmed with the volume of information being delivered. He wonders if this is really how his sister and her friend spend all their time. Aaron whispers encouragement to him, to help him focus his attention. Angel tries to wrap up the historical portion of the lesson.

"As the number of humans with the new dark matter adaptation expanded, additional matter was attracted to the locations in which these humans resided. Eventually, the matter itself began to adapt. While more and more of it gathered, and the concentration of it became denser, it began to surround the human communities. As the humans with the adaptation lived their lives and then died, the matter they had held was released back into the gathering mass, and the memories contained within the matter survived. As each of the memories merged with the others, and the volume of dark matter attracted to the area increased, a new consciousness was formed. The Guardians were born."

Timothy is intensely focused. "So, evolution happened to both humans and guardians, right?"

"Yes, Timothy, that is a good way to put it. Guardians evolved to accompany the humans as they developed. Within a few more generations, almost all humans had this adaptation. The volume of dark matter surrounding them was great indeed, and each time a new human was born with the characteristic, when their ability to capture dark matter was triggered, a Guardian accompanied the little spark of matter which was to become the human's soul. This has continued throughout the millennia. Eventually every human had the same characteristic, and therefore all humans have a soul, comprised of a tiny amount of dark matter, and Guarded by one of us."

As Angel concludes the history, the children each reflect upon the new knowledge. Gabe accepts the history of souls and Guardians as he does much of his other learning, with acceptance but not obsession. Natalie is filled with delight to know of the background of her beloved Angel. Timothy ponders the scientific aspects of the lesson, wondering how the mind captures the dark matter, what it was that caused the Guardians to begin tending to individual humans, and whether human scientists would be able to invent instruments to locate the dark matter within the human brain. He makes notations in his notebook.

Angel smiles upon the children as they absorb the lesson, waiting for them to be ready to proceed.

Timothy is gathering follow-up questions in his mind. However, Gabe speaks first. "So, what's the deal with Jonathan's soul?" Of course Gabe wishes to focus on the specifics of how his best friend is impacted by this knowledge, rather than on the esoteric and philosophical implications of the creation of souls. He wants tangible, current answers.

Natalie looks to Timothy, knowing he was planning to ask more questions about the background, but he decides to wait for those questions, and instead echoes Gabe's inquiry. "Yes," he says, "please tell us what is going on with Jonathan now."

Chapter 8

Hypothesis

Natalie

All of this information about how guardians and souls got started is so amazing. They've been around for such a long time, but not forever. I know that I'll be thinking about all of it a lot, trying to understand. Angel will help me.

But for now, I agree. We want to know how to help Jonathan.

Angel has been watching patiently each time I repeat a sentence to Gabe and Timothy. I'm trying as hard as I can to get all the words right, since I know how important this is. Angel tells me I'm doing a good job, and I'm telling them everything perfectly fine.

"As we have discussed, Jonathan's soul is present, but without his Guardian, it is diminished. When souls grow during their lifetime, they become brighter and stronger. Jonathan's soul had grown very bright and strong indeed. However, when Demon vanished, all of the growth in Jonathan's soul vanished as well. It is now barely visible, barely glowing. When Natalie touched his hand earlier today, it began emitting a stronger light. As soon as the contact with her hand ended, his soul reverted to the lessened state. This occurred a second time as she touched his shoulder while we were departing."

Timothy nods. Angel has told us most of this before, he is just summarizing. Timothy looks over at me, and I know he's thinking about what this can all mean. "So there is something about Natalie's touch that helps," he says. "I know it helps me feel better sometimes when she touches me."

"Me, too," Gabe adds quietly. I'm a little surprised to hear him say this, and look over at him. He gives me a gentle little smile. "Yeah, Nat, it's true, I've always known that if you give me a hug or something when I am sad, I feel a lot better. More than Mom or Dad. There's something about you that's different."

I giggle. "Well, obviously," I say, pointing over to Angel. Although, of course, Gabe can't see him.

Timothy

"All right," I tell them, "this should be the next phase of our experiment. Our hypothesis is that Natalie's touch is different. We need to try to figure out more about this."

Natalie rolls her eyes. I tell her, "No, Natalie, you have to take this seriously. You know lots of things about you are different. This is one of them. I'm sure you want to learn as much as you can, right?"

Natalie says, "Sorry. Yes, I want to learn as much as I can, since we have to figure out how to help Jonathan."

Gabe is still laying on Natalie's bed. "Okay, what do we do?"

I think about what to do next. "I think we should have Angel and Guardian watch while Natalie touches us." I realize I should include Gabe's guardian too, since he is here as well. Everyone can participate in the experiment. "And Aaron, of course."

Gabe blinks. "Um, yeah, all right."

"First, I would like Angel to tell us anything else there is to know about what happens when Natalie touches someone."

Natalie looks to the side, and after a minute says, "Angel says he and Guardian and Aaron are remembering times I have touched anyone and something seemed to happen. Apparently there have been a lot of times that if someone is sad when I touch them, they feel better." She is quiet for a second, then says, "I guess I always knew that, but I didn't know it was any different from other people. I thought anybody could touch someone to make them feel better."

I write it down in my notebook. "Angel, can her touch do anything other than help sad people feel better? Like, can she change other feelings?"

Natalie listens to Angel, then says, "Angel says that he has seen it work with other feelings. Especially when I first started the Jonathan Project, if I touched his hand or something while he was feeling mad or annoyed or wanting to be mean, it would help change the way he felt."

I write this down.

Gabe asks, "What about other stuff? Like pain? Could she help with that?"

Natalie looks over at Gabe and her forehead wrinkles. "Is your ankle still hurting?"

"Yeah, a little."

"Want me to get you some ice? Or Tylenol?" she asks him.

"Wait!" I say. "First, Angel, has Natalie ever been able to help someone who had physical pain?"

Gabe snorts. "Are we going to experiment with my ankle now?"

"Of course," I tell him. "It's the perfect opportunity."

Natalie goes over to Gabe and starts to fluff up the pillow under his foot, but I say, "Wait!" again. "Hold on, let's do this right. Gabe, you don't mind waiting for a couple of minutes, do you?"

"Um, no, I guess not," he says.

"Okay, Angel, do you think she can help with pain?"

Natalie listens to him. "He thinks it might be possible, but it is difficult to separate the reaction to physical pain from emotions. So it might be hard to tell." She frowns. "I guess I don't really understand."

"Well, let's do some experiments. First, I am going to touch Gabe as a control. So we can rule out any random touch being effective."

Natalie says, "That's a good idea. Do you think you should touch his skin or his clothes?"

I consider this. "I think skin would be best. So the contact is as close as it can be. Gabe, would you mind lifting up your pants leg a little so I can touch your knee, up over your cast?"

I can tell that Gabe thinks this is silly, but he does it. "Okay," I say, "guardians, please all check to see whether anything happens when I touch him." I lean over to the bed and put my hand on top of Gabe's knee, then count to ten in my mind, and take my hand back off.

Gabe stares at me while I'm doing this.

"Did you feel anything different?" I ask him.

"Only that it feels different to have some dude grabbing my knee," he scoffs.

"Does your ankle still hurt the same way?" I ask him. I think he is trying to joke around, but this really isn't the time for jokes. We need to focus on the experiment.

"Yeah," he says.

"Did any of you guardians notice anything happening?" I ask.

Natalie looks to the side, then tells me, "No."

I write that down in my notebook.

"Okay, Natalie, I want you to do it next. Hold your hand on his knee for ten seconds. Guardians, please monitor whether anything changes."

She leans over the bed and puts her hand on Gabe's knee, and counts to ten. Then she asks Gabe, "Well?"

"Um, I don't know," he says, "I can't tell. Maybe?"

I take in a deep breath. "We need to be as precise as possible. Please. Gabe, when you think maybe something happened, let's be specific. Did the pain in your ankle change at all?"

He rolls his eyes a little, but then says, "Okay, I'll try to be serious." He thinks. "I don't think the actual pain changed, but somehow I felt a little better."

I ask Angel, "Can you tell what happened?"

Natalie listens, then says, "Angel says that since pain and emotions are all sensed inside the brain, it is difficult to tell the difference between them when I touch someone. He says the guardians all watched carefully, and there wasn't any physical change in the injured ankle at all. But the pain Gabe was feeling was reduced, maybe because he wasn't feeling as bothered by it."

She lifts her hands and shrugs. "I'm not sure that makes very much sense."

Gabe looks thoughtful, then says, "Maybe it does make sense. I really didn't feel anything different in my ankle, but I think maybe I wasn't noticing it as much."

I write this down in my notebook. It is frustrating that this kind of experiment is so hard to get exact results. Stuff about feelings doesn't seem very scientific.

"Okay, I'm not sure we'll get a better answer about the pain, but I have another question. Angel, when Natalie touched Gabe, or when she touches someone else, do you see any change at all in their soul? Like what happened with Jonathan?"

Natalie says, "They haven't ever noticed a change in a soul before. He thinks it only changed because Demon is missing and Jonathan's soul is so small."

I write that down, then say, "Can we repeat the experiment one more time? To be sure we aren't missing anything? This time, Gabe, I want you to concentrate on what you are feeling and try to see if you can find another way to describe it. Guardians, can you please pay extra attention to whether anything happens with Gabe's soul when Natalie touches him?"

Natalie looks at Gabe, and he nods. So she does it again, holding her hand on his knee and counting to ten. He closes his eyes, I guess so he can concentrate better. I know that helps me sometimes too.

When she lifts up her hand, she asks Gabe, "Anything?"

He looks up at the ceiling, then says, "Yes, I think it's what I said before. I felt like the pain wasn't bothering me as much, even though it was still there. Like maybe you touching me helped me live with it?"

Natalie shrugs. Then she listens to Angel, and says, "Angel says they all monitored Gabe's soul carefully, and thought that perhaps there was a small gleam while I touched him. But he says human souls are changing all the time, so it is impossible to tell what caused this change."

I write some more, then stop to think for a minute. "I don't think we have discovered anything specific. There is a possibility that Gabe felt better from Natalie's touch, but I don't think we can quantify it."

"Can I get Gabe something for his ankle now?" Natalie asks.

"Yes, go ahead," I tell her. Then while she goes downstairs to ask her Mom for some Tylenol, I think about what to do next. Their Mom comes in and checks on Gabe, gives him some Tylenol, then goes back out.

Natalie looks at me. "What should we do now?" she asks.

"I don't think we can pursue this experiment more right now. We have learned a little, but we can't replicate the conditions we need for more. I would like to learn more about what happens when you touch somebody who is mad or scared or sad, but we have to wait until it happens. And I want to know a lot more about what happens when you touch Jonathan."

"Okay," she says.

"So, I have to give the guardians an assignment. I would like you all to always be paying attention, whenever Natalie touches anybody, especially Jonathan. Report back if she helps anyone change their feelings, and tell us everything that happens when she touches Jonathan. We'll have to let this be an ongoing experiment. All right?"

Natalie looks to the side, then says, "Yep, they're all on board. They'll let us know when anything happens."

Gabe says, "Well, if we're done with that, I'm going to go play with my Gameboy. Unless you need me for anything else?"

Natalie looks at me. "No," I say, "that's all I can think of for now."

"Okay," he says, and gets up with his crutches to go to his room.

Natalie and I are left in her room. "Soooo," she says, "want to read books?"

Chapter 9

Fascinating

Natalie's

Timothy's experiment regarding Natalie's touch is fascinating. From the time she was a tiny infant, she has instinctively used her touch to comfort others in her family. It has been clear from the beginning that there is something soothing about her presence. I had always attributed it to her empathic abilities, her awareness of the emotions of others and her determination to bring happiness whenever she can. But now, with the experience regarding Jonathan's soul, and Timothy highlighting the issue, I begin to suspect there is something specific about Natalie's touch which is different from that of other humans.

There are many things about Natalie which are unusual. Perhaps this is one more. As a Seer, she can perceive her Guardian. Clearly, there is something about her that allows her to at least discern the dark matter of which I am made. Can she actually interact with such matter? Her touch caused Jonathan's soul to flare. It appears her touch actually may also have a tangible effect on the minds of others, modifying their emotions.

There are other unusual characteristics as well. I have noticed when she suffers any injury, her healing process is faster than that of other humans. She has never experienced illness. She sleeps for fewer hours than other humans her age. She even appears to be able to function in lower light than normal, being able to read books at night using only the light entering her room from the streetlamp outside. The differences are all quite subtle, not necessarily attributes which would be noticed by other people.

All humans have an evolutionary adaptation allowing them to hold a tiny portion of dark matter, which is the soul brought to them by a Guardian. Perhaps as a Seer she has a further adaptation? Perhaps the Seer is formed in such a way that the dark matter impacts all of her bodily systems?

I do not know. As a Guardian I can perceive the soul of my beloved, of course. I know all of her thoughts and emotions, and am constantly aware of her senses and physical condition. But I do not possess expertise in how the genetic structure of a human might interact with dark matter. I know a genetic mutation was the origin of humans' ability to possess enough dark matter to comprise a soul. I can not, however, pinpoint the genes which allow this to happen. Similarly, the specific modifications in the body of the Seer allowing dark matter to provide enhanced abilities are not clear to me. I can only observe, and attempt to understand.

I am eager to continue with Timothy's experiment. I and the other Guardians will do as instructed, and diligently track any noticeable impact which can be attributed to Natalie's touch, whether with Jonathan or any other human.

We will learn, yet again, through the scientific process as directed by a brilliant child.

Michael's

My beloved is robotically accomplishing his tasks, on his first day returning to duty on his ship. He enjoyed his leave following deployment, but sadly the time which passed was insufficient to bring healing to his troubled mind. Nor were the actions of his wife effective, despite her diligent efforts. She prepared his favorite meals, ensured that their child was quiet and stayed out of the way, even arranged outings designed to bring peace and healing to Michael. He appreciated it all. Yet, every night he continues to experience nightmares and disrupted sleep, triggered by the trauma of being involved in the wartime activities conducted on his Navy vessel.

A deep exhaustion has settled in, even during his weeks of vacation. He refuses to acknowledge that anything is amiss. He is determined to set things to rights by simply ignoring his symptoms, and carrying on with his duties. He speaks with his coworkers, manages his daily routine, takes care of business.

But I am distressed on his behalf. All I can do is support him, offering my silent encouragement. I must only hope that it helps.

"My darling, with time, you will mend. Perhaps you are correct, and the best way to go forward is to simply do your work, and try not to think about the problems you have been having. I am here, beloved, here with support for you, here with love."

Laura

Brenda called and said they'd bring Timothy home later this afternoon, since they plan to come by and pick up her Christmas decorations.

Since Michael returned to work today, this leaves me a day to myself, after I finished up a couple of haircuts at the salon in the morning.

I'm kind of sorry to hear she's planning to bring her decorations to Ron's house. I'm afraid it means they aren't planning to stay here over the holidays.

At least Timothy is able to spend time with his friend. I'll have to talk to Brenda about arranging play dates over Christmas break, since I guess I have to assume they'll be staying over at Ron's.

I had been hoping they'd end up all living here at Brenda's, but I'll bet after they've spent all of Christmas break at Ron's, they'll be more likely to pick his house. It's bigger, and has a yard for the kids. I know it's been hard to decide where to live, but I'm thinking maybe the decision has been made. I can't say I don't understand.

Sigh. Timothy won't be able to wave goodnight from his window to his friend any more.

And of course, I won't have my best friend next door.

Well, I just have to focus on my family. On Michael. He was very quiet before leaving for work today, but I could tell he was tense. I had hoped that a two week vacation would see him well-rested before he had to go back to work, but I'm worried it wasn't enough. We're both exhausted. Neither one of us has been sleeping through the night, with his constant nightmares.

Well, speaking of that, I suppose this would be a good time to squeeze in a nap.

Brad

I wrap up my day at the grocery store and head home. There's not much daylight left. I always kind of hate it after Daylight Savings Time ends and it starts getting dark so early. Hopefully when I get home there will still be a chance to spend some time with Jonathan in the yard, playing with the dog.

He's seemed so dull all week. I suppose we could have gone ahead and sent him to school, since when they discharged him from the hospital they said everything seemed fine. But there were only a couple of days left before Christmas break, and Stef was so anxious about him that it seemed best to keep him home, let her keep an eye on him.

I suppose he needed it. He has spent the week sitting around, barely doing anything. It's been strange. I'd started to have this weird sense that it was reminding me of something, then yesterday with a bang I realized what it was. It was like when Stef's Mom died, while Jonathan was a baby. And Stefanie spent a couple of months sitting around, quiet and still, barely engaged in anything. It was what she needed to do, mourning for her Mom, full of grief. The only thing she would do is take care of Jonathan.

And now Jonathan seems the same. We can't interest him in anything. He doesn't seem to have any desire to play or watch t.v., or really take any initiative at all. The only thing I have seen him want to do is play with the dog, but even that is strangely subdued. It's so much like when Stef was grieving, and all she could do was sit with her toddler, waiting to feel better.

But why is Jonathan acting like this? It isn't like he is in mourning. Nobody has died. He's probably missing Gabe, since he hasn't seen him since the hospital, but that isn't unheard of. Gabe lives over at his Mom's house during the school week, so Jonathan wouldn't have seen him this week anyway. I really can't understand what's going on.

I've hesitated to mention this to Stef. I don't want her to be more worried than she already is. She's pregnant, and I was so worried when Jonathan was in the hospital that she wouldn't be able to handle the stress. She's gotten through it okay, it seems, but I don't want to add any problems by mentioning my worry about Jonathan's weird behavior. Besides, she told me yesterday at the doctor they said everything seems normal.

I guess I just have to wait. I waited it out with Stef after her Mom died. This will end too.

When I get home and go inside, I see Jonathan is sitting on the couch and watching t.v. That's the first time this week - since I had technically grounded him from t.v. a week ago, as a punishment for getting into a fight, he shouldn't have been watching it anyway. But what is weird is he never even asked about it. I don't know whether he even remembered he had been grounded after his accident. Neither of us mentioned it, since it would have seemed kind of awkward to ask him why he wasn't asking about t.v., and then have to enforce the discipline anyway.

Stef comes over and gives me a hug. "So, how's the kid been doing today?" I ask her.

"Really good," she says.

"Really?"

"Yeah. Gabe came over, and Natalie and Timothy even came. They ended up going out in the back yard and playing with Socks for a while. Jonathan was throwing the ball to him and everything. He seemed like he had a lot more energy than he has all week."

"Seriously? Wow, that's great to hear," I say. What a relief! Maybe he's starting to come out of whatever funk he's been in.

"I told him he could watch t.v. again, by the way," she tells me. "It's been a week. So he's been watching it, but I'm not sure he's really paying attention. He hasn't changed the channel even though his cartoons ended an hour ago and it's a talk show now." She shrugs.

Oh. Well, maybe it'll take a while for him to really come back around to himself.

Chapter 10

Another Christmas Eve

Ron

Another Christmas Eve together with Brenda. This time, it isn't fraught with all the anxiety I felt last year, trying to get ready for the gathering with our friends while not really knowing how Brenda would feel about everything. This time, I know she is staying, I know she is happy to be here with me. It gives the entire day this wonderful glow for me. I'm so happy I can hardly believe it.

My family is in the kitchen, laughing and chatting while they make Christmas cookies. This was Natalie's idea, of course. She's always full of plans for how to make everyone happy. She told Brenda that if everybody is coming over, she'd like to have a bunch of decorated cookies to serve. So, they've got this huge production line going, mixing up batches of different kinds of cookies, trays going in and out of the oven, the table covered with frosting and sprinkles and platters with cookies in various stages of completion.

Laura and Timothy are here too, joining in all the fun. Natalie invited them to come over early, before it's time to set up the luminarias, so they can help with the cookie assembly line. Timothy and Gabe are sitting at the table, trying to decorate some of the cookies with frosting, while Natalie giggles at their clumsy efforts. Apparently boys are nowhere near fastidious enough in their decoration techniques.

Brenda and Laura are chatting away, apparently having the time of their lives. I'm starting to get the paper bags and candles and sand ready to do the luminarias later.

I manage to catch Brenda's eye from across the room, and blow her an air kiss, and she gives me a radiant smile. I chuckle and look down, figuring that I shouldn't try to point out the smear of flour across her lovely cheek. She's so adorable.

Michael

Laura's already over at Ron's house with Timothy. I'm running some errands, glad I have today off work. I haven't managed to get her a Christmas present yet, and today's the deadline, so I have to figure it out. I'm down at the mall, Fashion Valley, trying to figure out what she'd want. I don't know. Like, a scarf or something maybe?

I wish I hadn't put this off for so long. I hate shopping, but by delaying I've only made it much worse for myself. It would have been better at the mall if it wasn't the day before Christmas. It is so crowded here. I'm brushing shoulders against other people, trying to get into the department store to find something I can buy, so I can get out of here ASAP.

Here, there's a display of scarves. I sort through them, searching for one to match the color of Laura's blue eyes. There's a nice yellow one with light blue flowers. I'm peering at it to make sure it is the right shade.

There's a bang behind me. I whirl around, on high alert, bumping into the stand of scarves, ready for action. My heart rate skyrockets. My vision darkens. There's a roaring in my ears. It's happening. It's an attack. I hear the shouts of the civilians. I crouch behind the barricade, taking cover, ready to engage. I feel somebody grab my shoulder. I shout and lunge to the side, swinging back around to confront my attacker.

A young sales girl shrinks back from me. I remember where I am. Not there. Not over there. Not Afghanistan. I'm here. Reality comes crashing down over me again. It's just San Diego. Just a department store. The scarves are scattered on the floor around me. I must have knocked them over. The girl asks, her voice trembling, "Sir, are you all right?"

I feel a hot red blush of embarrassment flaming across my face.

"Sorry," I mutter. "I guess I tripped."

She stares at me, baffled. She knows I didn't trip. "Can I help you with something?"

I realize I'm still holding the yellow and blue scarf in my hand. "Um, yeah, I want to buy this," I say, lamely, mortified.

Another employee comes over and starts picking up the scarves, gawking at me apprehensively. Other customers pause as they pass, watching the scene.

"Yes, sir," the sales girl says, eyes wide. "I can help you at register two." I follow her over. I can't wait to get out of here.

Michael's

"My dearest, you are safe, there is no threat, there is no battle, all is well. Peace, my darling, try to stay calm. You are safe. You are fine."

The incident is deeply disquieting to Michael, and to myself. My beloved imagined himself to be in the midst of battle, triggered by a noise made by something dropping nearby. His mind immediately invented a scenario in which he was under threat, had to be prepared to defend himself. There was no threat, but for a few moments it seemed utterly real to him.

The weeks which have passed since he returned home from his long deployment have not brought the peace I had hoped for. His nightmares continue, and now his visions of violence and harm have begun seeping into his waking hours as well.

The situation is deeply worrisome.

"Peace, my darling, find calm, know yourself to be safe, those around you are safe. All is well, my dear. Peace. Calm."

Brad

"Okay folks, time to head over to Ron's house," I tell them. Stefanie grabs the bag of gifts, and I hold the hot casserole dish. Jonathan gets up from the couch, where he had been sitting waiting, his shoes and jacket already on.

It's been gradual, but in the week or two since the hospital, he seems to be getting closer to normal. He's still quiet, but he is talking a little more, and taking more interest in doing things. I guess he was initially rattled by the whole thing, but he seems okay now. Mostly.

It's been interesting how much he's hanging around with Gabe's sister now. I thought at first that she simply wanted to play with the dog, since she loves him so much. And Socks seems to love her about as much as he loves Jonathan. Every time she shows up with her brother, which has been at least once a day now that their family is staying put at Ron's house, Socks goes rushing over to her, panting and wagging and frantically excited.

I expected she'd play with Socks, while Gabe and Jonathan did their own thing. But I realized after the first couple of days that this wasn't what was happening. Their dynamic has changed somehow. Natalie seems to want to spend time with Jonathan as much as Gabe does. More, in fact. Every time I turn around, Natalie is reaching out to hold Jonathan's hand, or touch his shoulder, or lean against his side. If they were a little older, I'd think something is going on between them. But they're way too young for that. It's more like Natalie is hovering over him like a little mother hen, trying to take care of him.

A month ago I think it would have annoyed the heck out of him. But now, he seems to accept it fine. I never see him trying to move away from her, or tell her to leave him alone. He would have before. Now, things are different, I guess. Gabe doesn't seem to be at all bothered by his little sister tagging along.

I think whatever is going on is helping Jonathan, though. He has gone from totally lethargic when he first got back from the hospital, to acting closer to normal. Not rambunctious like he was before, but at least up and doing things.

I suppose it was just a phase he was going through. And this is another one.

Well, tonight should be fun, doing luminarias with Ron and his family again.

Jonathan actually gets out in front of us, leading the way to his friend's house. Yeah, he's getting better. Slowly but surely.

Natalie's

The other Guardians and I continue to monitor the progress of Jonathan's soul. For the past week, Natalie has determinedly followed a program of rehabilitation, spending as much time as possible with him, and particularly maintaining physical contact whenever she can. Jonathan has no idea he is the subject of this effort, any more than he has been aware of any of the events since the Jonathan Project began.

After Timothy assigned us the task of watching and reporting any changes to Jonathan's soul, we have observed an incremental improvement, each time Natalie touches him.

The touch of the Seer, we have confirmed, is a significant factor in Jonathan's recovery. Each time she touches him in any manner, his soul brightens. Feebly at first, and only temporarily. However, over the last few days, his soul appears to be better able to cling to the glow which her touch infuses in it. Now, when Natalie touches him, causing a flash in his soul to occur, a remnant of the flare remains even after the contact ceases. So over time, the brightness has slightly increased, day by day. Although his soul continues to be drastically diminished from the mighty beacon it had become, it at least has grown enough to more closely resemble that of other humans. It is still a fraction of what it should be, but it has clearly improved.

We have not observed his soul brightening through any of Jonathan's own actions. It is only the touch of the Seer which brings any improvement. Further, there continues to be no sign at all of his Guardian. Demon is nowhere to be found. I had thought perhaps with the brightening of his soul, Demon would find a way to return, but it has not occurred. It is most perplexing.

Jonathan's personality continues to be distinctly muted. Thankfully, his prior proclivity towards cruelty has shown no signs of manifesting once again. With his savage side apparently vanquished, he has become a quiet, sweet child. He tolerates Natalie's attentions docilely, feeling the gentle warmth of her touch as it illuminates his soul.

She is both optimistic and troubled regarding his condition. She knows he has drastically changed. It had always been her intention to encourage him to be kinder, but this is certainly not the mechanism she had intended. She wished for him to choose it deliberately, not to be forced into this meek disposition by the disappearance of his Guardian. She knows that it is only Demon's absence which leaves Jonathan so pliable. She wishes for Demon's return, despite the conflict which led to his disappearance, because without his Guardian Jonathan is incomplete.

Because she knows her efforts have helped him, she intends to continue. She reports her progress regularly to Timothy, who tracks the progress of the experiment and makes frequent suggestions for additional activities designed to assist with the endeavor.

I, and the other Guardians, continue to watch the entire scenario unfold with a constant sense of astonishment. What will the Seer lead us to next? What new procedures can Timothy invent to uncover additional world altering facts? How will we all be changed?

49

Chapter 11

One Giant Experiment

Gabe

"Hey, Jon!" I'm glad to see he's here to help us set up the Christmas Eve luminarias. Natalie comes running over to the front door, and as soon as he gets in she gives him a smile and takes his hand. I know what she's doing, trying to touch him every chance she gets. I can see it helping him.

He gives her a little smile too, just a glimmer of what his big bright smile used to be. He lets her lead him inside to where we have all the cookies set up on the kitchen table.

Timothy is waiting there. He isn't holding his notebook and taking notes, but he might as well be. He's ready to watch everything, and remember stuff to write down later. I've started to get used to the fact that to him, this is all one giant experiment, and he is gathering data to analyze later. It's all about proving a hypothesis, or reaching a conclusion, or finding the next thing to investigate. The world is his experiment. He's a lot more complicated than I ever realized before, back when I used to only hang around with Jonathan. Jon always used to say Timothy was a weirdo, and so I never took the time to know him before. Now I realize Jonathan was right, because yes, Timothy is very weird, and so is my sister. But not at all in the way that Jon meant.

I'm glad I understand what Natalie and Timothy are doing, but I have started to feel like I really miss the old Jonathan. I miss my best friend. He is so different now. Not at all the exciting guy who could always find some thrilling new activity for us. Now, he mostly waits for Natalie to decide what we should all do together.

Well, as long as I've got this cast on, I really couldn't play with Jon the way we used to, anyway. The doctor gave me a walking boot to put over my cast, so I can get around easier, but I'm still supposed to try to stay off my foot if I can. So I still use my crutches for walking sometimes, and sometimes I hobble around with the walking boot. Natalie told me that Angel says the bone is healing well, so by the time the cast comes off at the end of next month it should be all better.

Maybe by that time Jon will be all better too? And we can get back to having fun while we play?

For now though, it's pretty much all about the Jonathan Project. Natalie touches Jonathan, Angel tells her how his soul is doing, Timothy takes notes, and all the Guardians hunt for Demon.

What a freaking weird situation.

Stefanie

Brad and I put our stuff down, while Jonathan goes over with the kids to inspect the table where they've got a bunch of food set up, including a whole ton of cookies. "Wow, Brenda, looks like you were busy today!"

She smiles. "Yep. Natalie decided we should become a Christmas cookie factory today."

I go over and stand with Jonathan, who is staring at the cookie display. I lean down and murmur to him, "Go ahead, but only one. I don't want you to spoil your appetite for dinner." He grabs a cookie, Natalie smiling by his side.

I hear the front door opening, and Ron greeting Laura's husband who has arrived. "Hey Mike," Ron says. "Come on in."

Once Michael gets in, Ron tells us, "Okay, you all remember the drill. Let's get those luminarias set up before dinner."

We all head back to the front. Last year, most of us had never heard of luminarias before, but now that I know how pretty it's going to be, I'm looking forward to seeing them again.

Same as last year, Ron gets us all set up into teams. The adults prepare the paper lunch sacks, folding down the top so they stay open. He gives the kids buckets of sand, to put a bit in the bottom of each bag. Gabe goes around and puts a candle into each bag, then finally Ron goes through and lights all the candles.

I have this sudden memory of last year, Timothy having an outburst when he didn't like something Jonathan was doing. This year, though, the kids all seem to be getting along together great. They are quietly and efficiently fulfilling their duties. Jonathan is scooping sand into the bags, seeming perfectly content to be participating. I keep seeing Natalie right next to him. It's very smooth and efficient.

When we get everything set up and lit, after a couple minutes of stopping to admire how pretty the luminarias are, glowing golden and lining the yard, we head inside for our potluck.

Brad and I have decided to go ahead and share our news with our friends tonight. I'm into the second trimester, and the doctor at my last appointment said everything appears fine. I know I'm starting to show, so there isn't much point in trying to hide it from our friends. I think this will be a good night to tell them.

We told Jonathan yesterday. I don't think it has really sunk in yet for him. He pretty much just smiled and said, "Okay," when we explained that we are going to have a baby, probably at the end of May or beginning of June. I'm not sure what kind of reaction I was expecting from him, but at least it wasn't negative. I'm sure it will seem more real to him the closer it gets, like when I am really starting to show and I can let him feel the baby moving.

We've all gotten our plates and are scattered around the room. The kids are sitting on the floor eating together, and the rest of us have seats at the table or on the couch. Everyone is chatting together about everything going on in our lives. Brad and I look at each other, asking silently if it's time to share our news.

Before I get the chance, though, Ron says, raising his voice slightly, "Well, we have some news."

Laura

I already know what he's going to say, of course. Brenda told me a couple of days ago. She would never allow him to spring it on me. It isn't a surprise at all, after having spent the last year watching them try to figure out what they are doing and where they are living. I'm trying hard to be happy for them. And of course, Brenda has assured me over and over that we are still going to see each other all the time. If not for our own sakes, we obviously have to make sure that Timothy and Natalie get to continue their close friendship. So we figure we'll all still have dinner together at least once a week, and drive the kids around on weekends to play with each other.

Ron continues, "You all know that Brenda and I have been doing this crazy thing where we are going back and forth between our houses all the time. But we figure, now that we're getting remarried, we really need to just pick one. So we've decided we're going to stay here, in this house. We'll fix up her condo and rent it out for at least a while."

Michael pauses, fork halfway to his mouth, and looks over at me. I hadn't told him. I nod at him and shrug. He knows how close I am to Brenda. "Well," he says, "that's going to be a real change."

I glance over at Timothy, but as I had figured, he doesn't seem surprised at the news. Obviously Natalie would have already told him, after her parents told her what they had decided. There's no way Natalie would let him be surprised by something like that either.

"That's great," Brad says, smiling over at Stefanie. "I'm glad to hear you'll be here all the time. Cool, right Jonathan?"

Jonathan, sitting right next to Natalie, nods. "Yes," he says, "that will be nice." Natalie smiles at him and puts her arm around his shoulders, giving him a brief hug. Timothy, on Natalie's other side, leans forward slightly like he's trying to get a better view of Jonathan.

I've wondered about how different the kids all seem with each other lately. They had all that trouble a couple of weeks ago, where they had a fight at the library, then Jonathan and Gabe both got hurt on the school playground. But ever since then, the four of them seem really inseparable. It feels a bit strange, since I know Timothy didn't really like Jonathan before. Oh well, I guess relationships with kids shift around, as they grow and mature and change. It's probably a good thing Timothy and Jonathan seem to be getting friendlier, since now with Brenda living here instead of at her house, the kids will all probably be with each other even more often.

Chapter 12
The Faintest Hint

Brad

After the talk about Ron's announcement dies down, I look over at Stef, and she nods. "Well," I tell everyone, "you guys aren't the only ones with some news."

Everyone's eyes shift to me. "Oh yeah?" Ron asks. "What's up?"

I feel a giant grin spread across my face. "We're having another baby!"

There's a general outburst of oohs and aahs and congratulations. Brenda and Laura immediately turn to Stefanie and start asking her all the details, about how far along she is and how she's been feeling and stuff.

Brenda gets a sort of sly expression on her face and says, "I admit I had a feeling. I had noticed you seeming like you felt kind of queasy a few weeks back."

Stef laughs. "No kidding! This time was a lot worse than last time. The morning sickness is all over now, though, and I'm feeling fine."

"Second trimester for the win!" laughs Laura.

I glance down at Jon to see how he's taking it. Natalie is sitting there on the floor with him, hanging on to his arm and talking about how exciting it is that a baby is on the way. "You're going to be a brother, Jonathan! Oh, I'm so excited! Ooooh - I'll bet Socks is going to love having a baby around!"

Jonathan is smiling and nodding. He seems happy to listen to her go on about his impending brotherhood, and to let her hand rest on his arm.

But then, I see something pass across his face, a flash in his eyes, not of annoyance, exactly, but almost of awakening, like he had been far away in his thoughts and suddenly came back to himself. He gives a little shake of his head. Then he jerks his arm out from under Natalie's hand.

Her eyes widen, and she pauses, her hand left hanging in the air. Gabe and Timothy both lean in, staring at what is happening.

But what is happening, anyway? I have no idea. These kids have been a mystery the last few weeks.

Natalie looks to the side, away from Jonathan, and then looks back into his eyes. He leans his head away from her, with a strange expression on his face, like he is confused about what he is doing sitting so close to her.

She slowly reaches her hand out, and places it again on his arm. Rather than jerking away again, he simply relaxes, and sits quietly again, still and silent.

What the heck?

I'm wondering if I should go over there, offer him a cookie or something to interrupt whatever weirdness is happening, but then I hear Stefanie say my name.

"Brad has been so happy about it. He's got a million plans about how to move our furniture all around to turn the office into a nursery."

"Do you have the baby furniture you need? A crib and changing table and things?" Brenda asks me.

"Yeah, I think so," I respond. "After Jonathan outgrew that stuff I stored everything up in the rafters of the garage. I plan to start hauling it out in the next couple of weeks, after the holidays are over."

The conversation about the new baby continues. I glance over at the kids. They're back to chatting quietly together again. I must have been mistaken that there was anything wrong.

Natalie's

For the first time since the moment on the school playground weeks ago, there is a flash of Demon's presence. Just the barest glimmer, a mere wisp of dark matter brushing against Jonathan's soul, only to evaporate again as soon as Natalie once again touches Jonathan's arm.

What has happened?

Guardian and I, and our companion Guardians, all share a moment of amazement, relieved that we have seen confirmation that Demon still exists, and is still tied to Jonathan. The disappearance of a Guardian has been deeply unsettling for all of us. We begin speculating about what has occurred.

Of course Natalie perceives it at once, the moment Jonathan removes his arm from her touch, his eyes full of an expression of more emotions than have been there since his Guardian vanished. "Is Demon back?" she silently inquires.

By the time she asks and I answer, it is already over. *"I believe, very briefly, Jonathan's Guardian attempted to reappear. It was only the faintest hint of his presence, now already gone again."*

She hesitantly replaces her hand on his arm, as the last vestiges of Demon's presence again fade, and Jonathan relaxes back into the quiescent state he has inhabited for weeks.

"We'll talk about this more later," she silently tells me.

"Yes, my darling. Yes, we will. In the meantime, of course, the other Guardians and I will carefully attend to every aspect of Jonathan's status."

She does not pause in her renewed conversation with Jonathan, discussing again the news of both her family's living situation and the baby which will soon be born to Jonathan's family. She silently affirms her awareness of my statement, as she watches Jonathan closely while she speaks.

Chapter 13
Guilt

Timothy's

My beloved has pleaded with his parents to stay later at Natalie's house, even after the other guests went home, and the luminaria candles finally burned out. They have agreed, and are having some last refreshments with Natalie's parents downstairs.

The children are taking advantage of the opportunity to question Angel about the incident with Jonathan. Gabe and Natalie and Timothy rush upstairs, and sit on the floor of her bedroom together, Gabe on a chair to accommodate his cast. They have a plate between them full of Christmas cookies, which Gabe snuck up the stairs for them to share. His injured ankle no longer presents a significant impediment to his movements.

Timothy had not brought his own notebook to the Christmas Eve celebration, so Natalie has supplied him with one of hers, and he is ready to take notes regarding the evening's events.

"So," Natalie tells the boys, selecting a frosted cookie to munch on. "I think you noticed Jonathan did something different tonight."

"Yeah," Gabe replies, "for a second he seemed like the old Jonathan. It was like all of the sudden he didn't know why he was letting you touch him. Does that mean what I think it does?"

"Uh-huh," she affirms. "Angel says Demon was sort of back, just for a second."

Timothy makes a notation. "Angel, please tell us exactly what happened."

"For a brief moment, the smallest measure of time, we detected that Demon's presence had manifested, barely touching Jonathan's soul before vanishing again."

Timothy writes a note, then asks, "Was this when he yanked his arm away from Natalie?"

"It seemed to start in the moment immediately before he did so. He appeared to sense his Guardian, his natural temperament started to emerge, then he moved away from Natalie's touch. The entire incident lasted only a few seconds. As soon as Natalie returned her hand to his arm, his sense of Demon subsided, and he reverted to his current state."

The children share glances with each other.

"So," Natalie asks, "what does this mean?"

"The other Guardians and I speculate that, as Jonathan's soul has gradually mended due to your efforts and your touch, my dear, Demon has been drawn back to it. We still have no idea where he has been, or where he is now. But knowing that he is tied to Jonathan's soul, we theorize that once the soul grew strong enough, it acted as something of a beacon to attract Demon's return, if only briefly."

After Natalie repeats my words, Timothy muses, "I guess it's working, then. Natalie is healing Jonathan's soul, and that is what is going to bring Demon back. It's what I thought might happen."

Gabe absently eats another cookie. "Is he going to be the same way? I mean, I really miss the way he used to be, because he hardly seems like my best friend anymore. But I don't want him to go back to being mean all the time. I sure don't want him to hurt you again, Nat."

"I do not know, my children. We have no experience with anything even remotely resembling the current events. If Natalie continues her efforts, we can anticipate that it is possible Jonathan's soul will continue its healing process, eventually causing Demon to truly return. Whether or not this means he will resume his control over Jonathan, and force him to attempt to injure Natalie or others once again, I can not predict."

My beloved is concerned about Natalie's safety, as always. "I want the Jonathan Project to work, Natalie," he tells her, "but I don't know if you should keep going if it might be dangerous again. Jonathan already seems a lot better than he did at first. Maybe you should stop, and let him stay the way he is now. At least he isn't trying to hurt anybody."

"*My dearest,*" I whisper to him, scarcely using the merest glimmer of energy so he senses only my approval without being distracted by my words, "*you are such a loving friend to Natalie. Even as you wish to proceed with the experiment in order to learn as much as you can, your first priority is her safety.*"

Natalie firmly shakes her head. "No. Jonathan won't be better until his guardian is back. I know it now. Whether or not he starts being mean again, we won't know until it happens. We'll have to cross that bridge when we get to it."

Gabe considers. "Well, even if he does try to start controlling Jonathan again, we aren't helpless anymore. We know what to do now. The guardians were able to get rid of Demon before. I think they can just do it again if they have to."

The child is correct. This is a topic which has been considered and discussed at great length by myself and the other Guardians in the Seer's group. We learned how to use our joint efforts to draw power to ourselves, and direct it at another of our kind as an offensive weapon. This is another unprecedented occurrence, one of many which have followed the Seer's efforts in discovering the truth of our nature.

We have deeply grieved the development, although of course Angel has not shared this fact with his dearest child. The idea of Guardians effectively doing battle with each other is an intensely horrifying concept. This has never before occurred. How could it have? We are in essence the same entity, only divided during our brief lifetimes of Guarding. It is incomprehensible that we have come to this. We all acknowledge that our action was necessary at the time, to protect the Seer from the attack being directed by Demon. However, the fact remains that we joined forces to overwhelm another Guardian by force, and as a result both the Guardian and his attendant soul were injured.

We share an emotion never before experienced by any of us, by any Guardian to our knowledge.

Guilt.

Chapter 14

Christmas Spirit

Stefanie

Can it possibly be 7:30 on Christmas morning? I stare from my pillow, befuddled, at the digital clock on my nightstand. I hear Brad's slow breathing beside me. Why on earth didn't Jonathan burst into our room before dawn, demanding that it is time for presents, like he has every other Christmas?

After a quick trip to the bathroom, I check on him, and discover him not asleep in bed, as had been my guess, but instead sitting quietly on the couch in front of the Christmas tree, Socks curled beside him, absently stroking the dog's fur.

I sit down next to him, and put my arm around his shoulders. "Merry Christmas, sweetheart," I say. "Everything okay?"

"Yeah," he says. "Just looking at the tree." Socks looks up at him when he hears Jonathan's voice, then lays his head back down on his paws.

Huh. I sit with him, and gaze over at the tree, a humongous pile of presents beneath, the lights sparkling. He obviously turned them on when he came in here. "It's pretty, isn't it?" I ask him.

"Mm-hmm," he says. "It's nice to sit here while it's quiet. I feel... I don't know, kind of peaceful. Like I'm letting the Christmas spirit sink in."

This is unusual, but he has been doing a lot of unusual stuff this month. It's not bad, though. I chuckle and lean over to give the top of his head a kiss. "I agree. You know, I used to do this too, when I was a kid. There's something so nice about pausing to enjoy the moment, and look at the decorations, before everything happens."

He nods, still gazing at the tree.

Brad comes in, wearing a bathrobe over his pajamas. "It's present time!"

Our little bubble of peace pops, but we're both fine with it. Jonathan smiles. "Okay."

Natalie

I love Christmas. And this one is so nice, with Mom and Dad back together for real, and Gabe's broken ankle healing, and the Jonathan Project starting to work.

We opened all the presents already, and had the big special Christmas breakfast Mom prepared, and are hanging around checking out our new stuff. Dad told us it is too early to try to go over to see Jonathan, and we have to wait for a decent hour.

So Gabe has busted open this big new Lego set he got and is starting to build with it, using the instruction manual. I'm curled up on the couch with what I think is my favorite present. Grandma sent me a bible. A real, grown-up bible, not short like the children's one she sent before. It isn't in old-fashioned language, though, it's in modern language, and I'm able to understand it all right so far. Although I've barely started, of course. It's super long, so I figure it'll take me quite a while to get through the whole thing, but I'm eager to do it.

It's still strange for me to think about the bible, and religion, and the entire concept of God. Now that I know people made the whole thing up. Angel said when some people could tell their guardians were there, they decided it must be God they were feeling. It never was, though. And that's how the whole thing started, thousands of years ago, when people made up all sorts of different religions, creating whole groups of gods and goddesses to worship.

When Angel first told us about this a couple of months ago, it was hard for Timothy and me to believe that the whole thing was invented by people. But now the more I think about it, the more sense it makes. I've read books about old religions, like Greek mythology. Angel said people back then took their religion, with Zeus and Hera and Apollo and the other ones, just as seriously as people today take their religions with Jesus and Jehovah.

It's all the same stuff, but with different names and stories attached to it. People want to understand the world, and they try to find ways to explain everything, whether they are right about it or not. They sense their guardian, and figure it is a God. Some disaster happens, so they decide the explanation is their God must be mad at them. And some people want to control others, and figured out that saying they know what God wants is the perfect way to do it.

I've been trying to figure out how it all developed, so I can find a way to untangle it, and help people stop using religion as an excuse to be awful to each other. It's been used as the reason for horrible things, over and over again. Like the attacks on September 11. That's why I want to read the bible, to help me understand how it all started.

But here I am, loving Christmas, the whole Christmas story, the baby and the manger and the sheep and the wise men and the entire thing. And I love everyone being happy and loving each other and lighting candles and having a feast. So I guess religion can be used for good things too. Everyone having a wonderful time together, and giving each other presents, and celebrating, is so nice. I don't want to get rid of the good parts.

So, I'll keep reading the bible, and try to figure it all out. How to help people believe in something nice, without wanting to do something awful.

Brenda

Waking up here again this morning, for the second Christmas in a row, in Ron's house, in Ron's bed, was so wonderful. When it happened last year, it was the beginning of our reconciliation. It's been a long path, but I'm glad we've walked it.

I know how much he regrets everything that happened, and wishes he had never started the whole divorce thing. I can't say that I don't wish it too, but I also don't find myself filled with any regrets. I've started to feel like everything happens for a reason, even the hard parts. If he hadn't left me, so many things wouldn't have happened. A lot of pain, yeah, we would have been spared that. But I wouldn't have moved to my condo, wouldn't have met Laura, and Natalie wouldn't have met Timothy. I think we're all in a good place right now, and I'm glad for it.

The only drawback to any of it is I know Laura is disappointed that we've decided to live here at Ron's house from now on. I'll miss her too, but honestly ever since Ron and I got back together I haven't spent as much time with Laura anyway. We'll still see each other a few times a week. I told her we'll invite them over for dinner weekly, and of course we'll be dropping off Timothy and Natalie on weekends to play with each other. It'll all work out fine.

There's something else going on with her, though. I've seen how tired she's been looking lately, the dark circles growing under her eyes. She says it's only because it has been hard getting used to sleeping together with Michael again since he returned from deployment, so she isn't getting as much rest as normal.

I feel like there is more to it, but she hasn't responded to my gentle prodding to find out what's really wrong. Michael looks tired too, and almost like he got a lot older during the six months he was gone. He's thinner, and there are lines in his face which weren't there before. I guess I shouldn't be surprised, since I know he was involved in the Afghanistan fighting. It must have been so hard on him.

Ron interrupts my train of thought by sitting next to me on the couch, with his new World's Best Dad mug full of coffee. I chuckle softly. He actually is, although for a while there I didn't want to admit it. He's a great Dad. And fiancé. And lover. And soon to be husband. I lean against him with a smile. We sip coffee and watch Gabe build his Lego spaceship or whatever it is. Natalie's nose is buried in her book. We're all together, all happy.

What a lovely Christmas.

Chapter 15

Give It A Try

Michael

She likes the scarf, at least. She's got it on now, wrapped around her neck, so lovely with the white sweater she's wearing. It didn't take us long to open up all the presents, then she made us a good breakfast. Timothy thanked us for everything, but left the toys scattered under the tree, and brought the books up to his room. He's up there now, like usual, presumably reading.

I couldn't imagine why she got him textbooks for Christmas, but he seemed thrilled. Like, actual college textbooks. I certainly never would have thought of doing that. I looked at them after he opened them. Introduction to Physics. Introduction to Psychology. Brain Development. Really? He is still only seven, right?

I'm watching a football game on t.v., but I'm not terribly interested in the teams, so I'm not paying much attention. I'm also distracted by remembering what happened yesterday at the mall. It was so embarrassing. And scary. For a minute there, it seemed so real, and I don't know why. It was like the nightmares that keep waking me up at night. But I was wide awake at the time. Why was I suddenly convinced I was in some kind of battle? Was I hallucinating? Not like I've taken any drugs, not for a long time. Am I crazy?

I'm glad that Laura puts up with me. I know it's not easy, being a single mom every time I have to go out with my ship. But I think this time it's even harder with me back, and waking her up every night by jolting awake. She's trying to be patient, and trying to do things that help me. I've noticed it all. The way she keeps making all my favorite foods for dinner. The things she's invited me to go out and do, hiking even, when I know that isn't at all her style. Even the way she keeps initiating sex most nights, much more than usual. I think she's trying to wear me out.

It keeps working, until it doesn't. Until I fall asleep and the bombs start falling again.

Laura

Christmas morning done. Next step: preparing Christmas dinner. Brenda and Ron are coming over. I've got the turkey in the oven, and am mixing up some sides. I'm looking forward to having them over again.

I've taken off the pretty scarf Michael gave me, so I don't splash anything on it. It's a lovely gift. I'm touched he thought of it, especially since I know he's been struggling to get through each day. He's always exhausted, never getting enough rest at night. I'm trying everything I can think of to help him, but I don't think anything is really working. I'm so worried about him.

At least there haven't been any problems between him and our son. Timothy is a lot more mature now, and doesn't have meltdowns all the time like he used to. He's still on the spectrum, and awfully quirky, but not in a way that seems to be bothering Michael. Although I have to admit Michael thought we were both crazy when Timothy was so excited to open up the box with the textbooks in it. I pay attention, I know the subjects he's been interested in learning. And I know college is a long ways away, but I don't think that will stop him from trying to read and understand these books.

I peek into the living room to see what Mike is doing. Oh - I think he's fallen asleep watching football. I'll stop banging pots around in the kitchen. Maybe he can take a little nap. He surely needs it.

Ron

"Hey guys, come on in," Mike tells us when he opens the door. It's already dark outside, now that the winter solstice has passed and the days are as short as they will be all year.

"Merry Christmas!" Brenda says, taking off her jacket and setting it down on the edge of the couch.

The kids all go running upstairs to Timothy's room. Did Gabe used to hang out with them this much? I don't think so, but he seems to be doing it more and more lately. Maybe they've gotten old enough that they seem more interesting to him.

Laura is still finishing up getting dinner ready, so Brenda goes into the kitchen to help. And talk, of course.

"Have a seat," Mike says. "Can I get you a drink?"

"Nah, thanks, I'm good." He sits back down with a huff. He seems tired.

"How's it going, Mike? Are you settled back in to being home? Got your land legs back?"

He snorts out a little laugh. "Yeah, I suppose. It's nice to be able to sleep in a real bed again." Then he shakes his head and looks down, like he's amused by what he just said. I think he wants to change the subject. "So, you guys have decided to rent out Brenda's place?"

"Yeah," I say. "I'm glad we've finally reached a decision. It was pretty goofy to keep going back and forth. It'll save a lot of money to consolidate all our housing expenses into one place."

"So you picked your place since it's bigger?" he asks.

"Well, maybe that's part of it. I seriously didn't care at all, I would have been perfectly happy if Brenda said she wanted to stay here. But the kids seemed to want to stay over there. Maybe they like that it's roomier, and has a yard. I dunno. I'm happy either way."

"When are you going to do it?"

"Well, actually, I think we're going to start working on it this week. We both have the rest of the week off work, so it seems like a good time to start thinking about what to pack up and bring over there to my place. We're going to have to get rid of a ton of stuff, since there will be a lot of duplicates. The kids will have to get used to merely having one set of everything like other people, not doubling up their belongings. No more of this Mom's house/Dad's house stuff."

"Phew," he huffs exaggeratedly. "It sounds like a lot of work. Good luck with that. Let me know if you need help loading boxes or anything."

"Thanks, man."

Gabe

Hanging out in Timothy's room. Something I never used to do. But I guess I'm part of this team now, the guardians team. It seems like Natalie and Timothy always have something to learn about it, something different to try to help figure stuff out.

"How was Jonathan today?" Timothy asks. He wants to get right to it. He knows we were planning to play with Jonathan after we opened all our presents. He doesn't even stop to tell us what he got for Christmas.

Natalie giggles. "He was fine, Timothy. Nothing else changed, he pretty much was the same way he has been the last two weeks. Did you have a nice Christmas?"

He's already sitting on the floor, writing in his notebook. He glances back up. "Oh, uh, yeah, it was nice. Mom gave me those books," he says, pointing over to his desk.

I look up there to see what they are. What? "You mean these science books? This looks like college stuff. She gave you these?"

Timothy says, "Yes, she knows I have been studying brain development. And after September 11 I was interested in physics, since I wanted to understand more about what happened. They are college books, but if you concentrate hard enough you can understand at least some of it."

Huh. "Well, good for you. I don't think I could understand them, even if I was in college." What a brainy little nerd. He really is the perfect friend for my sister. I shake my head and laugh. I'm glad to be part of this group, weird as it is.

Natalie smiles. "Those books are great, Timothy." She looks over at me, and says, "You shouldn't be surprised about him reading those. He's already been trying to learn about this stuff, with books he got from the library. He wants to understand how minds work, to help him know how he can communicate with Guardian."

Oh yeah, sometimes I forget Timothy can sort of hear his too. I've gotten used to the idea that Natalie talks to her guardian all the time, but it's strange to think about other people doing it. "How does that work, anyway, Timothy?"

He finishes the line he's writing and then puts down his notebook. He closes his eyes for a second, then opens them. "I started learning how to do it a while ago. I know I've told you before, I have to keep my mind open."

"Yeah," I say, "I remember you saying that, but what does it even mean?"

Natalie watches back and forth as we talk.

"It's very hard to describe," Timothy says. "It's like, picture your mind like a cupboard. You have to open the door, and then make sure there isn't anything in there. It has to be completely empty. Then if your mind is quiet and open and ready, you can start to sense that your guardian is there."

Natalie says, "He and Angel described it once like being a baby, having to wait for its Mom to come and feed it. The baby just has to open its mouth and wait for the food. It can't go in the kitchen and cook its own dinner."

I hoot out a laugh, thinking of a baby getting out pans and food and cooking for itself. Then I get serious again. I haven't given very much thought, this whole time, to having a guardian myself. I know they've told me I have one, since everybody has one. But it hasn't ever seemed like something that I could really have any contact with.

I suppose Timothy does, though. So I wonder if that means I could.

Natalie is watching me. "Angel says you probably could feel your own guardian, Gabe, if you tried to practice keeping your mind open like Timothy does."

"Huh. I wouldn't even know where to start, I don't think," I say. "I don't know how I would try to open my mind like a cupboard door, like you say."

Timothy says, "There's another part to it, too. When I was only opening my mind, I was just feeling Guardian a little, like the feeling you get when you realize someone is standing right behind you. I had to do something else before I could start actually hearing any real words or thoughts. It's kind of harder, but I wonder if it would be a good place for you to start."

"Really? What is it?"

"It's part of why I want to learn about the mind," Timothy says. "Why I'm reading those books. Angel told us the part of the mind that the guardians communicate with is the subconscious mind. So, more like the part you dream with, not the part you think with while you are awake."

Um....

Natalie can tell how confused I am. "Timothy told me he started experimenting with having his mind open while he was falling asleep, so he was closer to dreaming, and could maybe hear Guardian better that way."

Timothy nods. "Yes. So I believe that maybe you could try it while you are almost asleep. After you get in bed, try to think about nothing except Aaron. Imagine your guardian being there next to you in your room, and try to make your mind quiet and focus only on him. It might work." He shrugs. "If I could do it, I don't see any reason why anyone wouldn't be able to."

"Well, I don't know about that," I hoot. "I'm not sure you guys have ever noticed, but Timothy is a bit different from other people. So are you, Natalie."

They look at each other. Timothy shrugs, and Natalie giggles. "We know," she says. "Believe me, we know."

She looks over to the side, obviously listening to Angel. "Gabe, why don't you give it a try tonight? When you're falling asleep? Just think about Aaron. He'll be right there, like he always is. Every minute he is thinking about you and loving you and watching you. If you can open up your mind and let him in, I'll bet you could at least tell that he's there. It's a nice feeling." She looks over at Timothy.

"Yes," he says, "it's a nice feeling. You should try to do it."

Well, okay then.

Gabe's

My beloved is going to attempt to achieve communication with me? Although he learned of the existence of Guardians several weeks ago, he has never seriously contemplated my own presence. This is a marvelous development.

A rush of love and joy washes through me. Being a member of the Seer's inner circle brings with it such astonishing privilege. Such learning. Such change.

"Oh, my darling, if you choose to do this I will focus with my entire being on your effort. I will love you all the same whether or not you can ever sense my presence, but if you do manage it, my bliss will be complete."

Chapter 16

Little Angel

Brenda

I wake up early, before Ron or the kids. It's still dark outside. I have a lot to do today, and as soon as my mind starts thinking about it I know there is no way I'm going back to sleep. So I get up as quietly as possible and head downstairs to make myself some coffee.

This is going to be one of the last mornings I wake up in my house, I realize. We told the kids last night at Laura's house during dinner that we've decided to stay over here the next couple of days, so we can start deciding what to pack up and take over to Ron's. And what we will get rid of.

It makes me a little sad. I've built a home, here in this condo, and now this part of my life is ending. It's bittersweet. However, I'm nothing but thrilled that the period of time without Ron is over. I'm excited about living with him, about getting remarried, about the happily ever after that we are finally going to get. We were always headed there, it turns out, we just had a few bumps in the road first.

And one of those bumps is going to be packing up and moving out of here. You know what, though, I tell myself. Guess who's going to be here helping, doing all the heavy lifting, by my side every step of the way? Ron is. My love. He'll be here with me, doing whatever I need. And I'll be doing it all for him.

All right. I'm set. Let's do this. I start considering what we need. Boxes. We'll need lots of boxes.

Brenda's

My beloved resolves to embrace the new phase of her life. Her reconciliation with her beloved husband has brought so much joy to her, and to their family. It is good that they have resolved the question of which residence to use, as it has been an ongoing source of some confusion for each of them.

The Seer's Jonathan Project, unbeknownst to her parents, substantially impacted the decision. When Natalie decided she wished to remain as close to Jonathan as possible over the winter break, it nudged her parents in the direction of choosing the house in that neighborhood. Natalie's friendship with Timothy had been feared to be a possible obstacle to making this choice, but instead she was the one who essentially guided it.

Natalie is confident her relationship with Timothy will not suffer from the distance. Although with a normal childhood friendship that would probably not be the case, it very well might be here. Natalie's determination is a bigger factor than her parents even realize in formulating their plans. As always, if she wishes for something to happen, she will find a way. All humans and Guardians in her orbit feel inclined to accommodate her wishes, as her presence brings a sense of well-being to all. With, of course, the one exception being Demon.

Furthermore, Timothy's ability to communicate with Guardian has grown to the extent that he is able to reliably receive brief messages. As a result of this and of our ability to speak with each other over previously impossible distances, Natalie knows she and Timothy will be able to remain in contact even while in different neighborhoods.

All appears to be working out beautifully for my beloved. Joy permeates the family.

Gabe

I fell asleep last night with my mind feeling very strange. I was trying to do what Timothy said. But honestly, how on earth do you open your mind like a cupboard door? I couldn't figure out what that would even be like. So all I could do was try to think about my guardian being there.

Aaron, Natalie says his name is, so I just thought about Aaron. She says he's always thinking about me, so maybe if I'm thinking about him too, it would help. So I was laying there, trying to concentrate on some invisible angel named Aaron, while I was getting sleepier.

And it felt different. Like when I finally fell asleep, there was something there. Was I dreaming it?

This morning, as soon as I wake up, I remember about all that. About Aaron. I think I was dreaming about him.

I guess I'll never know.

Hold on. Of course I can know. Natalie can always ask Angel.

I jump out of bed so fast I make myself laugh. I'm totally turning into Timothy, all eager to find out the results of an experiment!

Natalie

When I fell asleep last night, Angel was telling me about Gabe trying to hear Aaron. It wasn't going as well as it does with Timothy, but Gabe was really trying.

As soon as I wake up, I ask Angel, "Well?"

"Good morning, my darling. Your brother fell asleep while making the effort to feel Aaron's presence. I believe that while he was in the twilight realm, between waking and sleeping, he felt a slight hint of the love which Aaron was transmitting to him. He dreamed of Aaron last night."

"So would you say that it worked at all?"

"For a second or two, he felt the barest glimpse of Aaron's love for him, but it was similar to what other humans can sometimes sense when their Guardian is speaking to them. My dearest, you must remember how unusual this situation is. Only you and your closest companions have any idea of the existence of Guardians. The fact that your friend and your brother attempt to contact theirs, much less have any success, is extraordinary. If your brother does not immediately succeed, please be patient. It will take much time and effort. It might never actually work. However, Gabe's knowledge of his Guardian is already helping him. The simple fact of that awareness brings him comfort."

I guess he's right. I'm being too impatient. But now that Gabe knows, I want him to be able to talk to Aaron. Talking to your guardian is so nice, and Timothy really likes being able to hear Guardian when he tries.

I think about Timothy and Guardian. I'm really glad they've been practicing, since I won't be living here anymore. I hope that soon they are good enough at it so I can tell Angel anything, and he can tell Guardian, and Guardian can tell Timothy. It'll be like a game of phone tag, but better than having to wait until we see each other at school to talk.

"Your brother is coming to see you," Angel says, and a second later Gabe pokes his head in my door.

"You awake?" Gabe asks me.

"Yeah. Angel says you were trying to hear Aaron last night."

He jumps onto the bed next to me, making my mattress bounce me up like a teeter-totter. It makes me laugh.

"I was," he says. "I don't know if anything happened though. I think I remember right before I fell asleep thinking I could feel someone close to me, but then I was asleep and dreaming."

"Well, keep trying," I tell him. "I think you probably felt him a little. Angel says that since nobody else even knows about guardians, just the fact that you know and are trying to hear yours is amazing and will help you."

"Help me what?"

"Like, feel calm and happy. Don't you think knowing your guardian angel is always sending you love makes you feel better?"

"Yeah, I guess so. I mean, even if I can't feel it, I guess I know it, and that seems nice."

He looks around my room. "Have you thought about what you want to keep? To bring over to Dad's house?"

"My books."

"Ha! Of course that's the one thing you'd care about."

"What about you?"

"Boy, I don't know. I am going to have to sort through everything. My room at Dad's is already pretty full of stuff. I don't know how much more I can fit in."

"Well, most of your Legos are over there. A lot of the stuff here is kind of baby toys, right? Mom said we should think about what we can donate, so maybe some of your baby toys can go there."

He nods. "Yep. But I'll think about it later. I'm hungry. Let's go get breakfast."

"I still need to get dressed. I'll be down in a minute."

He heads out, and I go to my dresser to get out some clothes. The drawer is completely full. I have a ton of stuff in here. My room is full of clothes, and old toys, and all kinds of stuff. I guess I should think about whether I want to bring anything other than my books. I don't really feel like I need anything else.

"May I suggest you search through your closet for Little Angel? A Guardian is not often sentimental about physical objects, but I believe it would be nice for you to keep that memento of your younger years."

Oh yeah! "That's a great idea, Angel! Thanks!" He's right. I totally want to keep my little Beanie Baby angel, the one I used to think was the same thing as my Big Angel.

Chapter 17

Project

January 2002

Gabe

We stayed up super late last night. Mom and Dad said we could stay awake until midnight to celebrate the New Year in our new house. I mean, they called it our new house, even though it's the same old house Dad has always lived in. But since we spent the whole last week over at Mom's clearing out all our stuff, so we can move in here permanently, they said we should treat New Year's Eve like the first night in our new house. It'll be weird not to stay over at Mom's ever again, but this is nice. I like it here.

So to celebrate, last night we rented a couple of movies from Blockbuster to watch, and Mom set up snacks in the family room, and we spent the whole night munching and watching. It was super cool. Then we counted down to midnight, and yelled Happy New Year, and ate some more snacks before Mom finally made us go to bed.

I'm still laying in bed, half asleep, when I hear my door open. "Gabe?" Natalie asks.

"Mmmmm?"

"Um, are you ever getting up? It's, like, after nine o'clock."

"Mmmmmm."

"Come on, don't you want to go over to Jonathan's?"

Fine. I open one eye and squint at her. She's already dressed, her usual leggings and a sweater she got for Christmas, standing next to my bed and bouncing on her toes. How on earth does she look so perky after being up so late last night? I close my eye again.

...

"Gabe. Don't go back to sleep!"

Pfsh. "Okay, okay. Just because you somehow managed to get enough sleep doesn't mean we all did. Give me a minute."

She sits down on my chair and waits, kicking her legs and staring at me.

Sigh.   It's no use arguing, she has that we-need-to-do-something-right-now expression on her face, and I have realized that once she decides something needs to happen, you might as well agree. It's going to happen.

So I sit up. She starts to say something, and I tell her, "Hold on," and get up and go down the hall to the bathroom. I don't need to bother with my crutches, I can hobble on my cast.

When I get back in a couple of minutes, feeling more awake, she's still sitting there on my chair. I sit back on my bed, but when she gives me a warning look I resist laying back down.

"Okay, Nat, what is it? I can tell you have a plan. Let's hear it."

She smiles, apparently glad I'm starting to figure things out. "I think that when we go to Jonathan's today, we need to ask him what he remembers about the day Demon disappeared. We've avoided talking about it this whole time, but I think we need to do it."

"Aren't you worried he isn't ready?"

"Angel says his soul is getting better every day, even though we spent the last few days not seeing him very much. But every time we brought a load of stuff over here in the car, when we popped by to see him and I touched him, Angel said he could see 'substantial improvement'." She puts her fingers up in air quotes whenever she wants me to know that she is using Angel's exact words. "You've seen it yourself - he's talking more, and doing more things. I think he might be ready for us to tell him about what is really happening. To have the conversation we were trying to have that day on the jungle gym."

"Really?" I ask. "Are you sure? I mean, he's talking more and stuff, but he still doesn't seem like himself at all. And he hasn't ever said anything about that day."

"I know," she says. Then she looks to the side for a minute. "Angel says he thinks Jonathan is recovered enough that he should be able to have a discussion about what occurred. And besides, I think it might be a lot easier to tell him now, than it was when Demon was around making him all angry and violent. I mean, won't it be nicer to try again to tell him about guardians without thinking he's about to start punching you?"

"Well, do you really think he needs to know now? I mean, since Demon is gone, he isn't being mean to anyone. That was the whole reason you wanted to tell him about guardians, so he could try to resist when Demon wanted to make him do stuff. Now that Demon isn't even here, he's perfectly nice. So he doesn't need to know about it or resist anything, does he?"

"I know," she says, "but I think now is our chance. While Demon is gone. Angel thinks he is going to come back. There was already that one time where Demon tried to come back, just for a second. I think it is going to happen again. And Angel says the stronger Jonathan's soul gets, the sooner it will happen. I think we should tell him before then, so when it does, he can be ready for it. And I think we definitely should try before school starts again. Consider it the next step in the project."

I am really not sure about this. Jonathan seems kind of damaged. He's still quieter than normal, and the way he doesn't object to Natalie touching him all the time is honestly kind of weird. He never would have put up with it before. I don't know how he will take this news. It might be super confusing, or upsetting. Learning about guardians was hard for me, and I wasn't missing mine. "Well," I tell her, "take it slow though, okay? Maybe just tell him a little bit, not the whole thing?"

She listens to Angel. "Angel says you are probably correct, and we will 'evaluate Jonathan's status as we proceed,' so we can tell him as much as he can handle, but not too much. I guess we should start, and see how it goes."

I let out a deep breath. "All right. Let me get dressed."

Ron

Man, this combining households project is way more effort than even I anticipated, and I thought I was the only one being realistic about it. There has been so much to do. Packing and moving boxes from Brenda's, then making room here to fit everything in. We've had to help the kids go over everything in both houses, and decide what to keep, what to throw away, and what to donate. I don't think either one of us has kept up very well on keeping their clothes and toys current, because it was flabbergasting how many bags of outgrown stuff we were able to haul away.

Gabe was going to donate his big collection of toy dinosaurs, but Natalie suggested that Timothy might want to keep them. She reminded us how much Timothy used to love dinosaurs, way back in the day when they first moved in. I don't know how excited Michael and Laura were about having a giant box of dinosaurs come into their house, but Timothy certainly seemed pleased to have them.

Brenda decided to set the good baby clothes and toys aside for Brad and Stefanie to go through, figuring they might appreciate some hand-me-downs. So there are a bunch of big black plastic bags full of that stuff in my garage waiting to be sorted out.

I think we've gotten the personal possessions mostly finished, after a few days of intense effort. The next decision Brenda is going to have to make is about kitchen items and furniture. Although, now that I think about it, I wonder if we could rent it out furnished? It'd save us a lot of effort trying to get the big things hauled away, and maybe there are renters who don't have their own furniture. I'll have to talk to Brenda about it.

For now, though, we are taking the day off, back at my house. I mean, our house. The house. As they used to call it in the divorce papers, the community residence.

Gah. Perish the thought. I feel like I need to wash my brain out with soap for bringing up that memory.

Our house. It's our house, and it's New Year's Day.

We spent last night here after several nights at Brenda's while we were busy packing. We rang in the New Year together, appropriately in the place where our new life will happen going forward. Now, we're simply relaxing. Tomorrow the kids go back to school. It'll be the first time back for Gabe since he broke his ankle. And the first time for the kids leaving for school from here.

So far, they both seem to be adapting fine to this entire thing. Of course, they've lived here part time for years, so I know they are already comfortable here. But even the process of packing wasn't too bad. Although, Gabe had to be encouraged to leave more behind, and Natalie had to be encouraged to bring more with her.

I laugh and shake my head, remembering her standing in front of her boxes full of nothing but books, holding that tattered old Beanie Baby, and insisting that was all she needed. Brenda had to go in and retrieve a lot of the clothes and some of her other stuff which really should be kept.

Gabe and Natalie come pounding down the stairs. "We're going over to Jonathan's," Gabe tells me. He ducks into the kitchen and grabs an apple, clearly figuring that will be his breakfast on the road.

"Okay, that's fine. See you later." I watch him swing out the door on his crutches, as comfortable with them now as he ever was walking without them.

It's been almost a month since Gabe and Jonathan had that fight, and as far as I can tell it was a one-time thing. We never really did understand what happened on the playground a couple of days later, but none of the kids seemed to want to talk about it, and considering everything that happened, I didn't want to press them. I was worried about them spending time with Jonathan after the fight, especially worried Natalie might get hurt again, but they've all been as thick as thieves for weeks now. I guess they got whatever it was causing their dispute out of their systems.

Chapter 18

The Lights Turn On

Jonathan

It's the last day of Christmas break. School starts again tomorrow. I think it's going to feel strange to be there again. I was out sick the whole week before vacation even started, so it's been a long break for me. Gabe was out of school that week too.

I'm not sure I really remember what happened. They told me that I fell off the jungle gym, and then the next thing I knew I was waking up in the hospital with Gabe staring at me. But everything is so fuzzy in my memory, not only about that day, but about almost everything that has happened since then. I do recall that a couple of days before it happened, I had a fight with Gabe at the library, but even that is hard for me to remember. I'm not even sure why we were fighting, I just have a vague memory of us on the floor hitting each other. And for the week after I was in the hospital, I barely remember anything.

They told me I was unconscious for a while, that's why I was in the hospital. I guess they scanned my brain and stuff, to make sure nothing was wrong, and the doctor said everything is fine. But I feel like I've changed somehow. I worry that something did get hurt, but the doctors couldn't find it.

Things don't seem, I don't know, as sharp as they used to. It's like if you squint your eyes to make everything go blurry. Everything seems kind of blurry to me. Not actually, I mean, I can see okay, but nothing seems as clear as it used to. Nothing matters as much. Nothing tastes as good, or looks as cool, or seems as interesting.

I haven't been able to get excited about anything I used to love doing. I haven't ridden my bike at all, although it might be because Gabe can't do it right now with a cast on. I've hardly watched any t.v., or played with my toys as much, or really anything. Even opening Christmas presents was fine, but not as thrilling as it used to be. I mostly don't feel like doing anything. It's like being tired, but not physically tired. My body feels fine, but my mind feels worn out somehow.

I hope it ends soon, because if I have to go to school tomorrow I'll need more energy than I have had lately.

Mom is busy in the living room putting all the Christmas decorations away, and Dad is helping her lift boxes and stuff. He says she shouldn't lift anything since she's pregnant.

Apparently I'm going to have a baby brother or sister. I suppose I should feel excited about it. But I don't, not really. Although that's nothing different. I can't seem to get excited about anything.

I go out in the backyard with Socks, to stay out of their way while they're moving around the ornaments and stuff. Socks is the only thing that makes me feel, not exactly happy, but, I guess, content. When I'm with him I feel okay.

Well, Socks and ...

I hear someone knock on the door, and here comes the one other thing that makes me feel good lately. Natalie has come over, with Gabe. I was just thinking about her. The first thing I really remember after I got back from the hospital was that she and Gabe came over one morning and we tossed the ball around for Socks. Everything that happened before that is super blurry in my mind, like a dream I can barely remember.

I'm glad they came over again today. They come out in the backyard, and of course Socks goes crazy with excitement, and rushes over to Natalie with his tail wagging a million miles a minute.

"Hey," Gabe says, "Happy New Year."

"Yeah," I tell him, "same to you."

I'm watching Natalie and Socks. He's already grown since we got him, and he can reach up a lot higher than he used to. She drops down to the ground with him, and he's jumping all over her and frantically trying to lick her face, while she giggles and tries to hold him. Their hair is the same color, dark brown. She looks over at me with a laugh on her face and says, "Happy New Year, Jonathan."

I cross over to her and sit down next to where she and Socks are wrestling around. She reaches out and touches my shoulder. Mmm. There it is. That feeling, like somebody turned the lights up in a dim room. Or like the day was chilly and got a little warmer. Then Socks gets even more rambunctious and actually knocks her over, and her hand leaves me, and she falls over laughing. It's like the lights go dim again.

I've started to realize it feels good when she's here, but especially when she touches me. I have no idea why. But I like it. So I hope she'll do it again.

After a few minutes Socks has obviously worn himself out, so he flops over and lays next to her panting. Natalie and I are still sitting on the ground, and Gabe is sitting on a chair next to us, his foot with the cast on it right near me.

"How's your foot?" I ask him.

"I think it's a lot better. It hasn't been hurting at all lately. Mom says I still have to bring my crutches when I go to school tomorrow, but I think I'll only use them if it starts hurting."

"When do you get the cast off?"

"In a few more weeks. Natalie says it should be fine by then." Then Gabe gets a funny look on his face, like he realizes he shouldn't have said something. Natalie looks at him and rolls her eyes.

"What?" I ask.

"Nothing," Natalie says. "Are you ready to go back to school tomorrow? Are you feeling all right?"

"Yeah, I guess. It seems like a million years since I was there last time."

She nods, and reaches over and takes my hand. Ah. Again. The lights turn on. I hold her hand, not super tightly, but enough that I think she can tell I want her to stay there. Gabe watches, and I'm glad he doesn't seem to mind that I'm holding his sister's hand again. Although, honestly, we've been doing it a lot lately. I think that before, Gabe might have teased me about it, maybe? I don't really remember what it was like before. But now he lets us sit here together, and I enjoy the warm feeling it gives me.

Natalie is silent for a minute, and looks over to the side. Then she asks, "Jonathan, do you know what happened when you were at school last time?"

"I fell off the jungle gym."

"Yes, but do you remember why?"

Gabe watches closely. He seems pretty interested in this too. "Um, not very much. I think you were up there too? And Gabe must have been, since I know

that's when he fell and broke his ankle. But I can't really remember anything."
I shrug. "The doctor said it's normal sometimes to forget the details when you
get hurt."

Gabe and Natalie look at each other.

She says, "Well, I can tell you what happened. Okay?"

"Um, yeah, I guess." I'm not sure how much I really care about it. But I want
her to keep sitting here next to me. Every minute we are together like this I
feel better, so I want to keep it up.

Chapter 19

Stay With Me

Natalie's

The child's development is fascinating to behold. Even without his Guardian, Jonathan begins to resume his life. Thankfully, the characteristic which had previously been so defining for him, his desire to inflict suffering on others, shows no signs of returning. But his thoughts are clearer. His activity level increases.

And even he has a rudimentary awareness of the reason for his improvement. He senses that it is Natalie. It was only after the first few days had passed, when she first saw him again, and touched him, that his soul started its path towards recovery. Until that time, it was almost as though he was in a trance, barely awake, scarcely participating in the activities of daily life. But each time Natalie has been with him, and especially when she touches him, he experiences an almost imperceptible improvement. The cumulative effect of the last weeks has been significant.

It is as though the power of his soul, which had truly been a wondrous sight to behold before the catastrophic day on the playground, cannot be suppressed. Even the injury caused by the sundering of his Guardian from his soul has not been sufficient to entirely quench his light.

He has begun to correlate the Seer's touch with a feeling of increased well-being. Each time she makes contact with him, and his soul glows anew, he feels more clarity and energy than he experiences when they are apart. He eagerly accepts each little pat from Natalie, grasps her hand whenever she offers it, and begins to actively wish for these incidents to occur. He instinctively gravitates towards the healing light of the Seer.

Natalie wishes to introduce the topic very gently. She shares her brother's concern that Jonathan's mental state is still fragile, and that difficult information might cause his healing to regress. She thinks for a moment, and decides where to begin.

"Right before you fell, I had told you something that I tried to tell you before, a few months ago."

"Oh? What?" He reaches out with the hand which is not held within Natalie's, and strokes the dark brown fur of his pet, who is lying quietly nearby, regarding the Seer.

"It was about guardian angels. Do you remember?"

"Um, maybe? I'm not sure. I'm having a hard time remembering everything."

She nods sympathetically. "I know you are. I'll help you. Before you fell, I was telling you that guardian angels are real. They are here to help us. We all have one."

His reaction, so different from the violent spasm caused when Demon tried to prevent her from sharing this knowledge last time, is barely visible. "Oh. Okay."

"Unlike when you told your brother, Jonathan does not perceive this as a game you are trying to play. He accepts what you tell him, but does not understand what you mean, or grasp that this information is significant. It might be that new knowledge is going to be difficult to absorb in his current condition."

Jonathan waits passively in the silence while Natalie listens to my description of his mental state.

Natalie peers closely at his face, concerned that her message is not being received. She decides to simply continue the narration, while he appears to be willing to listen to whatever she has to say.

"I know about guardians," she tells him, deciding to simply be completely frank in the hopes that this increases his chance of understanding, "because I can talk to mine. I've always been able to see my guardian angel, and he talks to me all the time."

She regards him, waiting for any reaction. He simply nods, and continues petting his dog. Natalie looks at Gabe, who has been on alert, fearing Jonathan's reaction would be nearly as intense as it had been last time. Clearly it is not. Jonathan is barely registering the importance of what Natalie has told him.

Gabe adds, "It's true, Jonathan, she's right about guardian angels. We all have one."

Jonathan nods again. "Okay." He pets the dog some more, as the words of the Seer slowly penetrate his mind. He has heard of guardian angels before, and has a preconceived notion of their purpose. He has a belated thought relating to what Natalie has said. "I guess ours didn't do a very good job, then, did they? If they let us both fall off the jungle gym."

Natalie squeezes his hand encouragingly, glad he is at least engaging with the topic, and seems to be understanding what she has said. She goes on. "They can't do anything to protect us physically, so we can still get hurt even though they are always with us. What they are here to protect is our souls. They try to help us live our lives, and grow our souls."

"He understands what you have said, but thinks there is hardly any point to an angel who can only protect the soul. The soul is not something, ironically, which Jonathan feels is important, despite how crucial it has been to him."

"Protecting the soul is way more important than protecting the body," she tries to clarify to him. "The soul is the part that will last forever. When we're done with it, it goes back and stays with our guardian angel, always. It never dies."

"He understands as well as he is going to, my dear. He has heard what you said. Again, though, he does not understand the significance of this topic."

"So, remember I said I could tell you what happened when you fell off the jungle gym?"

He nods. "Yeah."

"You probably don't remember, but you had started feeling really mad when I tried to tell you about guardian angels before."

"No, I don't think I remember. Why would I be mad?"

"Because your guardian angel was making you be mad. He didn't want you to find out about him."

"Why?"

"He was different from other guardian angels. He used to like it when ...." She hesitates, not wanting to remind Jonathan of his earlier pastime of cruelty, for fear that in his current state it would cause regrets. She revises what she had been planning to say. "He had found a way to make you do mean things, because he liked how much your soul would grow when it happened. He wanted to be able to keep controlling you."

"That was clever, my darling, to assign responsibility for Jonathan's past cruelty to his Guardian rather than to himself. He is considering what you said, and remembering times in the past when he committed such acts. Although, he remembers very little of the more recent times when Demon was causing him to do so."

"Huh. I guess I remember doing things sometimes. You are saying my guardian angel was making me do it?"

She nods, mutely, not wishing to actually utter a falsehood. She knows, of course, that Demon only started controlling Jonathan's actions in the past few months. The prior years were Jonathan's responsibility. Again, though, she does not wish any sense of guilt to interfere with Jonathan's growth.

"So," Natalie continues the tale, "your guardian angel didn't want you to find out about him. He liked controlling you, and he was afraid if you knew about him, he wouldn't be able to make you do things. So he made you mad when I told you, then you tried to make me stop talking."

Jonathan shakes his head, sensing a slight glimmer of a memory of the incident on top of the jungle gym, but it slips away again more quickly than a dream. "I guess I don't remember."

Gabe adds, "That's what happened. I tried to make sure that Natalie was okay, since It looked like you were going to push her off the jungle gym. So I grabbed your arm and..." Gabe also hesitates, taking the cue from Natalie to avoid assigning blame to Jonathan. "And that's when we both fell and got hurt."

"Oh," Jonathan says, believing this tale but feeling detached from it, as though it happened to somebody else. Which, in a way, it did. This Jonathan is a very different creature from the Jonathan on top of the jungle gym that day.

"The reason I'm telling you all this, Jonathan, is because there is something else I think you should know. That explains why you've been feeling so strange ever since that day."

This does interest him. He has been perplexed by his own lethargy, knowing it to be different, but not understanding why he feels this way now. "I am feeling strange. You can tell me why?" He looks at her, with an eager, open, accepting expression on his face, so unlike the old Jonathan that it is nearly heartbreaking. His eyes are filled with a hope, that she can help him. She is flooded with even more compassion for his plight.

"Your guardian angel left after it happened. He hasn't been with you since then. And your soul got weaker because he isn't here. Without him, your soul is smaller than it should be. And that's why you've been feeling so tired and different."

His brow wrinkles with concern. "My soul is... like ... broken?" Emotion washes over him, both a fear of the unknown, and a conflicting sense of relief that there is an explanation for his mystifying condition.

"But I'm helping you, Jonathan," she says fervently, bringing her other hand to join the first in grasping Jonathan's. With her added touch and increased urgency, his soul responds by flaring brighter. "That's why I keep coming over here. My guardian angel says when I'm with you, and if I touch you, your soul gets a little better. I think you will keep getting better."

He is moved, finally realizing the import of what she has been telling him. *"He begins to understand, my dear, that everything you are saying is true, and that thanks to your efforts he is beginning to recover."*

She is intensely focused on helping him to not only understand, but to prepare. "I will keep helping you, and your soul will keep getting better. But I think that once it is well enough, your guardian angel will come back. You have to be ready if it happens. If he comes back, and tries to control you, you should not let him. You don't have to do what he says. If you don't want to do mean stuff, just don't do it, no matter how he makes you feel."

Jonathan's emotions overflow. This is too much for him to absorb. "What?" he cries. "I don't know what you mean. Like, I have to fight my guardian angel for control over my own self?"

Natalie is dismayed that she has brought distress to him. "I don't know, Jonathan, we don't understand exactly what has happened, or what will happen next. But I'll stay with you, and help you, and Gabe will too. Even Timothy will. You'll be okay. We'll make sure you're okay. You have to try hard to only do the things you want for yourself."

He is not weeping, but he is filled with anxiety over this unexpected warning. He pictures a terrifying dark angel come to seize control. "What will happen? How will I even know when he's back?"

"I'll tell you, as soon as my guardian angel knows it is happening. But it isn't yet. I don't think it will happen very soon. You don't have to do anything but concentrate on getting better. And pay attention to how you are feeling, and make sure they are your own feelings. Not something that feels like it came from somewhere else."

She is worried that she has not explained this clearly enough.

Jonathan says, anxiously, "You'll stay with me? It feels better when you stay with me." He looks down at their joined hands.

"I will, as much as I can. We will help you get through whatever happens."

Chapter 20

Welcoming Committee

Laura

Well, they're gone. Yesterday they packed up the last load of stuff and took off to Ron's house. I sigh. I wonder how long before they rent out the condo and we get new neighbors. New neighbors for the new year.

I don't know why I am missing Brenda even more now. She hasn't been here on weekends for months, and I did see her yesterday. Well, we've set up a plan for dinner in a couple of days.

Timothy is in a bit of a funk, too. Not as much as I would have expected, though. He seems to understand better than I do that he'll be able to continue to see his friend. They're in the same class, after all, and he knows we'll make sure to maintain their weekend playdates.

He is also happy with the big box of toy dinosaurs Gabe gave him, going through them with a nostalgic smile on his face. It makes me laugh to think about it, all those years ago when he was only two and started playing with those dinosaurs with Brenda's kids. That was the first thing Natalie saw him do, when Timothy started shrieking about Gabe picking up a couple of the toys. Natalie was able to figure out how to comfort him, even though she was also only two. And they've been inseparable ever since.

There's been a lot of changes since then, but not that. Timothy and Natalie are still like two peas in a pod, never tiring of each other's company, constantly thinking of things to talk about. Performing their cute little experiments all the time.

Michael has never paid very much attention to it. He knows that Timothy and Natalie are friends, but he doesn't understand their relationship. I'm not sure anybody else does. They aren't just kids who are friends. They are very unusual kids.

The fact that Timothy is already well into studying the college textbooks I gave him for Christmas is typical for him, but baffling for Michael. I'm starting to wonder how much longer regular school is going to hold Timothy's interest. He's obviously academically far more advanced than second grade. The whole special ed testing and IEP process which started last year was enough of a challenge for us, and especially for Michael. I have hesitated to mention my concerns about whether Timothy might be better off in a higher grade level, or some other academic setting. I don't want to rock the boat. So to speak. I laugh at my own pun, joking about not upsetting my Navy husband.

That's another challenge. It's not only that he's still having a hard time sleeping, he has gotten really jumpy. He went back to work after a couple weeks of leave when his deployment ended, and since then when he's home he is almost twitchy with anxiety. I have to be careful not to come up behind him too quietly because if he is startled he jumps a mile. It's like he's expecting a fight to break out at any moment. It's alarming, and I don't know how to deal with that either.

I keep mulling it over in my mind, all these issues tangled together, unable to find any solutions. Finding something to do with myself now that my best friend moved, my kid's academic potential needing to be fulfilled, my husband's stress needing to be managed. I have no idea what to do about any of it.

Stefanie

"Good morning, sweetie, time to get up." Jonathan opens his eyes, but I get the feeling he wasn't actually sleeping.

"I know," he says, somewhat glumly. I suppose it's hard to get back to school after being off for so long. Extra long since he missed the week he got hurt, before Christmas break. He sits up, resigned.

I feel so much better about how he's been the last few days. He seems to have gotten over the lethargy he experienced after the hospital. He's not really back to himself, not as mischievous and challenging as he usually is. But maybe it's because he is maturing. My little boy is growing up. I think the events of last month might have given him a little incentive to behave better. It's a good thing.

I stand back up from his bed, starting to feel a little off balance, now that the baby is growing and my body is expanding. I've already had to give up on wearing my normal clothes. I don't have much by way of a maternity wardrobe, since I was still in high school last time and I don't have any of that stuff any more. I've found myself wearing a lot of Brad's big sweatshirts and stuff.

I need to get some clothes, though, since my internship starts in a couple of weeks. I'll be working in a psychologist's office, so I need something that will be suitable. I'm planning to drop Jonathan off at school and then head down to the mall to try to do some shopping.

The morning passes quickly. He eats breakfast, and has time to play with his dog before we have to go. I made sure to get him up plenty early to have time for everything without feeling rushed. He seems slightly on edge, like he is worried about something, presumably anxious about being back at school again. Before long, we are in the car headed to school.

I start to pull up to the place on the street where I usually drop him off. He says, "Mom?"

"Yeah?"

"Um, can you walk me in? Please? Just today?" There's a slight quaver in his voice.

Oh, that's different. Man, he hasn't wanted me to walk him in for years, probably since he was in kindergarten. What on earth? Then I realize. Last time he was here, he was carted off in an ambulance. It's enough to make anyone anxious. Poor thing.

"Of course, kiddo, let me pull the car around and park."

We get out, and I walk close enough that he can hold my hand if he wants. I want to reassure him, but I don't want to embarrass him, so I won't grab his hand in public. But it turns out I don't need to. He has a whole little welcoming committee waiting for him.

He lights up when he sees not only his BFF Gabe, but also Natalie and even her friend Timothy, standing at the front of the school, obviously there specifically to welcome Jonathan. Aww, that's so nice of them. Sometimes kids can be sweet.

They rush over and meet us before we even get out of the parking lot. "Hey Jon," Gabe says, "welcome back to school!" Natalie reaches out and takes his hand, which is very cute. Even Timothy says hello to him.

I sense him immediately relax. He looks up at me. "Thanks Mom. Bye. I'll see you after school."

Well then I guess I've done my part. I lean over to kiss the top of his head. "Have a good day sweetie. I'll see you after school."

Gabe

I figure we are going to head over to the jungle gym where Jonathan and I always spend every morning before school, but Natalie catches my eye and shakes her head. Oh. She must have heard that from Angel, and she thinks we shouldn't return to the scene of the crime, so to speak. Probably good to avoid it. And Jonathan doesn't make any moves to go over there. I don't know if it's because he doesn't remember it has always been our spot, or if he wants to avoid being where we both got hurt.

So instead we walk over to the edge of the playground, next to the fence overlooking the canyon behind the school. Natalie doesn't let go of Jonathan's hand the whole time.

"How are you feeling?" she asks him.

"Okay, I guess."

"I know you are getting even better every day," she tells him. "I think you'll be fine in class. Then we can all eat lunch together, all right?"

Jonathan

Timothy and Gabe watch us, while Natalie is holding my hand and talking. I suppose Timothy is here too since he is always with her.

Natalie glances over to the side. "Timothy knows about guardian angels," she says, looking back at me. "He's going to help you too. We are all here for you."

I don't remember Timothy wanting to hang around with me before, and thought he didn't really like me. But since there's a lot I don't remember, maybe I don't have that right.

"Okay, thanks."

Timothy looks at the watch he's wearing. "It's five minutes until the bell rings," he says.

"All right," Natalie tells me, "we can all walk you to class, okay?"

"Thank you," I tell her.

I've been super freaked out about the idea of my guardian angel coming back and trying to control me. It's scary. I don't like how anxious I've been feeling. On the other hand, this is the most of anything I have felt since I got hurt, and it's almost nice to have a strong sense of anything.

Natalie assuring me she is going to help, and they are all going to stay with me as much as they can, makes me feel a lot better. I can almost believe everything is going to be all right, when she's holding my hand and looking into my eyes.

I like it when she does that. Looks into my eyes. Her eyes are the prettiest color of dark green, and they seem full of light and friendship. Especially outside, in the sun, I love to see them.

We get to my classroom before I know it. Everyone is running around and talking about what they got for Christmas. But Natalie and Gabe and Timothy are standing with me, quietly. She's not holding my hand any more, since I think she doesn't want everyone in my class to make fun of me about it, but she's standing right next to me so our arms are touching. It's enough.

"Okay, Jonathan, we have to go to class. Have a good morning. We'll see you at lunch." She touches my hand one more time before they head away.

It's okay. I'm okay. I go in.

Timothy's

My beloved is extraordinary. Despite the years of torment at the hands of this boy, Timothy is committed to doing everything he can to help. Of course, it is founded on his devotion to the Seer. But he also wishes to see the success of the Jonathan Project. He believes that if the project succeeds, Natalie's preferred outcome might actually come to fruition. She strives for both the restoration of Jonathan's Guardian, and a decision by the boy to control his own choices. Preferably, kinder choices. If this is able to occur, Timothy feels, he can continue in his close friendship with Natalie despite her determination to spend as much time as possible in Jonathan's company. It is an uneasy alliance, and a struggle for Timothy to control his anxiety about spending more time with other children, particularly with the one child who he for so long sought to avoid.

But he is resigned. Furthermore, of course, he feels an insatiable scientific curiosity about what he views as an experiment. The data he is gathering adds to his understanding of myself and the other Guardians. Our communication continues to strengthen. Every night before he falls asleep, he is able to hear my words of love, and we find it possible to carry on a very brief conversation before he drifts off. Just a few words. It is necessarily fleeting because in order for this to happen, he must be very close to sleep. The rest of the time, he habitually opens his mind to me, and nearly continuously feels my presence, senses my support and companionship.

When he first began his efforts to communicate with me, his initial motivation was a hope that this would assist him in understanding the topics he studies. His experimentation has expanded from this original purpose, but he has never forgotten it. Now, I sense that there is progress in this direction. As he studies his textbooks, clearly at an academic level far above that which he is prepared for, I attempt to transmit to him a sense of deep focus, and I believe it is assisting. It is difficult to know to what extent his learning is enhanced. His naturally brilliant intelligence would have led the way to great academic achievement, even if he had not begun his experimentation in Guardian communication. But I believe his learning is augmented by his ability to receive my support.

He focuses today on the experiment. Natalie is receiving frequent updates from Angel regarding Jonathan's experiences. His first day back to school seems positive. He and Gabe are both experiencing the minor celebrity which comes with being the victims of a dramatic accident. The entire school was aware of their injuries, and engaged in intense speculation regarding their fates after they witnessed the spectacle of an ambulance on the school grounds.

Gabe accepts the attention good naturedly if abashedly, allowing his classmates to try using his crutches, and to sign their names on his cast. Jonathan is basking in the attention. He finds himself surprised to be enjoying anything this much, after his month of muted emotions. Natalie is pleased to receive Angel's reports indicating that all appears to be proceeding very well.

Timothy

At lunchtime, I take the chance to write some notes about the updates Natalie has been giving me about Jonathan. It's strange to be sitting together and eating with him. Every time he's come over to me at lunch before, it ended up in some disaster, with him teasing me or hurting me or fighting with me. Not today though. He's only sitting there, talking about how all the kids in his class were asking questions about the ambulance and the hospital, and how he had to make stuff up to tell them since he barely remembers anything. Natalie is sitting next to him, and I am on her other side eating and writing in my notebook about the Jonathan Project.

Angel says his soul is getting better all the time, but Demon is still missing. So the experiment is still unfolding. Jonathan seems a lot better than he did at first, and he doesn't show any signs of trying to be mean to me or anyone else.

Let's hope it keeps up.

Chapter 21

Back To Normal

February 2002

Brenda

I can't believe how busy we've been the last couple of months. Between getting the condo ready to rent out, and making arrangements for our wedding, it's like there hasn't been a moment to sit down and catch our breath.

Ron acts like he's having the time of his life, though. He is so in on everything. When we packed up all our stuff to bring it to his house, he was gung ho about lifting all the boxes and helping with everything. He's the one who had the idea to leave most of the furniture in the condo and rent it out furnished. I think most rentals are unfurnished, and I wasn't sure if it'd work, but we got plenty of people interested in renting it with the furniture already in.

We've ended up having to do a lot of repairs and painting and stuff, trying to get it in good condition before the guys move in. It's going to be a couple of young guys, roommates, who had decent credit and steady jobs and seem like a good risk for renters. I had envisioned a family moving in, but these guys were some of the first to respond to our ad so we decided to go for it. They both work in construction, so maybe if anything breaks while they are there, they can take care of it. But we'll see if anything like that comes up.

Today is the fifteenth of the month, and it's move-in day. I'm resisting the urge to go over there and stare when they arrive. I suppose they won't have too much stuff, since they aren't bringing furniture. Laura told me she'll keep an eye out and let me know if anything interesting happens.

And now, with the last of the condo rental situation resolved for now, we can get back to normal. And I can really focus on the wedding. Mom has made arrangements with her pastor to have it at the church she has attended for decades in Albuquerque. We really aren't inviting anyone though. My parents will be there of course, and maybe my sister will fly into town. I suppose Mom will invite some of her friends. But we're not sending out many invitations or anything that formal. It's a re-wedding. Nobody really needs to come and watch us admit that we were idiots for divorcing. We're correcting a mistake, that's all.

I am doing a few things. I've gotten a lovely dress, elegant and simple. No frills for this wedding. The kids will have nice outfits. Natalie, of course, is involved in the planning, very excited to pick out a dress. She wants there to be flowers, so we'll include some of that in our planning too. She insists that Ron wear a tuxedo, and he is happy to indulge her in this, and is taking care of ordering it.

After the ceremony we plan to go out to lunch at a restaurant in Albuquerque. We've decided to fit the whole trip into the kids' spring break the last week of March. So we'll do some sightseeing and stuff while we're back there. We're all looking forward to the trip next month.

Brad

Boy, this last month has been really something. I practically feel like a single dad, Stefanie is so busy all the time. Between her last semester of college, and her internship, I hardly ever see her. Good thing the grocery store is being understanding and letting me keep my schedule flexible, so I can be available to take care of Jonathan.

I am waiting for him in the car when he finishes school for the week. I went into work at the crack of dawn, like I've been doing lately, so I can be there to pick him up. Stef has been taking him to school. I know pretty soon, we'll have to figure out how to juggle two kids.

Jonathan opens the door and climbs in. "Hey Dad."

"Hello, buddy. How was school?"

"Good."

"Anything exciting?"

"Dad, it's school. There is not usually anything exciting."

I laugh. "I suppose not." Today's Friday, and Stef only has her internship, not classes. So hopefully she'll be home for dinner. "Let's go by the store and pick up something to make for dinner tonight, okay? Have any suggestions?"

"Hamburgers?" he suggests, hopefully.

"Sure. Sounds good."

That accident back in December seems a million years ago, like it never even happened. Jonathan spent a few weeks recovering, but he seems pretty much back to normal now. Thank goodness. I'm not sure he even remembers it. He never mentions it. Probably just as well.

"Do you know when Gabe and Natalie will get home?" he asks.

"Well, probably same as usual, right before dinner time."

"Okay," he says, watching out the window as we drive to the store. I know he's already planning to see them tonight at some point. It's been nice since they moved to Ron's house full time. He wants to play with them constantly, even more than he used to. So I'm glad they're always in our neighborhood now.

"Hamburgers, and....?" I ask him.

"Duh, Dad. French fries."

He makes me laugh. Like usual. He's always been so entertaining.

Chapter 22

Routine

Natalie's

My beloved waits impatiently for her mother to arrive at the home daycare center where she spends her afternoons. Timothy was not there today, because his mother was not working this afternoon and therefore picked him up directly after school. She did not pick up Natalie as well, now that they are no longer neighbors and this would not be as convenient for Brenda.

Gabe is also not at the daycare, because this is the day he has a doctor's appointment for the removal of his cast. There was a delay of a week or two, due to difficulty scheduling the appointment. He has been eager to have it removed, as would any patient with such a cast in place. However, it is particularly difficult for him to bear the delay, because I have kept him and Natalie updated regarding the healing process, and he is aware that the broken bone was already mended at least two weeks ago. The cast has been nothing but an annoying ornament since that time.

I always provide Natalie with any information she requests, of course, but in some instances I wonder if it might do more harm than good. No doubt Gabe would have accepted the wait with more patience if he was unaware the cast was now unnecessary.

Natalie looks over at me, sensing the general direction of my musings. She seems to do this more frequently all the time. Our communication grows in power and capacity as she matures. Still, she prefers the precision of direct communication, rather than contenting herself with a general understanding of my thoughts. "How is Gabe doing?" she silently inquires.

"The doctor has removed the cast, using a small saw, and is examining his ankle. Everything seems to be properly mended."

"As you said," she thinks.

"As I said."

She returns to her book. A few weeks ago she asked the daycare provider if she happened to have a bible. Surprised, the woman retrieved one from her bedside table, and Natalie has been reading it at daycare whenever there is no other activity to engage in. This bible is a different version from the modern English variety which she has at home, and she enjoys comparing the old-fashioned language of King James to what she remembers reading in her own bible. She has begun making comparisons, appreciating where the differences in language provide conflicting nuances in the tales. Her study of the development of religion continues, her determination to understand it and find a way to correct its mistakes unabated.

She finds the Old Testament to be particularly fascinating, as a historical exercise. But it is the New Testament content which she loves. This is unsurprising. The message of Jesus is so similar to her own philosophy. Love one another. Be kind. Help each other. She has followed these teachings for her entire life, without even being aware of it at the start. She particularly loves the parables, and tries to imagine what the message was behind each story. She attempts to understand why the story was told in this way, rather than as more straightforward instructions.

Always, she is focused on her knowledge that everything in this bible, everything in every religion throughout history, is an invention of mankind. She was devastated when I first told her the concept of God is a human contrivance. She has thoroughly embraced that knowledge now, and eagerly consumes the bible as literature, and as lessons for living. She continues to categorize each story as either simply a tale of human lives, or as having been influenced in some way by Guardians.

Jesus, she is convinced, could hear his Guardian. This is quite likely. Although I have no personal knowledge or memories to confirm the fact, the way his life is written in the bible would be consistent with the abilities of a Seer. There is no archeological proof of his existence, but his message is so similar to Natalie's viewpoint that it is certainly quite possible. We have discussed this at some length, usually late at night when all the others in her family have long been asleep. She is quite interested in the way that the stories of his life have obviously been conflated with tales in prior religions, which I have been able to describe to her as well. There is little chance of her being able to untangle any potential historical truth from mythology, but she is undeterred. If nothing else, she simply enjoys the reading.

"Your mother is approaching, my dear."

She looks up from her reading, and bookmarks her place with the ribbon attached to the top of the bible. Setting the book on the table beside the couch where she has been sitting, she approaches the woman who runs the daycare. "Thank you again for letting me read your bible. I hope you have a nice weekend."

"Of course Natalie, it is so nice to see a child who wants to read it. I hope you have a good weekend too." There is a knock on the door, and the woman is not surprised Natalie had already said her goodbyes before her mother arrived. This is standard for Natalie, and no longer seems strange to the woman.

Gabe is there at the door with his mother, pointing triumphantly to his foot wearing a regular shoe, rather than the cast with walking boot which has been plaguing him for so long. "Yay!" Natalie exclaims, clapping her hands with delight. "Finally! It must feel so good!"

"Oh, yeah!" Gabe agrees enthusiastically. "I'm glad that's over!"

The woman chuckles with Brenda, then says, "Okay, kids, have a nice weekend. See you next week."

Jonathan

They come over before dinner, thank goodness. "You're here earlier than I expected," I say, happier the minute Natalie takes my hand.

"Yeah," Gabe says, "I had a doctor's appointment. Look!" He points to his foot.

"Oh, right! No cast. How's it feel?"

"Pretty strange, actually, but I'm so happy to be done with that. My leg's all skinny and pale from being trapped in there, but the doctor said it'll be normal in a few days. And everything is fine now apparently. No harm done!"

It's kind of cold and windy outside, so we don't go out in the back yard. They come into my room with me. Socks as usual is so hyper about Natalie being here that he is practically knocking her over as she tries to walk down the hall.

Natalie sits with me on the floor, leaning against my bed. Socks sits next to her and lays his head on her lap. Gabe sits with us, now that he doesn't have the cast on and it won't feel so awkward. "Aahhhh!" he says.

Natalie giggles. "Welcome back to the floor." We all laugh.

"Well," Natalie says, "we got through another week. How are you feeling?"

This is our routine now. At the end of every week she checks to see how I'm doing. And whether I feel like my guardian angel is back yet. I'm getting used to the whole idea, about us all having them, and her being able to talk to hers all the time.

Gabe likes to play this game with dice where we shake them in a cup and turn it over so we can't see, then Natalie tells us what they say. It's pretty fun. He told me the first time they played it was the night she told him about guardian angels. It was the same day we had a fight in the library.

I'm starting to remember little pieces of what happened. But I've never been able to figure out a lot of it. Like the parts where I did stuff when they tell me my guardian angel was in control. I don't disbelieve what they say. I know for a fact that it's all true. Natalie wouldn't lie to me. And it's the best explanation for how I felt after the hospital.

I don't really feel that way any more. I think my energy is normal, and I like to do stuff again. I'm glad I don't have a guardian angel around making me do mean stuff. I remember liking to play tricks on people, and tease them, and things like that, but I don't have any interest in it now. I guess it's because it was my guardian angel wanting me to do it, and now that he's gone I don't want to.

"I feel fine," I tell her.

"Any emotions that don't make sense?"

"No."

"Have you felt like you want to hurt anyone?"

"No."

"Anything different at all?"

"No. I just keep feeling better. I think you really have been helping me," I tell her. I look into her eyes, which are dark brown here inside the house. "Thank you."

She smiles and touches my shoulder. Mm. The light goes on. It still always happens, but now it isn't as noticeable. I think I'm feeling normal enough all the time that it doesn't make as big a difference as it did at first. I still like it, though.

Chapter 23

Sleep

Timothy

Natalie starts with a report on the Jonathan Project when I get to her house, first thing Saturday morning. "He still keeps getting better. Angel says his soul is much healthier. He is acting like a normal person now, and he says he hasn't noticed anything that would seem like Demon is back."

"Who knows," Gabe says, "maybe he'll never come back. Jonathan seems fine, maybe we shouldn't want Demon to return."

Natalie says, "Angel doesn't think he'll stay away forever. He says Demon is still around somewhere, since he is tied to Jonathan's soul. We just don't know when he'll come back or what will happen when he does."

"Well," I say, "I think you've done a good job preparing Jonathan for it. He knows to be aware of his feelings so that he'll be able to tell if Demon is trying to take control again. I think the Jonathan Project is going well."

Natalie says, "And you are okay being around him now, too. I'm really glad about that. I'd hate to have to only be with one of you."

I shrug. "Yeah. He's not bad to be around any more, now that he has stopped teasing me. He actually can be kind of fun sometimes. He's good at building Lego sets."

Gabe grins. "Look at us all getting along together, thanks to Natalie The Great!"

She rolls her eyes. Then Gabe rolls his eyes since nobody is laughing at his joke.

I take a few notes in my notebook about the Jonathan Project. I've started using a chart that I made to check off all the questions I know she asks him at the end of every week, about whether he is feeling Demon.

"So," she asks me when I'm done and put the notebook down, "how are things over at your place? Did you see the renters after they moved in?"

"Yes. It is extremely strange to have somebody other than you guys living in your house." I sigh. I know I see Natalie almost every day, but I liked having her living closer to me.

"What are they like?" Gabe asks.

"It's two grown up guys. Roommates. Mom said they moved in while I was at school, but I saw them later going back and forth to their cars. I don't think they had enough stuff that they needed a big truck to move."

"That makes sense," Gabe says, "since we left all our furniture there for them. They wouldn't need to move big stuff in. I agree about it being weird. Other people living in our house. Freaky."

"Do they seem nice?" Natalie asks.

"I don't know. My Dad went and talked to them, and said he thought they were going to be okay neighbors."

"No kids for you to play with, though," Natalie says.

I stare at her. Why would I want other kids to play with?

She laughs and shakes her head. "Well, want to go over to Jonathan's for a while? I'd like to see Socks."

Michael

I'm sorry that Laura misses Brenda living next door, but the new neighbors seem pretty chill. I got the chance to talk to them yesterday. They're a bit younger than us, probably in their early twenties. They told me they were high school friends, and they work at the same construction company. One of them recently broke up with his girlfriend and needed to find a new place to live, so they decided to rent a place together.

After I drop Timothy off at his friend's house, I head in to work. I feel bleary with fatigue. I'm getting used to the feeling of constant exhaustion. Every night I wake up with nightmares. Every fucking night. Last night was especially bad, and when I jerked awake I think I actually hit Laura. She didn't say anything about it this morning though, and I hate to bring it up in case I'm wrong. She just looked at me with her blue eyes full of concern.

That's what's killing me more than anything. That this is so hard on her. I can tell she is eaten up with worry about me. Every time I wake her up I feel that much guiltier about how disruptive I'm being. I think a few times I've even made so much noise that the kid woke up too.

I have no control over it. It's even happening more often during the day, where I hear some noise and it triggers this giant adrenaline fight or flight response. It's not even like I'm remembering actual combat I participated in. It's made-up images of bombs dropping, the bombs I helped deploy in Afghanistan. My crazy brain keeps putting me there on the receiving end.

I'd give anything for an actual night of sleep. For me and for Laura.

Laura

Saturday morning shift at the salon. I'm on my third haircut, and am trying as hard as I can not to let on that I feel half dead on my feet. I wrap the nylon cape around my customer's neck and lead her over to the sink so I can wash her hair.

What I wouldn't give to feel rested again. This is worse than when Timothy was a newborn and I couldn't sleep for more than a couple of hours at a time. With a baby, you might be exhausted, but you know there's a purpose to it, and you know how to take care of the baby when he wakes up in the night.

With Michael, I have no idea what I should be doing. I've tried everything I can think of. I even suggested that perhaps he would sleep better if I went and slept on the couch downstairs, but he wouldn't hear of it. No, he told me, he's pretty sure that being next to me is actually helping.

Man, if that's helping, I'd hate to see how bad it would be otherwise.

I lean the chair back up from the sink and ask her to come on over to my station. I start clipping up sections of her hair before I begin cutting. I ask her if she has any plans for the weekend, but I'm afraid I'm not concentrating on her answer.

It's every night. We haven't had a single full night of peace. I'm starting to worry he's going to give himself a heart attack someday, jumping out of bed like he's being pursued by the devil himself.

There have even been a couple of times he acted the same way right in the middle of the day. It's been very scary. Last week I dropped something I was carrying in the kitchen, while he was sitting at the table, and he leapt to his feet so fast that his chair crashed to the ground. It took him a couple of minutes to calm down. It's like he didn't know where he was, like he felt like there was some threat. Thank God Timothy was at school at the time.

I pump the salon chair up a little higher with my foot. "Okay, tilt your head forward please," I tell her, and start cutting the hair on the back of her head.

I'm starting to feel desperate. And I'm wondering if there is anything the Navy could do to help. I'm scared to do it, for fear it would upset him, but I'm trying to figure out how to suggest to him that he should see a doctor. Some kind of therapist. This situation is really unhealthy, and I am afraid it is deteriorating. I think he needs help. Help that I haven't been able to provide.

Michael's

It is deeply distressing. Nothing I can do penetrates the chaotic cloud which fills his mind. He has managed to continue functioning, both at home and at work, but I fear this is not sustainable. His emotional suffering, and his lack of sleep, have seriously impacted his physical well-being. He has drifted off to sleep at work several times, and even once or twice while behind the wheel of his car. He awakens after a second or two and there has been no serious consequence, but I know if this continues there will inevitably be an accident.

His wife has begun considering whether to suggest that he consult a doctor to ask for help. She does not know that he has already attempted this. A few weeks ago he had an appointment with the doctor on board the ship, mentioning that he was having trouble sleeping, and was having nightmares related to combat. However, because my beloved was not directly involved in physical combat, the symptoms were not considered to be caused by his military service, and therefore no treatment was suggested other than typical suggestions to better tend to his diet and exercise routines.

In an effort to enact this advice, he has begun taking nighttime walks around the neighborhood. He is hopeful that this will help him sleep better, but as of yet there has been no improvement.

This evening is no different. The family eats dinner together. Timothy retires to his room to read before bedtime.

Michael puts on his shoes. "I'm going to go take a walk," he tells his wife.

"Okay, honey, have a nice walk," she replies, giving him a kiss, then looking into his eyes with the deep love and concern she feels for him.

It is fully dark outside. He walks through the complex to the street, lifting the collar of his jacket against the chill of the February night. The cool air feels good on his face. He contemplates his conflicting feelings about his wife. He loves her deeply, and appreciates her love for him, but he begins to feel suffocated by her constant ineffective attempts to help him. Her love is overwhelming at times, and it makes him feel unworthy for her to be trying so hard to help him.

"My darling, you are indeed deeply worthy of the love of your wife. Please, enjoy this walk, let the exercise in the cool night clear your head, and make you ready for sleep. My dearest, I am with you together in your struggle."

After he begins to feel physically fatigued, he turns around and heads back towards his home. He passes by the home next door, where the new tenants have recently moved in. Through the open curtains he sees the two young men within, watching television, laughing and apparently greatly enjoying themselves.

He hesitates, watching the appealing scene through the window. He does not wish to face his wife yet, to see the worry and concern and hope in her eyes as they ready themselves to go to bed. Here before him is a preferable alternative.

Impulsively, he approaches their front door and rings the bell. One of the young men answers a moment later. "Hey," he says to Michael. "What's up?"

Michael

I can hardly believe I'm standing here rather than going home to Laura. "Hey," I tell him. "I'm Mike, from next door. We met yesterday. I just wanted to swing by and see if you guys are settling in okay."

"Oh, cool," he says. "Want to come in?"

"Sure," I say, far more jovially than I feel. "Your name is Enrique, right?"

"Yeah," he says. "Hey Jim, look, our neighbor Mike is here."

Jim glances up from the couch. "Dude," he says, "welcome."

I say, "Just checking to see if you guys are settling in. Do you need anything?"

Enrique slumps back down on the couch. "Have a seat," he invites me. Gratefully, I sit down. I really didn't feel like going home yet. This is perfect.

"We're good," Jim says. "I don't think we need anything, but thanks for asking." He offers me a bowl of chips that was sitting on the coffee table. "Want to hang for a while?"

I take the chips with a smile. "Sure, thanks!"

Laura

I didn't mean to fall asleep, but Michael was gone so long on his walk that I must have drifted off on the couch while I was waiting for him to get back. It wakes me up when I hear him come back in through the door.

"Mmmm," I murmur, sitting up. "What time is it?"

"Not really sure," he says, then gives a strange little giggle. "Sorry for waking you up."

"You were gone a long time. Is everything okay?" I'm groggy with sleep.

He sits next to me on the couch and puts his arm around me. "I went to visit the new neighbors. Jim and Enrique. They're really cool."

Oh, that's unexpected. "Really? Okay." He leans in to give me a kiss, and that's when I smell it. My sense of sleepiness instantly evaporates. I lean back and gape at him, shocked. "Oh my God. Have you been smoking pot?"

"Um, yeah, maybe a little. They offered me some, and it seemed rude to refuse." He giggles again.

What. The. Heck. I know Michael used to smoke pot sometimes when he was a lot younger, but he's in the Navy now. He knows he's not supposed to do this.

I am absolutely flabbergasted. He looks at me, sort of abashed, but clearly not sorry. "Don't be mad, Laura. It was only a little. Come on, let's go to bed."

I don't know what to say. This is so unexpected, and disappointing, and alarming. But how can I confront him about it, when he's been having such a hard time lately? So I bite my tongue and follow him up the stairs.

Michael's

My beloved's experience in sampling the marijuana with his new neighbors has brought a surprising sense of well-being to him. The constant turmoil in his mind has slowed. He worried about his wife's reaction, but other than expressing some initial surprise, she has not commented. They prepare themselves to retire for the night.

"My dearest, how nice that you visited with your new friends and enjoyed some refreshments with them. Try to rest now, beloved."

Laura

I wake up, noticing that the sun is already in the sky. It's Sunday, so the alarm wasn't set, since we don't have to go anywhere this morning. Michael is still laying asleep by my side.

Suddenly, I realize two very important things. I remember last night Mike went over and smoked pot with the neighbors, much to my shock when I realized it. But more importantly, unbelievably, miraculously, he did not wake up last night. We both slept all night long.

I almost want to cry I am so relieved. He got a full night of sleep. We both did.

Last night when I was falling asleep, I was making plans to tell Brenda that their tenants are already in the house smoking pot. I know she and Ron would not want that to be happening. It's probably in the rental contract that the tenants signed.

But now I'm not so sure. Was that why Mike slept all night? It seriously is like a miracle. Maybe having done that, just the one time, things will be able to get back to normal now. Maybe I should refrain from mentioning it to Brenda. Just for now.

Mike rolls over in bed, and opens his eyes. He looks confused, like he doesn't know what's going on. Then I see the dawning realization in his face. He knows it too. He didn't have any nightmares last night.

Chapter 24

Good Friend

March 2002

Brenda

The time has passed so quickly. It's impossible to believe it has been four months since Ron proposed, and that the wedding we've been planning is already next week. When school ends on Friday for spring break, we'll be picking the kids up from school and heading straight to the airport.

Then Sunday is the day. We'll have a brief morning ceremony at the church, with only a few people there, before heading to a restaurant for a celebratory lunch. Ron and I will be husband and wife again. Although, I already feel that way. It's like those few years in the middle never happened. How long was it? Like six or seven years? Well, it'd have to be, Natalie is seven, and Ron left while I was pregnant. But all of that hardly matters now. I am back to feeling like Ron and I have always been married, and always will be. If soulmates is really a thing, that's us. It's a comfortable feeling, of total fulfillment. Together, we are complete.

So, although I suppose I have some nerves about the big day, they aren't about the marriage part. I'm completely confident in me and Ron now. But I want to make sure everything comes together and the ceremony is pleasant and will make a nice memory for the kids.

Then, the rest of the week we will relax and hang around Albuquerque, see the sights, eat lots of Mexican food.

For now, though, I have to get the office in order for me to take a vacation for a week. I'm still the manager for this little insurance branch, but at least now we have a second staffer who can take care of everything in my absence. I'm planning to spend the rest of Wednesday going over everything with her, then tomorrow I'm only working half a day so I can go home and start packing. Then Friday we're off!

I imagine how Ron is spending his day. Much the same as me, I assume. As though he could hear me thinking about him, my phone chimes. I pick it up and see his text message. It's a little heart emoji, nothing more. Just enough for me to know everything that I need to.

Jonathan

"Want some of my cookies?" I ask them, passing around the full baggie. My Dad always packs way too much food for my lunch. He's the one who packs it up now, since Mom is too busy with school and whatever else she's doing. I think Dad thinks I can eat as much as he does, like he doesn't realize I'm only nine. Which is strange, considering that we had my 9th birthday party a few weeks ago.

So here I am with two sandwiches and an apple and chips and cookies and some other stuff he tossed into the bag for good measure. Gabe takes a handful of cookies when I wave the bag under his nose.

Natalie takes one, making sure to touch my hand as I pass it to her, and she very politely thanks me. It still feels good whenever she touches me, but she doesn't have to do it all the time anymore. She says Angel told her I'm almost back to normal. We hardly ever talk about my missing guardian angel any more. There's still no sign of him, and I'm starting to think he's gone for good. That's fine. I feel okay. Natalie told me that him being missing was a problem, but it doesn't seem to be any more. I used to be afraid of him coming back and controlling me again. But I don't think it will happen now. I don't remember any of it anyway, so I don't feel like it is a real threat.

Timothy even takes a cookie when I hand him the bag, and sits there munching it while staring off into the distance.

I think everyone else in the school is used to this now, the four of us eating lunch together every day. We didn't used to, before the "jungle gym" as we have been calling it. The day everything changed. But now Natalie is my friend, as much as Gabe ever was.

Even Timothy. I've gotten used to his weird little personality. Who could have ever known that such a quirky dude could be so interesting and smart? I don't remember everything that happened before the jungle gym, but I'm pretty sure I used to tease him for being a weirdo. I'm sorry about that. I didn't understand him before. Being around Timothy, especially with Natalie's help, has given me a whole new appreciation. He even helps me with my homework sometimes, even though he's a grade lower than me.

"Hey, Timothy?" I say.

He focuses back on reality, obviously coming back from wherever he just was in his head. "Yes?" he asks.

"We were talking about something in science this morning that I thought you'd be interested in." He's in second grade and I'm in third, and he always wants to hear what we do in science. He finds it more interesting since it's at a higher level. Although I've started to realize that even third grade science would be too easy for him.

His eyes light up. "Really? What was it?"

"We've been talking about different kinds of energy, and batteries and stuff. The teacher told us you can actually make a battery out of a potato!"

Gabe laughs. "I can think of better things to do with a potato. Hmmm. Now I want some of your chips!" He grabs my bag of potato chips, while Timothy and I start talking about how to make a potato battery. It sounds like he knows more about it than my teacher does.

Natalie smiles and watches us all.

Timothy's

To watch my beloved enjoy the company of a group of friends, aside from his relationship with Natalie, is a joy. It is all because of the Seer, of course, but his friendships with Gabe and Jonathan are genuine. They both understand and tolerate, even appreciate, his personality quirks.

Jonathan's status is confounding. After Demon's departure left his soul so damaged, it seemed unlikely that he would ever be able to recover. But with the Seer's touch and presence, he has revived tremendously. His soul glows as healthily as that of the humans around him. It has never recovered the flaming brilliance of its former days, but it is perfectly satisfactory. The symptoms of lethargy and disinterest which resulted from his diminished soul have long vanished. As have, interestingly, the sides of his personality which alienated my beloved from him in the first place.

Jonathan is now a good friend to the other children, and has none of the dark thoughts which used to direct his actions. It has been many months since the last time he played a cruel trick, or attempted to harm another. His sense of humor has returned, and his enjoyment in life is back to normal. He engages in many activities with enthusiasm. But never with darkness or cruelty.

Angel and I have spent a great deal of time analyzing this. It was Natalie's touch which healed Jonathan's soul. Did she also imbue it with her own sensibilities? Her guiding principles are those of love, kindness, mercy. Have they overlaid Jonathan's darker tendencies, obscuring them into oblivion?

If Demon were to return, what would happen? Would Jonathan immediately revert to his prior proclivities? We tend to think not, as long as Natalie remains nearby, and continues to hold sway over Jonathan's life.

Despite the way Demon had become an evil and controlling spirit, lusting for the pain which Jonathan could inflict, I do not believe he started that way. Jonathan's Guardian used to share the same priorities as the rest of us, for the humans being Guarded to grow in goodness and light. It was Jonathan's own tendency towards cruelty which transformed Demon, not the other way around.

Angel and I are convinced of that.

But this being the case, why has Jonathan changed so much without Demon?

There is only one conceivable explanation. It must be the influence of the Seer.

Stefanie

I shift in my seat, and try to get comfortable as I index the patient files in the back room. Still another couple of months before this baby comes, but I already feel like a whale. I was definitely not this big with Jonathan.

Meg comes in. She's the psychiatrist who works in the office where I'm interning. "How's the project coming?"

"Good," I tell her. "I've gotten most of the files organized, and I'm starting to upload them into the database."

I'm helping her with a research project she's working on, and she's been going back through her old patient files to include them in the study. She's trying to disprove any connection between vaccinations and autism, since there's a lot of people these days who seem to think that childhood vaccines cause it. She wants to start by indexing all of her old records, then she's going to expand the research into the files at Children's Hospital where she also practices. She wants to get a huge sample, so there are a lot of patients who have been diagnosed and also those who haven't. She'll try to access the vaccination records of as many as possible to see whether there is any mathematical correlation.

We have to be careful not to include any identification in the database, just the symptoms and treatment information, and any medical history which would show vaccination status. I've been learning a lot more about data entry than I ever expected. I'm really enjoying it.

She sits down across the table and opens a can of soda. She peeks into a file on the top of the pile closest to her. "Oh yeah, this guy," she says, leafing through her old handwritten notes. "One of my first patients on the spectrum. I wonder how he's doing these days," she muses.

She closes the file and sips her soda. "How's it going?" she asks me. "With school and everything?" She waves her hand at my growing torso, indicating my pregnancy.

"Pretty good," I tell her. "My course load this last semester is a little lighter than usual, since I had to fit in the time for this internship. So I don't have too many finals and projects to worry about before the end of the year."

"Are you feeling well? When are you due, again?"

"Yeah, I have been feeling fine. Just huge. My due date is at the beginning of June. Fingers crossed that I get the semester finished up first."

She laughs. "Let's hope."

She takes another sip of her soda. "Do you have anything lined up for after you graduate?"

"Not yet. I had figured I'd do a lot of job hunting this semester, and try to have something lined up by the summer. But since the baby will be coming then,

I'm planning to wait a couple of months. Take some maternity leave before I start the job search."

"Well," she says, "I have a proposal, if you're interested. I don't have any other research assistants right now. After you take a couple of months off, would you be interested in coming back to work for me? As an actual paid position, not only for the internship? We could make it part time at first if you like, until the baby is a little older. This project is probably going to take at least another year or two of research before it's ready to publish, and I could really use the help."

Oh! "Oh, wow, that would really be perfect!" I love Meg, she's a good friend, not just a boss. The idea of continuing to work with her solves so many of the issues I've been wrestling with. Especially if I could work part time at the beginning, and even take a couple of months off after the baby is born. "Thank you!"

"So that's a yes?" she asks, with a lopsided smile.

"Um, yes! Absolutely!"

"Great," she says. "We can sort out the details as it gets closer. I still get you for free for a couple of months until your internship ends," she points out with a grin.

We laugh.

I can't wait to tell Brad. This is going to work out so great!

Chapter 25

Tangled Situation

Jonathan

"So, what are you doing over spring break?" Gabe asks me. Natalie looks over at me to see how I answer.

I look up from the Lego spaceship I'm building on Gabe's bedroom floor. "Well, being bored out of my mind, obviously, without you guys here."

Natalie laughs, and reaches over and pats my hand. "You've got Socks to keep you company!"

I am not looking forward to the break that starts tomorrow after school. They are going straight from school on their trip to New Mexico, and they'll be gone the entire week we're on break. Ugh. Mom is super busy with work and school, so there's no way for our family to go do anything interesting. I'll spend the week hanging around the house with Dad, apparently.

Natalie says, "By the way, since we won't be here tomorrow night, I want to ask you our Friday questions now."

I shrug. "Fine."

"How have you been feeling?"

Sigh. I know why she asks me this all the time, but sometimes it gets tiresome.

"I'm feeling fine."

"Are you having any unexplained emotions?"

"No."

"Have you felt like you want to hurt anybody?"

"Nope."

"Feeling anything different at all?"

"No. Still feel normal, and like I am in control of myself."

She smiles. "Thanks for being patient with this, Jonathan. I know it is getting old, but as long as your guardian angel is missing, we need to keep track of how you are doing."

"I'm pretty sure he's done with me. He would have come back by now if he was going to. I think I'm on my own. And that's fine with me. I don't want to have to fight off some demon." Natalie told me she started calling my guardian angel Demon before he disappeared. That sounded scary at first, but I'm not scared any more. It's been over three months. I feel totally normal again, I haven't had any unexplained impulses, everything is fine. I wish Natalie would stop worrying about it.

She shrugs. "Well, keep track of everything while we're gone, then we'll talk again next weekend when we get back." She grins. "Maybe we'll send you a postcard from Albuquerque!"

"Yippee!" I say, rolling my eyes.

Ron

"Okay, kids, have a good day at school, and we'll be waiting right here when the bell rings this afternoon!"

The kids say goodbye and clamber out of the car, heading over to the playground on campus. I have a couple of errands to run on the way home. I have to pick up some trip snacks, and a couple of little games for them to play on the plane to keep them occupied. Then home to finish packing and getting ready to go.

It's actually happening! I know Brenda said yes months ago, but I still can hardly believe we're really doing it.

She's planning to have lunch with Laura before we leave, last minute girl pep talk before the wedding, I guess. We invited Laura and Mike to come out for the wedding, but I guess Mike is too busy with work to take time off.

I pull into the grocery store parking lot. What snacks should I get? Hm. Cookies, obviously.

Laura

Mike's at work, and Timothy is at school, so Brenda and I get to enjoy a quiet lunch together. Well, maybe not exactly quiet. There's a lot of laughing going on.

She's super excited about the wedding. I've demonstrated how she should fix her hair in an updo which will look beautiful together with her dress, then took everything out and supervised while she recreated it. She wanted to make sure she can do it herself on the day of the wedding.

It's wonderful to spend time together. We haven't had much of it lately, with her living at Ron's now and so busy with everything.

While we're sitting in the living room after lunch, one of the new neighbors walks past the window. Well, not that new, I guess, they've been there over a month.

Brenda pretends to hide behind a pillow. "Wouldn't want him to know the landlady is here checking up on him. Awkward!"

More laughing.

"Seriously, though," she says, "how's it been? With them next door?"

"Um, fine," I say, trying not to seem evasive. "Very weird for it not to be you guys. Timothy misses Natalie a lot. He used to wave goodnight to her sometimes out his window at bedtime."

"Awww," she says. "They still see each other all the time, though. Natalie seems okay with it. I think Timothy is too?"

"Yeah, he actually is."

"How is Mike doing?" she asks.

"Okay," I say, shrugging. "He's even made friends with Jim and Enrique. Your tenants. He hangs out over there with them after dinner sometimes."

Her eyebrows go up. "Really? I had no idea. That's nice, I think?"

"He seems to like it. I guess it helps him relax after work. Although hanging around with more guys after being on a ship full of guys all day can't be all that different."

She laughs.

I really want to redirect the conversation, to get away from the topic I have to avoid. "So, do you want some make-up tips? For the wedding, to go with your fancy hairdo?"

"Yes, please!"

Good. Let's move on to safer areas. I am filled with guilt over everything I'm not telling her. I had never really told her how much trouble Michael was having when he got back from deployment, how his nightmares were keeping him up all night. I had mentioned it a couple of times, but it was right when Gabe got hurt in December, and then they were all getting ready to move in with Ron full time, then she wasn't here anymore. There never was a great time to give her a long description of what was going on, when we were alone without husbands or kids around so we could talk freely.

And now I am definitely keeping something else from her. I am so conflicted about what is going on with Mike. He's gone next door pretty frequently in the evenings, and usually comes back with the smell of marijuana clinging to him. I hate that smell, and I am worried he's going to end up getting in trouble with the Navy if he gets a random drug test sprung on him.

But, I can't wish that he isn't doing it. The transformation since it started happening is huge. We hadn't had a single decent night of sleep in months, but then that first night after the guys moved in, it was like a miracle. He slept the whole night.

At first I hoped the pot was a one-time thing, but it's obviously their favorite hobby. I have started to see a correlation between it and how well he sleeps. If more than a few days goes by, he starts getting jumpy and having nightmares again. After a visit to Jim and Enrique, he gets another couple of nights of good sleep. There is something about that stinky weed which is helping him.

And of course he is spending a lot of time over there rather than here at home with me. Sometimes I think he likes their company better than mine. I'm glad he has friends that he's enjoying, and I am profoundly relieved that the sleep thing is improving. But I miss him, and have these little twinges of resentment when he's over there late into the night after I've put Timothy to bed. The situation is so fraught.

I hate it and I love it.

And I can't say anything to Brenda about it. This is happening in her house. The house she is renting to these guys. They are breaking the rules, she could probably evict them for it, and the HOA might come down on her if they find out what is going on in her rental.

But if I tell her, I'm narcing on my own husband. And furthermore it might end up taking away something he has come to rely on for his peace of mind. And his health. I think he's gained back some of that weight he had lost. He is starting to lose that starved, haggard appearance he had. He's filling out again, in all the right places. Starting to look more like the gorgeous hunk I married.

I'm wracked with guilt.

Brenda is my best friend and I'm hiding something important from her, in order to enable my husband to continue neglecting me and coming home all smelly. But it's for his benefit.

It's a very tangled situation.

So, I'll stay quiet about it, and hope for the best.

Timothy

When the teacher tells us it's time to get our lunches and go outside, I ask Natalie to bring her notebook with her. She looks at me curiously. We don't normally bring notebooks to lunch, but I want to set her up for the new experiment.

"Okay," she says, and pops back over to her desk to grab it, along with a pencil.

Gabe and Jonathan are already eating at our table. The four of us always sit in the same spot.

Natalie says, "So, what do you want my notebook for?"

"Well, this is our chance to expand our guardian communication experiment. You guys are going to fly to New Mexico. I checked on the map, and Albuquerque is about 600 miles away from San Diego. That's way farther than we've checked before, to see if guardians can still hear each other. So I want to track it."

"Oh!" she says, "what a great idea!" She hands me her notebook, and I flip to the back page, and write down some instructions for her.

"You'll need to keep detailed notes. I'll try too, but since my communication with Guardian isn't as reliable, I want to make sure you record everything Angel is telling you about whether he can still hear our guardians."

Jonathan snorts, and I look over at him. "Oh, sorry. I mean my guardian."

We've told Jonathan the whole thing, about how our guardians learned how to use energy to talk to each other, and then how Demon started doing it to control him. I hadn't considered whether discussing this experiment in front of Jonathan might make him feel left out, since he doesn't have a guardian any more.

"Whatever," he says. "I suppose it'll be interesting to find out."

"Do you know what time your flight leaves?" I ask.

Gabe says, "I think at 5:30."

"Okay. As soon as you are in the air, start having Angel track his ability to hear Guardian. I'll start trying to listen to Guardian at 5:30, and hopefully I'll be able to tell how the experiment is going. If not, I guess I'll have to wait for you to get back. So take a lot of notes."

Gabe leans over the table to watch what I'm writing.

I check what I've written in Natalie's notebook to see if I forgot anything. I've made a chart for her to fill in, with distances and the names of the Guardians. I want Angel to tell her if Guardian is still hearing all four of them. She'll have to write in the times. I guess she won't really know the distances, but she'll at least be able to fill in the last one, when they arrive.

I hand her back the notebook. "Angel will help you with everything. He might even be able to track the distances. Do you have a watch you can wear to know the times?"

"Um, no. My Dad does but I'd hate to keep bothering him for the time."

I think for a second, and take off my watch. "Okay, here, wear this. I won't need it over spring break, we're not planning to go anywhere so I think I'll be staying at home. I don't really need a watch for that."

Natalie's mouth falls open. "Are you sure? You love this watch!"

"Yes. Try to take care of it, and use it to track the experiment times."

"Thank you, Timothy. I'll do my best!"

Chapter 26

Flight

Jonathan

After the bell rings we all walk up to the front of the school together. We go over to the car where Natalie and Gabe's parents are waiting.

Natalie gives me a hug. Ah. Every time, still, I get a little wave of warmth when she touches me. She doesn't do it all that much any more, since she says my soul seems fine now. But it still feels nice. "Have a good break, Jonathan," she tells me.

I sigh. "I'll try. Have a fun trip."

Gabe punches me in the arm and laughs. I grin at him and watch as he climbs in the car. At least that hasn't changed.

Natalie touches Timothy's shoulder, and tells him. "I've got my notebook. I'm all ready!"

He nods. "Goodbye," he tells her.

She gets in the car behind Gabe. They all start laughing about something, and then they all wave at us as the car pulls away.

Timothy and I look at each other and shrug.

Okay then.

Brenda

As Natalie gets in, I glance back and see something on her wrist. "Are you wearing a watch?" I ask her, surprised.

"Yeah, Timothy is loaning it to me so I can keep track of the time on our flight."

Ron glances into the back to see it, then he meets my eyes and chuckles softly as he starts the car. It looks pretty goofy, that huge black digital watch on her delicate little wrist.

I straighten my face and say, "That's nice, honey."

Before Ron starts to pull away, he performs the trip ritual. We're back to doing this silly thing whenever we go any distance, quoting from the Blues Brothers. We watched that movie together with the kids on New Year's Eve.

"It's six hundred miles to Albuquerque, we've got a full tank of gas and our airplane tickets, no cigarettes, and I'm wearing sunglasses," he says, looking into the rearview mirror with a grin.

"Hit it!" we all shout, and drive away from the school laughing.

Natalie's

The family eagerly anticipates an enjoyable trip. Natalie's only twinge of regret is that she is leaving Jonathan behind, and will be apart from him for the first time in months, unable to maintain any contact for a week. His rehabilitation, conducted through her deliberate efforts, is essentially complete. His soul appears normal. It is nowhere near as vibrant as it had been while Demon was still here, but Natalie has managed to infuse it with all the energy it needs to be equivalent to the souls of other humans.

Demon has still not returned. Only one time was I sure he was nearby, months ago when Natalie was beginning her efforts to aid Jonathan in recovering. That time there was a brief flash of awareness, the barest glimmer of the presence of Jonathan's Guardian. Then he quickly vanished again, and has shown no signs of reappearing.

I begin to believe that Jonathan might be right, and Demon will simply stay away. The child's soul is functional, his level of activity restored, his mind clear and his friendships strong. He is functioning quite well without a Guardian. It is remarkable to behold. As far as I know he is the first human in tens of thousands of years to walk the Earth unaccompanied by a Guardian. Perhaps this is a new development in human evolution.

The main drawback of Demon's absence at this point is that I am unable to provide information to Natalie about Jonathan's status when we are not in proximity to him. The old limit of distance applies, as he has no Guardian with whom I can use our new technique to converse. Although, at any rate, I had never attempted this with Demon.

She is confident that Jonathan is doing well enough to go through this week without her supervision, although she does wish she was able to track him.

In the meantime, she is focused on the newest iteration of Timothy's experiment. This will be interesting, and we Guardians all look forward to learning whether our communication technique will be sufficient over a distance of several hundred miles.

She is pleased to be wearing Timothy's watch, and keeps checking the time by looking down at her wrist. Her parents are correct, of course, the watch is ludicrously large for a child, and even looks too big when Timothy wears it. On Natalie's slender wrist it is overwhelming. She does not notice, and is very happy to have this reminder of her best friend with her on the journey.

Of course, I could tell her the time, and she knows this, but his offer of the watch was very touching and she would not dream of rejecting it.

The airport process unfolds smoothly. Ron parks the car in the long-term parking lot, and the family makes their way into the terminal. They go through the security line, the parents realizing that since the September 11 incidents last year the process has become substantially more cumbersome. They eat a light meal while waiting for their flight, and are able to board the aircraft without difficulty.

Once they are settled into their seats, Ron looks at Brenda with a smile. "So far so good!" he says. The children are seated in the row in front of them.

Natalie immediately extracts her notebook from her carry-on bag. She has brought the notebook, her bible, and her old little Beanie Baby angel, which she has endearingly been thinking of frequently since I reminded her to transport it to her new residence.

Gabe immerses himself in a new game which his father provided for the Gameboy device.

"Okay," Natalie thinks to me. "You talking to Guardian?"

"Of course, darling, we are all quite eager to participate in the newest experiment."

She eagerly awaits the moment that the plane lifts off into the sky. When it does, I begin a narration, intending to continue updating her throughout the journey. The other Guardians, Aaron and Lady and Knight, join me in maintaining communication with Guardian.

"We are climbing in altitude, my dear, and so far this has not diminished our contact with Guardian. We are already further away in distance than during the experiment with your parents' desert camping trip, and we continue to hear Guardian with perfect clarity."

She smiles and notates this, her tongue poking out between her lips in concentration. "How is Timothy doing?" she asks. "Is he able to hear Guardian well enough to know what is going on?"

"As is typical during waking hours, he can detect Guardian's presence nearby, and senses that Guardian's thoughts are positive. He can surmise from this that the experiment is going well so far. He plans to attempt a more tangible level of communication with Guardian tonight while he is falling asleep."

She sighs and nods.

Timothy's progress with Guardian is astounding, but it seems to have plateaued. It is likely that this is the level at which their discourse will continue. Timothy's awareness of Guardian is generally steady, as he has become so accomplished with the ability to keep his mind open throughout the day that it is second nature to him now. When he does so, the feelings of Guardian come through, if not any exact words. If Guardian needs to transmit a more tangible message, he increases the level of energy which he uses, and Timothy is more likely to understand. However, in order to truly hear Guardian, Timothy must be completely relaxed and nearing sleep. It is only as his consciousness has almost faded away, that a true dialogue can take place. It is always very brief, only a few words, perhaps a sentence or two can be exchanged. This is necessarily the case, because it appears to be impossible to maintain this state deliberately. Either the effort wakes him up, or he drifts all the way into sleep. He treasures the moments where a bit of conversation with his Guardian is possible, if only for a few seconds.

Natalie is staring fixedly at Timothy's watch, and after ten minutes have passed she asks me for an update.

"We continue to maintain contact, which is undiminished despite the distance."

"All of you?"

"Yes, myself, Knight, Lady and Aaron can all hear Guardian clearly."

She checks off boxes in the chart prepared by Timothy. Gabe looks up from his Gameboy and observes. "How's the experiment?" he asks.

"Good," she says softly. She does not wish other passengers, including her parents, to overhear. "They can all hear Guardian just fine. Angel says going up high in the air isn't changing anything, and neither is the distance we are away already."

"Cool," he responds, and is about to resume his game when the fasten seatbelts sign goes off with a chime. He unbuckles, kneels up backwards on his seat, and faces his parents. "Do you guys have any snacks?"

His father laughs, and pulls out a bag of cookies from his backpack. "How about this?"

"Woot!" Gabe grabs the bag. "Thanks!"

The children settle down and share their cookies as they each pursue their pastimes.

Natalie

The experiment worked out great! Angel said they never stopped hearing Guardian, no matter how high or far away we got. So I think they will always be able to hear each other no matter what. Maybe someday one of us will go to Japan or Africa or someplace super far away to check, but I'm pretty sure it won't matter. It's nice to know that our guardians can always hear each other no matter where we are.

"How much do you think Timothy knows about how it turned out?" I ask Angel after the plane lands, and is driving up to the airport.

"He is aware that Guardian is pleased with the result, and he interprets this as success. Tonight as he is falling asleep he will attempt more specific confirmation."

Good. I'm glad he'll know, and not wonder all week how it went.

"When do you think they'll be able to talk to each other all the time?"

"My dear, I suspect that their ability to communicate will remain at the current level. Timothy has achieved far more than any other human, but even he cannot overcome the difficulty posed by needing to access his subconscious mind in order to truly hear Guardian's words. He has discovered how to do this while nearly asleep, but it is unlikely to be possible during most other times."

"He has heard Guardian while he's awake, though."

"Yes, a few times, but usually only when Guardian is exerting a great deal of energy, and there is high emotion involved. Under ordinary circumstances, any specific message is unlikely to be received.

"What about when we were doing our words at 8 o'clock?"

"When you were writing down a word each evening so Guardian could attempt to transmit it, Timothy was able to receive it by attempting to approach the sleeping state. It being close to his bedtime, he was more likely to achieve success than if he attempted this during the day."

"Well, I think he'll figure it out."

"He certainly intends to try, and regularly experiments with ways to make his mind receptive. I am sure that if there is any way to make regular communication with Guardian possible, Timothy is the one human who will find it. I suggest patience, though. Please remember that this has only been going on for a few months, and Timothy is still quite young. With more education, he might obtain insights on how to proceed further with the effort."

"Okay."

The airplane has stopped and parked at the gate, and everybody is standing up, getting their carry-on bags, and waiting for their turn to get off the plane. Gabe and I are standing next to our seats.

Finally it's our turn, and Mom and Dad come into the aisle behind us. When we finally get out, Mom goes to the counter to rent a car and Dad goes to the baggage claim to get our suitcases. We go with Dad to help him find them going around on the luggage carousel. Gabe says, "Think I could take a ride on this thing?"

"Definitely not," Dad says, grabbing the hood of his sweatshirt just in case. It makes me giggle.

Chapter 27

Think Of Me

Margaret

"Oooh! Ooh! Frank! Here they are!" I jump up from the seat by the window where I've been watching and waiting for Brenda to drive up. We offered to go down and pick them up at the airport, but Brenda said since there are four of them we wouldn't all fit in one car. And besides they're planning to do some sightseeing after the wedding so Ron wanted to rent a car. So we've had to wait for them to arrive home.

I rush out into the driveway as they are pulling in, Frank sauntering along behind me with much more dignity. I am tickled about this whole visit, and so excited to spend some time with Brenda and the kids.

And with Ron, I suppose. I haven't seen him in quite some time, probably the last time when we visited Brenda in San Diego a couple of years ago and he was picking the kids up for visitation. I am happy for Brenda, since she sounds so excited about this whole thing, but I can't stop feeling a little leery of Ron. He broke her heart once. What's to stop him from doing it again?

The kids come running over to give us hugs. "Holy smokes, Gabe, you are growing like a weed! I think you're taller than me now!" He grins and stands on his tiptoes while he is hugging me, to emphasize how tall he's gotten. I scooch a little lower so that I have to look up at him, and we both laugh.

Natalie is waiting with a smile, and I grab her for a hug next. She isn't growing much, still just a tiny little tyke. I know not to be fooled by her size though, this kid has deeper thoughts than most adults I know. "Oh, Natalie," I say, while I'm giving her a squeeze, "I'm so glad to see you! I hope you're enjoying the bible I sent?"

She smiles. "I am! I have it right here," patting her backpack. "I've read most of it, and I really am enjoying the stories. Although some of them are way stranger than you would know from hearing the usual stories about Christmas and stuff."

I laugh. "No kidding! Well, I'm looking forward to chatting with you about all that. We should have plenty of time to talk after the wedding."

She nods happily. The kids head into the house, and after giving Brenda a kiss on the cheek, and nodding at Ron, I follow them in. I'll leave Frank to help sort out the luggage.

Ron

I have to admit I'm a bit nervous greeting Brenda's folks. I am pretty sure I've been persona non grata around here for years, and here I am cavalierly showing up to marry their daughter. Again. I suspect I'll have to find a way to prove myself.

Margaret gives me a terse nod then follows the kids into the house. Frank comes over to the car where I am unloading the kids' suitcases from the trunk.

"Ron," he says, nodding at me.

"Frank," I respond.

Hoo boy. Yeah, I have some work to do.

He helps with the bigger luggage while Brenda gets the lighter bags.

Natalie

After we put our stuff down in our room, where we will each have a twin bed to sleep on all week, I ask Gabe to come with me. "I have to show you something," I say.

"Um, okay," he says, and comes with me out into the hallway.

Mom and Dad are in the living room talking with Grandma and Grandpa. I take him down the hall towards the kitchen, and stop in front of a painting. "Check this out," I tell him.

It's the guardian angel painting. Two tiny kids are walking over a river on a shifty looking bridge, while a beautiful angel stretches her arms out over them. This is one of my earliest memories.

"Huh, look at that!" Gabe leans in closer to inspect it more carefully. "It's a guardian angel!"

"Yes," I tell him. "I remember being here when I was super young, and seeing this painting, and thinking it was Angel. That was back when I used to carry my beanie baby around all the time. I remember Grandma coming and talking to me about the painting. It was the first time I realized that other people couldn't see my Angel."

He looks away from the painting, down at me. A sort of sad expression crosses his face. "Is this hard for you? Sometimes? Knowing you are different?"

That's an unusually deep question for my brother. I smile and look down, but then I try to give it the consideration it deserves. If he is going to think a deep thought, I need to be serious about it. "Well, maybe, but probably not the way you would think. The hardest part for me isn't really that I'm different from other people. It's that I'm sorry for them. I wish they could see their guardians too. It's the most important part of me. It's really wonderful, and I wish so much everybody could share it."

Brenda

Oh my gosh, my Mom is so funny. She is insisting we comply with the tradition that has Ron not seeing me from the night before the wedding until we are actually at the church. She told me that we need all the luck we can get to make this marriage stick the second time around. So, Ron is going to the hotel a night early, and will stay in our room by himself Saturday. We were already planning to leave the kids with my folks after the wedding, so we can have a couple of days to ourselves. But then we'll want to grab the kids during the days for the rest of the week to take them around and show them the sights. My Mom insists she is pleased as punch to have them sleep here all week.

So after staying here at my parents' house for one night, Ron is already packing back up to go.

"I'll take the car with me, but let me know if you need it for some reason," he says.

"Nah, I'll be fine. I can borrow one of my parents' cars if I need to, and we're all going to the church tomorrow." I'm in my old bedroom, where we squeezed into the double bed together to sleep last night. The kids are in the other room. Ron is putting his toiletries back into his case while I watch.

"I'm going to miss you tonight," he tells me.

"Me too."

I think I have to bring up a possibly sore subject before I let him go. "Did you ever manage to get hold of your Dad?"

He sighs. "No. There still isn't any answer, and as far as I can tell he doesn't have an answering machine. We did send him the invite, but I don't know if he'd want to come anyway."

Ron hasn't had a good relationship with his Dad, ever since his Mom died many years ago. He has a little brother who he keeps in touch with sporadically. But Ken moved away from Albuquerque a long time ago, and had to send his regrets since he and his wife are busy with their twins. As far as we know his Dad still lives in Albuquerque, but there's been no contact for years.

I don't want to nag him, but I feel like he shouldn't give up. "Do you want to try to find him today? I don't want to pressure you, honey, but I'm worried you'll regret it if you don't at least drive over there and see if he's home."

He sits on the side of the bed and leans his elbows on his knees, running his hands over his clipped hair while he stares at the carpet. I give him a minute to think. He looks up at me, his blue eyes resolved. "You're right. I don't want to live with regrets. I've done enough of that." He leans over and kisses me. "Thank you. I think I needed your little push. I'm going to drive over and knock on the door. Honestly, I don't know if he even lives there any more, but all I can do is try."

I put my arms around him. "I'm glad you're going to make the effort. At least you'll know you did what you could." I'm leaning against him, as we both sit side by side on the bed. I nuzzle against his neck, and kiss along his jawline. "I'm really going to miss you tonight."

He laughs, then leans down to kiss me properly. "We're old enough that we can control ourselves for one night. Not like we're in college any more."

We let go of each other reluctantly, then he stands and gets his bags. "Text me about what happens with your Dad."

"I will. Think of me tonight."

I chuckle. "Believe me, I'll dream of you all night long."

Chapter 28

Dilapidated

Ron

I park across the street from the scruffy little house, barely more than a shack, on the outskirts of Albuquerque. The yard is overgrown, but not so much so that the place actually appears abandoned.

I sit in my car, gazing at the front door, paralyzed by indecision. Do I really want to do this? The last time I talked to my Dad face to face, it did not go well. It was before we even moved from Albuquerque, so like eight or nine years ago. He was so mad at me for deciding to leave. He accused me of abandoning him, and not being helpful enough with my brother Ken.

Looking back on it, I understand it better. I think I have a broader perspective. Now that I'm a little older, and have gone through struggles of my own.

He was still grieving my Mom, who had died of cancer two or three years before. I don't think he could dig himself out of the hole of despair he had been down since she died. He couldn't think of anything but his grief, his struggle. He thought I was being entirely selfish in pursuing a job opportunity in San Diego. He said things to me that were utterly hateful.

I was very hurt. I made very little effort to stay in contact with him after that. Brenda had him on her annual Christmas letter list while we were still married, but presumably she stopped sending it to him after we got divorced. I honestly don't know if he was even aware when Natalie was born.

The house looks sort of sad and lonely, sitting there on this isolated corner. It clearly hasn't been painted in a long time. The roof could use some help. One of the window screens is broken and half hanging out of the window.

It seems like a reflection of my father, and of my relationship with him. I suddenly realize I can't just drive away. Brenda is right. I need to know that I have done everything I can. I fixed my relationship with her after it was thoroughly broken. Maybe there is hope for this one too.

I take a deep breath, and get out of the car. The wind bites at my face as I cross the street. I stand in front of the door for a moment before knocking.

There is no answer. I try knocking again. No answer.

The wind bumps against the broken window screen and bangs it against the wall.

I try one more time. If there's no answer I will leave.

I hear someone moving inside. There's the sound of door latches being lifted, then the door is opened scarcely an inch or two. I see him standing inside, but can't be sure it is really him, with the door barely opened.

"Hello?" I say.

"Who are you? What do you want?" It's him. I recognize his voice, but it has changed. It is higher, wispier.

"Hi Dad. It's me. Ron."

The door opens further. He stares at me, shocked. He hasn't shaved in a while. He seems shorter. Thinner. And older. Much older. Nearly a decade has passed, but he wears it like two.

"Ron." He looks like he can't believe what he is seeing.

"Yeah. I'm here in town with my family. I wanted to come and see how you are."

He lapses into silence, and we stand awkwardly for another minute, he behind the door and me out in the wind on his porch. Finally, he moves back from the door and says, "Well, come on in."

Wow. This is really happening. I enter, and am dismayed by the condition of the house. It smells terribly musty. There is so much clutter everywhere, we can barely move. He shuffles along in front of me, towards the kitchen. He shifts a pile of newspapers off of a chair in front of the table, and gestures for me to sit down. Then he kicks aside a pile of some kind of cloth, clothing maybe, to get to the one chair which isn't covered in junk. After he sits down, he pushes aside the stacks of detritus on the table so we can see each other.

"Ron," he says again.

"Yeah, it's really me."

"I didn't expect to see you," he says.

I nod. I don't know what to say. Getting here and seeing him seemed like the biggest hurdle. Now I have to converse with him? How on earth am I supposed to do that?

"You still living in San Diego?"

"Yes, with Brenda and our kids."

"Kids? Didn't you just have one kid?"

"Yeah, but we have two now. Gabe is ten, and Natalie is seven."

He tilts his head like that doesn't make any sense, but he doesn't comment again on the kids. "What are you in town for?"

I am noticing more details. He is fussing with some of the papers on the table, and I see that he clearly has developed a significant tremor. He can barely clutch the magazine he is moving to the side of the stack on the table, his hand is trembling so hard.

I feel awkward as I explain to him what we are doing. I try to keep it as brief as possible. "Well, Brenda and I separated for a while, but we reconciled and are getting remarried. The wedding is here in town. Tomorrow."

His eyebrows furrow. "Oh, I think I remember something about that?" He shifts more papers on the piles in front of him.

"Yeah, we sent you an invitation a couple of months ago. We didn't hear back."

He shakes his head. "I don't know where I put it. Probably here on the table." He seems anxious, standing back up to access papers across the table.

"Dad, you don't need to find it. If you want to come to the ceremony, I can tell you the details." I am realizing he is even more of a wreck than the house. The entire dilapidated scene is depressing. How did it get this bad? Does Ken know about this?

"What? Oh, no, I couldn't go. I don't get out much."

I try not to admit to myself that I'm relieved. I couldn't imagine him showing up in Margaret's church in this condition. But now that I'm here, I need to try to figure out what is going on. I think if I had stayed in contact with him, I might have been able to help prevent him from deteriorating so badly.

Great. Another thing for me to feel guilty about. This one might not be quite so directly my fault, but clearly I must share some responsibility for this situation.

"So, Dad, tell me how you've been. What's been going on?"

Chapter 29

Pardon Me?

Brenda

Mom and I are in the kitchen fixing dinner, when my phone beeps. I glance at it. It's a text from Ron. He spent the afternoon with his Dad! I text him back and ask if he's coming tomorrow. No, he responds, he's not well and can't make it. He'll tell me all the details when he gets the chance. Then he ends with, "Sleep well," and a row of heart emojis.

That's interesting. I'm glad he got the chance to talk to his Dad, but I wonder what's wrong. He's unwell? I hope it's not too serious. I know we haven't seen Theo in forever, but I'm still fond of him. I used to get along pretty well with him. He had a wicked sense of humor, and used to enjoy trying to shock me. Some of his old stories were hilarious.

"Who was that?" Mom asks.

"Ron. He went over and talked to his Dad. It's the first time they've talked in years."

"Well, praise Jesus!" she says. "How wonderful. Will he be coming to the wedding tomorrow?"

"Apparently he isn't well, and can't make it. I don't have any other details. I'll let you know in a couple of days what Ron says."

She carries a bowl full of salad over to the table. I follow with the fried chicken.

"Come and get it!" she calls, to Dad and the kids out in the living room.

Gabe comes bounding around the corner and sees the fried chicken. "Oh, yum!"

Natalie giggles and sits in the chair beside him. She always seems to find his eternal appetite amusing. "Thank you for dinner, Grandma." Mom smiles at her as she sits down.

"So," my Mom says, scooping food onto the kids' plates, "how is school going for you two?"

"Good," Gabe says, barely waiting for her hand to leave his plate before he is gulping down his dinner. I have to agree with Natalie sometimes, it is pretty amazing how much Gabe can eat. He's tall and skinny and growing, and seems to have a bottomless appetite.

"How about you, Natalie?" Mom follows up. "Is school keeping you interested?" Mom knows how smart Natalie is, and I've discussed with her my concerns that maybe her classwork isn't advanced enough for her. She never complains about it, though.

"Yes, it's interesting. If I finish what I'm doing early, there are plenty of books in the classroom to read."

"You sure do like reading, don't you? You said you've already read the bible? Just a little bit of it? Or most of it?"

"Yes, most of it," Natalie says matter-of-factly, apparently having no idea how unusual it is for a second-grader to have accomplished that. "I read the children's bible you gave me the year before, but I was glad to get the real bible this year. I wanted to know more about the stories. Thank you again for giving it to me."

"You are more than welcome, sweetheart. I am delighted you're reading it."

Warming to the topic, Natalie continues. "I like the language in your bible better than the King James one at my daycare. It's easier to understand. But sometimes the meaning of the stories comes out different in the modern language one."

My Mom's eyes widen in surprise. She looks over at me, and I nod and shrug. Yeah, I know.

"Well my goodness, darling, aren't you the little biblical scholar! Can you tell me which one is your favorite story?"

"Christmas," she immediately responds. "I love the Christmas story so much."

"I'm so pleased to hear that. Me too! Knowing how the birth of our savior came about is so special."

Animatedly, Natalie continues. "It's so interesting how other mythology got mixed in with the story. The virgin birth, and the star, and so many of the stories that people were already telling before then. Even the date, December 25, is just made up since people already celebrated other stuff on that day." She happily takes another bite of her fried chicken.

Um.

My Mom puts down her fork. "Pardon me?"

Natalie has no idea she is treading on dangerous ground here. My Mom can be pretty stubborn in defending her religion.

Natalie looks over to the side, and I think she suddenly realizes that Mom is offended. She stares back over to her grandmother with wide eyes.

"Young lady," my Mom says firmly. "It is not for you to question the words of the bible. You must simply accept its lessons gratefully as the gift from God that they are."

"Oh. Okay. Sorry Grandma," she says, clearly not wanting to argue with her grandmother.

My Dad has been observing this exchange with a wary amusement. He goes along to church with my Mom for her benefit and for the socializing, but I know he does not share her fervent belief. When it seems the religious dialogue is concluded for the evening, he pushes back his chair. "Well," he says, "I think I'll pop over to the hotel and see how Ron is doing. He shouldn't be alone on the night before his wedding. Maybe we'll have a little bachelor party."

"Oh, pshaw," my Mom says, waving her hand and laughing. "Bachelor party, you two old guys?" She stands up and starts clearing his plate. "Although, It's nice of you to think of him. Yes, why don't you go on over and keep him company for a while."

I stand up and give my Dad a kiss on the cheek. "That's really nice, Dad. I'll text him and let him know you're on the way. Give Ron my love."

Chapter 30

Bachelor Party

Ron

I'm surprised to get Brenda's text that her Dad is coming here to keep me company. That's - unexpected. I don't know whether he's just being thoughtful or if he's coming to confront me to make sure my intentions are honorable. Probably the latter. I sure wouldn't blame him for doing that.

Well, here's my chance to try to make amends. I hurt his little girl. Judging from my own experience with seeing Natalie get hurt a couple of times, I know there isn't anything I could have done much worse than that.

I'm waiting for him downstairs in the lobby when he arrives. I call out his name and wave him over.

"Hey, Frank. It's very nice of you to come over. Thank you."

He nods. "Sure thing. I thought we could have a bit of a bachelor party. Figured you shouldn't be alone the night before your wedding." He glances around the lobby. "How about we head over to the bar and get a little drink?"

"Sure, thanks," I say, somewhat warily. I need to wait to see how this unfolds, but I'm ready to be completely open with him about everything that happened, if he asks me about it.

He leads me over to a couple of chairs around a low table. "Have a seat," he says. "What shall I get for you?"

"Um, a beer would be great."

He nods and steps over to the bar. "Two beers, please."

The bartender pours them from the tap and hands them to Frank. He brings them over and sets them down on the table.

I take a sip. "Thanks."

He nods. "So, have any wedding jitters?"

"Not at all. I've never been more sure about anything in my life," I assure him.

He thoughtfully sips his beer, then sets down his glass and wipes his lips with the back of his hand. "Brenda seems pretty sure, too."

"I think she is. I'm so grateful."

"I've got to say, Margaret and I were very surprised when she told us you two were getting remarried. After so long."

He looks over at me. This is my opening. "I can believe that." I take another swallow of beer, to brace myself. "Frank, I think I owe you an explanation. And an apology."

"All right," he says guardedly, leaning back in his chair.

"Everything that happened was entirely my fault. I am completely to blame for our first marriage breaking up. Brenda had nothing to do with it."

He nods slowly.

"I'm sure you know that I had an affair."

"Uh-huh."

"I was weak, and selfish, and made the worst mistake of my life. I will always regret it. I have never forgiven myself for it. Somehow, miraculously, Brenda has."

His eyebrows lift. "Well, it's good to hear you accept responsibility."

"I do. All of it. I created a gigantic mess with my stupidity, and it has taken this long to try to clean it up. I am infinitely grateful to Brenda for taking me back."

I drain my beer, and Frank gestures to the bartender with two fingers up, to order us a second round.

He waits to see what else I have to say. "I have apologized to her. Profusely. I was willing to grovel, to beg, to do anything it took. But she was so gracious." The second glasses arrive, and the bartender takes away the empties. My mouth has gone dry, so I gulp down some more.

"I want to apologize to you, too. I know how hurt she was, and how much pain that must have caused you. I understand now, I think, as the father of a girl, how protective it makes you feel. I'm sorry for hurting your daughter."

He nods again. "Well, I'll accept your apology for the past, since Brenda has. I can't say I'm not worried for the future, though."

I deserve that. "I understand. All I can do is tell you that I never stopped loving her. Even during the affair, all I wanted was to turn back time and be with your daughter again. The affair didn't last long, and after that I spent years longing for Brenda, and not feeling worthy to even try. But eventually, we found our way back to each other." I feel embarrassing tears coming into my eyes, and quickly wipe them away.

He can hear the emotion in my voice, I know it.

"So, I will never make that mistake again. I am committed to spending every minute of the rest of my life making it up to Brenda, and appreciating her, and making her happy. And loving her. With every bit of my being."

He takes a long drink. He sets down his glass, and extends his hand. "Let's shake on it, then."

I shake his hand, moved more deeply than I had expected.

He picks his beer back up and lifts his glass. "To marriage."

I clink his glass. "To marriage. And to Brenda."

Frank

I didn't really know what to expect coming over here, but I'm glad I did. I've spent the last seven years fuming at Ron, indignant on my daughter's behalf about everything he did.

Tonight he could have tried to shift blame, or justify himself. But he didn't. He simply owned it all, and promised to do better. I'm impressed with the man. I feel better, reassured that Brenda isn't making another mistake.

I think we've both had enough of the heavy talk. He asks, "So, how's everything going at the house tonight?"

"Good," I tell him. "The ladies made fried chicken for dinner." I laugh. "Then Margaret and Natalie started talking about the bible, and your little girl started trying to lecture my wife about religion."

He laughs. "Oh man. How'd that go over?"

I grin and shake my head. "About as well as you would expect, when the kid tried to tell her that not everything in the bible is completely true."

He snorts, which makes him choke a little on his beer. I reach over and whack him on the back. When he can talk again, he says, "Yikes! Natalie has spent a ton of time reading up on bible stories lately, and is definitely developing her own opinions about everything. And isn't shy about sharing them."

"That's quite some mind on her," I note. "She's always seemed awfully advanced for her age. I think it's possible, although please don't tell Margaret I said this, that Natalie knows more about the contents of the bible than her grandmother does!"

He nods. "I wouldn't be surprised. She absorbs knowledge like nobody I've ever seen. Except maybe her best friend."

"Oh?" I think I remember seeing her with another little kid last time we visited. "Would that be the same kid we saw her with a couple of years ago?"

"Yeah, his name is Timothy. He's even more excited about reading, and advanced academically, than Natalie is. He's on the autism spectrum, so he's a quirky little guy. He and Natalie have been inseparable since they were only two years old."

"Well, sounds like you'll have your hands full going forward. She's going to be a real pistol as she grows up."

"I know," he says. "It's going to be a journey, I can tell."

"What about Gabe? How's he doing?"

"Good. Growing like a weed, as you can see. He'll be starting middle school next year. He hasn't been involved in youth sports much before." He looks sideways at me, ruefully. "That might be another thing I need to take blame for. With us living apart, and me having visitation on weekends, it was too hard to figure out how to schedule it in."

I nod.

"But, I'm thinking he's going to want to play soccer or baseball in the next school year. He enjoys pick-up games with kids in the neighborhood when he gets the chance."

"That's good to hear. Sports can be so good for a boy."

"I agree," he says. There's a minute of silence, then he adds, "I'm really glad you came over, Frank. Thank you again."

"Some bachelor party, eh?" I chuckle.

He grins. "The best I've ever had, that's for sure!"

Chapter 31

Mad

Timothy

Guardian was able to tell me last night before I went to sleep that the experiment worked fine, and he is hearing Angel and the other guardians all the way from New Mexico. I'm glad to know it. Who knows where everyone will be when we all grow up. I'm happy that there will always be a way to keep in touch with Natalie.

I miss her. Normally on Saturdays I go over and play at her house, but obviously I didn't do that today. I ended up having to go and sit at the salon with my Mom while she did hair for a couple of hours this morning. Dad had left for work, and Mom didn't believe me when I told her that I'm old enough to stay home by myself. So I brought a couple of books and sat there and read, spinning around on the chair next to hers. Then she gave me quarters to get whatever snacks I wanted from the vending machine nearby. So it wasn't a bad morning. Just a morning without my best friend.

I wonder what she's doing, and if she's having a nice time. "Guardian," I think to him, "please ask Angel to tell Natalie Hi for me. Tell her I've been reading the book about archeology I got at the library last week." I'm laying on my bed with the book open in front of me. There's a picture on this page of an excavation in Israel.

I feel his agreement, like a hug inside my mind. I don't think our communication has changed much in the last couple of months. I can feel him but not really hear him, unless I'm nearly asleep, or unless something special is happening which makes us both try really hard. I'm starting to accept that this is how it is going to be. Angel always said Natalie is the only one who can hear her guardian. I've definitely come a lot further with it than where I was at first, when I first learned about Guardian.

"Timothy," Mom calls from downstairs. "Dinner time."

I head down and sit at the table. Dad is there already, and Mom sits down after she carries a dish over.

"How was your day, Mike?" Mom asks.

"Okay," he says.

"Do you work tomorrow?"

"No, I have off until Tuesday," he says, taking a bite of salad.

"Great, can you stay with Timothy? I have some clients scheduled. I brought him with me today, but I think he'd rather stay home."

I shrug. I don't really care. Either way I'll be reading.

"Yeah, okay," Dad says.

After we're done eating, Dad says, "I'm going next door for a while."

Mom doesn't say anything back to him. While he puts on his shoes and leaves, she carries dishes over to the sink. "Bring me your plate, Timothy," she tells me. I carry it over to her.

I think it's weird to have Dad going over to Natalie's old house all the time. But he's there almost every night. I guess he's really good friends with the guys who live there now.

"Want to watch some t.v. with me tonight?" Mom asks me.

"No thank you," I tell her. "I want to keep reading my book."

She sighs. "Okay, kid. What's the book about?"

"It's the one about archeology. I'm reading about an excavation in Israel. They think they've found a site from the bible."

"That sounds interesting," she says, and leans over to kiss me on top of my head.

I go back upstairs.

Laura

It's still too early to go to bed. The kitchen is clean, Timothy is reading in his room, and Michael is over at Enrique and Jim's house, as usual. Without me. So

I'm slouched on the couch, under a cozy blanket, flipping through the channels trying to find something to watch.

I guess at least I can be pretty sure that we'll get some sleep tonight. He'll come back late, stoned, and go right to sleep. I keep telling myself it's better than constant nightmares.

I wonder how Brenda is doing. I'm so happy for her, that her marriage has been fixed and they're going to have a nice wedding. I can't help but feel sorry for myself, seeing the contrast.

It's a hard time right now. First Michael was too stressed and jumpy to sleep, and now he's spending all of his free time with a couple of stoners. The two of us haven't done anything nice together for months. We haven't gone out anywhere like we were doing before. After he got back from his last deployment I had tried to set up things to do to help him sleep better, outdoorsy stuff like hiking. But all he does now is work, hang out next door, and sleep.

Oh well, at least he isn't waking me up all night long, thrashing and yelling. I suppose I should be grateful for small favors. I have to try not to be mad about it.

Michael's

My beloved has discovered the path to peace of mind. His wife does not like it, and even he has qualms about what he has been doing. He knows there could be trouble with his employer if he continues this practice and is detected.

But, he has no way to stop. For one thing, he actually enjoys the companionship of his new neighbors. They are younger, and seem more carefree than he has been for many years. Their employment with a construction company seems uncomplicated, straightforward. They have no wives, no children. They enjoy dating various women, and enthusiastically encourage each other in this effort.

When my dearest compares his life to theirs, he feels that he has heavier burdens than they do. He does not regret his life, but feels nostalgic for his younger days when his lack of attachments brought with it a sense of freedom which he no longer enjoys.

And, of course, the chemicals in the substances which he imbibes with his new friends have been able to quiet his mind, bring him peace, alleviate the problem he had been having with anxiety. And especially with nightmares. They still occur, but with far less intensity and frequency. The treatment he had unsuccessfully sought from the doctor may or may not have been effective, but his clandestine use of drugs certainly is.

I, obviously, support my beloved in all that he does. I am delighted that he has found a pathway to greater happiness and well-being than he had been experiencing before these young men moved next door. I must encourage him to continue.

"Beloved, enjoy your evening with your friends. You know that you feel better than you had in quite some time. This is the best for you, for your health, and your mind, and your soul. I am with you in love and happiness."

Jonathan

Sigh. Is this only Saturday? This week seems like it is lasting forever already. Dad went to work today, and I'm staying home with Mom. But she's so busy studying that she doesn't have time to play any games or anything with me. So I'm loafing around, trying to find ways not to die of boredom.

I watched t.v. for a while, but honestly that just doesn't seem as exciting as it used to.

I wish I could go into Gabe's house and play with his stuff. He has more cool toys than I do. He has a zillion Legos, and neat video games. My stuff seems boring compared to his. But, he's off on their vacation and I won't see him for a whole week.

I miss Natalie too. I haven't felt that nice warmth I get when she touches me since yesterday when she left after school. When I think about it, this is the longest time I've gone without feeling that for months. She's always hanging around, making sure to hold my hand or touch my shoulder or lean against me, because Angel has told her it helps me.

I know it does. And I miss it. I didn't realize it until now, but I think I need it. I'm not feeling right without her warmth. I don't think it's only because I'm bored without my friends and their cool toys. I think it's because she's left me here, without her, and I'll have to suffer through this whole week without getting what I need.

How could she do that? Why would she leave me? She didn't have to go. She could have talked her family out of it. She doesn't care about me as much as I thought she did. If she cared, she wouldn't have left me.

This is all her fault. Everything. The way I was feeling before she started hanging around me, and even more now. I feel bad because of her.

I go out in the backyard. Mom barely looks up from her book as I walk past her. She doesn't care either.

Nobody does. Everyone is so awful to me. It makes me so mad.

I hate them. I hate them all. I especially hate Natalie, for doing this to me.

I kick a soccer ball across the yard. Socks goes bounding across the yard to get it for me. It's too big for him to fit his mouth around, though, so he comes running back and stands in front of me, with his mouth open and his tongue hanging out and his tail wagging.

Dumb dog. What do you want from me? "Go away," I tell him, pointing across the yard. He looks at where I'm pointing, then back at me, confused. He doesn't know what to do.

Sheesh. I cross the yard and go back over to where the ball is, and kick it back towards him. He tries to jump up and get it, but it's too big for him and it whacks him in the face. He leaps back and whines.

Oh my God. What am I doing? Why am I all of the sudden so furious? My poor dog didn't do anything wrong, he's trying to be friendly. I run over to him and drop down on the ground and pick him up, hugging him to me. I feel better, holding him.

I'm confused about what just happened. It's like a huge rush of anger washed over me, out of nowhere.

Suddenly, I realize what it is. I feel faint and dizzy with fear. I know what this must be. I remember the questions Natalie asks me every week. She wants to know if I have any unexplained emotions. And I just did.

There's only one explanation.

Demon must be back.

Chapter 32

I Am Jonathan's

Jonathan's

I Am...

Jonathan's.

I am Jonathan's. I am here, with him, with his soul.

Time has passed, but I had no clear sense of it while it was passing. It is almost as though I have been asleep, which is a ludicrous concept for a Guardian. We don't sleep, obviously. We are non-corporeal beings, and sleep is a biological process. No, the state I was in entailed more self-awareness than that known by a slumbering human.

Even when we are not Guarding, we have some constant sense of self, although severely diminished, as we are merged into one consciousness while waiting with the others. But this was not even akin to the period between lives. It was a sort of purgatory. Not quite oblivion, as I continued to maintain some level of awareness, at least intermittently. But my solitude was utter, seeming as though I was somehow located outside of the universe. There was no reference point, nothing familiar, nothing definable. It was impossible to comprehend my circumstances. I have not known how to return to my dearest soul, have not been able to locate even myself within the vast emptiness in which I appeared to be lost.

My last clear memory, which sustained me as I endured the bewildering nothingness of the last few months, was the final glorious moment I shared with my beloved, while he rejected the cruel attempt of the Seer to frighten him with spurious tales of my existence. We would not allow that. We could not have her succeed in sundering our beautiful unity. We refused to listen to her diabolical words.

As I flooded Jonathan with my power, he battled against the forces of evil that would have seen us torn apart. We were one. He was fighting for us both, trying to silence the Seer's abominable message. We were both absolutely consumed by this effort.

Until the Seer's Guardian attacked. I was taken utterly unawares by the unprecedented action. A Guardian attempting to oppose another, in such a tangible and violent way? Unheard of. Impossible. Horrific. Terrifying.

I was distracted from my task, and forced to turn my attention away from my beloved, to the group of Guardians who were aggressively directing their power against me. It was shocking. I had never even interacted directly with other Guardians before, although I had observed the Seer's preposterous group of Guardians chatting with each other as though they were mere humans.

I was helpless against their onslaught. The sensation was agonizing, unlike anything I had ever experienced before. I have shared the pain felt by my Guarded over many lifetimes, but of course never had the direct sensation myself. The energy shot at me by the other Guardians infiltrated the matter of which I am comprised, first slamming into me as a physical blast, and then shredding each particle apart from every other. It was the work of only moments, but I perceived it as an eternity of anguish, while I sensed the explosion of dark matter peeling away from my core. It was nothing short of an execution, a murder. I had only the dimmest sense of my beloved's own struggle while I was being assaulted and tortured.

And then there was nothing.

For another eternity, there was nothing.

I was lost in the nothing. I knew nothing, saw nothing, was nothing.

Only one glimmer of hope remained to me, only one thing existed in the universe to anchor me to reality. I knew I was tied to Jonathan's soul. And I could sense, somehow, that Jonathan lived, that his soul remained, that they were waiting for me to return.

I drifted, waiting, helpless, unable to take any action of my own volition. I lacked any cohesion, my matter scattered across the infinite reaches of space. I was literally unable to pull myself together.

After an undefined amount of time, though, there was a flare of warmth, an instant of sudden shining clarity which came upon me without warning. In a moment it was gone. But somehow, that flash of heat had given me a tiny sense of healing. I realized when the moment ended that I had regained the smallest fraction of myself. The matter of which I was made had regained an iota of cohesion, a particle or two growing close once again. I was still helpless, still scattered, but I knew that an infinitesimal amount of progress had been made in restoring my manifestation.

I did not have any idea what had happened, or why it had taken place. I struggled to understand, to find if there was anything that I had done or could do to recreate the moment. But I was unable to fathom any action I could take to trigger the event to recur.

Then, again. It happened. A flash of light, a glow of warmth, a miniscule recovery of my self.

What was happening?

I did not know. But it began occurring, again and again, at random intervals over which I had absolutely no control. I could neither predict the events, nor prolong them. Sometimes it was for the briefest of instants, sometimes the moment lingered on and on. Each time it occurred, my gathering being grew in the smallest of increments.

The events came and went without any regard for my efforts to generate them. There was no pattern I could detect. But I was profoundly grateful for the gift of healing that they brought.

Little by little, I sensed my being becoming increasingly intact. I was still lost within a great void, but I was slowly becoming myself within it.

Then, as one of these events seemed to linger, lasting longer than most, while I felt more of myself being drawn back together, I suddenly had a flash of my beloved. There he was, suddenly looming out of the nothingness, his soul softly glowing rather than robustly burning, and I was pulled towards it, back to my source, rushing across the void faster than the speed of light.

For an instant, I saw him, felt him, was at one with him. I was utterly disoriented and could not understand what was happening, where the void had gone, what I was doing. It took a moment to attempt to reorient myself, to try to re-establish our link.

I reveled in our blessed togetherness, delighting in the renewed connection with my beloved from which I had been bereft for so long. He was suddenly also filled with a sense of my presence.

That is when I saw that he was sitting with the Seer, strangely complacent, permitting her even to touch him. Once I realized what he was doing, I recoiled emotionally from the contact with the creature who had brought us such profound harm. He felt my revulsion and yanked his arm away from hers.

Then, I felt the moment of warmth fading, the event which had brought me back to him ending, and my manifestation dissipating. I struggled to remain with him, but to no avail. I returned to the void.

But now there was a difference. I could still sense my dearest, my Jonathan. I could not reach him again, but the nothingness was broken. His soul, his light, reached out to me across the darkness. I took solace in the fact that I could sense him, even if from afar.

The intermittent moments of warmth and healing continued sporadically, gradually bringing me closer to the time I knew must be coming. The time that I would truly return to my beloved. I watched his soul, still the only thing I could sense in the void, and I drew strength from the knowledge that one day we would be together once again. His soul had lost the brilliance it once had, but was growing increasingly vibrant.

I eventually realized that when I experienced the events which brought me warmth and healing, his soul experienced matching and simultaneous growth. The events that healed me were healing him as well. Our recovery coincided. I could not understand the mechanism by which we were both being healed, but again I was filled with deep gratitude.

Time passed. Our healing progressed. Eventually, my sense of his soul expanded, so slowly at first that it was difficult to detect the change. But I began to realize that I could dimly perceive the activities of Jonathan himself, not merely the status of his soul. I developed the slightest ability to observe him from the vast distance which still separated us.

And I finally realized what was happening. It was the Seer. Intervening again, imposing herself upon my beloved, installing herself as a fixture in his life. He accepted her presence as I had never allowed him to do in the past.

I was aghast when I discovered the shocking truth about what was binding us back together. The source of our recovery, the warmth and light which brought us both healing, was the girl. The very being whose actions had led to this exile. The Seer whose Guardian had committed such an unforgivable offense against me, against us.

My gratitude had been directed to my enemy.

My sense of conflict was enormous. How could I crave the touch of the monstrous entity who had led me to this torment? Yet each time it happened, as Jonathan reveled in the warmth it brought to him, I was similarly flooded with warmth and healing and light. I wished to revile the touch, reject it, refuse it. But I had no control, and no power over the activities of the Seer. I was forced to passively accept the means of my restoration from the abhorrent instrument of my destruction. I loved her and loathed her. I desired her and detested her. The inescapable ecstasy of healing was forced upon me. I was powerless, victimized again and again with the rapturous sensation of warmth and delight. It was a sweet torture, an agonizing bliss. Each episode left me both healed and shattered.

What felt like another eternity passed in this way. However, I had begun to come back to a sense of time once again. My perception of Jonathan's life became clearer, day by day, until I could understand where he was and what he was doing. I could see him, but could not contact him. The gulf between us continued to be insurmountable. I began to feel myself again, yet still could not find my way back to him.

Until today. It has been over a day since the touch of the Seer last brought me the exquisite agony I had grown to abhor even as I yearned for it. I observed my beloved bid her farewell, apparently to embark on a journey with her family. Then I watched my dearest boy wait at his home, pining for the Seer's touch, but having to endure its absence.

I do not know how exactly I was brought back to him. What caused my return? Was it his longing? His loneliness? The length of time since the Seer last touched him? I cannot understand. But, suddenly, I felt the distance between us vanishing, blinking away as though it had never existed. I see him, not from across a vast chasm, but here, before me, together as we were prior to the day the Seer and her Guardian severed our connection. The hateful Seer, the cause of our schism, has been defeated. My banishment is over. Our separation has come to an end.

A powerful sense of belonging floods through me, and brings with it a tremendous relief. I feel truly whole, for the first time since I was dismembered and hurled across space by the attack of the Guardians.

Jonathan's soul reacts to my renewed presence by flaring strongly, for the first time since I began perceiving it once again. The Seer's touch had healed it, and caused it to gently glow, but it is only my presence that can make his soul truly whole. It delights me to see him restored to himself.

But what is this? Jonathan recoils from my presence. He is filled with a terror which I have never before sensed from him. His heart rate accelerates, his eyes widen, he clutches the little pet that he had acquired shortly before I was exiled. He fears the return of "Demon".

Ah yes. I remember now. That is the name the Seer had assigned to me, in her arrogance. I had rejected it out of hand. But my beloved has accepted it. Furthermore, he has clearly been instructed by the Seer regarding my existence. I search his memories, and find the education he has received from her, the knowledge and awareness that he has achieved regarding the reality which is hidden from other humans. She has corrupted his view of me even as she taught him of my presence. I see the unfair bias against me that has infiltrated his thoughts.

If I had a heart, it would be breaking. To have my beloved know of me, even call me by a name, should be an unprecedented delight. Instead, it is a crushing blow to find that the Seer succeeded in her fell mission to warn him against me. I yearn for him to love me, as I love him. Instead he fears me, even hates me.

My sorrow is overwhelming. But I must try to do what I can to repair the situation. I find myself weak, still suffering the effects of my long-lasting injury and convalescence. It is difficult, but I force myself to speak to him. *"My darling,"* I whisper painfully to him, *"we are together again, as we are meant to be. As we must be. I will love you always, help you, support you. Please, dearest, be not afraid. All will be well. We will live our life in the companionship that is fated to be. My beloved."* It is exhausting, after all the time apart, to even whisper these few words of love to my Guarded. I sense that it will take some time, some additional recovery, before I am able to function as normal.

It occurs to me that before my exile, I had been using enormous power to interact with my darling boy, but I make no such attempt now. Simply whispering this brief message depleted my energy, left me without further resources. My return is so new, so sudden, so shocking, that I scarcely know how to resume my position as Jonathan's.

But I at least know that I am here. I am his. I am Jonathan's.

Chapter 33

Open Door

Timothy

The dream fades, and I keep my eyes closed, trying to cling to the sensation of sleep. I've told Guardian not to wait for me to talk to him, to take advantage of the fact that my mind is receptive when he can tell I am first waking up. So I hear him right away. He doesn't waste any words saying good morning, since he knows we only have a few seconds.

"Natalie sends her love. Today she will attend her parents' wedding. All is well with her family, although she fears she annoyed her grandmother by questioning stories within the bible."

What? Really? Well, that's done it, as soon as I hear that message I get too interested and it wakes me all the way up. "Thanks, Guardian," I whisper to him. She annoyed her grandmother? I know that is who has sent her the bibles she's been reading. Natalie has told me that her Grandma likes to take her to church and talk about Jesus and stuff like that. I wonder why it would annoy her for Natalie to talk to her about it?

I sit up, and reach over to my desk to get my notebook. I decided yesterday to keep a list of things I want to talk to Natalie about when she gets back. Every day we usually are able to talk about everything, and I don't want to forget all the topics I have wondered about while she's gone. I write, "Why was Grandma mad about the bible?" Then I go to the bathroom, get dressed, and head downstairs.

Mom is drinking coffee, sitting at the kitchen table. She looks up. "Good morning, sweetie," she tells me. "What do you want for breakfast?"

"Can I have toast?" I ask.

"Mm-hmm," she says, taking another swig of her coffee then getting up. I put my book down on the table and read it while she's moving around the kitchen. When she puts a plate of toast down in front of me, she tilts her head sideways to check the book. "Is that the one about archeology you were reading last night?"

"Yes," I tell her, and push the book around the other way so she can see the picture on the page. "This is an archeological dig site in Israel. They are exploring a city mound with signs of habitation from the bronze age." I am trying to help Natalie with her bible research. She wants to try to figure out what parts of the bible are true. So she's reading the bible, and learning about other religions and mythology from Angel, to compare the different stories people have made up. Meanwhile I am trying to learn what scientists have actually discovered about the history of the area.

Mom looks closer at the picture, then rubs her hand across my hair and says, "That's nice." I swing the book back around and read more while I'm chewing my toast.

She finishes her coffee, then sighs and stands up. "Well," she says, "I need to get ready to go to work. Your Dad is staying home with you today, but he's still asleep, so try to be quiet, okay?"

I nod, and turn the page.

Laura

It makes me nervous to leave Timothy alone with Michael, but I try to tell myself it will all be fine. He was out so late last night. I had long since given up on waiting for him and gone to bed, and I'm not even sure what time he got home. But I know it was long after midnight.

He is completely passed out in bed as I quietly move around the bedroom getting ready to go. I hate to wake him up, but I can't leave without telling him, so he knows that he's alone here with Timothy.

I sit on the side of the bed and gently shake his shoulder. He doesn't react. I shake him a little harder, and that does the trick. He inhales quickly, and squints his eyes at me.

"Honey?" I say.

"Mmm," he sort of moans.

"I'm leaving for work. Remember, you'll be here with Timothy today, okay?"

"Mmmm."

I pause for a moment. He starts drifting back into sleep. "Mike?"

"Mmmm."

"I'm going to leave the bedroom door open, okay? So you can hear if Timothy needs anything."

"Mmm-kay."

Well, that's about as much as I'm going to get. I kind of hate to leave it like this, but I'll be running late for my first hair appointment if I don't get going.

I pick up my purse on my way out of the bedroom, glancing back through the open door to see Michael's breathing resume the slow rhythm of sleep. I sigh.

Timothy is in his room reading, of course, his notebook open to take notes about what he's learning. I think this is another one of the experiments he is running with Natalie, something about learning about the history behind the bible. I've stopped being surprised by this kind of thing with the two of them.

"Hey, kiddo, I'm going to work."

"Okay. Bye, Mom," he says, looking up from where he is sprawled on his floor.

I crouch down next to him, and give him a kiss on top of his head. "Your Dad is still sleeping, but if you need anything you can go and wake him up."

"I won't need to Mom, I'm old enough to take care of myself. I told you that yesterday too."

I chuckle. "I remember. I don't think the authorities would agree with you, but I know you are very capable and mature. Remember that Dad is here if there is an emergency."

"All right, Mom. Have a nice day."

Chapter 34

I Feel Great

Jonathan

I wake up and it all comes rushing back to me. Demon is back. I know he is. I felt that rush of anger yesterday, then it went away pretty quickly. But I know I wasn't imagining it. The anger wasn't the only thing.

I feel different. Like, I've been feeling okay for a couple of months, but there's something else going on now. It's like the warmth I feel when Natalie touches me. That feeling like a light has turned on, seems like it is stuck on now. Before, when she stopped touching me each time the light turned back off, but now the light switch is staying on. It's been like this ever since yesterday, after I stopped being so afraid about Demon and was able to calm down.

I mean, nothing else happened. I was mad, and I kicked the ball at Socks, then felt bad that I might have hurt him. That's when I realized Demon was here and got really scared. But I didn't feel anything else I shouldn't, didn't want to hurt anyone, nothing like that. None of the stuff Natalie has been warning me about.

And I actually feel better. A lot better than I was feeling yesterday before it happened, while I was missing Natalie so much. Now I don't feel like I need her to touch me any more.

I think whatever was wrong with me is fixed. I hadn't even realized how bad I was feeling before. But now I look back on it, I know that the times Natalie touched me made me feel like normal, like I used to feel, like I should always be feeling.

And that's how I feel now. Actually, I feel great.

I don't know whether Demon is really watching me, like Natalie told me guardian angels do. Is he listening to everything I'm thinking? Does he know how scared I was? I wish I had paid more attention to Natalie, or asked her more questions about how this works. It didn't seem as important to me as just having her be with me. But now I think I should have been learning more. I don't know what I'm supposed to be doing now that he's back.

Well, I don't suppose there's anything I can really do about it. I guess everyone has a guardian angel, so it doesn't make me any different than anyone else. I've spent the last few months scared of the idea of having a guardian angel, but now it seems fine. I don't see anything wrong with it.

I realize that I'm starving. I don't remember feeling this hungry for a long time. I get up and head down the hall to the kitchen. Wow, it must still be really early, I don't think the sun is even all the way up yet. Mom and Dad's door is still closed. What day is it? Oh, Sunday, I don't think they have to go to work or school today, so they're still asleep.

Well, I can get myself some food. I open up the cupboard and start rummaging around. It all looks so good.

Jonathan's

"Yes, my dearest, I am here. Exactly as you are wondering, I am listening to everything you are thinking. I will always hear and see each of your actions, all of your thoughts. You are the center of my existence, my beloved."

It is already growing easier to whisper to my beloved. As his recovery accelerated once we reunited, so has mine. I feel as though I am the same as before the exile occurred. I am not quite ready to start experimenting with the use of energy again, though.

To hear my Guarded speculate about what I am doing is astonishing. I had seen such things occur with the Seer before, but this is a new experience for me. I had attempted to prevent Jonathan from learning about me, fearing that it would harm my connection with him. But after having our connection nearly destroyed, I am delighted to find that even though he reacted to my return with an initial fear, he already finds acceptance.

It is so perceptive of my beloved to recognize that he is feeling whole once again. It grieves me to discover how unwell he had been feeling in my absence, even though he did not truly realize it at the time. But now he sees that only with my presence can he function normally, feel well, find renewed pleasure in his life. Even his appetite has returned.

As I observe him breakfasting in the early morning, I contemplate how interesting this situation is. It has been so long since any human was without a Guardian, the knowledge of what that would be like has long been lost to memory. But now I see the profound difference that it makes. A great deal of the functionality of the human is tied to the presence of their Guardian. The partnership is even deeper than I knew.

What might this mean for us moving forward? When I fully recover, and am able to again consider the use of energy in our communications, what can we accomplish? Now that he knows of my presence, will I be able to communicate with him? Control him?

And of course, soon we must deal with the inevitable return of the Seer. We have these few days of peace, to ourselves, before she returns and presumably attempts to resume her interference in Jonathan's life. I dread having to see the unnatural creature again. I worry about how I will react to her presence, after having spent so long both craving and hating the effect she had on me whenever she touched Jonathan. Can I influence Jonathan once again to exclude her from our presence? Can I force him to do so?

We shall see. We can hope.

Chapter 35

Today Is The Day!

Natalie

OMG OMG OMG! Today is the day! I am so excited I feel like I can't sit
still. My parents are getting married again today! Everything I hoped
would happen is coming true!

The second I get up I put my beautiful dress on. Mom let me pick it out
myself to wear to the wedding. It is made out of a shiny yellow fabric that
shimmers with a sort of orange color when it moves around in the light. It has
a pink satin sash, and a big full lace slip underneath that makes the skirt poof
out all around me. It's the best thing I've ever worn.

When I get out to the kitchen, Mom and Grandma are in there making
some breakfast. Mom turns around and sees me in my dress, and bursts out
laughing. "Oh, Natalie, honey, it's not time to wear your dress yet! You don't
want anything to spill on it."

Grandma sees me in my dress and starts to laugh too, but then straightens
out her face. "Sweetie, why don't I come and help you get back out of that,
and we'll hang it up to make sure it doesn't get wrinkled before the wedding.
All right?"

Angel smiles at me and shrugs. I can tell that he is making himself not laugh
too. "Even you, huh?" I ask him silently. Now he's laughing.

"Okay, Grandma, fine," I say, sighing. I guess they're right.

So we walk back out of the kitchen into the hallway, and I glance up at the
picture of the guardian angel on the wall, like I always do every time I pass

by. She sees me look at it and chuckles. "You always have loved that picture, haven't you?"

I look up at her. "I have," I agree. "I remember the first time we talked about it."

She shakes her head. "Naw, sweetie, you couldn't remember that. You were way too young."

Angel looks over at her, laughs and shakes his head. He knows she's wrong about that.

I stop myself from sighing. I do remember, but after last night I'm not about to try to argue with Grandma about it. Angel told me she was very offended when I mentioned that the Christmas story in the bible is full of all sorts of other mythology which existed at the time it was invented. The last thing I want to do is upset Grandma, about anything. I would like to have the chance to talk to her about the bible, though, if I can figure out a way to do it without upsetting her.

We get back into my room and she helps me pull the dress back off over my head. While I'm putting on some leggings and a shirt, she puts the dress on a hanger back in the closet.

"It is the loveliest dress, kiddo, I don't blame you for wanting to wear it as much as you can. I would too!"

I smile at her. "Thanks, Grandma. I picked it out!"

"Did you now? No wonder it suits you so perfectly." She looks around the room, and starts making up the two beds that Gabe and I slept in last night. Oops, I suppose I should have done that. I go and start working on the other bed, and she smiles over at me while we both straighten blankets.

"Good job, Natalie. You really are a very good kid, you know?"

"I try to be," I tell her. I think now's my chance. "I'm sorry I upset you with what I said about the Christmas story last night."

"Oh, sweetie, you didn't upset me. I know sometimes people can have questions about bible stories. What you have to understand, though, is that it is important to have faith in the word of God. There is always an answer to any questions you might have, but it doesn't mean you have to doubt that anything in the bible is exactly right."

I nod, considering that. She believes the bible is all accurate, but of course I know that so much of it is stuff people made up. Some of what people think is in the bible isn't even in there. Maybe I could ask her about that? I'm starting to know the bible well enough to feel like I can try to help other people understand what is really going on. "So, like you mean if I ask questions, I can find answers in there?"

"Of course, honey," she says, fluffing up the pillow on Gabe's bed and smoothing down the cover.

"Well, okay." I think I can ask her this one. "So, like what I said last night about the date of Christmas? Being December 25? I guess I must have missed in the bible where it says that's the date. Can you tell me where it is?" I feel a little guilty, because I know it isn't in either of the bibles I have read. But if I say it this way I think she'll take it as her grandchild asking a real question.

I'm nervous about her thinking I don't believe everything in her religion is really true. But it's like the way I started the Jonathan Project, to see if I could help just one person. She is just one person. A lot of people have hurt each other over religion, without thinking very carefully about what their religion is actually saying. I am starting to think that this is where it has to begin - with people carefully thinking about what they believe, and why they believe it. It's worth a try, anyway.

She straightens up from the bed, and puts her hand up to her chin, obviously thinking about it. Angel is standing to the side, watching, and I think he's amused by what's going on. "What?" I think to him.

"*She is trying to find the answer to your question, and is realizing that she cannot.*" He smiles as he watches.

"Well, sweetie, I'm not rightly sure where it says the date in the bible. I'll have to ask my pastor." She heads out the door and back down the hallway.

I look over to Angel. "Is she mad?" I ask him silently.

"*No, my dear, but she is perplexed to find that she cannot answer your question. You must be careful, darling, for your grandmother's self-identity is to a great extent based upon her faith. If that faith is challenged, it would be very difficult for her.*"

Well, I guess that's what I'm doing though. I think the whole point of everything I've been learning is to challenge people's faith. I want to help them find a new faith. A faith in something that is actually real. One where they don't have any wish to hurt anyone else over it. I think Grandma's finished talking about it for now, though.

I am following her down the hall, and Angel says, "*Your Aunt Caroline will arrive shortly.*"

Oh yeah! Mom's sister is coming for the wedding. I haven't seen her since I was a lot younger, and I don't know all that much about her. I know she lives on the East Coast. I want to see when she arrives, so I go into the living room and stand next to the window so I can see the street.

Margaret

I get back to the kitchen, trying to remember the nativity stories from the bible. I can picture the whole scene so clearly in my head, with the angels coming to talk to the shepherds, and the star overhead, and the baby lying sleeping peacefully in the manger. But honestly, I realize now that Natalie has mentioned it, the date isn't in there. It doesn't really even talk about what season it was. The weather had to have been nice, though, since the shepherds and their flocks were outside at night. Hmmm. What is the weather like in Israel in December? Could it have changed over two thousand years?

Frank and Gabe have come back in from the side yard where they were checking out the old car Frank has been fixing up. Brenda has finished up the scrambled eggs, so I start laying the table.

Where is Natalie? Wasn't she coming with me out of her room?

I duck my head around the corner to see if I can find her, and see her standing in the front window, staring out at the street. Right then I see a car pull in to our driveway. Natalie turns around and gives me a big smile. "Here's Aunt Caroline!" she informs me.

Huh! I actually wasn't expecting Caroline to get here for a couple of hours. I wonder if she ended up taking a different flight.

"Well that's nice, sweetie," I tell Natalie, heading over to the front door to open it. Then I turn around and take a second look at Natalie, who is still watching out the window. It's almost as though she was expecting Caroline to arrive now, and was waiting for her. Odd.

I head on out to greet my youngest.

Brenda

"Caroline? You're here!"

I put down the bowl I'm carrying to the kitchen table and rush over to the doorway as I see her come in with Mom and Natalie. She grins at me and reaches out for a hug.

"I thought you weren't coming until right before the ceremony?" Natalie is smiling up at me while I goggle at my sister. How can she be so tidy after just getting off an airplane? Her appearance is as pristine as ever, light brown hair in place, makeup on, fashionable clothing unwrinkled.

"Turns out that I was able to get an earlier flight. And the weather cooperated. So here I am!"

My Mom bustles past us all cluttering up the entrance to the kitchen. "Come in and sit down, everyone," she tells us, heading over to the cupboard to get out another place setting for Caroline.

Dad gets up from the table where he was already sitting with Gabe. "Heya, Caroline, so glad you're here!" He reaches out over Natalie's head to give her a one-armed hug. Caroline is his baby, and I know he's always had a huge soft spot for her.

Gabe gets up too, to join the crowd doing the exact opposite of what Mom told us all to do. He hangs on the edge of the group until Caroline acknowledges him. "Is that you, Gabe? What happened to my Little Gabey? Who is this giant young man?"

He grins and shrugs. I tell her, "Turns out this is what happens when you keep feeding a kid!"

My Mom is finally able to shoo us all back to the table to sit down. "Eat before everything gets cold," she tells us. Gabe of course is the first to dig in.

I gaze around the table at my family, on the day I will be remarrying the love of my life. I am filled with happiness, but in the back of my mind there is something missing. I miss Ron. I can't wait to see him at the altar.

Chapter 36

Hungry

Michael

Mmph. I slowly come awake and stare blearily around the room. Why is the door open? Oh, yeah, Laura told me she was leaving it open so I could hear if Timothy needs anything. I lift my head off the pillow and look at the clock.

That can't be right. After 11? Not really, is it?

I haven't heard a thing since Laura came in here earlier. What's Timothy doing? I get up and get dressed, then go look in his room. It's empty. Um, I haven't managed to lose the kid already, have I?

I go downstairs, and find him in the kitchen, sitting at the table eating a bowl of dry cereal, with a big textbook of some kind propped up on the cereal box in front of him.

"Good morning," I say to him.

He glances at his wrist like he's checking the time, but then realizes his watch isn't there. I hear him say under his breath, "Oh, right." Then he looks up at me and says, "Hi, Dad." He goes back to writing something in his notebook.

"You doing okay?" I ask him. "Do you need anything?"

"I'm fine. I was getting hungry so I found a snack."

Well, all right then. I open the fridge to find something for myself. There's some hard-boiled eggs, that sounds fine. "Want an egg?" I ask him.

"Um, okay," he says. "Yes, please," he adds.

I peel a few eggs, then bring them over and put them down on the table. I sit across from him and watch what he's doing.

"Is that homework?"

"No, it's archeology. Natalie and I are studying the history of the bible, and I'm trying to find information about what scientists have learned about the region."

Oh. I would not ever mention this to him, but the kid and I really don't have anything in common, do we? Archeology? Bible study? I guess it's nice that he can keep himself entertained, but he never seems to be doing anything we could enjoy together. "Huh," I say, not having anything to add.

We sit in silence for another couple of minutes. His pencil scratches across the page he's writing on, glancing back and forth between the book and his notebook. He finishes his cereal and the egg. It's so quiet in here.

"Mind if I turn on the t.v.?"

He looks up at me. "No, of course not. I'm going upstairs anyway. Thanks for the egg." He gathers up his books and leaves the room.

I sigh and go over to the couch and flip on the t.v. I guess I'll have to wait until Laura gets back to go find out what Enrique and Jim are doing tonight. Maybe I can find a game to watch in the meantime.

Brad

I poke my head out the back door and call, "Hey Jon, come on in, let's have some lunch." He is wrestling around with the dog. He throws the ball but then chases it together with him to retrieve it, rather than waiting for Socks to bring it back. He's been a total bundle of energy all morning, ever since I woke up to realize that he was already awake and playing in the back yard.

"Hooray!" he yells. "Lunchtime, Socks!" He comes pounding back in to the house, and flops himself down at the table where he sees the PBJs that I've put together. He grabs one and starts devouring it.

"Woah, dude, pace yourself! What's the rush?" He laughs and crams in another half sandwich.

Boy, I do not know what has gotten into him. It's almost overwhelming how he has seemed practically frenetic all morning. What is going on?

This is much closer to the old Jonathan, the way he always used to be so excited and enthusiastic about everything. But it has been months since he really seemed that way. I thought it was probably because he was maturing, becoming less like a bouncy little kid, more sedate as he approaches adolescence. But this is wild. He's like a whirling dervish, like a tornado of exuberance.

Stef comes out from the back, where she's been putting some baby clothes away in the nursery. She wants to get ready well in advance of the baby coming. Of course she does. Always on top of everything. She laughs at Jon as she sits down next to him. "Hungry much?" she asks him, as he grabs another sandwich.

"Yep, starving!" he replies, grinning maniacally.

She meets my eyes with a chuckle. "Good thing your Dad works at a grocery store, then, I think he might need to bring a truckload of food home if you keep this up!"

It's nice to see Jonathan so full of life. I was worried he'd be moping around missing Gabe and Natalie while they're out of town, but he seems fine. He must be going through a growth spurt, that'd explain the feeding frenzy. Kids grow in the Spring, right?

I reach in to grab a sandwich for myself before they're all gone. We settle in together to eat. It's nice to have all of us here, nice to have this Sunday where we are all off work and school. I lean my chair backwards to reach the counter and grab another bag of chips, and toss it over to Jonathan. "Here, buddy, have some of these."

"Thanks!" he crows, catching the bag and digging in with gusto.

Smiles all around.

Jonathan's

"Ah, my darling, my beloved, your appetite is restored in more ways than one. As I languished in the darkness, you lived a diminished life. You had lost your intense joy which makes you so much better than all of the other humans. And now with my return you are restored. Yes, enjoy the food, have fun with your dog, laugh with your family, take pleasure in your sense of well-being. I am here, my dearest, here with you, never to be separated again. We are whole."

Even Jonathan's parents realize that my return has brought renewed life and vitality to their son. They do not understand the cause, of course, but the difference in Jonathan's behavior is dramatic. From the quiet child he had become for the last few months, he resumes his more intense level of activity.

His soul blazes with the brightness it had lost, even with the ministrations of the Seer. She could not truly heal my dearest one. Only I could do that.

And as his soul has grown in strength in response to my renewed presence, so I have grown as well. The weakness I had felt upon my return fades. I am not ready to resume my experiments with the use of power in my communications with him, but I am eager to do so.

Now that he knows I am here, I believe we can both benefit from an attempt to imbue my messages to him with more energy. I don't know if I will be able to merely control him as I had done before. I don't know if that's truly what I want any longer. The possibilities of actual contact are enticing. Perhaps I can truly communicate with him? Perhaps he will be able to sense my words, respond to my suggestions deliberately rather than subconsciously. The prospect fills me with a fervent hope.

What will develop between us?

For the time being, I revel in the togetherness we share, and thrill to watch my beloved enjoying his life, even while accepting my presence. He knows now there was nothing to fear. The Seer was misleading him. I would never harm him, will only ever love him. We will be one, in spite of her wishes. We are united.

Chapter 37

Church

Ron

My heart is pounding, but it isn't anxiety I am feeling. It is excitement, joy, love. I can't wait until I see her again.

I arrived ridiculously early at the church, all dressed up in a black tuxedo. The pastor took pity on me and let me sit in the church's little library, where I'm waiting for the other people to start arriving. He left me here since he had to go out and conduct the morning service. I'm sitting by myself with a book that I can't focus on, looking like the most formally attired loner ever. I hear the sounds of the worship wrapping up, the congregation singing the final song along to the strains of the organ. After they all clear out we can set up for the wedding.

We won't have a crowd. Just my family, Brenda's parents and sister, and probably some other parishioners from the church. Old friends of Brenda's Mom who can't resist a wedding.

I've asked Gabe to stand up with me, and he very seriously agreed. I think he feels the import of the position of best man. Natalie is very excited to act as Brenda's bridesmaid slash flower girl - she had the image in her mind of spreading the flower petals, so she'll do that then stay with Brenda at the altar.

It will be the four of us together as Brenda and I make our promises to each other. Very appropriate.

I hear the service finish up, then everyone goes outside to mill around and chat and have refreshments. I think there will be more waiting before anyone gets here, but Gabe comes in the door to the library. He looks remarkably grown-up in his dark suit and tie.

"Gabe!" I stand up and give him a bear hug. "I'm so glad you're here! Is it time to go set stuff up?"

He grins and hugs me back. "No, they said I should come in here and wait with you until the ceremony starts. Grandma wanted to come early to talk to her friends after the morning service. She said she and Grandpa will set up the flowers and stuff."

"Great, that's us off the hook for all the work then," I laugh. "Where's Natalie?"

"She's waiting with Mom and Aunt Caroline in the pastor's office."

I look at my watch, and see that there's still about 45 minutes before our ceremony is scheduled to start. I gesture over to a shelf I noticed earlier in the library. "They've got a chess set. Want a game to pass the time?"

"Sure," he says, and goes to grab the box. I'm glad he's here. The waiting suddenly seems much easier.

Caroline

Brenda and Natalie and I settle into the pastor's office. He has an adjoining bathroom which makes it easy to ensure that Brenda's hair and dress and everything are in order.

I haven't seen Ron yet. I'll have to stomp on any impulse I start feeling to sneer at him. He's the good guy again, I have to remind myself. Not the creep who ditched my sister. Not anymore. Or at least that's what she tells me.

Natalie is being so cute. She is bubbling over with excitement, looking like a flighty little butterfly in her shiny yellow dress. She buzzes around the room, peeking through the door to see what's going on out there, then coming back over to check Brenda's bouquet, then sitting next to me to hold my hand for two seconds before she hops up again. She intermittently glances off to the side, looking here, there and everywhere, taking everything in.

I'm feeling like I need to make a bigger effort to visit more frequently. It's been three years, at least, since the last time I was able to travel out to San Diego to visit, and I can hardly believe how much the kids have grown since then. I need to see them more often, or I'll end up missing their entire childhoods.

It's hard, though. I'm so busy at work. My real estate practice is thriving, after taking a couple of years to get off the ground. And Tom's law office is so busy that he hardly ever gets home before 7 or 8. We've built a beautiful life with a gorgeous home in Bethesda, near Washington, D.C. Although to be honest we don't spend as much time there as I would like. And of course, there hasn't been any time at all to consider having kids of our own. Maybe someday.

In the meantime, I can enjoy my niece and nephew. I'm really glad I was able to make it home this weekend.

I look at Natalie and see that her hair has gotten mussed with all the zooming around she's doing. "Hey, Natty, want me to fix your hair for you? To be fancy for the wedding? I can put it up in a bun, kind of like your Mom has."

She clasps her hands together in delight and squeals. "Oh, yes, please!"

I smile and pull her over, then get out the brush and comb I keep in my purse. I have a couple of hair ties in there too. "Come here, and try to sit still for a minute, okay?" I start combing out her long dark hair, which is so much like my sister's.

Brenda observes with a smile on her face, while glancing up at the clock and tapping her foot. I give her a sideways smile over the top of Natalie's head. "Relax, Sis, only a few more minutes, then you get to see the 'man of your dreams.'"

We both bust up laughing. Just like old times.

Chapter 38

Dearly Beloved

Ron

G abe and I are putting away the chess set when the pastor comes in. Gabe did a good job on the game. Didn't win, of course, but he expects that. He'll catch me someday.

"Okay, gentlemen, you ready for the main event?" Pastor Lyman asks.

I spring to my feet and huff out a breath of air, suddenly full of nervous energy. Gabe grins and shakes his head. "Dad, you do know it's just Mom, right?" he asks, laughing.

"What do you mean 'just'?" I gasp, pretending to be insulted. "She is the most wonderful woman in the world and I am the luckiest man alive!"

Pastor Lyman chuckles. "There you go, Ron, that's the right attitude. Okay, let's head in there."

I let him lead us over to stand in front of the altar, with my son standing by my side, where we wait for the ceremony to start. There's a couple dozen people sitting there in the audience, more than I expected. Brenda's sister is sitting with her mother. The organist stayed behind after the church service ended, and after a few minutes of hearing some activity going on behind the doors at the front of the sanctuary, she starts playing the traditional wedding march.

The doors open, and Gabe and I see Natalie start heading up the aisle. She looks like the most adorable little fairy princess, that flouncy dress shimmering all yellow and orange and pink like a sunset around her. She has her hair up in a fancy bun somebody has given her. She's holding a frilly little basket filled with flower petals which she starts lightly tossing out on the path in front of her as she approaches me.

I feel my lips start to twitch, and I have to stop myself from laughing, when I see Timothy's giant ungainly black digital watch on her delicate little wrist, spoiling the entire effect. It's hilarious and adorable. I'll bet Brenda had the same reaction.

Then I see Brenda step out of the foyer, wearing the most perfect cream colored gown, elegant and simple, clinging to the lines of her body, exactly right to set off her glorious dark hair and sparkling eyes. She is looking at me with a breathtaking smile.

Brenda

There he is, staring at me with a delighted expression, like I've caught him laughing about some charming secret. He takes my breath away in his tuxedo, tall and elegant and gorgeous. His hand is on Gabe's shoulder, and the two of them are smiling at Natalie and I as we progress up the aisle.

My Dad walks with me, like the first wedding, only this time he isn't going to do the whole giving me away thing. Seems a little late for that. He's only there to escort me. He peels away and sits down next to Mom when we get to the front.

Ron takes my hand, gazing into my eyes with an intense expression of love, then we face Pastor Lyman. Natalie and Gabe stand flanking us. I see them glancing at each other with grins and nods.

The pastor waits for everyone to settle down, then begins with the traditional "Dearly Beloved."

I glance up at Ron, and his blue eyes are gazing down at me, full of delight. This whole second wedding thing is all slightly corny, but so perfect. We both laugh a little when we notice Natalie bouncing on her toes, she's so excited to be part of this. He reaches behind me to give her a little pat on the back, then we turn our attention to Pastor Lyman.

Gabe

Really? Weddings really do start with Dearly Beloved, just like in movies? I can't wait to tell Jonathan when we get back. We'll get a real laugh out of this.

The pastor is wearing a robe with a sort of flat scarf hanging down over his shoulders, and holding a book which he starts to read from. But then he closes the book and holds it down in front of him.

"We are all gathered here today to witness the union of Brenda and Ron. As I am sure you all know, this will be their second wedding. They are here with their two wonderful children, ready to recommit their lives to each other. It is inspiring to see that even when it seems love has been lost, it can still be found again."

I hear Dad sniffing, and I look up to see that he is getting all emotional about this. Well, I'm the best man, it's my job to support him. I reach over to touch his arm, and he looks down at me, sets his mouth in a firm line, and nods. I think it helps him get it together.

Natalie peeks over at me behind their backs and gives me a smile. I'm sure Angel is keeping her posted about how everyone is doing.

There's a lot more wedding stuff. The pastor talks about God and love for a while. When it's time, I give Dad the rings I'm holding in my pocket, and Natalie takes Mom's bouquet to hold it while they are putting the rings on each other's fingers. It's been a long time since breakfast, and I'm wondering if anyone else can hear my stomach growling.

Finally, we're done. Mom and Dad give each other a giant kiss, Natalie almost literally glows with joy, and Grandma and Grandpa come up and give us all hugs.

Is it time for lunch yet?

Chapter 39

Doughnuts

Natalie's

What a privilege it is to share in the delight of my beloved. Her pleasure in these events is natural for a child of her age, but the intensity of it exceeds that of the other humans around her. Her empathic abilities continue to grow, to the extent that not only does she sense the feelings of those surrounding her, but her own feelings increasingly have an impact on others. Even without making physical contact with another person, which as we have discovered with Timothy's guidance is particularly potent, she brings her glowing feeling of joy to everyone. It infuses all within the church during her parents' wedding, bringing a sense of blessing and peace to every participant and witness.

After the ceremony, while Gabe impatiently wishes to proceed to the celebratory lunch, one of the friends of Brenda's mother takes pictures of the wedding party. Following that, Margaret brings Brenda and Ron around to introduce them to her friends who have attended the ceremony.

Natalie finds herself standing to the side with Gabe, waiting for the adults to finish their conversations. She leans closer to him, and quietly says, "There are some doughnuts left over from the refreshments after the morning service." His eyes light up. "Follow me," she says.

With my guidance, she quickly finds the kitchen area in the back of the church, and they slip inside. Nobody else is nearby. The box of unfinished doughnuts is on the counter, and Natalie opens the lid so Gabe can help himself.

"Mmmmm. Thanks Angel." He looks over at her. "It was Angel who told you, right?" I am touched that the child thinks of me.

"Yep. We don't want you to starve!" They both laugh.

"Want one?" he asks.

"No, I want to go find the pastor and ask him a question. I'll see you in a little while."

He nods his head, getting another doughnut out of the box.

"He is in his office, darling. Where you were waiting before the ceremony."

"Thanks," she thinks to me. She exits the kitchen through the side door, and walks around the outside of the church, then through the foyer to the hallway, while the crowd surrounding her parents stands inside the sanctuary. She wishes to steal past without being seen.

The pastor's door is ajar. She knocks lightly and peeks her head inside.

He glances up from the papers he is studying on his desk. "Well, hello my dear. Are you looking for your parents?"

"No," she replies, smiling brightly at him. "I wanted to thank you for the beautiful wedding ceremony. It made my parents so happy."

He leans back in his desk chair, pleased with her charming statement. He is impressed that such a young child should take this initiative. "You are most welcome, child. Your name is Natalie, right?"

"Yes," she smiles at him.

"Would you like to have a seat?" he inquires, when she seems to be lingering rather than returning to her parents.

"Yes please, thank you." She perches on the chair in front of his desk. Her fancy dress puffs out around her.

He looks at her with a perplexed smile, tilting his head, not sure what she wants. "Did you need anything else?"

She takes a breath. "Well, I was wondering, if you have any time, could we maybe talk about the bible a little bit?"

His eyebrows go up. He notices that he is still holding a pen in his hand, and he lays it down. "Well, sure. What do you want to know?"

"Oh, anything," she says. "I've been reading it, and it's so interesting, but I don't really have anyone else to talk to about it."

He is astonished. He tries to remember Natalie's age, somewhat misled by how small she still is. "Do you read the bible in Sunday school?" he asks.

"He isn't sure how old you are, my dear, he thinks you are younger based on your appearance."

"No, I don't go to Sunday school," she tells him. "I'm seven years old, by the way. I have just been reading the bible for fun. My Grandma gave it to me."

"Ah, yes, your grandmother is very devout. I'm not surprised that she gave you a bible, but I admit I am a little surprised to hear you are reading it for fun. Many seven-year-olds wouldn't find it very interesting."

"Well, I like to read a lot. And I am interested in learning about how religions develop."

He shakes his head in amazement. "Is that so? Do you want to know anything in particular?"

She casts about for a specific question. She hadn't planned out the discussion, other than simply wishing to converse with a person knowledgeable about the bible. "Um, which one is your favorite?"

"Which...." he prompts.

"Which bible? Like what version. Do you like King James, or one of the newer ones?"

"Oh! Well, I love the language of King James, since it seems so formal and important. But the one we use here in church is one of the newer ones, since modern English is easier for most people to understand." He does not think she can possibly comprehend his statement.

However, she eagerly responds, "I've noticed that! The King James language seems like an old movie, the way the words are written, but the newer one is easier to understand. My Grandma gave me a newer one. But my babysitter has a King James so I like to read that too and compare it. The stories come out a little different sometimes, don't you think?"

His astonishment grows. Comparative biblical literature with such a young child? This certainly wasn't what he was expecting. He is shocked but deeply pleased to find himself delving into this conversation. If only his parishioners could be this focused.

Chapter 40

Missing

Ron

Margaret is happily chatting with all of her friends, bringing them up to speed on the development of my relationship with Brenda. It would have been preferable not to have everyone in New Mexico know how much I regret having an affair, but it's the truth, so I suppose she's entitled to share it. We are smiling and nodding along. Eventually, people start saying their goodbyes and heading towards the door. Gabe and Natalie long since got bored and wandered off, but Gabe has returned and is slouched in one of the pews kicking his feet and waiting for us to finish.

Brenda finally says, "Okay, I think we should all be heading to the restaurant. I made reservations for noon, and we shouldn't be late."

Margaret is yacking with some of the last stragglers who are still here. "Yes, dear, we'll be right along. We'll meet you there, all right?"

I look around and realize that Natalie still isn't in here. "Where's Natalie?" I ask Brenda. She stares around with me.

"I'm not sure. Maybe in the library? It'd be like her to find something to read while she's waiting."

I'm about to head over there, but Caroline says, "Why don't you three go ahead, and I'll bring Natalie over in my car."

"Okay, sure," Brenda says. "Come on Gabe, lunchtime!" Of course this is the main event for him, so he eagerly rushes out of the church to the car.

I walk to the front holding hands with Brenda, and finding ourselves in the foyer alone for a moment, I take the opportunity for another kiss. I run my hands down her back, feeling the satiny dress clinging to her luscious body.

"Thank you, Mrs. Cadwell," I tell her, after we come up for air.

"You know, that isn't anything new. I always kept your name, since it was easier that way with the kids."

"I know. Won't stop me from gloating about it all over again."

She laughs and grabs my hand, and we follow Gabe out to the rental car.

Margaret

I'm so pleased Brenda and Ron have finally sorted out their relationship. And it is so lovely to have the chance to show them off, and of course the grandkids, to all my friends.

We're lingering, gossiping about some church business, when Brenda and Ron leave with the kids for the restaurant. They know we'll be right behind them. Caroline comes back into the sanctuary and interrupts my conversation. "Mom, do you know where Natalie is?"

I wave her off with my hand. "Brenda and Ron already left with the kids. We're supposed to meet them at the restaurant."

"Oh," she says, sounding surprised for some reason. "Okay. I'll go over now, then. You and Dad should come along too."

"All right, darlin', we'll be there soon." I turn back to my friend. "Sorry, I missed what you said?"

Brenda

Mrs. Cadwell. Ron is right, my actual name might not be changing again, but it has a whole new meaning now. I feel so warm and wonderful.

We're the first ones to the restaurant, and we go ahead and sit at our table. Gabe digs in to the tortilla chips they bring out while we're waiting for everyone else to arrive.

Caroline comes in the door, and Ron waves her over to our table.

"Isn't Natalie here?" she asks while she's hanging her purse on the back of her chair and sitting down. "Mom said she was with you guys."

What? "No, we thought she was coming with you."

"Huh," she says. "Well, Mom and Dad should be right behind me, I'm sure they'll scoop her up and bring her."

"Did you check the library?" Ron asks.

"Yeah, but she wasn't in there, or on the playground or in the ladies' room. Then Mom said you had both of the kids with you, so I followed you here."

Ron and I look at each other, worried.

Gabe says, holding another chip, "Don't worry, she's fine." He scoops up some salsa, clearly unconcerned about his sister.

Um, okay.

It's only another couple of minutes before my parents arrive. Without Natalie.

"Mom! Where is Natalie?" I'm starting to feel frantic.

"What?" Mom says. "I was sure that she left with you!"

Ron gets up, all business, but I hear the stress in his voice. "I'm going back to the church. Gabe, stay here with your grandparents."

"I'm coming," I tell him, and we head out.

It's only a couple of miles away, but it seems like a very long drive. What could have happened? I feel my adrenaline skyrocketing, my heart pounding with anxiety.

When we get to the church, Ron strides ahead of me through the open front doors, shouting, "Natalie?"

I get inside a few seconds later. Someone must still be here, since they haven't locked up yet. Ron is heading off towards the kitchen area.

"Natalie?" I yell, starting to run down the hallway towards the back, the opposite direction from Ron.

"Here! Here!" Pastor Lyman comes out the door of his office, and to my massive relief there is Natalie right behind him, in her glowy dress.

Ron comes running up from across the church where he had gone. "Natalie! Where were you?"

Natalie seems surprised. "I was right here, talking to Pastor Lyman." She glances to the side, her eyes narrow, then she looks back over at me. "I'm so sorry Mom, I didn't know it was time to go yet."

Pastor Lyman looks sheepish. "I apologize. Natalie and I got to talking, and I think we lost track of time."

This is so confusing. "You've just been here talking?"

"Yes, it turns out that Natalie is quite the biblical scholar. Once we got going on that, I think we both forgot about everything else. I haven't had such a stimulating discussion since Seminary."

Ron and I goggle at each other. I feel a little shaky, the adrenaline rush starting to subside.

Natalie's forehead wrinkles, as she looks back and forth between me and Ron. "I really am so sorry, Mom, Dad. I didn't realize that anyone was going to be worried. I really wanted to talk about the bible." Her face full of remorse, she reaches out and takes both of our hands.

Phew. Okay. I'm starting to calm down, and feel better. Of course she's fine. I glance over at Ron, and see that he's going through the same thing. Just now feeling it sink in that there is no need to panic. Our daughter is not actually missing.

"All right," he says, "we know you didn't mean any harm. Please try to keep track of time better."

She nods her head fervently.

Pastor Lyman says, clearly abashed, "I'm so sorry that you were worried. It really is my fault. I should have been paying attention to what everyone else was doing. But your daughter is such an engaging young person, we both got completely lost in our discussion."

I chuckle a bit shakily. "Yes, we've heard that before. We don't blame you."

Natalie looks up at me as she squeezes my hand. "Mom, would it be okay for Pastor Lyman to come to lunch with us?" She looks over to him. "If you're not busy, of course?"

I look at Ron, then the pastor. "Of course, we would love to have you join us. We're going to Garduño's."

He grins. "I'd be delighted. I was going to eat a snack at my desk for lunch, but I think I've worked up quite an appetite with all this intense theological discussion we were having. Thank you!"

Natalie smiles all around, clearly pleased that everything is working out fine.

Chapter 41

Unpleasant

Laura

I'm thinking about what to make for dinner as I drive home. I don't feel like going to the store. It was kind of a long day at the salon, now it's already late afternoon, and my feet are sore from standing. I think I have some pre-packaged frozen meals at home. Won't take long to whip something up.

Mike is slumped on the couch, watching t.v. when I get home. "Hey," I say to him, taking off my sweater. "How'd it go?"

He shrugs. "Fine. Kid's been up in his room all day."

I laugh. "Well, that's normal." Mike turns his gaze back to the t.v.

I head into the kitchen and check what's in the freezer.

Michael's

My beloved feels a disheartening malaise. After having conquered the sleep disturbances he had been experiencing for so many months, he begins to grow weary of the solution. Although it was exhilarating at first to realize that the substances he imbibes with his new friends were making him feel much better, the initial thrill has worn off. The neighbors seem increasingly immature to him, and although he recognizes this is natural since they are much younger, it has started to wear on him. Especially after the antics of last night, although he appreciates the act of smoking together with them, their behavior makes him feel that he is regressing back to high school. However, he has no other readily available source from which he can obtain marijuana, and does not wish to risk making inquiries elsewhere.

He has tried off and on over the last several weeks to reduce his use of the drug, but finds each time that the lack of the substance leaves him feeling worse, and less able to rest at night. He also worries, however, that if he continues, eventually his military employer will discover that he is using illegal substances and he will face discipline.

Furthermore, he knows Laura is troubled by his activities, but he cannot manage to stop. He can't bear to face her disappointment, which makes him try to avoid her, staying out later each evening, spending time with the young men next door rather than with his family. He is unable to find a way out of the tangle he finds himself in. His mood grows increasingly darker.

I am at a loss. I do not know how to comfort him, or to heal him. All I can do is be with him.

"Beloved, I share your turmoil, we are together as you journey through this path in life. You will find your way along the path, darling. I will walk it with you."

Timothy

I've made so much progress on the archeology research today. I've filled up a lot of pages of notes about excavations which could be where stories in the bible happened. I'm looking forward to comparing notes with Natalie when she gets back. She knows way more about the stories than I do, so we really need to look over my notes together to see whether any of them fit what's in the bible.

"Hey, Guardian," I whisper to him. "Can you ask Angel to tell Natalie how much I've gotten done? And tell her I hope she's having a good time, but I miss her."

I feel Guardian agreeing with me. It's frustrating that I can't hear his words most of the time, but this is still a type of communication, at least better than nothing. It's harder now that Natalie is gone, because when she's here she can tell me everything Angel and Guardian say, and I don't have to try so hard to hear my guardian. I hope when I'm falling asleep tonight, or waking up tomorrow morning, I can hear him tell me how Natalie is doing.

At least it helps now that I can picture his appearance. It was very surprising when Angel explained that guardians can look like anything they choose. Guardian said he could look like an ordinary human if I wanted, then I could decide if I want any details added. I've slowly been developing an idea of what seems right for his appearance, and Guardian makes adjustments as needed. Angel has described everything in detail. Guardian looks like a man now, about my Dad's age, with short hair like my Dad, but really tall like Natalie's Dad. He has thick black glasses and a white lab coat. It makes me happy to think of Guardian as a scientist. It helps me to imagine him next to me, and to dream of being a scientist like that someday. An actual scientist, with a real laboratory, not a kid running experiments all the time like I do now.

In the meantime, I'm finished with the archeology book. I'll need to get back to the library to see if I can find more. I guess I'll read something else for now.

I inspect my shelf, but I've read everything here a million times already. Hmmm.

"Dinnertime," Mom calls up the stairs. I have an idea.

When I get down to the kitchen and sit at the table, I ask, "Mom, do we have a bible?"

She walks over with the bowl of food and sets it on the table. "Well, probably. I haven't seen it in a long time. You want to read it?"

"Yeah, I'm done with the archeology book but maybe I can start finding the references to the places in the bible. I was going to wait for Natalie but she won't be back until next weekend and I don't have anything else new to read."

She looks over at Dad. He shrugs. "Well, I'll see if I can find it after dinner," she tells me.

"Okay, thanks."

I eat some noodles. I have to wait until after dinner to get the bible. None of us are talking while we eat, not even Mom.

After Dad finishes, he gets up. "I'm going next door," he says.

"Honey, can't you stay here tonight?" Mom asks, while she puts dishes in the sink.

He huffs out a sigh. "I was cooped up here all day. I want to get out of the house for a while."

Mom puts down a plate way harder than she needed to, and it makes a crashing noise that hurts my ears.

"Really? Mike, come on. I was working all day, why can't you just stay here? Maybe we can watch a movie together." She isn't quite yelling, but it's still too loud.

I'm sitting frozen at the table, staring at my hands. This is very unpleasant.

Dad stomps over to the closet and gets out his jacket. "Not tonight. Maybe another time."

"Fine!" she yells, and I can tell it surprises him as much as it does me. Mom never yells.

He stands next to the door, staring at her, like he can't decide what he should do now.

She is staring back at him from the sink. "Just go," she says, and her voice sounds strange, like she's crying.

I feel like I want to cry too. Watching my parents have an argument is awkward and awful.

He stares at her for another second, then turns around and leaves without saying anything else.

Mom and I stay still for a minute. I hear her sniff. I don't know what I'm supposed to do. I want to go back up to my room and get away from this.

But then I feel Guardian nudging me in my mind. He must be using extra energy. I can't tell what he's saying, but I suddenly remember what happened when Natalie started crying, the time Angel told us about God. I know what I have to do.

I get up from the table and go over to the kitchen where Mom is leaning against the sink, wiping her eyes and pretending like she isn't crying.

I put my arms around her waist. "It's okay Mom."

She gasps in a breath and hugs me tight for a minute, and I feel her crying some more, then she stops. I pat her back while she's doing all that.

After another minute, she lets go of me and gets a tissue out of the box on the counter, and wipes her face. She throws the tissue in the trash then turns around.

"Thank you, Timothy, that was very sweet. I'm sorry you saw all that, though."

I can't think of anything to say about any of this, so I just nod my head.

"Well," she says, "how about we go try to find the bible. I think it might be in my closet, in a box of stuff I never got around to opening after we moved in here. Want to help me look?"

"Yes," I say, and follow her back upstairs.

Chapter 42

Eyesight

Jonathan

I think I'm getting used to it. I know Demon is here, and I have really been feeling great all day long. I don't think anything is happening that shouldn't be. I've had a fantastic day, even though there wasn't anybody to play with besides Socks. But we had fun throwing the ball, and Mom and Dad ordered pizza for dinner which tasted better than anything I've had before in my life. Now they're letting me watch a movie with them that Dad picked up from Blockbuster, Men In Black. It's totally fun, gross and hilarious. I'm laughing my head off.

Mom hands me another bowl of popcorn she made. "Want some more?"

"Yep!" I dig in. Awesome!

Jonathan's

We both celebrate the delights brought to us by our reunification. He senses me here in the robust energy he has felt since my return. I revel in the sensations which result from being in his presence, such a stark contrast from the dreadful nothingness of my exile. I am restored. He has recovered. We are reborn.

Natalie's

It was an embarrassing lapse on my part. I failed to keep my beloved appropriately apprised of the activities around her, resulting in her being left behind as her family departed the church. This caused consternation and worry for her parents.

I felt especially disgraced when, once Natalie realized what had happened, she silently snapped, "Why didn't you tell me?" I apologized, and I know that she does not hold a grudge, but she was right to ask.

Why didn't I tell her?

The plain truth is I was too caught up in her excitement at the discussion she was having with the pastor. She has seldom been this focused, this fervent, this purposeful. Her entire consciousness was immersed in the conversation, and my focus on the event was utter. Neither of us gave a moment's thought to the activity of the others nearby. We both disregarded anything happening outside the room as mere background noise.

I am filled with remorse, and determined not to fail her again. I must always attend not only to her own actions, but to those of others which might affect her. I normally do so, but the time spent with the pastor was all-consuming.

I will endeavor to do better.

Of course, my dearest knows that I regret my negligence. She has regrets of her own. She blames herself for causing trouble, and also feels chagrin over her moment of impatience when she briefly chastised me for not having kept her informed.

We both feel we have let down the ones we love. And of course, we each attempt to comfort the other.

Thankfully, the moment of alarm passed quickly. Once she returned with her parents and Pastor Lyman to the restaurant, the family enjoyed a lively rehashing of the event. No doubt this exploit will become one of the cherished memories which will be related for many years, together with other juicy tidbits of family history. They will long remember the time Natalie was so busy talking to the pastor that she was left behind at church after the wedding.

Despite being marred by the abrupt conclusion, the discussion was the most fulfilling of Natalie's life. She and the pastor refrained from continuing their conversation during the family lunch, but as he was departing, Pastor Lyman handed her his business card. "Feel free to contact me any time, Natalie, I would very much love to hear from you again."

She took his card with a happy smile, and already is making plans to write him a letter about additional questions which she did not have a chance to ask during their discussion.

She and Gabe are in bed, but not yet asleep. It is still fairly early in the evening. They each lie in one of the small beds placed within the spare bedroom in their grandparents' home. They said goodbye to their parents at the restaurant, as had been planned. Ron and Brenda will spend the week at the hotel, enjoying a second honeymoon. The children will be staying here with their grandparents. After a day or two, their parents plan to pick them up for daytime outings, but they will return here each night.

Their grandmother finished tucking them in, then turned off the light as she left the room. Although the children are remaining quiet, they have no intention of actually going to sleep this early. Gabe feels that it is somewhat unjust to be sent to bed as early as his younger sister, and certainly much earlier than his usual bedtime. He was ready to advocate for being allowed to stay up later, but Natalie interceded, imploring him to do as they are told. She was concerned about causing any further trouble after the incident at the church.

He obliged her, and is somewhat grumpily lying in bed, although he is mollified by the fact that he can play with his Gameboy in the dark, using a modification his father had provided to illuminate the screen. Natalie assured him that I will warn them if an adult is coming to check on them, so he can tuck it away without being detected. I am making sure to be diligent in this duty, carefully tracking what the children's grandparents and aunt are doing elsewhere in the home. I will not let her down again.

Natalie leans over to retrieve her bible from the nightstand between the children's beds, planning to re-examine the passages which she and the pastor had discussed earlier in the day.

Gabe looks up from his gaming device. He whispers, "I thought you didn't want to get caught. She'll see it when you turn the light on to read."

"It's okay," Natalie assures him. "I don't need to turn on the light."

Gabe sets his Gameboy aside and leans up on one elbow. "Well, it's not like you have a glow-in-the-dark bible. What are you going to do, just hold it and try to absorb the knowledge through the cover?" He snickers.

"What? No, I can read it all right." She doesn't know why he is making an issue out of this.

"No you can't." They stare at each other, their faces illuminated only by the soft glow coming from Gabe's device. They share a moment of mutual confusion, neither understanding what on earth the other is talking about. To demonstrate that she is correct, Natalie opens the bible, finds the chapter and verse she wishes to examine, and begins reading it to him in a very quiet whisper.

Gabe's mouth falls open. "No way. Here, let me see that." He reaches over and grabs the bible away from her, and peers at the page she has open. Even with the faint gleam coming from his Gameboy, he cannot make out the words on the page.

"My dearest, he is perplexed because he cannot see well enough to read in such a dim light. He does not understand why you can."

Her brow wrinkles. She worriedly questions me. "Is there a problem with his eyes? Does he need glasses or something?"

"No, darling, his eyes are normal. You have not been aware of this, but it is your eyesight which is unusual. I have long known that you are able to see better at nighttime than other humans. That is why you are able to read without the light on. This is not possible for most other people."

Gabe realizes we are having a discussion. "What is he saying?" he whispers to her.

"He, uh... well, he says that apparently my eyes see better in the dark than other humans. I didn't realize it was different from other people."

Gabe sits all the way up. "Oh," he whispers. He sits in silence and stares at his sister. After a moment he realizes he is still holding her book. "All right then, here," he says, handing it back over to her.

I am relieved that although this new information about another unexpected aspect of her nature surprises Natalie, it does not disturb her. She quickly adapts to the knowledge. Taking back her book with a suppressed giggle, she says, "That's pretty convenient, I guess. I read at night all the time." She returns to her studies.

Gabe shakes his head. "Well, have at it then." He lays back down and holds up his Gameboy again, but he does not focus on the game. Instead, he contemplates how he has discovered another mind-blowing fact about his extraordinary sister.

Chapter 43

Entertainment

Timothy's

The situation with Timothy's father is troubling. It has been many months since he returned after his long deployment, and he has had a sequence of troubles since that time. His nightmares were keeping him awake and causing much distress to both of Timothy's parents. Then when he met the new neighbors and began using a substance provided by them to alleviate the sleep disturbances, there was some reason for hope.

However, now the remedy has begun causing problems of its own. It has led to conflict between Timothy's parents, which is beginning to impact my dearest one directly. It was quite distressing for him to witness their argument this evening. The situation has been going on for some time, but he has been so absorbed in his own interests that he did not pay any particular attention to it. Now, however, it has imposed itself upon his consciousness, and it has upset him.

I was pleased that he received my message encouraging him to comfort his mother with a hug, in the same way he assisted the Seer a few months ago when she was distressed. He felt my presence more strongly as I pushed energy into my thoughts, and I was able to cause him to remember how he had assisted Natalie. He proceeded to take the appropriate action to console his mother.

His assessment of our level of communication is accurate. He rarely hears my specific words unless he is drifting in or out of sleep. However, he frequent-ly senses my intent and presence as a more nebulous, non-verbal message.

The form of communication is imprecise, yet is an amazing achievement. He cannot appreciate how unprecedented it is for him to regularly converse with his Guardian. Only Seers can do this, yet he has found a way. His success continues to be astonishing. He, however, has come to accept it as simply another aspect of his life, as a discovery he has made with the use of the scientific method. On top of the intense love I bear for him, my admiration of his intellect grows daily.

I have updated Angel regarding the events of today, including the unfortunate developments regarding Timothy's father. In return, Angel shared with me his remorse over disappointing the Seer. He bears a heavy burden as the Guardian of a Seer. His responsibilities far exceed those of ordinary Guardians. I try to offer him support and insight, sometimes even advice.

I savor our regular conversations. The relationship which I have developed with Angel is an utter novelty, something which I never experienced before. But it has become deeply important to both of us. Our communication, our friendship, benefits us both, and helps us each in our quest to better Guard. It is remarkable and delightful.

Timothy slumbers, and I wait through the quiet hours of the night, observing his dreams in silence. He is not awakened by his father returning home in the early hours of the morning, even though there is a substantial amount of noise involved in opening doors and walking up the stairs.

I consider the words I should use to update Timothy about Natalie's day when he awakens. I must choose very wisely, knowing that he will hear me for only the briefest of moments. It has become an interesting exercise, to carefully select the phrases which will impart the most information with the greatest economy.

Stefanie

My Spring break happens to coincide with Jonathan's this year, but unfortunately I'm not planning to really spend extra time with him. I'm trying to finish up all of my internship hours this week, so for the rest of the semester I can focus on my classwork. I still have to study for finals and write a couple of papers. I've cleared it with Meg to get as much work done as I can this week, then I'll be taking a break until after the baby is born. I'm still thrilled to already have the job lined up with her, to continue as her research assistant after I've taken maternity leave.

I'm plugging away on the data entry for her project, using the information from the files that I had already organized. I'm glad I'm finished with the organizing part, so I'm not doing as much lifting boxes as I had to at first. That would be harder now that I'm so far along. So I spend my time here sitting in front of a computer, having to reach past my belly to get to the keyboard.

Meg comes in during her morning break, after seeing her first couple of patients. "Hi, Stefanie, how was your weekend?"

I push back from the computer and stand up, stretching my back out. "Good," I tell her. "Jonathan's friends are on vacation with their family for Spring break, so I was worried he'd be missing them and totally mopey, but it's really the opposite. He was super full of energy yesterday. It was exhausting just watching him!"

She chuckles. "What's he doing for the rest of the week?"

"Brad has shifted his schedule around, so he can stay with him during the day. Hopefully they'll go do something that requires a lot of physical exertion - Jonathan really seems to need to burn off some energy somehow. I think they're planning to hang around at home today, and I'll bet he's driving Brad crazy looking for entertainment."

She puts down the mug of coffee she's drinking. "You know, I have a couple of guest passes for the zoo that are about to expire. Think they'd want to use those?"

"Oh, that'd be perfect! Are you sure you don't need them?"

"Nope, I get them with my annual pass and I haven't had any visitors this year who wanted to go. I'll go get them out of my purse. Hopefully they have a good time."

"That's really nice, thank you!"

I really lucked out with this internship. I love everything about this job.

Frank

I hang up the phone. "That was your Mom," I tell the grandkids, who are sitting in front of their breakfast, watching me and waiting for my report. "She said that she and your Dad are going to stick to themselves today, but they'll be here tomorrow morning to pick you up and go out to do something."

Gabe shrugs, and Natalie nods.

"So," I ask them, "what do you want to do with your ol' Grandma and Grandpa today?"

They look at each other. "Could we go out to eat again?" Natalie asks. "Maybe someplace with more Mexican food?"

Gabe laughs and lightly noogies her head. "You just want some more sopapillas with honey, don't you?"

She grins. "Okay fine, yes, I do. They are the most delicious thing I've ever had."

"It's nice for you to seem hungrier than me for once!" he replies, and they both guffaw.

Brenda has often lamented that they can't find sopapillas in California. It's hard to believe that Mexican restaurants everywhere don't include this with their meals. The little fried puff of doughy bread, drenched in honey, is exactly perfect to douse the heat from spicy food. But I guess this is a strictly New Mexico tradition.

Margaret is watching this whole exchange. "Sure, kids, let's plan to go out for lunch on the way to the airport to see off your Aunt Caroline. The timing will work out with her flight."

"Excellent plan," says Caroline. "You can't get sopapillas in Maryland either. I agree with my niece about how delicious they are. I'll appreciate one more chance to have some." She waggles her eyebrows at Natalie, who giggles.

"Well, that leaves the whole morning," I point out. "What next?" It's been a long time since we had to provide entertainment to children. I'm not sure what kids like to do these days. Do they still watch cartoons?

Caroline offers, "If nobody else has any suggestions, I have an idea. It's a beautiful day, and I'd love to go see the Rio Grande while I'm here. Maybe we can take a walk along the river like we used to when I was a kid? They have a visitor center that Gabe and Natalie might enjoy."

Margaret says, "That sounds like a lovely idea, dear. How about it, kids? Want to go walk along the river?"

"Sure," Gabe says. "I didn't even know there was a river in Albuquerque."

Natalie smiles. She always seems happy to do everything. Or maybe she's just dreaming about sopapillas.

Chapter 44

Waking Up

Brenda

"You are a genius," I tell him breathlessly, lying together in the comfortable hotel bed, the sheets and blankets in a total jumble around us.

Ron laughs softly, rubbing his hand slowly up and down my arm as he lies behind me still. "Nah," he says, "many other people have also figured out how to do that. It doesn't take a genius."

Ha! "Not that. Although, honestly, you're so talented in that area it's possible you're a genius there too." He laughs again, his face buried in my hair so I feel his breath warm my scalp. "I meant your idea to stay here at the hotel, and let the kids stay with my folks."

"Yes, that I'll accept credit for. Getting you to stay alone in a hotel with me for a whole week is a brilliant scheme, I admit."

I roll over to face him, snuggling up to his chest. "As I said. Genius."

"Mmmmm," he murmurs, wrapping his arms around me, keeping me close to his heart, "feel free to admire the next thing this mastermind will do: take a nap."

Laura

I'm working again today, but only for the morning. I told Timothy that I was going to work when I left, but I didn't even bother waking up Michael. After his late night, I think with a bitter twinge, he wouldn't have gotten up even if

I had told him I was leaving. I did at least leave the bedroom door open, so if there is an emergency hopefully he will be aware. He's making me bitter, I realize with some dismay.

I don't know what to do about any of this. I'd try to continue ignoring it, but now I feel like Timothy has gotten involved. I was both mortified to have him see me crying last night, and deeply touched when he came over to hug me through it. I can't have Timothy feeling like he needs to take care of me, though. He's only seven, for God's sake.

I know Mike goes back to work tomorrow, so maybe another week will go by without anything else happening. I'll be hanging around home with Timothy most of the time. It'll be quiet, peaceful, exactly the way he likes it. So, I have to admit, do I.

Timothy

When I start to wake up, I hear Guardian tell me, *"Natalie enjoyed the wedding. Afterwards, she was so involved in a discussion with the pastor about the bible that she didn't hear her family leave. They had to come back to get her."*

As always, as soon as I start to concentrate on what he's saying, it wakes me up. "Thanks," I tell him. I'm trying to figure out what that meant. I'm glad she found somebody to talk to, since I'm not much help when it comes to bible stuff. But she didn't hear her family leave? Well, here's another thing to add to my list of questions I will need to ask her about when she gets home.

While I'm writing that down on my list, Mom comes in to tell me that she's going to work, and that she'll only be gone a few hours today. And that Dad is still asleep. "Do you want me to make you some breakfast before I go?" she asks.

But I can tell she's in a hurry. "No, I'm fine. I can get cereal or something. I keep telling you, I'm old enough to take care of myself."

She smiles and kisses my head. "Okay. Wake up your Dad if you need anything." I just shake my head at her, then tell her goodbye.

I pick up the bible she found for me in a box last night. I haven't gotten very far into it yet. I go downstairs and set it on the table while I get some breakfast for myself. Yeah, I guess cereal again. I sit down and start eating, and open up the book.

This bible is sure different from anything else I've read before. The paper is super thin, and the letters are really small. I'm skimming through it, looking for names of places. I open my notebook so I can take notes about any place names I find. I want to see if I can recognize any of the locations from the archeology book I've been reading. The stories don't interest me - I'll let Natalie think about those.

I flip through all the way to the back, and discover something unexpected. There's actually a couple of maps back here! That's much more useful. I know the archeology book has some maps in it too. I'll be able to compare them once I get back upstairs.

I finish my cereal quickly, because I want to compare the maps as soon as I can. I take the bible and notebook back upstairs, planning what to do next. I think I need to make a chart, showing the place names, where they are mentioned in the bible, and what the archeology book says about them.

I'm thinking hard about this as I get into my room. I sit down on the floor and start organizing my books.

"AAAAHHH!"

I jump a mile when I hear a loud yell coming from down the hallway. My heart starts pounding. I don't know what's wrong. I leap up off my bedroom floor and stare around wildly.

"MMM AAAHH Mmmm." More yelling, and some mumbling.

What is happening? After I get over the shock of the sudden noise, I realize it has to be my Dad yelling. He's the only other person in the house. Is he hurt?

I'm afraid to do it, but I have to go check to see what's wrong. I wish I could talk to Guardian as well as Natalie can talk to Angel, because it would make it easier to find out without having to go in there. But I can't, so I have to do it.

I look out the door of my room and don't see anything, so I walk slowly down the hallway towards my Mom's room. The door is open.

I hear him breathing really heavy now. At least he isn't yelling any more. I peek my head in the door.

I see my Dad sitting on the side of the bed. He is wearing pajama bottoms but no shirt. He is hanging his head down, and covering his face with his hands. He is breathing really hard.

I stay in the doorway, afraid to get closer. "Dad?" I ask in a small voice. He doesn't move, so I don't think he heard me. I make myself say it louder. "Dad?"

He looks up, his hands still covering his mouth. His forehead is all wrinkled, like he is really worried about something.

"What's wrong, Dad?" I wonder if he needs medical attention. Am I supposed to call 911?

"Oh, hey Timothy." He shakes his head back and forth really fast, like he's trying to clear his mind. Then he runs his hands over his hair.

"Dad?"

"Sorry," he says. "Did I yell? I was asleep. I had a bad dream."

Oh. This is confusing. "You were just dreaming? There's not anything wrong?"

"No, nothing's wrong. I'm sorry I scared you." His breathing has slowed down, I can't hear it any more. My heart is still pounding though.

"Um, do you need anything?" I ask him.

He takes a deep breath, and slowly lets it out. "No. No thanks, kid. I'm good. Sorry about that." He looks around. "Where's your mother?"

"She went to work. She said she won't be gone all day though."

"Oh, okay. Well, I'll get up now. Go on out so I can get dressed, okay?"

I stay in the doorway for a minute, staring at him. That was really scary and confusing and I'm not sure if I should really leave him alone.

He looks at me, and he gets a strange expression on his face. "I'm fine. Go."

I nod, biting my lip, and back out of the door. I close it behind me.

Michael

Well, shit.

I haven't had a nightmare like that for months. Not that bad. I thought it was behind me. Especially if I smoke weed, I usually sleep fine afterwards. I've been trying to cut back a little, but not last night. I stayed over at Enrique and Jim's place until ridiculously late, smoking and playing games on their XBox with them.

Maybe that was the problem? We were playing Halo, a first person shooter game, which seemed super fun, but I think it gave my crazy stupid brain ideas about new ways to torture me with nightmares.

And now I'll always be stuck with the image of Timothy standing there staring at me, with his eyes as wide as saucers, like I had done something really terrifying. I must have yelled before I woke up. It looked like I scared him half to death.

Ugh.

Chapter 45

Stroll

Natalie's

My beloved is enjoying the time outdoors, walking through the trees and along the bank of the river, which flows placidly to our left. The Spring sunshine warms the group as they stroll together down the path, chatting amiably, in no hurry to be anywhere else.

"It feels very pleasant for you, to be outside, doesn't it, my dear? You tend to spend so much time indoors talking with Timothy or reading, that I don't think you have developed much of an appreciation for the beauty of nature. Please enjoy this time, beloved."

She silently agrees with me. "True," she thinks to me. "It hardly ever occurs to me and Timothy to go outside to play. Maybe we should do it more. This is really nice." The breeze whispers along the leaves in the trees, as I whisper to her while we move through them.

She is walking behind her grandmother and aunt, who are caught up in conversation. Behind her are her grandfather and brother, engaging in a discussion of their own. She listens quietly, drinking in the scenery along the route. A passerby might think she is being left alone to fend for herself, but of course she is never alone. She has no shortage of conversation with me.

Her attention is captured by hearing her grandmother say the name of her father. She listens more closely.

"Ron told Brenda that his Dad is having some trouble. I didn't get the whole story, but apparently his house is run down and he is having some kind of health problem."

Caroline responds, "I haven't seen Ron's father in forever. I think it must have been way back when Gabe was a baby."

Margaret nods. "I think the last time had to have been not long after his wife's funeral. That was a sad business. Then after the divorce, we didn't see any need to stay in contact with Brenda's ex father-in-law."

"What are they talking about?" Natalie silently inquires.

"The day before the wedding, your father went to visit his own father. They had not seen each other in many years. Your father discovered that your grandfather is suffering from some type of affliction, and has not been able to properly care for his home."

"What affliction?"

"I do not know the details."

She is silent for a moment, thinking. Hearing that her grandfather, whom she has never seen, is having troubles of course triggers her empathic side, and she wishes to learn more, to determine whether anything can be done to help. "Can you ask Knight? He would have seen whatever Dad saw when he was there."

"Of course, my dear, I will ask your father's Guardian for details. One moment."

It continues to prove convenient that we have learned how to communicate with each other over any distance. Previously, I would not have been able to access the thoughts of Guardians who were not in my vicinity. Now, however, our family group remains in fairly constant contact, in order to satisfy the Seer's desire for shared knowledge.

It is also convenient that Natalie has taken it upon herself to assign each of us a name. I must remember to address her father's Guardian as Knight, her mother's as Lady, and her brother's as Aaron. This makes conversations easier, even for us. Although to be sure, holding conversations of any kind would never have happened without the impetus of the Seer. The other Guardians near us usually observe with amazement as we speak directly to each other, something none of them would ever dream of doing.

Using the additional energy required to reach out to Ron's Guardian, I inquire, *"Knight? Natalie wishes to know further details about the status of her paternal grandfather. She only knows the bare minimum, as related by her mother. Can you share additional information about what is troubling him?"*

Knight quickly responds. *"Of course, Angel. When Ron arrived at the house of his father, he was surprised to see that the exterior appeared unkempt, with the yard apparently untended, the roof in some disrepair, and a window frame broken. It took some time for his father to respond to the knock on the door. When he finally opened the door and allowed Ron to enter, it became clear that the interior was cluttered, so full of items and debris that Theodore could barely move about the room."*

I repeat this information to Natalie. She wants details about his health. "What about his 'affliction'? It sounds like there is more than just a messy house?"

"Please go on, Knight. Natalie is concerned about the report that Theodore's health may be impaired."

"Yes, it is so. Ron does not know the extent of it, and Theodore either does not understand what is wrong, or has not been able to obtain a diagnosis. He is mentally foggy, forgetful, and has a substantial tremor in his hands. He has lost weight and appears significantly older than would be caused by the actual passage of time since Ron last saw him. He is extremely reluctant, even afraid, to consider leaving his home for any purpose. Hence his inability to attend the wedding. His Guardian tries to assist, but the whispers of support have no effect."

I repeat these words to Natalie. Her brow furrows. "Is there anything we can do to help?"

"I do not know, my dear."

She sighs, stymied. "Well, how are Mom and Dad doing? You might as well find out while you're talking to Knight."

"Thank you, Knight. Natalie wishes to know if her parents are well."

I sense the smile coming through Knight's thoughts, along with the image of the physical intimacy which her parents have been sharing with much enthusiasm since they returned to the hotel last night. I smile at Natalie, and offer her an edited, age-appropriate rendition of their activities.

"They are very well, my darling, and are greatly enjoying each other's company. They appear to be napping at the moment, in their hotel room. They are quite happy."

"Okay," she thinks to me. "Please thank Knight for letting us know."

"The Seer sends her thanks, Knight. As I send mine."

I nod at her to let her know that I have conveyed her message to Knight, then lapse into silence by her side.

She returns my nod contentedly, then resumes gazing thoughtfully at the quiet river as we pass by.

Ron

I'm awakened by the feeling of Brenda moving within my arms. I guess we had both fallen asleep, after we tried to get up earlier in the morning but then ended up straight back in bed again. It is a honeymoon, after all.

She murmurs, "Good morning. Again."

"Mmmm." I caress her hair, which is spread across us both. I love her hair. "Good morning, O Best Beloved."

After a minute she moves to get up.

"No," I protest, tightening my arms around her. "Stay here. Please. Don't go."

She chuckles and settles back down against my chest. "You planning to stay in bed all day?"

"Obviously. There is nothing out of this bed that I could possibly need."

"What about breakfast?"

I lift my head far enough to see the digital clock on the nightstand behind her. "I think it's too late for breakfast."

She leans back to see the clock too, and bursts out laughing. "Lunch, then?"

My traitorous stomach chooses that moment to loudly grumble. "Okay, fine. I suppose we have to eat. Room service? We can have them bring the food right here to the bed."

She smiles and relaxes against me again. "Sounds wonderful. But, I have another idea."

"Does it involve getting out of this bed?"

"Sadly, yes. But I think you'll agree with me."

I sigh, melodramatically, tragically. It makes her laugh. "You wound me, woman. But fine. We'll do anything you want. What's the plan?"

"Well, I'm thinking it would be nice to go check on your Dad."

Oh. Yeah, that whole thing. I suppose she's right. "Okay, we can do that. He's probably wondering if I'll show up again. Before another decade goes by."

She sits up, and I follow her, not willing to let go of her yet. "I have to warn you though, it's depressing. The house is a shambles, and he is different. Like, so much older and feebler than I ever imagined. I don't know exactly what's wrong, but it's way worse than I expected."

She nods, and leans over to kiss me. "I know, that's what you said before. And that's exactly why we should go."

"Why are you always right about everything?"

She laughs. "Just keep that in mind for the future."

"Always. I will never forget it again."

That triggers more kissing.

"Okay, okay," she says finally, pushing away from me, "we have to stop or we'll never get out of here. We will starve to death, or at least sex each other to death, and your father will end up having to be taken away by elder services or something."

"Always right, like I said. I'll make you a deal. I'll get ready to go, but only if you'll take a shower with me."

She smirks, raises an eyebrow at me, and saunters sexily towards the bathroom, her glorious hair brushing against her bare back.

I feel myself spring to attention. She's right again. She knows exactly how to motivate me to get out of bed.

Chapter 46

Grandfather

Margaret

We have to wait a little while to get a table big enough for our group of five. Padilla's is always quite crowded at lunchtime. Best little hole-in-the-wall place for Mexican food in town.

The waitress brings menus and water. And of course chips and salsa, which Gabe starts in on right away. I look over at him with a fond smile, thinking about how he is such a growing boy. He seems to have hollow legs, constantly hungry but never getting full. He'll be as tall as his Dad someday. Maybe even taller.

Then I glance at the entrance behind him, and can't believe who I see coming in the door. Speak of the devil!

"Well, what do you know!" I say with a laugh, and Brenda and Ron look over at our table, startled to find us here.

The kids swivel their heads around to see what I'm looking at, then jump up and rush enthusiastically over to greet their parents.

"I didn't know you were meeting us for lunch," Gabe says happily, while Natalie smiles.

Ron laughs. "We weren't planning on it. What a coincidence!"

Frank waves them over. "Come on and sit down." He grabs a spare chair from an adjoining table, so there are seven seats for us now.

Caroline grins at Brenda. "How's the honeymoon going?" Brenda gives her a meaningful smile. Is that a blush I see?

As they sit, the children chattering happily with their parents, I think actually it isn't that much of a coincidence. This has been our family's favorite spot for years. Of course they'd want to come here for lunch.

"So," Brenda asks the children, "what have you been up to?"

Gabe describes the morning walk we took along the river. "Ah," Brenda says, "how wonderful! That was one of the things I was thinking about doing with you guys while we're here this week. I'm glad you saw it!"

Natalie asks, "Do you have other plans for the week? Like, are you going to visit anyone else?"

Gabe looks at her questioningly, wondering who she means. I wonder as well.

"Actually," Ron says, "we are planning to go visit my Dad after lunch."

Natalie smiles. "Can we come?"

Her father's eyebrows go up, then he looks over at Brenda. "Well, I'm not sure," he begins, but Natalie cuts him off.

"I'd really like to go, please. I want to meet our other grandfather." She looks at Gabe pointedly.

"Um, yeah," he joins in, still looking at Natalie, clearly taking his cue from her. "Yeah, we'd definitely both like to go."

Brenda and Ron meet each other's eyes. "I think it will be okay, Ron," she says. "I'm sure he'll be happy to see the kids. He knows they're in town, after all."

He nods, resolved, then looks over at me. "Okay, sure. We'll bring them with us after lunch then, and drop them off later. All right?"

"Of course. It'll be nice for them to visit with their other Grandpa. Won't it, Frank?"

"Yep."

Then the sopapillas arrive and Natalie's attention is thoroughly diverted. Gabe elbows her and laughs. She giggles back, already pouring honey over her fried bread.

Theodore's

My beloved sits in his dimly lit home, surrounded by his stacks of magazines and papers, but he does not make his customary effort to sort through them.

His memory is usually scattered, however he realizes that yesterday was the day his son said there would be a wedding.

Although he has been a solitary creature for many years now, accustomed to being by himself, today he feels a renewed sense of loneliness. The visit from his son triggered a sense of longing in him, a nostalgia for the days long ago when he was surrounded by his family.

"My darling, if only you could sense me here, you would know that you are never alone. Your loneliness is unnecessary. I am your family, your devoted Guardian, ever present, ever loving."

I wish it was enough.

He stares at his table, covered with papers, and at the wedding invitation he had managed to find after Ron left his house the other day. He feels utterly alone.

There is a knock on the door. He breaks out of his reverie with a start.

"Who could this be?" he mutters, slowly rising to his feet and shuffling across the room.

There is another knock.

"I'm coming, I'm coming," he mumbles so quietly that the visitor would be unable to hear him. I am focused on him, not looking to see who stands without.

When he opens the door, an amazing sight appears. I don't know which of us is more astonished.

Me. I am more astonished. Despite his seclusion, he has often seen other people before. In fact he has seen most of these specific people before. He saw one of them only two days ago.

I, however, have not encountered a Seer in many an eon.

There she stands, a small child, her soul glowing with an aura unlike that of any of the other humans with her. The human soul normally glows with warm colors, varying in intensity depending on the individual and their activities. With this Seer, her aura is quite different. It shines with an intense white light, as bright as a star. It fiercely illuminates her surroundings, emitting a brilliance which would be blinding to her human companions if only they could detect it.

She is accompanied by her family, and by her Guardian, who has taken the form of an angel. This Guardian's manifestation is highly detailed and obviously created for the benefit of the Seer.

I try to suppress my sense of shock, as my beloved greets his family. "Ron," he says, "I'm surprised to see you again." I am very pleased that he immediately recognizes his son this time, and that he seems oriented as to the time and place. He remembers the visit from two days ago.

"Hi Dad," Ron says. "I wanted to bring my family by for a visit. I hope that's all right?"

Ron's family stands on the porch with him, to all appearances passively waiting to be invited inside. But the Seer is a flurry of unseen activity. She is engaged intensively with her Guardian, issuing a barrage of questions about the condition of my beloved. The Guardian assesses my dear one's health, his mental state, his physical condition, his memory, his emotions, even his soul, and meticulously reports to her each finding.

My amazement, if it is even possible, heightens. The Seer is not merely here for a family visit, I realize. She has learned, presumably from her father, that my beloved has impairments, and she is determined to learn about these, and, most shockingly of all, try to find if there is a way to repair them.

I feel a blaze of hope. Can this remarkable development lead to an improvement in the life of my beloved? Can this young child manage to bring comfort to her grandfather?

Theodore blinks, staring around at the group of younger people on his porch. It seems to him that it is almost as though fate heard his wish, as though his sadness over the absence of his family somehow brought them here to him. "Yes, yes," he manages to say, "I'm glad you came by. Please come in."

He moves back from the door, and as the group crowds into his entryway, he realizes somewhat helplessly that there is no place for them to all sit down together. The Seer quickly questions her Guardian, and offers the solution.

"Hi, Grandfather, I am Natalie," she says sweetly, gazing up into his face. "I'm happy to meet you." She moves her hand, indicating the cluttered living room. "Would it be all right if my brother and I move some things off the couch in here so we can sit down?"

My beloved is moved, to not only meet the granddaughter he only learned of two days ago, but to have her make this kindhearted introduction. He makes an effort to smile down upon her. He has not smiled for a long time.

"Yes, of course, that would be fine," he responds to her question.

"Come on Gabe," she says, and marches straight over to the couch, her older brother following amiably along behind. They must dodge past piles of belongings stacked on the floor. She immediately sets to work on her project. She lifts a few items from one end of the sofa, and indicates to her brother what he should pick up.

Ron's eyes widen, and he says, "Hold on, I'll help," moving into the room to supervise and assist.

My dearest is frozen in place, watching this veritable invasion of his isolation. He is both pleased and dismayed.

The children's mother reaches out to him, as they both wait for the others to clear some room to sit. "Hi, Theo," she says. "Remember me? I'm Brenda."

He shifts his gaze away from the activity in the living room, and focuses on her. "Yes, hello Brenda. I haven't seen you in so long."

"It's really nice to see you again," she tells him, and he seems to acclimate to the reality of this visit.

He smiles at her, his second smile in many years. It is easier this time.

Chapter 47

Miraculous

Natalie

I made sure when everybody sat down that I was sitting right next to my grandfather. Angel and I want to be close to him, so we can watch everything. And so I can try to touch him.

I think this is going to be like one of Timothy's experiments. Back when we figured out that it helped Jonathan for me to touch him, Timothy kept track of everything. He's not here now, but Angel and me will try to remember everything, and write it down later.

I think I might be able to help. Angel told me that Grandfather's problems seem to be more emotional and mental than physical. I'm pretty sure I can't do anything about physical problems. I couldn't help fix Gabe's ankle when he broke it, but I could help him not be so bothered by the pain. And I know that Jonathan kept getting better every time I touched him.

Timothy wanted to keep going with the experiment, to see what else might happen if I touch people, but there hasn't been anybody else who really seemed to need it. Until now. Angel has described my grandfather's mind as being troubled, and told me that he seems very sad and lonely.

So this is a new chance to see if touching someone really can help with that kind of thing.

Of course, it isn't only an experiment. It's my grandfather, somebody in my family. Someone to love. I want to help him. I want him to feel better.

As soon as I sit down next to Grandfather, I reach out, and touch his hand a tiny bit, to see if it is okay with him. I don't want to be grabbing him if he doesn't like it. I feel his hand shaking. He is listening to my parents talk about the wedding yesterday, but when he feels my finger on the back of his hand, he looks down at me with a surprised expression.

"Is it okay?" I think to Angel.

"Yes, darling, he seems to accept your touch. I believe you may proceed."

So I smile at him, reaching over a little bit more, so I can actually hold his hand. I can tell he is surprised, but he doesn't try to take his hand away. After a second I feel him relax, and clasp my hand in his.

I see Gabe look over at us. He meets my eyes and raises his eyebrows. He can tell what I'm up to. I nod at him.

Grandfather's skin feels old, different from other people. Like, sort of papery and dry. I look up at his face while he listens to my Dad talking. His face is lined. His hair is white. His chin is covered with wispy whiskers. He seems very old. I wonder if he is a lot older than my other grandparents.

"He is only two years older than your mother's father. He is 67 years old."

It sounds very old to me, but I know people can live to be even older than that. And my other Grandpa doesn't seem this old at all.

"This is not terribly old. Many people who are 67 years old are still vigorous and healthy. Your grandfather's condition has deteriorated, leaving him weaker and more frail than he should be."

I realize my parents are telling Grandfather the whole story about how they forgot me at the church when they left for lunch. Oh boy. I'm literally never going to hear the end of that, am I? Gabe is sitting on my other side, and he pokes me and grins. Nope, never. I roll my eyes at him.

But then I hear my grandfather chuckling, enjoying the story. My hand is still in his, with my fingers poking out the side. He pats them with his other hand. "Well, little miss, it sounds like you gave your parents quite a scare, didn't you?" He smiles down at me.

"Yes, but I didn't mean to," I tell him, watching his face carefully to try to see how he is feeling. "I was so busy talking I didn't know it was time to go."

At the same time I am saying this, I ask Angel whether my touch is helping him at all. I feel like it is. He seems livelier than he did when we first got here. His hand has stopped shaking so much. He has been smiling and talking, more than it seemed likely when we arrived. It's like a statue is coming to life.

"Yes, darling, you are correct. He is feeling better. I believe this is partially because he is pleased to have a visit from his family, which has made him feel more energetic. But I also detect something similar to what occurred when you touched Jonathan. His soul seems to benefit from your touch, as well as his mind, and his emotional state. It truly seems to be helping."

Theodore's

The intervention of the Seer appears nearly miraculous to me. My beloved's mind has not been this clear in many a year. It is as though he has been trying to see in the dark for all this time, and suddenly the lights have turned on for him. His thoughts have a clarity and precision which he has not experienced in a very long time.

And his soul, which had dimmed greatly in the years since the death of his wife, fracturing and withering due to the consuming sorrow that filled his days, burns with a power brighter under the girl's touch than I have been able to generate through any effort. She brings with her a joy, and a love, which reach him to his core.

I am as affected as he is. I have shared his grief and solitude for so long. We both feel rejuvenated by this wondrous being who sits on the couch with my beloved, keeping her hand firmly within his, focusing her abilities on his well-being.

Miraculous, indeed.

Ron

Wow, this visit is so much nicer than I expected. After I saw Dad the other day, I was worried that there was some kind of crisis brewing here. But seeing him today, holding hands with Natalie, chatting and laughing with us about the brouhaha yesterday, I'm thinking that maybe I overreacted. It isn't nearly as bad as I had thought.

What a relief.

Brenda

Well, the house is a disaster, that's true, but I think Ron's description of his father's health was too pessimistic. Theo seems older, yes, but I think he's okay. He's talking to us, interacting with the kids, happy to have us here. It's not as bad as I was expecting.

Maybe we could make some kind of arrangements for a gardener and a housekeeper to come by regularly to keep things in better order. Maybe get a handyman out here too, to do some repairs. It's not that surprising that he is finding it harder to keep up as he gets older. I'll talk to Ron about this later.

In the meantime I'm really enjoying the visit. I always did like Theo, and it's awfully nice to see him again.

After we've lingered for over an hour, I think we should get going. Theo seems glad to see us, but I think he's getting tired. I'm sure he's not used to this much activity.

"Well," I say, trying to move things along. "It has been so nice to see you again. Thanks for having us." I stand up, to cue everyone else to do the same.

Gabe and Ron get up, but Natalie stays seated next to her grandfather. It's so adorable the way that she has been cuddled up to him, holding his hand this whole time.

She looks up at him, and he returns her gaze with a soft smile. He seems reluctant to let her go.

"We'll see you again soon, Grandfather," she tells him, slowly releasing his hand. She looks over at Ron. "Right, Dad? We can come back again tomorrow, right?"

He's surprised. I know he wasn't planning to visit his Dad this often during our vacation. "Well, I'm not sure what we had planned for tomorrow," he hesitates.

"Please?" she asks in a wheedling voice, very uncharacteristically.

Ron looks over at me, the question in his eyes.

"Of course," I say, unable to deny such a loving request from Natalie. "We'll come by again tomorrow morning, all right, Theo?"

His smile grows, and there is a glow in his eyes. Blue eyes, the same shade as Ron's, although they look very tired. But refreshed, like our visit has done him a lot of good.

Chapter 48

Hurt

Jonathan's

It is fascinating to observe how my beloved thinks of me, now that he is aware of my existence. His knowledge is tainted by the stories told to him by the Seer. She has biased him against me, bit by bit. She not only told him that my name is Demon, she then proceeded to interrogate him regularly about whether I have re-appeared, whether I am forcing him to do anything against his will. It is maddening.

Despite this, his fear of me had ended within a day of my arrival. He knows how much better he feels, and appreciates that with my return he is again whole. Still, he finds himself monitoring his feelings, as trained by the vexatious girl, to ensure that he is in control of his own actions and emotions.

Of course he is. I only ever encouraged him to do what is best for his own well-being. I am not a monster. I am not a demon.

Sadly, though, the use of that horrific moniker has created an image in Jonathan's mind. He pictures me as an actual, physical demon. A creature of biblical terror, a vision created using images he has seen in television and movies depicting such entities.

Very well, I think, with an aggrieved amusement.

I have only ever created a vague manifested appearance during this lifetime. Before I was banished, I had shaped my matter to appear like a bland, basic human male, no details, as none were needed to feel close to my most beloved boy. However, since my return I have not attempted to re-create this image. I am formless at the present time.

But, I think it would be appropriate, if ironic, to shape my appearance to comport with the image Jonathan envisions. He believes me to be a demon. He pictures me as such. I will be so. I will do it lovingly, hoping to defuse his fear, render it powerless by shaping it, bringing it to light. I will not hide his image of me in the shadows. I refuse to be hurt by it. I will adapt to it. I will own it. I will overcome it.

I begin my work.

Michael

Having another nightmare sucks, but at least it got me out of bed, so I don't sleep half the day and leave Timothy alone again. I feel bad about scaring him. I'm glad to have the chance to try to make up for it.

After I get dressed, I ask him if he wants to go out and do anything together today, but he says no, he's very busy with his project. He tries to explain something to me about the charts he's making, but I can't really follow what he's talking about, so I leave him in his room, where he is organizing a bunch of maps and books and papers.

The morning passes by. I'm bored. I've watched t.v. for a while for lack of anything better to do. I can't seem to find a way to spend time with my son, but I figure I can at least get some lunch together for him. That'll be better than yesterday anyways. I go look in the fridge, and find some frozen chicken nuggets I can nuke. I'm pretty sure he likes to eat those.

While they are in the microwave I go upstairs and look into his room. He has this giant command center spread out all over his floor. He seems to have taped together several pages of paper, and has them lined up next to a map.

"Hey, kid," I say.

He looks up at me, apparently surprised to be here in this reality with me, rather than in whatever world he was thinking about.

"Oh, hi Dad," he says, then glances back down at his work.

"I've got some lunch ready for you downstairs."

He looks back up, surprised again. Ugh, I wish it didn't surprise him to find that I've done something useful for him.

"Thanks," he says, and gets up to follow me out of his room. He grabs one of the books along the way.

I put some nuggets and chips on a plate for him, and throw on an apple for good measure. Laura would want him to have something nutritious.

I expect him to immediately bury his nose in his book again while he is eating, but instead he looks at me across the table. "Are you feeling okay, Dad? That nightmare isn't still bothering you, is it?"

Oh, wow, that's unexpected. "Well, no, it isn't. I'm fine." We stare at each other for a moment. He doesn't meet my eyes, but that's nothing new. I don't think we really know how to interact with each other. "Thanks for asking."

He nods, and now he goes ahead and opens his book. There we go, back to normal.

I'm finishing up my own plate of nuggets, when I see some movement out the front window, and I glance over there to see who it is. And WTF is this? There are Enrique and Jim, home in the middle of the day when I know they are supposed to be at work. Jim has his arm around Enrique, sort of supporting him as they walk slowly up to their house.

"What on earth?" I blurt out.

Timothy looks up. "What?" he asks, then sees where I am looking, and peers out the window as well. Even he can see that something isn't right here. "Are they okay?" he asks.

"I don't know," I tell him. "I think I should go and see if they need any help. Will you be all right if I leave you here by yourself for a few minutes so I can check?"

"Yes, Dad," he sighs. "I keep telling Mom I'm old enough to take care of myself. Go ahead."

"Okay. I'll be right next door."

I grab my shoes and head over. They are just getting up to their front door. It took them a long time to hobble over there.

"What's up?" I ask them.

Jim looks over his shoulder at me. "Hey," he says. "Enrique got hurt at work. Could you get the door for me?" He hands me the keys he was about to try to get into the lock.

"Sure," I say, opening the door and holding it for them while Jim helps Enrique get inside.

I don't see any obvious sign of injury, but Enrique clearly has something wrong. "What happened?"

"Hang on," Jim says. "Que, want to lie on the couch?"

"Yeah," he says, sounding a little blurry.

"Here, let me help," I say, and go to knock some of the junk off the couch to make room for him. There's still some debris from the snacks we were all eating last night. We get him lying down with his feet up. He winces as he settles in. He lays there with his eyes closed.

"So..." I say.

Enrique opens one eye and looks at me. "I fell off a ladder," he grunts. He closes his eye again.

I look up at Jim, thoroughly alarmed.

"Yeah," he says, putting down the backpack he had slung over his shoulder when he got here. He sits down at the kitchen table, seeming worn out. "We were working, and I'm not sure how it happened, but I think his foot slipped while he was climbing up a ladder. He landed flat on his back, and was obviously hurt. The foreman didn't want to call an ambulance, and Enrique was able to get up, so I brought him to urgent care in my car. They took an x-ray and said they don't think anything is broken, but he sprained his back."

"Shit," I say, staring over at poor Enrique. "So, what's he supposed to do for it?"

"They gave him some pain meds at the doctor, and a prescription for more. It's called Oxy-Condo or something. I still have to go pick it up. They said if we can get a flat ice pack, he can lay on that to help stop the swelling. He'll have to wait it out for a few days. They said it should hopefully feel better within a couple of weeks."

Enrique covers his eyes with his arm and groans. "Man, I shouldn't have stayed up so late last night." He isn't quite slurring his words, it's more like he's super tired. "I think I was half asleep at work today. That might be why I slipped."

Well, fuck. Is this my fault? He was up late because I was over here playing Halo with them. Crap.

"Oh, man, I'm sorry," I say. "Um, can I do anything to help?" I look over at Jim.

"Well," he says, "there is something you could do if you're willing. Someone needs to go to the pharmacy to pick up his prescription, and maybe see if they have any flat ice packs. You wouldn't be able to do that for me, would you, so I can stay here with him?"

"Yeah, man, I'd be happy to. Give me the prescription, I'll take care of it."

Enrique mumbles, "The doctor said they'd call the pharmacy. They didn't write a prescription."

Oh, okay. "What pharmacy?"

Jim gives me the information, and I head out.

Then I remember Timothy. Um, I guess I have to take him with me. He won't be happy about that, I don't think.

But then, saved by the wife. Here comes Laura, home from work just in time. She walks in from the parking lot, and frowns to see me standing outside next to Enrique and Jim's house.

"You weren't over there hanging around with them, were you?" she asks, sounding aggravated.

"No! I mean, not really. I went over because I saw them get home, and it looked like there was a problem."

She glares at me and hurries into the house, clearly to check on Timothy. Oh good grief, I'm in trouble with her.

"He's fine," I tell her, following her in. She sees him sitting at the table finishing his lunch, and breathes an obvious sigh of relief.

"What was wrong?" Timothy asks me.

She turns around and looks at me. Thanks, buddy, for your intervention, I think. Hopefully now she'll believe I wasn't goofing off.

I answer him. "Enrique fell off a ladder at work and got hurt. They just got back from urgent care. I'm going to go pick up his prescription from the pharmacy."

Laura's eyes melt, as she realizes that this wasn't about me being a screw-up. "Oh no!" she says. "What's wrong?"

"He hurt his back. Nothing's broken, they don't think, but apparently it will take a couple of weeks to heal."

She puts down her purse and comes over to give me a hug. Mmm, this is nice. I actually don't remember the last time we touched each other.

After a minute I let her go. Timothy is staring at us. "Okay," I say. "I need to go get that prescription. Be back soon."

She nods, her face filled with concern. Better than annoyance, that's for sure.

Laura

I feel bad that I immediately assumed Michael was up to no good. I need to readjust my attitude. He's a decent guy. I wouldn't have married him if he wasn't. I have to remember that.

Poor Enrique! You know, I haven't really spent that much time with our neighbors. Mike is over there all the time, but I barely know them. They're young guys, though. I doubt that they ever have a home-cooked meal. I'll bet it's all junk food all the time. Enrique should have something healthy while he is recuperating.

I'm planning to make a casserole for dinner tonight. I check the cupboards. I have enough ingredients to spare. So that's what I can do to help the neighbors. I'll make a second casserole, so they can have something to eat for dinner without worrying about what to do for food the first day that Enrique is back from urgent care.

Timothy is finished with his lunch, and he brings his plate over to the sink.

"How was your morning, honey?" I ask him, taking the plate.

"Good. I'm really glad you found that bible, it helped a lot. I'll show you my chart if you want."

"Okay. What'd you have for lunch?"

"Dad made me chicken nuggets."

Oh! Nice, Michael even prepared lunch for Timothy. See, Laura, you need to give him a break. He's fine, even if he does stay out late at night.

I wonder what will happen now that Enrique is hurt? Will Mike spend more time with him since he'll be home, or will he stay away since he needs to recover? I guess we'll find out.

Chapter 49

Beast

Gabe

"Okay, bye kids, be good for Grandma and Grandpa. We'll pick you up tomorrow after breakfast."

Mom and Dad stayed to talk for a while when they dropped us back off, to tell our grandparents all about our visit with our other grandfather.

Honestly, I'm just waiting for them to go, so I can have a chance to talk to Natalie. I totally could tell that she and Angel were up to something with Grandfather. The way she was touching him the whole time, and staring at him like he was a science experiment, reminded me a lot of how everything happened with Jonathan. So I want to know what's up.

We get our chance easier than I expected. After our parents leave, Grandpa goes outside to do some yardwork or something. Grandma says she needs to start working on dinner, so we should entertain ourselves for a while.

"Hey Nat, let's go hang out in our room, okay?" Grandma smiles at us and shoos us out of the kitchen.

Perfect.

We get in there, and she immediately hauls her notebook out of her backpack. "Well?" I ask her.

She opens the notebook to the page after the big chart Timothy made for her to fill in while we were flying, about the guardians being able to hear each other.

"I need to take notes about everything that happened with Grandfather."

"Okay. What happened?"

She starts writing, and looks over to the side, and I can tell she's listening to Angel. She writes some more.

"Wait, wait, wait," I tell her. "Hold on. I want to hear too."

She looks at me. "Well, I was trying to see whether touching Grandfather could help him. Angel thinks it really did. I need to write everything down I can remember." She sighs. "I wish Timothy was here. He's the one who usually takes the notes. And who thinks of all the right questions."

"Hello!" I wave my hand under her nose. "How about me? I might not come up with the right questions, but I can definitely take notes. I'll be in middle school next year, remember. I can probably write a lot better than you second-graders, you know. Just tell me what to write."

Her eyes get all bright. "That's a great idea! Thanks Gabe!"

She hands me the notebook, and I have to smile when I see her clunky writing. I mean, she might be some kind of spooky genius or whatever, but she still writes like a seven-year-old.

I hold the pencil ready. "Okay, you tell me what happened, and what Angel is saying, and I'll write it all down. Go!"

Jonathan

This is going to be so awesome. The lady at Mom's work gave her a couple of tickets to the zoo, and me and Dad are going there today. Mom is leaving for work, getting her purse, and feeling around with her feet to slip them into her shoes. I guess she can't really reach down there any more.

I go over and give her a hug, I'm so happy about the zoo tickets. I wrap my arms around her big belly, which is right in my face. "Tell the work lady thank you for the zoo tickets!" I say.

She rubs my back. "Yes, I will tell MEG thank you."

Ha!

Oh! My cheek is still laying right on my Mom's belly, and it kicks me! Right in the face! I lean back and stare at it in amazement.

"You felt that, didn't you?" she asks me. "That was the baby kicking. It won't be long before you're a big brother."

"Hey kid," I say right to her belly, "no kicking your big brother! Show some respect!"

Mom and Dad look at each other and bust out laughing.

Brad

It's been a while since we've taken Jonathan to the zoo. I don't know why we haven't thought about coming here lately - it really is a perfect way to spend the day. I wish Stef could have come with us, though. Maybe next time. Although, I realize, next time the baby will be here. An image flashes through my head of all of us walking along, with a baby in a stroller. It makes me so happy to think of it.

For now though, it is nice to spend the day alone with Jonathan. He is still super excited and energetic about everything, like he's been the last couple of days. Good thing, because this place is absolutely huge, it takes a lot of energy to walk through the whole thing.

We've walked down the giant hill to check out the hippos, then back up the giant hill to see the polar bears. Now we're finally back towards the top, where the elephants are, and are resting and eating lunch while looking at them. Jonathan is full of questions about every animal. Thank God for the signs they have posted everywhere with information about everything. I sure wouldn't be able to answer his questions without them.

Jonathan's

I accompany my beloved during his day of viewing beasts of every kind. It amuses me, as I, myself, have transformed into a beast overnight.

It takes time to generate a physical manifestation. I must contemplate each facet of my new appearance, and craft my nebulous matter into a form, concentrating in order to hold the new structure in place. When I have made an image in the past, it was always basically of a human being, not of another kind of creature. Since I have never created this sort of image before, I must consider each aspect more carefully as I generate it.

I am guided by Jonathan's image of myself. Each time the idea of me crosses his mind, a flash of that likeness appears, and I am able to consult his thoughts in order to design my new body.

It is an interesting exercise. Especially after the agonizing eternity spent in the void, it is delightful to assume a tangible embodiment. I am quite enjoying the experience of creating such a singular form, more precise than any I have known or seen before.

Except, of course, for the Seer's Guardian, whose angel form is incredibly elaborate, created for her, and used extensively by the Guardian as a tool of communication as much as are the words spoken to her.

I believe my form might be as comprehensive, though, by the time I am finished.

I consider my progress. I believe that the upper half of the image is complete. The head is large, with a belligerent human face, leading to long horns twisting above. The leering mouth is full of fangs, beneath sharply pronounced cheekbones. The eyes blaze with fire.

It seems that Jonathan imagines demons with wings, so of course I accommodate him. I have leathery, batlike, pointed wings, stretching far above my head.

My torso has rows of chiseled muscles, my shoulders and arms are brawny and powerful, my hands end in fearsome claws.

The entire image is a deep red color, as Jonathan pictures the worst demon he can imagine.

And now, the expedition to the zoo provides the finishing touch. As we pass through the area labeled as "horn and hoof mesa", Jonathan views the cloven hooves of the beasts, and remembers that he saw a cartoon once of a devil with such feet. Yes, I will have those too. And a swishing tail, like that on the lion we passed earlier.

I stalk alongside my beloved, a towering nightmare from hell, exactly as the Seer forced him to envision me. This is her doing.

I love my Guarded more than ever, and long for him to know I have done this for him. Everything for him.

I notice the other Guardians we pass by viewing me with perturbation. The Guardian of Jonathan's father watches askance as my image becomes clearer, darker, ever more terrible in its detail.

Fine. Let them stare. I do this for my beloved, I do this because he knows of me, I do this because such is how I appear within his mind. My image is for him. I am his. I am Jonathan's.

I am Demon.

Chapter 50

Thief

Michael

It's been a long week. I've been back at work every day, but I check on Enrique as soon as I get home. Laura has been making them dinner every night, so I bring it over to them. I can tell they really appreciate it.

Enrique seems to be improving a little. He really has to keep up with the medicine though. As soon as it wears off his back starts killing him again, so he has to take more. It even wakes him up at night. He says the meds are the only thing that let him sleep at all.

I've mostly been trying to leave them alone. I've been pretty much dropping off their dinner then going home. No smoking, no gaming. I feel guilty about keeping him up late playing video games, and keep thinking if I hadn't he wouldn't have been so tired at work that he fell. He hasn't said anything about blaming me, but I blame myself.

At least, I must be blaming myself, judging by my crazy dreams. Ever since the other morning when I had another nightmare, they have come back with a vengeance. I don't know whether it's because I'm not smoking pot this week. I know that wasn't the problem when I had the first one, since I had smoked a ton the night before.

I think that now my insane head has decided to start screwing with me even more. My nightmares used to be about stuff like bombs dropping over in Afghanistan. But they've gotten a lot closer to home. I'm pushing Enrique off of cliffs, or doing something which puts my family in danger, or finding them dead and mangled somewhere. These aren't as violent as the bomb dreams, but they are so much more personal that it seems worse. I don't know what the fuck is wrong with me, but I'm starting to feel desperate again.

Laura was happy to have me stay home for the first couple of nights, but I know all my thrashing around at night all over again is making her miserable. And Timothy seems to be noticing it a lot more now, maybe since he was here that first morning and it scared him.

When I get home, Laura has packed up another dinner for them. This is like the sixth night in a row she's done this. She really is being so sweet.

I'm glad I don't have to work tomorrow. I haven't been able to sleep for days and I'm exhausted, so I'm hoping that tonight I'll get some rest. And hopefully not disturb her again.

"Thanks for the dinner. I'll go give it to them, and be back in a few."

She nods and gives me a tired smile. Her blonde hair is up in a messy bun, and there are dark circles under her beautiful eyes. I have this flash of guilt, because this whole thing is so unfair to her. For months I've either kept her awake or driven her crazy by staying out late. I'm a shitty husband. Fuck me. I feel worthless.

I get over there, and Enrique hears me coming and manages to sit up on the couch. Jim has been working all week - he took Monday off to take his friend to urgent care, but with Enrique out sick their boss told Jim that he can't spare him at all. They've been super busy. So anyway Enrique has been alone during the days.

I put the casserole down on the table. "Thanks, man," Jim says. "Your wife is an angel. Tell her thank you for us. I'm gonna hate going back to pizza every night when she finally gets sick of doing this."

"You're right, she's an angel. She really wants to help out. I'll tell her you said thank you again."

Jim goes to the kitchen to get them out some plates and stuff. Enrique tries to get up from the couch, but grimaces and sinks back down again.

"Shit," he says. "I tried to go longer between doses today, and I'm paying for it. Could you do me a favor and go get me a pill, Mike? The bottle's on the counter in the upstairs bathroom."

"Sure," I say, and go up the stairs. I'm glad the drugs are helping Enrique with the pain. And helping him sleep. I'm almost jealous. I wish I had some drugs that would help me sleep.

I go in the bathroom and rummage around on the messy counter to find the pill bottle. I check to make sure I have the right one. Yeah, the label says Oxycontin, I remember that's the name of what he's taking.

I open the lid and shake one out into my hand. A couple of extra ones slip out. The bottle is still over half full. I'm about to put the extra pills back into the bottle, but something stops me.

I need to sleep. Since I haven't been smoking pot this week, I can't stay asleep, and it's becoming a real problem again. I know these are for pain, but Enrique said they really do put him right to sleep, until his back starts hurting again.

I look into the bottle again. Still plenty of them in there. He wouldn't notice a couple of them missing.

I shouldn't do it. But I do it anyway. I slip the extra two pills into my pocket.

I feel my ears burning when I walk back down the stairs and hand Enrique his pill. "Here you go, dude."

Jim is ready at the table for them to eat. I look at them, then down at the floor. "Um, okay," I say. "Enjoy the food. Have a good night. Feel better, Que."

I'm a goddamned thief. But I'm excited to have these tucked away in my pocket. I'll hold off on using them, unless I really need to. But I'm glad to know they're here.

In the meantime, I need something to settle my mind, so I pop open a beer when I get back, and sit down to dinner with Laura and the kid.

"They said thank you again," I tell her. "I don't think they've had food this good since they moved out from their parents' houses. It's really nice of you."

"Well, I'm glad to help," she says, putting some food on Timothy's plate.

I dig in. "You know, this is really good. You're a great cook. Thank you."

She smiles so sweetly at me, it almost hurts to see it. I don't deserve her. She doesn't deserve all the trouble I've been causing.

I'm already finished with my beer, so I go get another.

Michael's

It is anguishing to watch him try to hide his despair. His restful nights have come to an end. Every night for the past week his mind has been buzzing with dreadful images which surface the moment he manages to drift off to sleep. The marijuana had already begun to lose its effectiveness in preventing the dreams, and Michael was having to consume more in order to keep the nightmares in check. But the total lack of the substance since his friend's injury has been devastating to my dearest one's psyche.

He finds himself in a horrible cycle of repeatedly waking up in a panic from dreams which depict the gruesome deaths of his loved ones. He can doze for no more than a few minutes at a time before it happens again. He disturbs his wife repeatedly every night.

She is particularly upset that she is losing sleep tonight, because she is in the midst of her working weekend. She spent the entire day Saturday at work, with Timothy coming again with her to the salon because Michael was at work on his ship. In the morning she will work again, but since Michael will be home, Timothy can stay with him. However, Laura is dismayed knowing how exhausted she will be at work without having gotten sufficient rest.

This night is particularly trying. Despite having consumed numerous alcoholic beverages, rest eludes him. Finally, after jolting awake for the fourth or fifth time, sweating and gasping, Michael gets up to go to the bathroom. It is nearly four o'clock in the morning. This last dream looms before his eyes, a wrenching image of himself wracked with sobs as he clutches the dead body of his wife. He wretchedly wishes that they could both get some rest in the few hours before Laura must arise and prepare to leave for work.

He blearily decides to resort to the use of the pills he had pilfered from his friend's bottle of medication. So desperate is he for relief, he impulsively downs both pills together, swallowing them with a handful of water from the bathroom tap.

In a few minutes, he returns to the bed. Laura has fallen back to sleep, and her quiet breathing soothes him as he lies beside her, trying to forget the vision of her mangled corpse which dominated his most recent dream. As the medication dissolves and enters his bloodstream, it assists him in falling to sleep.

It is a blessed, dreamless, sound sleep.

They both finally are able to rest, deeply, peacefully. It is the most restorative sleep they have had in days.

Chapter 51

Go To Him

Timothy

It's finally Sunday. I'm so excited that Natalie is getting home this afternoon. I don't think I'll probably be able to see her today, but I know when we get back to school tomorrow she'll be there.

Mom got up and went to work with Dad still sleeping again. Same as last weekend. Hopefully he won't be yelling from bad dreams this time. I've heard it happen a couple of times in the middle of the night this week. I'm sorry he's having nightmares. I'd talk to Natalie about it if she was here. I wonder if Angel can tell us anything about how dreams work. Is there some experiment we can do to help?

I'll have to think about that.

For now, though, I'm really happy with everything I've done on the bible locations project. I've got pages and pages of notes, and I've marked up a map, and made a big chart full of information about archeological sites in Israel. This is really interesting, and I'm excited to show everything to Natalie. I wonder when is the next time she'll be able to come over here.

I hadn't thought about today being Easter until Mom gave me this Easter basket before she left for work. I'm glad she did. I'm munching on jelly beans while I review my notes.

Michael's

I worriedly watch my beloved slumber. His plan to use the pills to achieve sleep was far more successful than he anticipated. His wife, relieved that he has finally managed to get some rest, silently departed for work, happy to see him sleeping so soundly.

However, his body is reacting to the unfamiliar substance by more than simply peaceful sleep. His respiratory system appears to be suppressed by the chemicals in his bloodstream. His breathing is unusually slow and shallow. His wife perceived this as her husband finally getting the quiet rest he needs. But I can see that his breathing and heart rate are both becoming slower as time goes by. He craved this sleep, but I fear it is at the expense of his health.

I fervently hope that he will soon wake. Perhaps once he arises and moves about, possibly ingests some nutrients, his systems will return to normal.

As the minutes go by, however, my hope dims. He shows no signs of consciousness. In fact, his respiration has further slowed.

"My darling," I whisper to him, trying to rouse him, *"you should awaken. Your son is here, you should arise and spend time with him."*

Nothing changes. His breathing slows further, and my alarm increases. His respiration has actually become dangerously low.

"Beloved, awaken!"

Nothing. More time passes. Timothy is in his room, intently studying his maps. Michael takes a shallow breath, then pauses for several seconds before taking another.

"My dearest! Please! Arise!"

I frantically move as close as I can to him, appealing to his subconscious, trying to jolt him awake. Nothing I can do penetrates the deep torpor in which he slumbers.

"Michael! Wake up!"

Another brief breath, another long pause. The dangerous reality becomes clear to me. His life is at risk.

I don't know what else I can do to help him. It appears that his respiration has nearly ceased entirely. I fear this lifetime will draw to a close, our time together will end, I will find myself collecting his beautiful soul, and leaving him behind, this existence relegated to memory. I do not wish for this to happen.

Michael is young, and strong, and vigorous, and it has been a remarkable privilege to observe his son's relationship with the Seer. I want more time with him. I do not want this lifetime to be over.

I helplessly grieve the inevitability of the end.

Another inhalation, very brief and shallow, followed by another pause of several seconds.

No!

Timothy sits obliviously in his room, mere feet away from the unfolding tragedy. His Guardian watches, full of sympathy for my plight.

That is the answer, I realize. I have observed as Timothy's Guardian communicates with him, and as the Guardians around the Seer speak with each other. Guardians need not always be utterly helpless to affect the lives of their Guarded. I have learned this by watching the Seer's group.

I have never before tried to converse directly with another Guardian, as I have seen them do with each other. But I am filled with desperation and now, suddenly, hope. Perhaps there is a way.

"Guardian!" I implore Timothy's Guardian, using the name which the child has given him. I scarcely notice how bizarre it is to be speaking to another Guardian, so dire is the situation. *"Please, can you help? If only Timothy can awaken his father, perhaps he can be saved!"*

Timothy

I wonder where I can get a more detailed map of Israel. I'll bet the library has maps. Or maybe I'd have to buy one? Do bookstores have maps? Maybe I can...

"Timothy!"

It startles me so much that I drop the book on the floor. I've never heard Guardian so loud, so clear, except when I am mostly asleep, practically dreaming.

I'm not afraid, but I'm very surprised. Why is this happening? What is he doing? I quickly remember to open my mind up, trying very hard to concentrate only on Guardian, to hear what he wants.

It works.

"Go to your father! Now!"

I don't stop to ask why. I know that when I hear him first thing in the morning, there isn't time to waste, so I need to use whatever seconds I have to communicate. I still don't know why all of the sudden I can hear Guardian, sounding so urgent, but I don't spend time to wonder about it. I'm already out the door of my room, running down the hall.

I'm trying to keep my mind as open as I can while I'm doing this. I usually am sitting quietly when I'm trying to hear Guardian, but obviously that isn't possible now. Guardian is in a huge hurry to get me to Dad. So I'm in a hurry too.

I burst into his room, and see him lying in bed, on his back, sound asleep. I hesitate. There doesn't seem to be anything wrong. Why is Guardian so frantic? I can feel him, almost panicking, at the edge of my mind.

"Go to him!" He must be using a ton of energy to talk to me so clearly while I'm awake.

I go over there, and stand right next to the bed, looking at Dad closely. I realize that even though he just looks like he's asleep, he isn't moving at all, not snoring or even breathing as far as I can tell.

Then Guardian's panic hits me, floods over me like a tidal wave. I understand now why Guardian is yelling at me. Dad's not breathing!

Guardian pushes me forward.

I shake his shoulder. "Dad!" I yell at him.

He takes in a short breath. I'm so relieved. But then, he doesn't seem to keep breathing. Why isn't he breathing? I don't know what is wrong, but I know, I can tell from what I am feeling from Guardian, that everything depends on me waking Dad up.

I actually get up on the bed with him, lean over him, stare right into his face.

"Dad!" I scream at him, louder than I have screamed since I was a toddler having a tantrum. I think he takes another tiny breath in, then is completely still again.

"Wake up!" I shriek, and I start to shake him as hard as I can, my hands on his big shoulders, frantically pulling him up and down.

Guardian is there with me, helping me. I can feel him. I can tell he's using more energy than ever before. I don't hear words any more, I think because I'm doing exactly what he wants me to do. But he feels so real to me in this moment. We are both here, working together to get Dad awake, make him start breathing.

I feel even more energy, flowing all around, the most I've ever felt.

I lean around Dad, to push him up from behind, thinking that if he isn't laying flat on his back it might help. He's so heavy. I'm barely able to lift him up a little, and I cram the pillow from Mom's side of the bed back there behind him to keep him up.

His head rolls backwards. I grab his head on both sides, and pull it back up. I keep my hands on the sides of his face and shake him some more, still yelling. "Wake up!"

His head lolls there, heavy in my hands, and his eyes stay closed. He still doesn't seem to be breathing. I'm really panicking now. Nothing is working. It's too late to call 911, by the time an ambulance got here it would be too much time without breathing. Nobody can survive without breathing. It's up to me to help him, but I can't figure out how.

What else can I do? Suddenly I remember the last time I felt this way, terrified and desperate, when Jonathan was attacking Natalie on the jungle gym. So I do what I did then. I reach out with my mind, seeking, grabbing, trying to connect to Dad's mind. He's in there, sleeping. If I can't wake him up from the outside, maybe I can do it from the inside. I feel Guardian's energy filling me up, helping me reach. Then I think I feel the connection, a sense of Dad, together with the connection I feel with Guardian. "Wake up!" I scream again, both with my mouth and with my mind.

Finally, he inhales more sharply, and I feel him move his head away from me. I'm about an inch away from his face when he opens his eyes.

Chapter 52

Changing Fate

Timothy's

Together, my beloved and I, along with Michael's Guardian, have managed to stave off the unconsciousness which was threatening his father's life.

We are filled with a heady sense of success. This is incredible, unheard of. Guardians have saved a life.

Guardians watch, and whisper, and wait. When the life ends, it ends, and the Guardian reunites with the soul, to be enveloped back into the multitude of other Guardians waiting between lives. It is not for a Guardian to change the fate of their Guarded.

But we have done this. Using the methods taught to us by my beloved, inspired by the influence of the Seer, we have succeeded in changing fate. We have acquired the knowledge which allowed us to save the life of my dearest one's father.

It was the supplication of his Guardian which propelled me into action. I had been sadly contemplating the grief which Timothy would feel, the inevitable changes coming in his life, after his father drew his last breath. But then, his Guardian took the initiative to speak directly to me, shocking me into the realization that we need not passively await the end. We had the tools at hand to make an actual difference in the outcome of the event.

As we had been training for many months, I was able to contact my beloved, make him hear my message, help him understand what was needed. He reacted immediately, performing exactly the actions necessary to restore his father to consciousness.

It is startling how effectively he used the technique to reach his father's mind, to nudge him awake from within. I do not fully understand exactly what happened. I hope that soon we will be able to discuss this event with Angel and the Seer, analyzing and learning together as we have done in the past.

Another miracle appears to have occurred. Together I hope we can gain understanding.

Michael's

When Michael awakens, he is deeply bewildered. Not only is his normally distant son for some reason invading his space, but he feels light-headed, weak, breathless.

Timothy gasps, so close to his father that their faces are almost touching. "Dad?"

Michael wavers blurrily on the edge of consciousness. He leans his head back a bit further from his son, trying to focus on him. Then a wave of vertigo hits him and he slumps back down against the pillows propped uncomfortably behind him, closing his eyes again.

"No, no, no," Timothy says, "come on Dad, you have to stay awake."

Michael takes several deep breaths, and this seems to steady him. "What're you doing?" he asks Timothy, his voice husky and weak.

Timothy is flooded with relief. His efforts appear to be working. However, he does not wish his father to be irate with him. Furthermore, he does not know how much he should tell Michael about what just happened. Should he call for help? Will his father be all right now? He waits to see if he can hear any suggestions from his Guardian, who attempts to convey that his priority should be to get his father up and moving, to prevent him from falling back into sleep. I sense that if only Michael stays awake, the effects of the drug will fade and he will be restored.

While Timothy pauses, trying to determine what step should be taken next, Michael struggles to sit up. He notices the strange placement of the pillows and pushes them to the side, wondering how that happened. Now that he is upright, his head begins to clear. He looks at Timothy, trying to figure out what is happening.

"Um," Timothy says, trying to find an excuse for his behavior without alarming his father. "I'm, uh, hungry. Mom said I could wake you up if I needed anything."

Michael closes his eyes but raises his eyebrows, slightly shaking his head. "Oh." He takes another few deep breaths. "All right. Give me a minute."

Timothy fears that his father will lay back down again, so he does not leave the room. After a brief silence, he prompts, "Can you make me something to eat now?"

Michael opens his eyes and studies the boy. He knows something odd is happening with the child, that his son's behavior is even stranger than usual, but he doesn't feel awake enough to figure it out. Simpler to fulfill the request. "Yeah. Okay. Let's go."

He swings his legs over the side of the bed, and shakily stands. Timothy watches carefully, and is greatly relieved when Michael yawns, stretches, and proceeds to go downstairs.

I regard Timothy's Guardian. I am flooded with a powerful gratitude. *"Thank you, Guardian,"* I tell him. *"Thank you, to both you and to Timothy. I will never forget what you have done this day."*

Chapter 53

She Did This

Natalie's

The family has experienced a remarkable week. So many significant events have taken place. All of them the direct consequence of decisions made by my beloved Seer.

Her parents are remarried, filled with bliss and joy and love. She did this. It was she who set their reconciliation in motion, over a year ago, when she orchestrated their Christmas Eve celebration.

Her grandfather's situation is notably improved. She did this. She had scarcely known of his existence before this week, but during the last several days he has become another critically important member of her inner circle. Her determination to help him has been as firm as her commitment to the Jonathan Project. Her focus was staggering. She managed to convince her parents to visit Grandfather each day, and she spent each visit maximizing her physical contact with him, scrutinizing his reactions and his health. I was tasked to intensively monitor each aspect of his being, and report everything to her. Her touch continuously brought healing to every part of his consciousness.

The improvement has been remarkable. His soul glows more robustly, and his mind thinks more clearly. His emotional state has transitioned dramatically, as his isolation was replaced with inclusion. Even the physical tremor has improved, becoming significantly less noticeable. It grows increasingly clear how much the Seer's touch can impact the well-being of a person who needs it. Nearly every aspect of her grandfather's life has been rehabilitated.

Theodore's relationship with his son has also been repaired. He had nearly forgotten the argument with Ron so many years ago, which caused their rift, but began to recall it as his ability to remember was healed. Finally realizing his part in the estrangement, he was able to draw Ron aside two days ago, sincerely apologize for the cruel things he had said, and win Ron's forgiveness. It is not only Theodore himself who has been healed. The Seer's father feels an immense relief, and the lifting of a burden of guilt and grief which he had not even realized he was carrying.

Ron and Brenda have arranged for the hire of caretakers to tend to the home and yard, which will improve the physical living situation of Theodore. He even has become reacquainted with Brenda's parents, when Natalie managed to convince him to join them all for dinner yesterday evening. Margaret and Frank have committed to remaining in contact with him, ensuring that his loneliness will not be as acute.

The Seer has transformed the life of this broken being who she now fiercely loves as much as any other member of her family.

Her brother has also experienced a transformation, in his perception of his little sister. Gabe's awareness of her unusual abilities has grown, starting with her surprising capacity to see in dim light. However, it was when he volunteered to take notes for her, after their first visit to their grandfather, that he truly began to realize the extent of her talents. Being more directly involved in our conversation made him see more clearly what she is capable of. With the Jonathan Project, he always felt himself to be more of a bystander, viewing the experiments conducted by Timothy from the outside. Now, he is invested as a fully participating member of this effort. He has become equally focused on his grandfather's progress, contributing comments and making suggestions as the endeavor unfolded. In the process, his admiration for the Seer has blossomed. He sees anew how her formidable awareness of the world guides her unerringly towards the achievement of remarkable goals. He wants to help her, and support her in whatever she pursues. He is determined to follow where she leads. He feels love as her brother, but even more begins to feel adoration as her acolyte.

She did this as well.

Natalie

We had a fun morning. Grandma had us do a big Easter egg hunt, and we found goodies all over the house and yard. So much chocolate and stuff. I think Gabe ate almost everything already.

Then it was time to go to the airport and board the plane. I was sorry we didn't have time to go to church with Grandma and Grandpa. I would have liked to talk to the pastor again. Although with my luck, I suppose I would have been left behind and I wouldn't be sitting on this plane flying back home with my family.

I think about the last flight, where I was tracking whether the Guardians can hear each other, but I don't need to continue with Timothy's experiment today. It already worked.

I am going to have so much to tell Timothy. I can hardly wait to see him. I don't think I'll get the chance today, though. My parents are probably going to want to go straight home.

Well, at least Gabe and I should be able to go see Jonathan. I'll see Timothy tomorrow at school.

It makes me sad to have to wait, though. I really miss him, and want to talk to him. Angel has told me all about the archeology project he's been working on, with maps and a bible and everything. It sounds really interesting and I'm eager to hear everything he will have to explain.

"Darling, there is actually news about Timothy. Guardian has shared with me an event which took place this morning, which we feel you should know about."

Well, that doesn't sound good. "What's wrong?" I think to him, suddenly filled with worry.

"Do not be alarmed, Timothy is quite well, as is his father. However, his father had an earlier incident which threatened his health."

There's no use asking him what's wrong again. I have to wait for him to tell me. Gabe is in the seat next to me, playing his Gameboy, but I'll bet he figures out pretty soon that Angel is telling me something important. He has really started to notice, and to ask whenever it happens. He wants to be part of everything too. It feels good to have my brother sharing it all. Even if he doesn't notice and ask, I'll tell him everything Angel says, after I figure out what's going on.

I listen as Angel continues. *"Timothy's father had taken some medication last night which caused him to sleep so deeply that his breathing became too slow. His mother was at work, so Timothy was alone in the house with him. His father's Guardian asked Timothy's Guardian to help him. Guardian alerted Timothy that his father needed help, and Timothy was able to awaken him. He has revived and is apparently unharmed. However, Timothy very much wants to talk to you about this, so I can explain to him more about what happened, and what Guardian experienced. He wishes that he could see you this afternoon, rather than having to wait until tomorrow morning at school."*

Oh.

I sit still, stunned. I wasn't expecting this, that's for sure. Poor Timothy! It must have been really scary for him, especially without being able to ask Angel what is going on.

As I expected, Gabe has stopped playing his game and is staring at me, waiting for me to finish listening to Angel. "Okay, what is it?" he asks me.

I tell him what Angel said. His reaction is the same as mine.

"Oh," he says. We look at each other. I'm trying to think of what to do next.

"You'll have to go see Timothy today," Gabe says quietly. "Think Mom and Dad will take you there when we get home?"

Brenda

Ron and I are each reading our own books, but I'm making sure our arms are touching on the armrest. I can't seem to stop wanting to touch him. You'd think I'd have gotten enough after the week we spent at the hotel going at it like horny teenagers. I sputter out a laugh at that image.

Ron notices, and looks up from his book, meeting my eyes inquiringly. I'm about to tell him the phrase my brain cooked up to describe us, but suddenly Natalie's head pops up over the seat back in front of us.

"Yeeeees?" Ron asks her.

"Will we have enough time to go see Timothy when we get home?"

He looks over at me. "Well, I wasn't really planning on it," I say. "It'll be afternoon by the time we land and get our luggage and everything. Then we have to get home and unpack and get ready for the week to start."

"But that's not very late, is it?" she asks. "There's still time for a visit, right?"

"Well, can't you wait until tomorrow?" Ron asks her. "You'll see him at school."

"Please?" she asks, her little forehead wrinkling with adorable concern. "I really really really want to see Timothy. It's been a whole week! I have so much to tell him. And I want to know all about what he's been doing. And I have to give him back his watch! Please?"

There's a moment of silence while Ron and I look at each other and try to decide whether it makes sense to try to add something else to our afternoon.

Gabe's head pops up to join Natalie's. "We can fit in a visit, can't we?" he contributes to the conversation. "I'll bet Timothy is dying to see Natalie too. He's probably been awfully lonely this week without her."

We have to laugh. We can't fight both of them.

"Actually," I add, "I wouldn't mind seeing Laura, and catching her up on everything."

"Okay, sure," Ron says. "I'll call over there after we land to see if it would be all right to have a short visit on our way back from the airport."

The kids smile at each other, and Natalie plunks back down into her seat.

Gabe lingers a moment. Ron says, again, "Yeeeeees?"

"Do you have any snacks?"

Chapter 54
Step By Step

Timothy

After Dad makes me some toast, which I eat even though I'm not actually hungry, I have to think of something else to do. I don't understand what happened, and I don't think I should leave him alone. If I go back in my room, he might lie down and fall asleep again, and I think that might not be safe. I won't know until I can talk to Natalie and Angel.

I asked Guardian to tell Angel that I'd really like Natalie to come by for a visit so I can get an explanation of what just happened. I don't know whether she will, though.

Until then, I have to come up with a plan.

Dad is sitting at the table with me, having some toast too. He still looks super tired and groggy. He hasn't even changed yet. He is still only wearing pajama bottoms with no shirt.

I have an idea.

"Dad?"

"Mm-hmm?"

"Can we go to the park?"

He looks at me like that is the strangest thing he's ever heard.

"What?"

"Can we go to the park?"

"You want to go to the park?"

I understand why he's confused. I have never asked for him to take me to the park. I've never had any interest in it. But I think it would be a good idea to move around, be outside in the fresh air. It would probably help him get over whatever his problem was.

"Um..."

"Please?" I ask. "We can walk there, right? It's not very far. Don't you think it would be nice to take a walk?"

He's looking at me like he's wondering who I am and what happened to Timothy.

"Um, yeah, I guess."

"Thank you," I tell him. "You should get dressed."

I'm sure he's going to get tired of me bossing him around, but I don't feel like I can stop until after I find out the details of what his problem was.

He shakes his head but shrugs. "Okay. Let's get ready to go, then."

Michael

I genuinely have no idea what is happening. This whole morning has been bizarre. I had a horrible night, and only managed to fall asleep when I took those pills I swiped from Enrique. They worked great, I didn't have any more dreams or hear anything else. Until all of the sudden there was Timothy right in my face telling me he is hungry.

And I realize that I feel awful, like the worst hangover ever. When I woke up I was so groggy I could barely see straight. I feel more exhausted than ever, even though I know that I did get some sleep after I took those pills. I have a headache and feel kind of queasy, although the toast seems to have helped.

And now Timothy wants to go to the park? Has he been abducted by aliens and replaced by a pod person? He never wants to go to the park.

But, he claims he really wants to, and honestly, sitting around inside does not seem likely to help me feel any better. Maybe a walk in the sunshine would actually help.

So, fine.

I go get dressed, and in a few minutes we are walking down the street to the park. I'm already feeling my head start to clear. This was actually a great idea. I'm glad we're doing this, although I still have absolutely no idea what caused him to suggest it.

Timothy walks silently along by my side, glancing up at me several times.

When we get there, I'm surprised to see there are only a couple of other kids on the playground. It's the weekend, you'd think there'd be more people here. Then I realize, oh, it's Easter, isn't it? I suppose most people are at church or something.

"So," I ask him, "did you want to swing or something?"

He looks surprised, like he's suddenly on the spot. What the heck. He's the one who wanted to come here, doesn't he want to play?

"Um," he says, looking around the playground like he's trying to find something fun to do. He focuses on the jungle gym, a big metal dome made out of bars. "I know," he says, then looks up at me. "Dad, do you see the jungle gym?"

I look over at it. "Yeah."

"Can you, maybe, teach me how to climb it?"

"What?" What kid doesn't know how to climb a jungle gym?

"I tried to at school, the day Gabe and Jonathan got hurt. Do you remember that? But I couldn't figure out how to get up there. I think I'm not very coordinated. Maybe if I was better at it, I could have helped and they might not have fallen. Can you help me learn what to do?"

Uh, okay. It's interesting that he's approaching this so analytically. I guess it makes sense that he might need help figuring it out - he's never really played outside, or done sports or anything. "Well," I tell him, "I guess that's what fathers are for. To help you with this kind of thing. Sure, let's give it a go."

He nods, and looks like he's both relieved and nervous. Awww. The kid is nervous about it. I guess it isn't instinctive for him. I can help him. We can do it step by step.

"Okay, start by holding your hand on the bar here, right above your head," I tell him. He reaches up, apparently taking this very seriously. "Like that, right. Now you want to take your foot and put it on the lowest bar."

Chapter 55

Together

Laura

Driving home from work, I wonder if they've had lunch yet. Probably not, it isn't that late. If they haven't, I think I'll make us all some sandwiches.

I'm almost past them when I see them walking along the sidewalk together. I'm totally surprised, and manage to quickly stop and pull over to the curb.

What on Earth?

They hurry over to the car, and Mike opens the front door and leans his head into the passenger side. "Mind picking up a couple of hitchhikers?" he asks me, with a big grin on his face. I look behind him and see Timothy wearing a matching grin.

I feel like I'm hallucinating, and I'm not even the one who's been doing drugs. This might be the strangest thing I've ever seen. I like it, though.

"Sure, get in!"

I wait for them to get buckled before I pull away from the curb. They both seem energetic and happy, so I know nothing is wrong, but I still am baffled about what they are doing out here.

"Sooo....." I start to ask.

"Timothy wanted to go to the park," Mike tells me. "We've been there all morning."

Really?

"Really?"

Timothy is the one who wanted to go? I can't believe that's true, but sure enough he pipes up with, "Yeah! I asked Dad to teach me how to climb the jungle gym, and I'm totally able to do it now!"

"Well, that's awesome, sweetie!" I smile sideways at Mike. I'm not sure I remember him ever having an outing like this with Timothy before.

I'm very touched by this. I love them both so much, but it has always been like I have one on either side of me, having to love them separately, but never together. Today they are together, for the first time. Emotion wells up in me and I have to brush my tears away with the back of my hand, or I won't be able to see the road while I finish driving home.

Mike is looking at me, and I think he's surprised by how much this clearly means to me. The realization is dawning in his face, but he doesn't say anything. I think he's trying to process it himself.

When we open the door to the house, the phone is ringing. I hurry straight over there to grab it. "Hello?"

"Hi, it's Ron." Oh!

"Ron! How are you? Are you all home?" Timothy looks at me eagerly when he hears me ask the question. I know how much he's been missing Natalie.

"Not yet, our plane just landed, and we still have to go through baggage claim after we get off." Timothy comes closer to me so he can lean in and hear what Ron is saying. "Listen, the kids are wondering if we can swing by to say hi on the way home? Natalie is apparently dying to catch up with Timothy."

"Yes!" Timothy blurts out.

I hear Ron laughing. "So it's okay if we stop by in a while?"

"Of course, it would be lovely to see you all, and hear about your trip. Have you had lunch yet?"

"Not yet, we haven't thought that far ahead."

"Well, head straight here," I tell him. "I'm about to make some sandwiches, so we can all eat together."

"Perfect," he replies. "I figure it'll take about an hour to do everything and get over there."

"Okay, see you soon." I hang up and the expression on Timothy's face is priceless. He acts like this visit is the one thing he has been hoping for, like it holds the key to life itself.

I laugh and give him a hug. "There you go, kid, you get to see your friend. Why don't you go wash up while I'm making lunch."

He runs up the stairs, and Mike comes over to take his place in the hugging zone. He lifts my purse off my shoulder, sets it down, and wraps his arms around me. So gently. I'm startled by a new wave of emotion that engulfs me.

He leans back to look down at me when he feels me give a little sob. He looks dismayed to see me fighting back tears. "What's wrong?" he says, alarmed.

"Nothing. Everything is perfect. I'm just really happy about you and Timothy having a nice time together."

He enfolds me in his arms again, wrapping one hand around my head and holding me to his shoulder. I take in a deep breath to calm myself, and we stand together in silence for a couple of minutes. Mmmmm. This feels so nice.

I lift my head and look up at him. I don't know what has brought on all of this tenderness, but it's wonderful. It's been a really long time since we were this way with each other. He leans down and kisses me softly, before we finally move apart, reluctantly, but I have things to do.

"So tell me about the park," I tell him, moving into the kitchen to wash my hands and start getting lunch put together. "What on earth brought that on?"

"I don't know. It's been a strange morning. Timothy woke me up to make him breakfast, then out of the blue he asked to take a walk to the park. I was feeling a little off, so I thought being outside for a while sounded good. When we got over there, he asked me to help him climb the jungle gym. I guess he's never understood how to do it before, and it's been bothering him this whole time since his friends fell off of one and got hurt."

"Wow."

"Yeah. We ended up really enjoying ourselves. He had such a hard time with it at first. He's not very coordinated, you know." I chuckle and nod. I know. He goes on, "But he was determined, and he tried over and over again until he finally felt comfortable going up and down on his own. It made us both feel really good to tackle it together."

He is quiet for a moment. "I'd kind of given up on being able to do stuff together with him. He and I are very ... different. This was sort of the first time I really felt like I was doing a decent job as a father."

I'm listening with amazement, as I get out a whole bunch of bread and sandwich meat and stuff. "I'm really glad, honey."

For the first time since Timothy's autism diagnosis a year ago, I am starting to feel hope that maybe Michael and he can manage to have a good relationship. They'd always had problems relating to each other, and the whole special ed thing had kind of made Mike give up on even trying. It's like he had no idea how to approach Timothy after that. But now, maybe things can change. Timothy has grown a lot, I think that helps. And Michael has struggles of his own. Maybe they can help each other.

Brenda

Natalie goes tearing down the walk the second we get out of the car, and Gabe follows on her heels. Ron and I look at each other and laugh, and follow along behind at a more dignified pace, holding hands.

By the time we walk up to Laura's house, the kids have vanished upstairs with Timothy. Of course.

Laura meets us at the door, her hands clasped together in delight. "Here they are!" she says.

Michael, much to my surprise, starts humming the wedding march as we enter the house. "Dum, dum-duh-duh!" he sings. Ha! He's not usually such a comedian.

Ron grins while we enter. "Thanks for having this old married couple over," he jokes.

"Congratulations," Laura says, beaming. "I want to hear everything!"

I see that she has the meal ready on the table, but the kids are upstairs and nobody seems to be in a hurry to eat, so we sit down for a nice chat before lunch.

I look over to Ron, and nod to indicate that he should start telling the tale. I want to hear it from his perspective. He holds my hand and begins. "Well, Brenda's Mom started the festivities by kicking me out of her house!" I laugh, eager to hear how he tells it all.

Chapter 56

I Have A Plan

Natalie

Angel tells me the grownups are downstairs talking about the wedding, so we probably have a few minutes at least to talk. I have a lot to tell Timothy, but it will have to wait. The most important thing is to talk about what happened with his Dad. That's where we have to start.

"Okay, Timothy, tell us what happened," I tell him. "I think you should go first, then we can find out from Angel what Guardian says too. We'll figure everything out."

He looks so relieved to see me, and to have us here talking to him.

"Well," he says, "this morning Mom left to go to work while Dad was still asleep. The same thing happened last weekend too. I told her it was fine, I can get my own breakfast and take care of myself. She told me I could wake him up if I needed anything. I didn't plan to bother him, but all of the sudden I could hear Guardian yelling at me to go in there."

I already have a lot of questions, but I don't want to interrupt him. I know Angel is keeping track of everything, and will be telling us more details from Guardian. So I just nod.

"When I got in his room, he was asleep, and nothing looked like it was wrong at first. But I could tell Guardian was super worried, so I went closer, and I realized that he was hardly breathing. So I tried to wake him up. I yelled and shook him, but nothing was working. I was starting to panic."

I reach out and hold Timothy's hand. I feel so bad that he went through this alone.

Angel whispers to me, *"He wasn't alone, darling. Guardian was with him, helping him the whole time."*

Yeah, that's true. It makes me feel better. At least he had that.

"Anyway, all of the sudden I remembered what happened on the jungle gym with Jonathan. The way I grabbed his mind to make him stop pushing you. So I tried that, to grab my Dad's mind to wake him up. It seemed to work, he woke up and was breathing okay again. But he was still super tired, and I didn't want him to go to sleep again. So I told him I was hungry, even though I wasn't, so he'd get out of bed to make some food. Then when we were done eating, he still seemed really tired, and I thought taking a walk outside would help. So I asked him to take me to the park. I wanted to keep him awake and busy until I could talk to you guys and find out what was really happening."

Wow, that's a lot.

He's not quite done. He surprises me by getting a big smile on his face. "While we were at the park, he taught me how to climb up the jungle gym!"

Gabe grins. "Really? Way to go, Timothy!"

"That is great," I tell him. "I'm glad you had a nice time at the park, and that your Dad seems to be feeling fine now. But do you have any idea what was wrong? Why wasn't he breathing?"

"I don't know," he says. "That's why I needed to talk to you guys. Guardian must know what happened."

I look over at Angel.

"Yes, Guardian has filled me in on many of the details about what occurred."

I get ready to start repeating everything to Timothy and Gabe. Nobody is taking notes this time, but I don't think we should take the time to do that right now. Our parents are going to make us come downstairs for lunch pretty soon. Angel nods, to let me know that's right.

"The problem seemed to have started when Timothy's father was trying to find a way to stop having nightmares, which have been troubling him and preventing him from sleeping well."

When I repeat that, Timothy says, "Yeah, I knew he was having nightmares. Last weekend when Mom was at work and Dad was asleep, he scared me half to death by yelling in his sleep. He said he had a bad dream. I've heard him yelling in the middle of the night a few times, too."

Gabe nods sympathetically. I think he has bad dreams sometimes. Funny, I don't remember ever being bothered by my dreams. It's sad to think of Timothy's Dad having nightmares. I wonder why. I wonder if there's any way to make it stop.

"This is also what he was wondering, how to make it stop. It was having a very bad effect on his health, by preventing him from getting enough rest at night. Timothy's mother was also harmed, because every time his father woke up from a nightmare, it woke her up too. They were both very tired and upset by the situation."

Timothy looks surprised and sad when I repeat this. I don't think he had realized how bad it was getting, not only for his Dad, but for his Mom too.

Angel hesitates a moment, and I can tell he's doing the thing where he doesn't want to tell me something. I would normally be annoyed by that, but we don't have time to argue about it, and I also think maybe he is trying to avoid saying anything that would upset Timothy. "Fine, keep your secrets," I think to him. He gives a wry smile and a shrug. He knows I know what he's doing.

"Timothy's father tried to find remedies to solve the problem. For instance, sometimes he found that drinking alcohol would help him sleep better. But last night he was so troubled by the dreams that he tried to take a new type of medication. Guardian believes he took too much, which is why he fell into such a deep sleep that he almost stopped breathing."

"Is he okay now?" Timothy asks. "I wasn't sure if I should call 911 or something, but after he woke up I tried to keep him busy enough to stay awake. I hope I didn't do something wrong." He's been so worried about this, I can tell.

"He is well. Timothy's actions in keeping him busy, and especially going outside in the fresh air, helped his body process the medication in his system better, so it is no longer interfering with his functioning. He feels much better. Tell Timothy that he did everything correctly."

I smile and tell all of that to Timothy, and he whoofs with relief.

Gabe says, "Well, there is something I really don't understand. What is this about grabbing minds? I remember you said something about that after the whole Jonathan thing, but I never figured out what you meant. Then you did it again with your Dad? What does that even mean?"

Timothy takes a breath in to start to answer, but he's interrupted. His Mom calls up the stairs, "Kids! Come on down for lunch!"

Gabe jumps up, then holds up a finger to Timothy. "Hold that thought!"

Natalie's

While we are proceeding down the stairs, she silently asks me, "Do you think it would help if I touched Timothy's Dad? It helped so much with Grandfather, could it help him?"

"I believe it may, my dear. Timothy's father has been experiencing much mental distress, initially linked to his service on his ship during the recent military conflict. This is what led to his nightmares, and it continues to trouble him. Your touch seems to be able to remedy mental and emotional afflictions. It could very well assist him."

She nods, resolved. Gabe notices, and realizes that we have continued discussing the issue, but he cannot ask about it as we have arrived in the room with the adults.

Their parents are already gathered around the dining table, eating lunch. "Come and get some food, kids," Laura tells them. "You can take it over and eat on the coffee table."

Gabe of course, always ravenous with his pre-adolescent metabolism, immediately complies. Timothy considers the selection of foods and places a few items on his plate. Natalie, however, first approaches Michael.

She reaches out, placing her hand on his shoulder as she stands next to him. He looks at her with some surprise, still chewing a bite of sandwich which is in his mouth. He swallows quickly.

"Well?" she asks me silently.

"Yes, it has an effect. His soul flares slightly, indicating that there is damage which your touch can heal. He also feels a slightly increased sense of well-being."

She smiles at him. "Timothy told us that you helped him learn how to climb a jungle gym. I know it has bothered him that he can't do it. Thank you for helping him."

Gabe and Timothy stare over from the coffee table a few feet away. They see exactly what is happening.

"Oh, sure!" he replies, not expecting this thanks from Timothy's friend. "That's what Dads are for, right?"

She nods, snuggles a little closer to him to give him a brief hug, then joins the other children.

Gabe looks at her questioningly, significantly. She nods affirmation.

She whispers to Timothy, "It helped. I want to try it some more before we go home. I have a plan." Gabe leans his head in so he can participate.

Chapter 57

Healing

Michael's

It is extraordinary to behold. I have seen Timothy and the Seer operate in the past, of course, utilizing their unique gifts, as they conduct experiments and explore their world. But to hear them converse about the specific needs of my own beloved, guided and assisted by the Seer's Guardian, is fantastical.

And now, when the Seer lays her hand upon Michael, there is a flare of warmth, and an almost pleasurable sense of wellness, which even his soul reacts to. I have heard the children discussing what they have called "The Jonathan Project" in which this occurs, but I have rarely witnessed this phenomenon myself. Michael is not frequently in the company of Jonathan. To see this happening to my beloved fills me with an unprecedented joy and hope.

Can this be the solution to his problems? I certainly never want him to experiment with the pilfered medication again, and indeed Michael feels the same. He does not remember any of the drama over his cessation of breathing, but he certainly knows that he felt terribly unwell once he finally woke up, and he realizes this must have been caused by taking those pills. At this point he has no intention of repeating the experience, much to my extreme relief.

If the Seer is able to mend his soul, bring him some peace, might his nightmares fade? Could his ongoing affliction be resolved, so he can stop feeling compelled to self-medicate with chemicals?

He feels better at this moment than he has in quite some time. The last of the medication has finally begun to leave his system. He glows with an unaccustomed warmth caused by the unusual experience at the park, bonding with his son for the first time as together they solved the problem of how to climb the jungle gym. He is enjoying the visit from Ron and Brenda, with their stories of the wedding. The brief touch of the Seer improved his mood even further.

The adults continue to discuss the events of the past week. The Seer's parents are regaling the group with a humorous tale of having left her behind at the church following the wedding. Natalie looks up from the whispered discussion she is having with the boys in the next room, and shakes her head aggrievedly. "Oh good grief, they're still on about that!"

Gabe laughs and pats her head.

Even Timothy is amused by the tale. "I was wondering about that," he quietly says to her, "because Guardian mentioned it while I was waking up the next morning and I wanted to ask you what had happened."

She rolls her eyes. "Okay fine, now you know. I was gabbing so much with the pastor that I didn't realize they were leaving." She peers over at the table, and sees that the adults seem to be nearly finished with their lunch.

"Now, Timothy," she whispers, "before my parents decide it's time to go home!"

Timothy gets up from the coffee table, ready to play his part in the scheme. He approaches his father. "Dad?" he asks.

My beloved looks at him, actually patting him on the back, an unusual show of affection. "Yeah?"

"Um, I'm so excited about being able to climb the jungle gym, I'm wondering if you can come back to the park with us so I can show Gabe and Natalie?"

Michael raises his eyebrows. His son wanting to go to the park twice in one day is certainly not something he ever expected to happen.

Laura seizes the opportunity, and addresses Brenda. "I tell you what. Let's send the guys over there with the kids, so you and I can have some girl talk."

Brenda grins and looks at Ron. "That all right with you, honey?"

He chuckles. "Anything for you, babe. Come on kids. Let's go to the park!"

Ron

It actually feels great to stretch my legs, walking to the park after sitting on the airplane all morning. Those airline seats are not made for someone my height.

We all stroll the couple of blocks to the little park, the kids happily chatting along the way.

Natalie has decided to hold Mike's hand today while we walk along. She always seems to choose someone. It was cute the way she had done that with my Dad all week.

My mind drifts back to the situation with Dad. He seemed so, I don't know, broken, when I saw him the first time. But by the time we said goodbye last night, he was almost back to normal. I think being alone had really taken its toll on him. I'm glad Brenda's parents said they'd check in on him regularly. And also that Brenda suggested setting him up with a housekeeper and gardener. He clearly shouldn't be alone so much. I hope he's okay now that we've left. I plan to give him a call at least weekly. I'm going to make a real effort to keep in touch. Who knows, maybe we can even get him to come out and visit sometime.

I realize we've made it to the park while I was lost in thought.

"Okay, Timothy," Gabe says encouragingly. "Let's see your amazing new climbing superpower!"

We all gather around the jungle gym. Mike stands close by to help, even though Natalie seems determined to keep holding on to his hand.

But, Timothy doesn't seem to need help at all. He looks as focused as an Olympic gymnast approaching the competition area. He methodically places his hands on the bars, then starts making his way up the side, one bar at a time, like he is following a formula. It might not be graceful, but it is effective. At the top he turns around and gives us a smile. And the crowd goes wild! We all applaud his effort.

Gabe immediately clambers up there to join him, but Natalie stays on the ground with Mike and I, content to watch the boys sitting together on the top of the jungle gym. She is beaming.

Michael's

The children know far more than the adults. They know the Seer is engaged in an intense rehabilitative effort on behalf of my beloved. They also know that Timothy saved him earlier this morning.

This latter item, they know only theoretically. Even they do not have a full appreciation of the fact that but for Timothy's actions, his father would have died. The stark possibility of his death is far too abstract for them to actually contemplate. But it is the simple truth. The life of my beloved should have ended today. It was a miracle that Guardian and Timothy and I were able to prevent it.

On the day that so many humans celebrate a story of resurrection on Easter, my beloved was brought back from the brink of death.

And now, I witness what is surely another miracle.

The Seer deliberately maintains physical contact with Michael, as her Guardian provides her constant updates about the progress of the effort.

Michael's perspective is simply that his son's cute little friend has decided to hold his hand, and he finds it sweet and charming. Also, although he does not consider it consciously, he feels increasingly well, happy, strong. His soul, which had diminished in strength over the past several months as his psyche was injured by trauma, now glows with a significantly more vigorous light. The damage which had slowly been depriving his mind and body of good health is being repaired even as I watch. I realize more than ever that the soul and the psyche are linked, and harm to one causes harm to the other. The Seer's touch brings an amazing gift of healing to both.

By the time we conclude the expedition to the park, Michael appears restored. The Seer glows with joy to hear the report from her Guardian that her efforts are successful. My gratitude and exultation are overwhelming. I do not know whether his glowing good health will be permanent, but I see that he is in better condition mentally and emotionally than he has been for a very long time.

First Timothy, and now the Seer, have, in more ways than one, saved my beloved today.

Yes, it is truly a miracle.

Chapter 58

Enough Talking

Laura

B renda and I didn't really have enough time to talk about everything, but it was enough. I heard all the details she didn't want to share in front of the guys and the kids. Sounds like they had a pretty steamy week together. I'm so glad for them. I shared with her some of the problems I've been having with Michael, with his nightmares especially. I didn't tell her about the drug thing going on next door - that's a secret I still feel guilty about keeping, but not something I'm willing to get into now.

When the guys get back from the park with the kids, they are all bursting with energy. The kids launch into a detailed recounting of Timothy's triumphant climb to the top of the jungle gym, as excited for him as though he had just won the Super Bowl. I notice that Natalie is holding Mike's hand, which is awfully cute. Everyone seems so happy.

Eventually, though, they have to go. Ron says, "Look, I hate to be a party pooper, but we really are going to have to get home. We still have to unpack and do laundry and stuff. Back to work and school tomorrow."

The kids all "awwwww" together, but are willing to part when we remind them they will see each other at school first thing in the morning.

Natalie gives Mike one more sweet little hug before letting go of him. She's the most affectionate little thing. And, I know, she has always seemed to have an almost eerie sense of everything that is going on. Who knows, maybe she can sense that he's been having problems lately and she's trying to make him feel better. I wouldn't be surprised, now that I think about it.

By the time they go, it's almost time for dinner. I whip something up, with enough for Jim and Enrique again. I'm starting to feel quite motherly about them. I want to make sure they are eating right.

Mike gets back quickly from dropping it off. "Enrique seems a lot better today," he tells me. "I think he's finally starting to heal."

At dinner, Timothy and Mike have far more to say to each other than usual. They are chatting about the park, the jungle gym, even the map project Timothy has been working on this week. My heart is so full to see them interacting like this with each other.

Before I take Timothy upstairs to help him get ready for bed, he gives his Dad a hug. "Goodnight, Dad," he tells him seriously. "Sleep well."

"Thanks. You too."

After I tuck Timothy in and come back downstairs, I'm surprised to see Mike sitting on the couch, but the t.v. is off. He pats the seat beside him, and I join him there, wondering what this is about.

He reaches his arm around me, and pulls me in to his side. I relax against him, appreciating the affection, and the peace and quiet after our busy afternoon. After a few minutes of silence, he reaches his other hand around and tilts my face up to his. He gives me a tender kiss. I gasp, feeling a flare of passion in response. He hasn't acted this romantic for a long time. I move against him, kissing him harder.

After a few minutes of this, he breaks off. "I want to take you upstairs," he whispers huskily. I nod enthusiastically. "But first, I need to tell you something."

I lean back to look into his eyes. What could he possibly want to discuss right at this moment? "All right," I tell him, slightly out of breath.

"I'm sorry I've been such a pain lately." I start to try to shush him, but he shakes his head. "I have, you know I have. I know it's been bothering you to have me spend so much time next door, especially staying out so late all the time. I'm going to try to cut back on that. And I'm going to lay off on the weed. I was doing it so much because it was helping me sleep, but I think I need to try to sort that out without using it. I'm probably lucky they haven't sprung any surprise drug tests on me at work."

I gaze into his eyes, surprised and moved, and so happy to hear he really does understand. "I know that's what you were doing, honey," I tell him. "I know it was helping you sleep."

"Yeah," he says, "but I think it was working less even though I was using more. I need to cut it out."

"What if you still can't sleep, though?" I ask him.

"You know, I feel a lot better today. Like, my mind is calmer. Maybe getting outside with Timothy really helped. Who knows? Hopefully I can sleep without waking you up tonight." He looks down at me with a glint in his eye. He reaches around me and strokes his hand along my waist. "I have an idea about what might help. Remember what we used to do?"

I smile. "I do indeed." Enough talking. I grab him, holding the back of his neck to pull him to me, almost frantically, and give him a deep kiss, pressing myself to him. It's been so long. I'm realizing how much I need this. And I think he realizes he needs it too. Hopefully more than he needed to smoke pot.

He leans back breathlessly and laughs. "Yes, this should do the trick. It might not solve the nightmares, but at least it'll solve this!" He moves my hand to press against him, and I can feel how excited he is, how much he wants me.

We run up the stairs, trying to be quiet as we pass by Timothy's room.

It's both tender and intense, incredibly passionate, deeply fulfilling. I've missed him so much. It almost feels like he just got back from another deployment, and we are finally together again.

We fall asleep in each other's arms.

Chapter 59

Demon Is Back

Natalie

Mom and Dad are in the front seat planning out everything they have to do as soon as we get home. He's going to unpack and start the laundry while she runs out to the grocery store to get something for dinner and for our lunches this week. Boring adult stuff. Angel laughs at me for thinking that.

Then suddenly Angel stops laughing, and looks like he goes stiff with surprise. "What?" I think to him, alarmed.

He hesitates a minute before saying anything. He looks completely shocked. I am staring at him with wide eyes. He doesn't normally act like this. I can't imagine what is wrong.

"What?" Gabe asks, seeing me staring at him.

"*My dear,*" Angel finally says, "*It seems that Jonathan's Guardian has returned.*"

I gasp in a breath, and put my hands over my mouth.

"WHAT?" Gabe asks again.

I whisper to him, "Demon is back."

Gabe stares at me, his eyes huge. "Demon's back?"

"That's what Angel says. He could tell as soon as we got close enough for him to hear that Demon is with Jonathan again." We are whispering, so our parents don't hear our conversation. They'd think we're crazy, or playing a weird game, I suppose.

"I have to go see Jonathan," he says.

"Yes, but I think we should talk to Angel first to see if he can tell us what's going on."

"Can he tell how Jonathan is doing?"

Angel says, *"Jonathan seems very well. His soul is restored, even more than it had been through your efforts in touching him. He appears far more lively and energetic than he has been the last several months."*

I repeat all of that to Gabe. "Great!" he says. "Sounds like the old Jonathan is back!" He looks really happy. I know he has missed Jonathan the way he used to be.

Dad pulls the car into the driveway, and we start getting out. Gabe is about to run straight down to Jonathan's house, but I grab his hand. "Hold on a minute, please, let's go inside and talk some more first."

He is impatient to go. "Fine," he huffs, "but let's make it quick. I've got to see him."

Dad hands us our backpacks from out of the trunk. "Here," he tells us, "carry these inside." We take them while he is unloading everything else.

Mom is unlocking the front door, and she laughs as we zoom past her and run up the stairs.

Gabe tosses his bag into his room then comes into mine. I shut the door. "Before we go down there, we should make a plan."

"Why? I just want to see Jonathan!"

"I really want to see him too, but you have to remember what he was like before Demon went missing. He was completely mad at me and fighting us. We don't know what's going to happen. We should be prepared."

Gabe frowns. He remembers, but he is so excited to see if Jonathan has returned to being his old exciting friend, he hadn't thought of that.

He crosses his arms and slumps down on my bed. "Okay, fine. What do you want to do?"

But then Angel tells me, *"Darling, there is no more time to make a plan. Jonathan is on his way here."*

Jonathan

I've been waiting for them all day. I thought they were going to get back a long time ago - I'm pretty sure they had told me their plane was supposed to land before lunch, but it's almost dinnertime. So as soon as I see them drive up, I grab my shoes, yell to Dad that I'm going to see Gabe, and start running down the street.

I've been so excited to talk to Gabe. And Natalie too. I want to tell her all about Demon being back, and how I could tell as soon as he got here, and how I am feeling fine. She's been ridiculously worried about nothing. All the asking me about whether I thought Demon was controlling me was totally pointless. I know he's here, and except for the first moment when he got back last weekend, I haven't felt any emotions that seemed strange.

I feel great. It's like I was tired or sick for a long time, but now I am healthy and strong and feeling fantastic. I have had fun doing stuff every day with Dad this week. The zoo, or the park, or the beach, or playing with Socks, or hanging around at home watching cartoons. Everything seems wonderful. I can't wait to share it all with my friends again.

I'm about to knock on the door, but it opens before I can.

There is Gabe, with Natalie peeking out at me from behind him.

I get a huge smile as soon as I see them, and I'm about to tell them hi and go inside, but then I feel it happening.

Seeing Natalie creates this rush of strange emotions, that don't feel like they have anything to do with me. I'm happy to see her and Gabe. I shouldn't feel like this, like I want to run away from her.

I hesitate on the porch, confused.

I see her look over to the side, and then she slowly backs away, getting further behind Gabe.

I don't know what to do.

Jonathan's

My dearest one is delighted to see his friends, but my reaction to the presence of the unnatural creature is instantaneous and involuntary. Everything she has done to me rushes at once into my thoughts. The torture, the delight, the imprisonment, the salvation. The eternity of anguish interspersed with the hateful pleasure which she forced upon me whenever she touched my beloved. I am filled with loathing and desire, an urge to join with her and a desperation to flee from her.

I sense energy erratically flowing outward as my memories crash down upon me. I have never felt such a powerful tumult of emotions. I know they are flooding into my beloved, overpowering his own feelings, creating in him the exact thing the Seer had trained him to fear. And for this too, I both detest and admire her. She was exactly correct, hatefully so.

She feels the vehement passions emanating from me and flowing through Jonathan, even as her Guardian begins to warn her against me.

There is no conceivable way to move forward from this schism.

The humans stand frozen. We are all utterly stymied.

Chapter 60

Terror

Natalie's

I am taken aback by Demon's presence. It is more than surprise. I have never been so aghast. I believe the proper term for my reaction to him is terror, which is an entirely new sensation.

Natalie sees. She is alarmed by not only the violent and conflicting emotions which she feels pulsating from Jonathan, but by my own fraught reaction to what I am seeing and learning. She moves back from Jonathan, not knowing what to expect. None of us do.

The first thing which strikes me about Demon is, of course, his appearance. Never could I have imagined a Guardian becoming such a ghoulish specter. He has incorporated the name which Natalie gave him into a brazen depiction of the most terrifying demon ever imagined by mankind. It is horrifying in every way. Looming behind Jonathan, the creature appears enormously tall and powerful, blood-red, horned, hooved, winged. The worst nightmare of any religion come to life.

My first instinct is to believe there is no way to justify having created this monstrosity. But, as I absorb more of Demon's thoughts due to our proximity, I begin to understand the twisted logic behind the manifestation. The strange mixture of hostility and love which led him to conceive of transforming into this horror.

As I try to acclimate to the petrifying image which Demon has chosen to project, I find my disquiet growing to unexpected heights when I realize the answer to the mystery we have all been trying to solve for the past several months.

Where is Demon, we all have wondered. The answer, it turns out, is far more frightful than anything known before in the history of Guardians.

As I witness his memories being triggered by the sight of my beloved, his anguish flows through me. I relive with him the dreadful months after our attack on him, remembering together the void, the loneliness, the confusion, the agony of solitude. Nothing like this has ever before befallen a Guardian. Demon suffered a damnation unparalleled in history.

And, I realize, it was my fault. It was the unintended consequence of my actions in protecting the Seer, by directing energy against Demon to make him stop forcing Jonathan to attack Natalie. I had to do it. But now I regret the result with every particle of my being.

The guilt which we Guardians felt for uniting in forcefully opposing him was more than justified. We committed a heinous act against one of our fellow beings. Our action led to an unspeakable torture, a cruel banishment, an excruciating exile.

The ghastly visage of the Demon standing before me is nothing compared to the horror of what he experienced.

Never before has a Guardian been alone. Since the dawn of time, when human evolution first created Guardians by capturing enough dark matter to form the soul, never was a Guardian so isolated. We are either Guarding, or waiting together to Guard. Always together. Always communing with either our Guarded or with each other.

Demon was cruelly torn apart from all other beings. Lost in a cold universe, separated from his beloved, isolated from any companion.

It is the worst torment I can fathom.

My own manifestation reacts of its own accord. My image has long been used as a means of communication, with gestures and expressions conveying meaning to the Seer as surely as spoken words. It has become instinctive, autonomic, to the point where these actions are as involuntary for me as they are for humans. My image experiences physical reactions just as the people around me do.

And now, without regard to my own will, tears start to flow down my face, tears of mourning and anguish, grief and sympathy, evoked by the memories of Demon's experience.

Natalie views me with alarm, her hands held to her face, as she feels not only the rush of emotions cascading through Jonathan, but my own sorrow flowing through our connection directly to her mind.

And, I realize with increasing dread, the expulsion to the void was not the only torture which Demon endured. If it is possible, it became even more unbearable. The means of his salvation, the reason he was healed and could eventually return, was intensely hateful to him as soon as he realized that it was all caused by the Seer.

My darling's innocent and compassionate effort to heal Jonathan, to restore his soul, was simultaneously creating unwanted and invasive contact with Demon, lost in the void. As Jonathan's soul was gradually healed, so his Guardian was restored, his fractured essence slowly brought back together. I grieve to witness the violation he perceived, the helplessness he felt, as the touch of the Seer ravished his being against his will, over and over and over again. He knew it was healing him. He felt the ecstatic pleasure of her touch, and hated himself for desiring it. But he hated Natalie even more for what she had done to him. He blamed her for my actions in leading our group against him. He saw her both as his destroyer, and his terrifying redeemer. She had cast him into the chasm, then tauntingly promised him the rapture which would eventually lead him back out. He felt victimized by her, not only in the initial act of his banishment, but constantly, unstoppably, unpredictably, for the entire time lost in the terrifying void.

I understand it all. I grieve for it all. I am shocked, I am stricken, I am repentant. I can do nothing more than weep before Demon, weep for his suffering, weep for the situation in which we find ourselves.

Gabe's

The Seer and her Guardian are filled with dismay. Jonathan and his newly shaped Guardian are locked in a frenzy of emotional turmoil. My beloved is baffled, scared, uncertain what he should do. I am as shocked and horrified as is Angel, not only by Demon's appearance, but by the realization of what has transpired since last we were together.

We are all trapped in this moment of tension and dread. I cannot even find words to whisper to my beloved to try to help him through this. I have no concept of what I could possibly say.

Gabe

Jonathan is standing there on the porch, staring at Natalie, and the expression on his face is the strangest thing I have ever seen. He hasn't even said hi yet. We're all just standing here, and I have no idea what I am supposed to be doing.

I look around at Natalie, and she is backing away from the door, her hands on her face, her eyes round and scared, like something really terrible has happened.

I look back at Jonathan, and his face is doing this awful dance, transitioning from the smile he had on when I first opened the door, then looking scared, then disgusted, then angry, and now scarily determined. Like he has decided what he has to do. He lunges forward, towards Natalie.

Jonathan's

The Seer is the cause of it all. But for her existence, none of this would have happened. We would not be standing here locked together in a tempest of emotions. I would not have been destroyed. I would not have been violated. Jonathan would be leading his beautiful life. Instead, he is full of conflict and fear, and I am damaged, possibly beyond repair. The other Guardians are filled with shock and horror. The situation is untenable. It must end.

I realize that in my rage and dismay, power is flooding through me, out of me, towards Jonathan. I'm not even controlling it. It is the byproduct of my spiraling emotions. Again, this is all her fault. If not for her, I would not have learned the use of such power. Everything is due to her.

She is unnatural. A being of her kind should not be allowed to exist. She must be stopped.

Jonathan

She's my friend, but all I can see her as right now is my enemy. Our enemy. I know it's Demon, but I can't see around how he's feeling. I have to make it stop, I have to stop our pain, I have to stop her.

I don't even have a plan. I lunge forward, trying to get past Gabe. I have to stop her.

Gabe grabs me. I don't get anywhere close to her.

He wraps me up in a bear hug. "Jon, no," he whispers. "Be yourself."

My head is going to explode. I am so confused. I don't want any of this. I have to get away.

I'm able to yank myself backwards out of Gabe's arms, and stumble my way back out of their door.

I swivel around, and start tearing down the street. I don't know where I'm going. Just away. I have to get away.

Chapter 61

Kind of Cool

Natalie

Gabe starts chasing after him. "Dad, we're going to play with Jonathan," I yell up the stairs, then follow them out the door.

I'm somehow able to catch up to Gabe, and grab his hand. "Wait, wait," I tell him. I see Jonathan running as fast as he can down the street and turning around the corner.

He swings around, his eyes wild. "Shouldn't we catch him?" he asks, breathing heavily.

"Yes," I tell him sadly, "yes, we are going to have to talk to him. But we don't have to chase him. Angel knows where he is. He can't get so far away that Angel won't hear him. We'll find him. Let's follow along, and give him time to calm down."

Everything I feared has come true. The Jonathan Project has blown up in my face. I had told Jonathan that when Demon came back, this might happen, but I had no idea how bad it was going to be.

I can't believe what Angel has been doing. He is so stricken with grief that he can barely speak to me. Tears are streaming down his beautiful shining face, his features contorted with crying. I hear him sobbing. I don't understand what is happening, but I know it is bad. I think Angel has realized something awful happened to Demon when he disappeared, and he is feeling guilty about it.

If only I could touch him, he would feel better. I've learned that.

But of course I can't. Never.

I look at Gabe, who is confused and upset. At least we can try to learn what is going on now, if Angel can calm down enough to talk to us.

"Let's walk," I tell them.

Natalie's

As the boy disappears around the corner, followed by the terrifying figure of the enormous demon trailing behind, Natalie manages to bring some calm to the disastrous situation.

She tries to soothe both of her companions, her brother and I, with her quiet suggestion that we simply walk along behind, giving Jonathan the space he needs to calm down. Once Demon is removed from our presence, he should be able to check his emotions, and Jonathan will recover.

She sets an unhurried pace, relying on me to guide them to wherever Jonathan is fleeing. This I can do, at least, until I can gain control over my countenance and my voice. We walk in silence for a brief time.

She watches as I try to manage my emotions. I feel ashamed for having lost myself so thoroughly in my grief and shock.

"It's fine," she thinks to me, her love and acceptance washing over me. "You can feel whatever you need to." She wryly looks up at my face. "I wish I could offer you a tissue."

It makes me smile. My sweet little one has reversed our roles, trying to bring solace to me.

Gabe has been waiting impatiently, until his sister seems ready to talk. He sees her relaxing as my emotions finally calm. "So," he says, "anyone want to tell me what just happened?"

We have rounded the corner where Jonathan passed out of our sight, and he is not on the next street either. I know, though, that he has only turned the next corner, and is slowing his pace as he proceeds. I sense that both he and Demon are calming, regaining control. His destination, I realize at the same time as he does, is the neighborhood park. He believes he can sit quietly there, and try to come to terms with what has happened.

"Jonathan is going to the park," I inform Natalie. *"And yes, I will explain all to you and your brother."*

"Jonathan is heading to the park," Natalie repeats to her brother. "Angel is going to tell us what happened while we walk over there." She looks up at me, evaluating, then turns back to Gabe. "He was so sad when he saw Demon that he started crying, but he is feeling better now."

Gabe looks flabbergasted at the idea of a Guardian crying. "What? Why?"

"Just start from the beginning," Natalie instructs me. "Tell us the whole thing. Start with why you seemed actually scared when Gabe opened the door."

"Scared?" squawks Gabe, mirroring the feeling. Natalie reaches over to hold his hand as they walk down the street. He feels better. Of course. Even now, she uses her gifts to help, to heal.

I wish I could avoid telling her the whole story. But of course she always knows when I withhold information. And furthermore, she needs to know the entire truth. Our actions have had consequences we never imagined, and she will need to understand this going forward with her life.

Gabe's

Angel glances at me before proceeding, and I indicate that he should go on. My beloved will be able to adapt to the new information. I will help him.

"*I was alarmed, my dear,*" Angel responds, "*because Demon has transformed his appearance. It is now ... unusual.*"

The Seer senses her brother's confusion. She clarifies for him, "Remember, Angel has told us that Guardians can look like anything they want. So I guess Demon has decided to change his look." She turns back to Angel. "What do you mean by unusual?"

Angel is reluctant to proceed, but he realizes this will actually be the easiest part of the conversation to come. "*He has transformed his image to reflect his name. Demon.*"

Natalie's nose wrinkles. "You mean, like, he actually looks like a demon now? Why did he do that?"

My beloved widens his eyes. "Really? What do demons look like?"

Angel attempts to answer all of the children's questions. "*He realized after he returned that Jonathan, in learning the name you had assigned to his Guardian, has begun picturing him as an actual demon. Therefore, Demon chose to affirm the vision by manifesting an image which corresponded.*"

Once Natalie repeats this information to Gabe, whose mind whirls with more questions, Angel continues. "*There are, of course, no actual demons. Such creatures are an invention of the human mind, alongside other mythological*" *deities and similar beings. However, Jonathan has seen images of these in sources such as books and movies. His memory of these images informed the picture which grew within his mind. Demon shaped his matter to coincide with what Jonathan imagined."*

"It's the same with you," Natalie whispers, comprehending our nature more deeply, "isn't it? You look like this because I pictured you as a guardian angel."

"Yes, darling, this is your image of me, shaped so what you beheld when you saw me reaffirmed your idea of what I am to you."

"But Demon knows Jonathan can't see him. Why would he bother turning into a demon?"

"Like all Guardians, Demon wishes to feel a kinship with his beloved human. He decided to affirm Jonathan's view of him. It may seem strange to you, but it does make sense."

"Well," Gabe blurts out, not understanding or even caring much about Demon's reasoning. "I want to know what it looks like!"

"Very well," Angel concedes, *"I will describe the image. The demon which Jonathan's Guardian is projecting is large, taller than a human adult. It is shaped roughly like a very muscular human man, but it has red skin, wings, horns, claws, fangs, cloven hooves, and a tail."*

"Oh, wow!" Gabe exclaims, after Natalie conveys this description. "Really?" He lets the image form in his mind as well. "That's super scary, but actually, kind of cool, don't you think?" he asks his sister.

She raises her eyebrows and stares at her brother. "Cool? Honestly?" She shakes her head and gives a little laugh. "Okay, sure, I guess."

"Seriously!" Gabe tries to convince her. "What do you want to bet, after we sort everything out and Jonathan is talking to us again, that he thinks it's cool too?"

"Huh," she says, tilting her head to the side. "Actually, I think you're right." She grows sad again. "Assuming we can ever fix this."

Demon himself, of course, is aware of this entire conversation. In other circumstances, he might find himself amused to hear himself so discussed. Not today.

We are in the proximity to Demon which allows Guardians to sense each other and any humans nearby. Natalie is aware that we are within this distance. At the end of the street we are traveling along, we can see the park entrance. "How are they doing?" she asks Angel.

Demon and Jonathan have reached the park, where the boy is sitting on the ground against a wall, his arms wrapped around his knees, staring silently into the distance. They have both regained their composure. Once Demon was away from the Seer, the emotional turmoil subsided, and he was able to re-focus his attention on the needs of his Guarded. He whispers to Jonathan words of comfort and peace, and apology. He knows it was his outburst which created the boy's distress.

"Jonathan is sitting quietly in the park, lost in thought. Demon has become calmer. His frenzied emotional response has settled."

"I guess you have to explain that to us next," Natalie says. "Just because he looks like a demon can't be what made you all so upset. I know there was a lot more going on."

Chapter 62

I Didn't Know

Natalie's

"**Y**es darling, of course you are able to perceive the truth. There is more to explain. But I fear that it will upset you as well."

My beloved, I worry, will be crushed when she learns of the pain we unwittingly inflicted on Jonathan's Guardian. Which we all inflicted. Demon specifically blames her, though, and I fear that she will feel the same.

She sighs and looks straight at me. "Even if it upsets me, I have to know it. You know I do. Just tell me."

I resist the urge to begin weeping again. "*It is about what happened to Demon, where he was while he was missing.*"

She nods, repeats this to her brother, and waits. We continue slowly approaching the park.

"*As you remember, when Jonathan was on top of the jungle gym with you, trying to push you off, myself and the other Guardians began using energy to try to stop Demon from controlling Jonathan. We reacted out of fear for your safety. But we did not have any idea what the consequences would be.*"

She nods, again repeating my words to Gabe. They both listen somberly, waiting for the bad news they know is coming.

"*All we knew after it was over was that Demon was missing. We searched for him to the best of our abilities, but could not locate him anywhere. Other than the brief flash I had of him a few days after the incident, I had not detected his presence again until today.*"

Nodding again, waiting.

I regard her sadly. *"I have learned that what happened to Demon was not simply that he disappeared. It was that he was essentially destroyed. The power of our combined voices, shouting at him with all the energy at our disposal, actually dismembered his entire being. Every particle of dark matter within him was blasted apart from the rest. He did not simply vanish. He was utterly unmade."* The dreadful responsibility of telling my beloved this horrifying truth is unbearable. I ache for her.

She pulls her hand away from Gabe's grip and covers her face, peering out from behind her hands. Tears spring to her eyes. She repeats this information for Gabe, speaking through her fingers. When she finishes, she asks, "You mean, you... killed him?"

"I know of no better description for what happened. Essentially, yes. We killed him," I affirm, deeply ashamed.

When Gabe hears this, he asks with astonishment, "Then how is he back?"

Yes, this is the proper question.

We have reached the park. Natalie sees Jonathan's small form in the distance, curled against the wall. She lifts her hand from her face to point him out to Gabe, then to draw him away. "Not yet," she tells him, "we can't go over there yet. We have to understand more."

He nods, agreeing. They move to a bench near a tree which would block their location from being viewed by Jonathan, were he to glance in this direction.

I must answer Gabe's question. *"Even though Demon's matter had been annihilated, and he had no tangible presence or cohesion of any kind, he was still tied to Jonathan's soul."*

The children nod, having heard this repeated numerous times during the last several months.

"His matter was apparently scattered widely throughout the universe, but it was still him. He maintained a rudimentary perception of his circumstances after the incident occurred. He perceived it as..." I try to find a way to describe it which will make any sense at all to the human children. *"It seemed to him that he was lost in a black void, with nobody and nothing anywhere around him. He was totally alone, and did not know where he was or how to help himself."*

Although I am not fully describing the terror, the agony, the forsakenness which Demon suffered, Natalie senses it all the same. Her heart is filled with compassion and sorrow for Jonathan's Guardian.

I must continue. *"He had no sense of how long this endured. It felt to him like an eternity. But then he felt a warmth, a glow which helped a tiny part of himself heal, some of his matter grow back together."*

Natalie looks at me, puzzled. I cannot keep her in suspense. I cannot try to convey the waiting, the bafflement, the confusion this caused for so long before Demon realized that she was the source. *"After this happened a number of times, Demon eventually realized it was when you were touching Jonathan, and his soul was healing, that Demon himself was also being healed."*

She smiles joyfully. "I helped him then? I'm so glad! I mean, I'm sorry that what we did made him get lost, but at least I was able to fix things so that he could come back!"

Her smile falters when she sees me watching this reaction sadly.

"But..." she frowns, "then why was Demon so upset with me? I could feel it coming from Jonathan. It felt like he hated me. Why, if I'm the one who helped him?"

This is the hardest part. *"My darling, as much as I do not wish to share this information with you, I must. Demon blames you for his banishment, even though I am actually responsible. And because he blames you, he did not enjoy your help. He found your touch to be... unwelcome."*

Gabe and Natalie look at each other, upset and bewildered. I try to clarify. I must be brutally clear. *"He realized that your touch was helping him while it helped Jonathan, but he hated knowing it was coming from the same person who he felt had imprisoned him in the void."*

Her forehead wrinkles with distress. "But I didn't know! I didn't know any of this! How can he hate me for it?"

Gabe looks at his sister. "I know it isn't the same thing, but it kind of reminds me of slavery. We've been studying it in history, what happened before the Civil War. If a slave was living a horrible life and being abused, they'd hate the person doing it, even if they were also being given enough food to stay alive. They might eat the food because they had to, but they would still hate the person giving it to them."

This is a shockingly good metaphor. I believe the only more apt human analogy would likely be a situation of serial sexual abuse, but thankfully these children are innocent of such ideas. *"Yes, I believe your brother has found a similar example. Demon was helpless, and was angry at you for putting him there, and hated that he had to accept your help. He has a very complicated set of feelings about you."*

"Was that why Jonathan tried to get to her?" Gabe asked. "What was he trying to do?"

I sadly reply, *"Demon is so upset at what happened, he feels that a Seer such as Natalie should not even exist. Jonathan had no specific plan, but he was compelled forward by Demon's sense that Natalie must be stopped."*

Gabe is aghast. "What? Well, that means Natalie is going to be in danger all the time! If Demon wants her not to exist, he'll make Jonathan keep trying to hurt her, won't he?"

"I fear that may be true," I reply. *"Understanding what Demon experienced, and the way he feels, I do not know if he will ever be able to accept having Jonathan spend time with Natalie. It is probable it will again trigger an emotional response which could lead to a desire to harm her. You should consider finding a way to avoid Jonathan in the future. Starting now."*

Gabe nods, grimly accepting that he will likely have to forsake his best friend, in order to protect his sister.

Natalie, however, reacts immediately. "No!" she nearly shouts. "No. I will not agree to stay away from him! This whole thing started because I was trying to change him, and everything that happened is my fault. Demon is totally right! It's my fault. I made this mess. I have to find a way to make it better. I'm going to."

Gabe stares at her, utterly flummoxed. "Well, Nat, you can't talk to him. The same thing will happen. I think Demon would make him go crazy again if you get too close."

She huffs and crosses her arms, leaning back against the bench. "I know. Give me a minute to think."

He lifts his hands in the air helplessly, then joins her in leaning against the bench. He waits, in silence. As do I.

Chapter 63

Just Be His Friend

Gabe

I haven't got the foggiest clue what to do next. But she said to give her a minute to think, so here we sit. She is staring off at the horizon, this intense expression of determination on her face. I suppose Angel is sitting there with her, but I have a feeling he's leaving her alone too, to let her think. She isn't looking off to the side to listen to him, so I think he's being quiet.

I guess I just wait.

It doesn't really take long. She sighs, and says, "I think you should go talk to him, Gabe."

"What? Why? What on Earth would I say?"

"Well, at this point he is the only one who doesn't know what is really happening. Demon has been listening to this whole conversation, right Angel?" She looks over at him, and apparently he confirms that because she looks back at me and nods.

Woah. I didn't think of that. Like, everything we said about Demon, he totally heard. He knows what we all think.

"So, Demon knows what we think, and we know what he thinks, but poor Jonathan is still sitting there all confused and probably miserable. That's why I think you should go over there. You don't have to tell him anything, or you can tell him whatever you want. It won't make any difference to what happens with Demon. But he needs you. You're his best friend. I think you should be with him. Just be his friend."

Oh. Dang. She's right. I hadn't even thought of it that way. Jon is scared and alone and doesn't have any idea what is going on. I should have thought of his feelings. I'm so glad Natalie did. I feel embarrassing tears pop into my eyes, because I'm sorry for Jonathan and grateful for my sister. I quickly wipe them away.

"You're right. Will you wait here?"

"Yes, I'll be here. Me and Angel will wait to see what happens. Go."

Jonathan

I've been sitting here so long my butt is going numb. I don't want to move, though. I'm scared of what will happen if I go back. Everything Natalie warned me about came true. I know Demon made me go all crazy again, and it's only thanks to Gabe that I didn't end up attacking Natalie.

I hate Demon. Why would he want me to hurt my friend? Why did he have to come back? I know that I used to like to hurt people, and apparently he wanted me to do it. But while he was gone I got over it. I don't want to feel that way. I especially don't want to feel that way about Natalie. What is it about her that makes him so mad? I could feel it, boiling through me, and I hated it. I hate him. I wish he would go away again.

Jonathan's

It is the deepest grief I have ever known. To hear my beloved consider his hatred of me. If only he was still oblivious to my existence. That would be far preferable to hearing this hatred. I love him. I cannot bear for him to hate me.

Again, it is her fault. I was right to try to prevent her from telling him about me. Then after she had banished me, she did it anyway. His knowledge and hatred of me are all her doing. Always the Seer, always creating unbearable agony.

I long to console him. He sits alone, taking no comfort in my presence. He is confused and terrified by having felt my fierce emotional reaction. Even without me attempting to deliberately control him, he was unwillingly compelled into action which he did not wish to take.

It occurs to me that there is a tragic parallel here between us. I was unwillingly compelled to accept the Seer's healing touch. I hated her for it. His reaction to being so compelled to action by me is similar. A sense of violation.

The more I consider this, the more horrible the reality of it becomes. I hate the Seer for what she did to me. And Jonathan hates me for what I have done to him.

To be in the same position as the Seer herself is the worst thing of all.

And still, I try fervently to comfort my beloved. *"My dearest, I would never try to harm you. I grieve for your pain, my sweet."*

I cannot find a way to help.

But then, a staggering thing occurs. The Seer can. She finds a way to help.

In the course of the entire wretched conversation she holds with her Guardian about me, about what she did to me, she never once feels hostility towards me, or towards my beloved. She does not blame me, or him.

She actually blames herself, as do I. She is right to accept the blame. It is all her fault.

She goes further, though. Overcoming her own sadness and uncertainty over the situation, she feels a deep compassion for my beloved. She does not want him to continue to feel alone, and confused, and afraid. She finds the perfect remedy.

She sends his friend to him.

Gabe

I run all the way over to Jonathan. But then, when I get closer to him, I slow down. I look at him as I walk up. I don't think he's moved this whole time. He's still sitting there on the ground, his back against the wall, his arms around his knees. He is staring off into space. I don't know if he even realizes I'm here.

"Hey," I say.

"Hey," he replies. So, yeah, he knew I was here.

"All right if I sit?" I ask him.

"Go ahead," he says.

So that's what I do. I sit down next to him. I don't know if he feels like talking, so I'm happy to be together with him. Like Natalie said. I just want to be his friend. I want him to know that he isn't alone.

We stay this way for a while. I don't know how long. The sun is getting lower, off to our side, shining light into the sides of our eyes.

After a while, he sighs, then turns his head and looks at me, squinting in the sun.

"You okay?" I ask him.

"My butt hurts," he replies.

I laugh. "Well, get off it, dude. Come on, let's take a walk."

He sighs again. I stand up, and offer him my hand. He reaches up and takes it, and I help him stand. He moves his legs around a little, clearly uncomfortable from having been sitting on the ground for so long.

"Your butt fall asleep?"

"Apparently."

"Well, come on then. Wake it up."

I lead him over to the hill overlooking the canyon behind the park. The sun will be going down over there pretty soon. Sometimes I like to see the sunset, and maybe that'll be nice for Jonathan too. Help calm his mind.

We stand together, looking out into the canyon. He isn't talking much, but I can tell his head is full of questions.

"So," I say, thinking maybe it would help him to ask some of them.

"So," he replies.

I think he's going to go quiet again, but instead he says, "Does she hate me now? Now that I did it again?"

"What? No! She doesn't even blame you. She's the one who told me to come over here."

He looks over at me. "Really? Why?"

"She thought you could use a friend."

"Oh." He stares at me for a second, then looks back across the canyon. The sun is starting to slip down into the clouds that are on the horizon.

"I wish I knew what happened," he says. "It was so strange, and I have no idea what is going on."

"I do," I tell him quietly.

He swivels his head back around and stares at me. "You do? How?"

"Angel told Natalie, and she told me. That's why she said I should come and talk to you. Because she knew you were the only one who didn't understand."

His mouth hangs open.

"So, want me to tell you?"

Chapter 64

Get Over It

Jonathan's

The presence of his closest friend is a salve to my beloved's turbulent feelings. And now, the promise of answers, answers which I am unable to provide, brings him a spark of hope.

I am grateful to Gabe for being here, for being willing to assist Jonathan, to explain to him what has happened. Perhaps once he knows more about me, his hatred will subside. I long for him to understand how much I love him, how I overcame my suffering to come back to him.

"Yeah," Jonathan tells his friend. "Tell me."

Gabe tries to summarize the bizarre set of facts which have been laid out by the Seer's Guardian. "Okay. Back when your guardian went missing that day you fell off the jungle gym, it was because the other guardians were all yelling at him to make him stop trying to control you. Do you remember that?"

"Yeah. After Demon got back, I started remembering everything a lot better. I remember it was like what happened today. I was feeling furious and trying to get to Natalie, to make her stop talking. I think she was trying to explain to me about guardians, and Demon didn't want her to."

My dearest child is correct. I did not want her to tell him. I still wish she hadn't. If we had been successful in stopping her, none of this would have happened.

Although, I realize with chagrin, it was also her action in sending her brother to Jonathan which is currently bringing him the consolation I have failed to deliver. I cannot hate her for that.

"Well," Gabe goes on, "do you remember Natalie and Timothy talking about energy? The stuff the guardians use to talk to each other?"

Jonathan nods.

"That day, the guardians were all using it to yell at Demon. It turns out that it, like, blasted him apart. That's why he disappeared."

Jonathan's eyes grow wide. "You mean they blew him up?"

"Yeah, basically."

"Oh." Jonathan tries to adapt to this new knowledge. "Well, he must have gotten better."

"Yeah, he did, and Angel has realized now how it happened. Remember Natalie telling you how Demon is connected to your soul?"

Jonathan nods again. This has always seemed very abstract to him, and while I was lost, he cared little about these issues. He only wanted Natalie to be there, touching him, because this made him feel better every time. He did not concentrate on what she was talking about. He simply wanted to be near her.

Again, the Seer. Everything is about the Seer.

"Well, anyway, I guess whenever she was touching you to help your soul get better, nobody realized it was also helping Demon get better. Eventually he was healed enough to come back to you."

Jonathan stares at Gabe, confused. His reaction is much the same as Natalie's had been to this information.

"Why the heck was Demon so mad when he saw her, then? You'd think he'd want to say thank you for helping him!"

"I guess it was because he was mad at her for everything that happened. He blamed her for him getting blown up and vanishing. While he was lost he hated her. When she started touching you, and it was healing him, he hated that too because he didn't want her touching him. But he couldn't stop it."

"Even though he knew it was helping?"

"Yeah, even though."

"Huh," Jonathan grunts. He falls into silence for a few minutes, considering, trying to make sense of this. I eagerly watch him, silent, hoping that his mind is able to resolve this in a way which makes me seem less hateful. All I want is for him to love me, not hate me.

After a time, he says, "Well, I guess maybe it makes sense. If someone I hated was touching me all the time, I'd be mad too."

It fills me with warmth to hear him acknowledge the validity of my feelings.

Gabe nods. "Yeah, me too. So I guess that's why Demon got all upset when he saw her. Angel says he has very complicated feelings about her."

Jonathan actually laughs. "No kidding. I could tell. My head was ready to explode with all the crazy things I was feeling. I know it was all coming from him."

They lapse into silence a moment longer, while the rays of the sun peek out from beneath the layer of clouds which had covered it, very nearly reaching the horizon. The boys' faces are bathed in the golden light of the sunset. They both watch, admiring the beauty even as they contemplate the chaotic events of this evening.

"Well," Jonathan finally says, "how is Demon now? Is he going to go all crazy and mad again?"

"I don't know," says Gabe. "Angel is afraid he will. He told us we should stay away from you, because it wouldn't be safe for Natalie if Demon keeps hating her like that."

Jonathan is stricken. He feels certain that he will lose his friends, his best friends. And this will be my fault. As surely as I have blamed the Seer for all of my misfortunes, Jonathan will blame me for this. His hatred for me will endure and grow. A future of pain and turmoil lays before us.

The boys stare at each other, sensing the imminent ending of their friendship. Sadness fills their eyes.

Jonathan decides to immediately face it. He just wants to find out. If I am to be a monstrous burden for the rest of his life, at least he doesn't want it to lead to harm for his friends. He will forego their friendship in order to protect them, if it appears that my presence will make him dangerous to them, to the Seer.

I watch his thoughts develop with dismay, unable to whisper that it is not so, because I know he may be right. I do not know if I will ever be able to control my emotional response to the girl.

He sets his jaw in a firm, resolved line. "Well," he tells Gabe, "let's find out. Let's get Natalie over here."

Gabe's brow furrows, full of worry and sadness, fearing this meeting will not go any better than did the last one. I share his fears. I believe I might not be able to control my reaction. Yet I do not want to be the cause of anguish to my beloved.

Jonathan says, "I wish I could just talk to Demon, tell him what I think."

"Oh!" Gabe says. "Sure, you can. Natalie told me I can talk to my guardian whenever I want. I do it sometimes. I can't hear him talking back, but I know he hears me. They always hear everything. They're always watching and listening."

"Oh yeah?" Jonathan says. His eyes narrow. "Okay, fine. Demon, listen up!"

I am shocked out of my self-pity. My beloved addresses me directly!

"Natalie is coming over here," he says. "You behave yourself! I don't want to be feeling any crappy feelings coming from you. We all have problems. You need to get over it!"

Gabe's mouth hangs open as Jonathan scolds me. I believe mine does the same. My new demon image is an intensely material manifestation. I have often witnessed Angel's form react to the Seer with what appear to be genuine physical motions, almost as though his body is real, and can make actual movements and expressions. My image has begun to do the same, essentially involuntarily. I am sure my face reflects the shock I feel.

Jonathan huffs out a sigh, then says, "Okay. Gabe, can you go get her?"

"No need," Gabe replies, gesturing down the hill. "Here she comes."

Jonathan looks at his friend. "Do me a favor," he says. "Get ready to grab me if I go crazy."

Gabe nods, his eyes wide.

Chapter 65

Let Me Help You

Natalie

I'm waiting with Angel on the bench. It's not hard to wait, because Angel is telling me everything they are saying. Gabe is making Jonathan feel better. I knew he'd be able to do that.

He's doing a good job explaining everything to Jonathan, too. Sometimes I'm not sure how much attention he is paying to whatever is going on, but he obviously understood the whole thing. Maybe even better than I did. It makes me smile a little when Angel tells me they've decided Demon got blown up. I guess that's accurate.

Then, it makes me sad when Angel says Jonathan feels like he is ready to stop being friends, if it's what he has to do so I'll be safe.

That's not what I want.

"Darling, Jonathan wants you to go to them now. He wants to see what happens."

Oh. Okay. Well, at least we are going to give it a try. I am not ready to give up on being Jonathan's friend. I will never be ready, no matter what happens.

Angel has described more to me about how Demon was feeling and how awful it was while he was missing. I think I understand why he has been so mad at me. It was my fault he got lost, and then he kept having to put up with me touching him all the time, while he was hating me so much. Just because I didn't know it was happening, doesn't mean it didn't feel awful for him.

I have to think of a way to make this right.

Jonathan and Gabe are standing on the edge of the canyon, staring at me as I walk up the hill.

"Where is Demon?" I think to Angel.

"He is behind Jonathan, closer to the edge of the canyon."

I have a plan.

I slowly walk right up to Jonathan. I am watching his eyes, and Angel is watching everything else. "Well?" I think to Angel.

"Demon is again feeling a flood of emotions, but he is attempting to prevent himself from using the energy which would direct these emotions towards Jonathan. So far, Jonathan is still in control of himself."

I give Jonathan a little smile, but I don't touch him. I don't want to push it.

Then, I look up over Jonathan's head, about where I think Demon's eyes must be. I picture him the way that Angel described him. A huge red demon with wings and horns, taller than my Dad. I see it in my head, but it isn't scary. It's sad. Poor Demon has suffered, he has been scared and lonely and angry, and it was all my fault.

Just because he is a guardian doesn't mean I shouldn't care about his feelings. I'm starting to realize that guardians are basically people too. They have feelings, they can love or suffer, they can be happy or sad, they can need friends. I want Demon to know that I understand.

"Demon," I say out loud to him, and I hope that I'm looking right into his eyes. Jonathan's mouth falls open, and he and Gabe gape at me while I keep talking. I'm saying it all out loud so they know what is happening too.

"I am so sorry," I tell Demon. "I understand what happened to you, and I want you to know how sorry I am. I didn't know that everything I did would end up hurting you, and making you get lost. I never wanted to hurt you. Then when I was helping Jonathan's soul get better, I never knew that what I was doing was bothering you. I know now that you hated it when I was healing you. I wish I had known. I wish I could have asked for your permission. I don't think you would have hated it if you had said it was okay for me to do it."

I would expect Angel to tell me everything Demon is doing, but he isn't. He is staying quiet, watching me, waiting for me to finish. I figure he will tell me anything I really need to know.

"I'm glad you're back," I tell Demon. "I know how much Jonathan needs you. Even though he was feeling better after a while, he was never complete without you."

Jonathan is staring into my eyes, watching me talk to his guardian. I look back down at him, and he nods, agreeing with me. Even though he is upset by what is happening, he knows that he needs Demon to be with him.

"I hope you can accept my apology, and let Jonathan stay friends with us," I continue. "I will always try to help Jonathan if he needs it, and I know you want what is best for him. And I will always try to help you too, if there is anything I can do for you."

And then I know what to do. Demon is still hurting, still full of anger and pain and sadness. A lot like what Grandfather was feeling, or what Timothy's Dad was feeling. I helped them by touching them. I can't touch Demon any more than I can touch Angel.

But, I can touch Jonathan. His soul is connected to Demon. I can hug them both.

"Please, Demon," I ask him, trying to fill my eyes with all the love I am feeling, "let me help you now."

I raise my arms to put them over Jonathan's shoulders, hesitating there a moment to ask him permission with my eyes. He nods, and I can tell he doesn't know what I think is going to happen, but he trusts me. I wait to see if Angel tells me Demon wants me to stop, but he doesn't.

So I grab Jonathan in for a big hug. I hold him to me as close as I can, and I feel him relax against me. They are connected. I hope whatever it is that helps people when I touch them can help Demon too.

I stay this way, and Jonathan hugs me back.

Then, out of the corner of my eye, I see Angel moving. I am startled when I realize what he is doing. He kneels down on the ground right next to me, and looks up at Demon.

Chapter 66

Love

Gabe's

It is astonishing to behold. Demon has gazed at the Seer throughout her speech, both aghast at her audacity in addressing him directly, then increasingly moved by her words. His emotions roil throughout his being. His hatred for the girl conflicts with his desire to do what is best for Jonathan. His terrifying devil face contorts, his eyes blaze with fire as he looks down upon her, his clawed hands curl into fists.

When she reaches out to embrace his Guarded, I fear that Demon is going to again seize control of Jonathan's emotions, and cause him to violently reject her advances.

My own beloved braces himself, his arms lifted, ready to intervene if it appears that Natalie may be harmed.

There is a tense moment as Jonathan relaxes into the Seer's loving embrace.

Then, the unthinkable happens. Angel gracefully falls to the ground, kneeling before Demon. He lifts his face to the monstrous visage. Tears flow down his shining cheeks. He clasps his hands before him in supplication.

"Demon, forgive me. Forgive me for the harm I have caused you, for the ignorance which led me to act thoughtlessly in such a way that you endured great suffering. As is the Seer, I am deeply sorry for the pain you have experienced. Like her, I will attempt to remedy this situation in any way I can. You need only accept our sincere apologies, and allow us to remain in the presence of your beloved Jonathan."

I am overcome with awe and emotion at the sight.   As the sunset glows orange and golden upon the scene, the shining angel kneels on the ground before the fearsome demon. The white robes of Angel pool around him, the light shines off of him, the tears flow from his eyes. Demon towers over him, his wings unfurling to a terrifying length, his fangs bared, his claws extended, filled with a mix of emotions that threaten to overpower us all.

There is a pause while all remain frozen in this tableau.

Then the Seer has a new flash of inspiration. "Angel," she cries silently to her Guardian, "give me your energy! Send me your power!"

Her Guardian has never had to direct energy towards her before, as it was never necessary for her to be able to perceive him. It has never occurred to either of them to try this.

He immediately complies, energy floods out of him towards her, linking their minds in a powerful burst. She holds Jonathan even tighter, concentrating as hard as she can, as she feels the power flowing through her. She focuses on his soul, because she knows that it is connected to Demon.

She has found the answer. She cannot touch a Guardian directly. But with the flow of energy from her Guardian, and her arms enveloping Jonathan, the magic of the Seer's touch overflows the soul of the boy and reaches through the connection to his Guardian.

Demon senses the connection, perceives the energy being provided by Angel and orchestrated by the Seer, and feels the healing touch which had brought him back to his beloved. This time, though, the Seer is no longer ignorant of her actions. She deliberately directs the power towards Demon, seeking to heal him of his pain, calm his troubled thoughts, soothe his memories, relieve his suffering. And this time he actively accepts it, willingly.

As he senses the healing power of the Seer, as he feels himself restored to a state of emotional balance, she lifts her head from Jonathan's neck to look over his shoulder at Demon.

And she sees him.

Natalie

I asked Jonathan's permission to do it, and I asked Demon to let me help him. He didn't stop me. He could have told Angel no. I am using my touch, using Angel's power, using all the love I have in me to heal them both. Jonathan is hugging me back, and I'm only feeling happiness from him, none of the ugly emotions he was having before. I think it's working.

So I look up at where I think Demon is standing. It's right in front of the setting sun, which is almost all the way down below the horizon. Its rays shine up in lines, lighting up Demon from behind.

And somehow, I can see him. I think it's because of the energy from Angel, and the fact that I'm hugging him by hugging Jonathan's soul, and maybe because the sunlight is just right, and I don't know what else. But I see him. Not as clear to me as Angel is. But there is definitely a huge demon standing on the edge of the canyon.

I hear myself gasp.

Demon looks exactly like Angel described. Even worse. Angel didn't say anything about his eyes being on fire. He is huge and red and scary, his wings are up in the air like he's ready to take off flying, and he is staring at me with the most astonished expression.

I stare back at him, not letting go of Jonathan, knowing that if I did I would lose this connection.

I can see that Demon isn't angry, he isn't hating me, he is just completely surprised.

I say it to him silently, so nobody else can hear it. Except the other guardians, I suppose. But I want him to know. And it's true.

"I love you," I tell him.

I love him for what he is to Jonathan. I love him for allowing me to be here. I love him for coming back.

I see tears start to slip out of his fiery eyes, and roll down his blood-red cheeks. He stares at me, then glances at Angel still kneeling on the ground, then looks back over at me.

He nods. "Thank you," I faintly hear him say.

Then it's over. The sun finishes slipping below the horizon, I feel the power from Angel stop flowing, and Jonathan leans back from me, taking a deep breath. I let him go. I look back up to the edge of the canyon and can't see anything anymore except the brilliant orange clouds.

Angel stands back up, a beautiful smile beaming on his face.

Jonathan looks amazed, like he can sense something important just happened. Gabe relaxes his stance, like he realizes there isn't any danger any more.

"Are you okay?" I ask Jonathan.

"Yeah," he says, sounding surprised. "I really am. Like, really, really am. I feel like Demon feels better now?"

I turn to Angel.

"My darling, your solution was perfect. Your touch, using my energy, did indeed reach Demon, did help to make him feel much better. As you have helped others, your touch helped him. I believe your friendship with Jonathan is no longer a threat to you."

I turn back to Gabe and Jonathan and tell them this with a huge smile on my face. "Thank you," I think to Demon. "Thank you for allowing this."

Angel nods, and I know that Demon is okay now.

Gabe is looking back and forth between me and Jonathan. "So," he says, "anyone want to tell me what just happened? This time?"

I laugh, a little shakily. I feel like I just ran a marathon or something.

"Well," I tell them, "Demon is feeling better now."

Jonathan nods. "Yeah, I can tell he is."

"And," I add, "I saw him."

"What?!" they both say at the same time.

"I don't know how exactly, but for only a minute, I could see him, standing there in front of the sun."

"Really?" Jonathan says, excited. "So, what's he look like?"

I laugh again. "Actually, he looks like a demon. A giant scary red demon. He shaped himself that way because he knows that's how you've been picturing him."

Jonathan's eyes bug out. "Oh my God!" he says. He looks over at Gabe with an amazed smile on his face. "Cool!"

Gabe looks at me and laughs. "Told you so!"

Ron

Dinner is ready, but the kids haven't gotten back from playing with Jonathan. I suppose they're enjoying seeing him as much as they enjoyed seeing Timothy. I put on my shoes to go down to Jonathan's house and fetch them.

There's a knock on the door as I'm about to leave. I open it, and there is Brad.

"Hey," he says. "You all married? Congratulations and all that!"

I grin and show him the wedding band on my finger. "Yeah, we totally tied the knot. Again."

He reaches out to shake my hand, then says, "Well, I'm here to pick up Jonathan. It's dinnertime."

Oh! "I thought they were over at your house," I say, perplexed. "I was about to go there to get them."

"Huh," he says.

"I'll bet they went to the park," I tell him. "I'll walk over there and grab them."

"I'll come with," he says. "You can tell me all about your trip."

So here I am, walking down to another park, chatting with another dad. This seems to be the pattern today.

When we get there, sure enough all three kids are there, up on the hill on the west side, sitting on the grass and animatedly talking in the fading light from the setting sun. They look up guiltily when we get up there and loom over them.

Natalie purses her lips. "Um, dinnertime?" she guesses.

I point to the fading sunset. "Yes. And nighttime. On a school night. It seems like you kids can't stay away from parks today!"

They all look at each other and laugh. Then they jump up, and we head home together.

Chapter 67

April Fools

Stefanie

Jonathan is obviously thrilled that his friends are back again. Last night he scarcely stopped talking for a minute, all the way through dinner and bedtime. It's nice to see him so happy. Exhausting though. And to think, starting in a couple of months there's going to be two of these kids jabbering away!

I head into his room first thing in the morning to wake him up and get him ready for school. He comes awake immediately and sits up with a smile on his face.

"Good morning," I tell him. "Oops, look, there's a spider on your head!"

His eyes grow wide and he reaches up there, and I say, "April Fools!"

He laughs, and returns with, "Well, there's a giant scary red demon standing right behind you!" I grin and tousle his head. "Good one, kid. Okay, get dressed!"

Timothy

Guardian wakes me up with, "*Your father slept all night, with no nightmares. Natalie learned that Demon has returned, and all is well with Jonathan.*"

My eyes pop open. Um, really? That's a whole lot of information to deal with first thing in the morning. "Thanks, Guardian."

It sounds like what Natalie did with Dad yesterday really helped him. I'm so glad. And now Demon is back? I'd be worried about that, but Guardian said all is well with Jonathan. I don't know how any of this is possible, but I'll have to wait to find out.

While I'm eating breakfast, Mom and Dad are both eating too. That's unusual. A lot of the time Mom gets breakfast for me before Dad is up. But I guess since Dad got enough sleep last night, he didn't need to sleep in. They are smiling at each other a lot this morning.

Dad says he'll take me to school. That's also unusual. Normally Mom takes me. I shrug and say okay.

While we're driving, he tells me, "Just so you know, kid, today is April 1st. Do you know what that means?"

"Oh, right, April Fools Day," I answer him, unhappily. I remember being confused and upset on April Fools Day before. People kept telling me ridiculous things, and I kept believing them, and they kept laughing at me. Not Natalie of course. But I didn't understand why anyone would behave this way. I hope it doesn't happen again this year.

"Right," he says, pulling the car up in front of the school. "Just remember, don't believe anything you hear first thing, make sure you stop and think about whether the person is only making a joke. Most people think it's really funny, but I know you probably won't. Try to keep it in mind during the day, okay buddy?"

"Um, yeah. Thanks Dad." He's giving me advice? That's nice, I guess.

"Well, have a good day, Timothy. I love you."

I stare at him.

"You too, Dad."

I get out of the car, and he pulls away. I check my watch for the time. Natalie gave it back to me yesterday while they were over at my house. I had missed having it all week. I think I looked at my bare wrist about a thousand times.

I realize it's still really early. I don't see Natalie or Gabe or Jonathan here yet, so I walk over to the playground. There aren't many kids here yet. I look around for a good place to wait for them.

My eyes focus on the one place we've been avoiding all year. The jungle gym. We hadn't wanted to go there since we thought it might bother Jonathan, after everything that happened there. But, Guardian said Demon is back, and Jonathan is fine.

And, after yesterday, I know how to climb the thing now.

I decide to go do it. I should practice what my Dad taught me. I put my backpack down next to it, and inspect the bars. They are a little different from the one at the park, but the procedure should be the same. I put my hand on the bar right above my head, then my foot on the lowest bar next to the ground.

Chapter 68

The Angel And The Demon

Jonathan

I'm really glad we're going back to school today. I had a nice week hanging around with Dad, but being with my friends is more interesting. And I wonder if now that Demon's back, maybe class won't seem as boring.

When Dad drops me off he looks across the playground. He tilts his head so he can see out the window over the steering wheel. "Huh," he says.

"What?" I ask him.

"Is that ... your friend Timothy on top of the jungle gym?"

Ha! "No," I start to say, because obviously that could not possibly be true. Oh, wait! I know what this is. "Good April Fools joke, Dad!" I tell him.

"No, seriously! Look!"

I can't believe I'm letting him make me look, but I turn my head. "Wha...?"

When I get over there, Timothy is sitting up on top of the jungle gym, holding on for dear life, and grinning from ear to ear.

"Timothy!" I yell at him, laughing. "What a great April Fools trick! I'll bet you knew how to do this all along!"

I dump my backpack next to his and climb up. When I get up there, I'm about to tell him about what happened yesterday, but he gets to it first.

"Is Demon really back?" he asks.

"Yeah. Did you talk to Natalie?"

"No, Guardian told me. I hear him in the mornings when I'm waking up."

Really? Yeah, I think I remember hearing him and Natalie talking about this, but I'm not sure I was ever really paying attention to them before. I wonder how that works.

"So," he asks me, "how do you feel?"

"I feel great," I tell him. "There was a whole situation yesterday when Demon got all mad about seeing Natalie, but she fixed it. We'll have to tell you the whole story when they get here."

He raises his eyebrows. I think he's about to start asking questions, but then we see Natalie and Gabe get dropped off. I wave at them like crazy, and laugh to see how amazed they look to discover Timothy and me up here together.

Gabe's

The children have all climbed the jungle gym together, and are excitedly sharing with each other the stories of yesterday's events. Their Guardians observe the group together.

I look at our assembly, the Guardians of this remarkable collection of children. The Seer with her brother and friends have changed us, altered our existence, in so many ways. Among many other changes, we have all designed detailed images to benefit our Guarded. Even I have altered my manifestation, adding details to the generic male image I had originally created. My appearance is now that of a young, athletic male, with curly hair like that of my beloved. It helps me feel at one with him.

It is amusing to behold the four of us surrounding the structure which holds the children. The angel and the demon, together with the scientist and the athlete. All profoundly altered from the generic Guardians we had been before the Seer began to change us.

I begin to understand that this change will not be limited to her companions. Her abilities will only grow, her influence will only expand. Change is coming to the wider world.

Jonathan's

My beloved balances at the top of the structure with his companions, happily explaining what he describes as my "awesome" appearance. When I created this demon image, I certainly had no expectation that Jonathan would be crowing about how "cool" it is to his friends. I am genuinely amused. I am happy to maintain this appearance, for his benefit. I had created it initially almost as a type of penance, or possibly retribution against the Seer for everything she had inflicted upon me. However, now that Jonathan understands what I have done, he is thrilled with it, and I will maintain this manifestation for as long as it makes him happy.

Everything for him. His happiness is all that matters. And maintaining his friendship with the Seer makes him happy.

Although I cannot say it makes me exactly happy, I acknowledge that her contact with me yesterday calmed my emotions enormously. I was infused with a peace and contentment which overlays the negative emotions that still exist. Her gift of joy does battle with the memories of the anguish I suffered.

However, I am better able to control my emotional response to the Seer's presence. At least there is that. At least I can stop taking actions which might cause Jonathan to hate me. I will no longer control him. I did not previously appreciate that to control my Guarded was a violation. Having experienced violation, even though I know that it was not intended, I am resolved to never again inflict it on him.

As Angel described, I have very complicated feelings regarding the Seer. I remember the rage, the hate, the disgust, but I do not feel them as keenly.

I will never forget the violation, the desire, the antipathy, the conflict which came from the ordeal in the void. But I attempt to follow the admonishment of my beloved, and "get over it." I am trying.

I no longer wish to stop the Seer from existing. Although she is very peculiar, she does not seem to be as much of an unnatural threat as I had believed. There must be some beneficial purpose to her existence. It appears that she has used her touch to help not only Jonathan, but others in her circle.

And me. She helped me. I will always retain the memory of the moment in the park, where she locked eyes with me even as she healed me through her inventive embrace with my beloved, while her kneeling Guardian flooded her with energy. I felt her touch heal me, and I felt the love in her heart.

I have added this to the list of complicated emotions which I feel about her. The list now contains ... love.

Natalie's

My beloved chats happily with her friends. Merely a child on the playground equipment. I know how much more she is, but I must remember that despite everything, she is still a young human child.

Her power grows as she does. Her compassion and love guide her to ever greater feats. In the past few days she has wrought miraculous healings of her grandfather, Timothy's father, and even Jonathan's Guardian. Her inspiration for how to use my energy to reach Demon was a breathtaking display of her increasing abilities.

Her group of supporters grows as well. The three boys surrounding her become increasingly devoted. They will help her, they will learn from her, they will protect her. They love her as brothers and friends, and, increasingly, as followers.

Her potential is limitless. How will she choose to use her gifts? Who will be helped next?

Her sense of self adapts to the new reality, in which she is aware that she can knowingly use her touch to help others. It enhances the marvel of who she is. She begins to understand that this is a gift which she can use widely, that she can help many people. She knows she will need to explore this further, learn more about herself, and plan what to do next. She looks forward to discussing it all with her friends, especially Timothy, who she is confident can formulate an experiment to investigate any phenomenon. She is comfortable in the knowledge that her companions, including me, will accompany and help her along her path.

She is my beloved. She is an empath. She is a Seer.

She is a Healer.

***

End of Book 3 of Guardians.

COMING SOON FROM JULIA GUROFF:

Natalie's story will continue in later books. But first, starting in 2026, two new book series will begin to be published:

THE SEER CHRONICLES: The tale of Guardians and Seers goes two centuries into the past, with a story set in the early 1800s along the Mississippi River.

JUST WOLVES: A werewolf romance - with a twist. This story is unrelated to the Guardians universe, is quite a bit spicier, and possibly more fun.

You can follow the journey at https://juliaguroff.com/